The shining splendor of our Zebra Lovegram logo on the cover of this book reflects the glittering excellence of the story inside. Look for the Zebra Lovegram whenever you buy a historical romance. It's a trademark that guarantees the very best in quality and reading entertainment.

A FIERCE LONGING

Sarah sighed, lost in her thoughts as the last of the soap disintegrated between her fingers. She never heard the door open. It wasn't until the cold draft that she realized she wasn't alone. She could feel his presence, could feel his gaze upon her nakedness. "I thought you'd be longer," she said.

She heard him clear his throat as he moved closer to the tub. Sarah knew her breasts were just visible beneath the soapy water. She raised her eyes to his, her cheeks growing warm as she found him staring. Suddenly, she realized that it didn't matter what he felt. She knew what she wanted. And she knew what she'd have to do to get it.

Sarah's hands reached slowly for the side of the tub for balance, her entire body trembling at her daring. Never before had she stood naked before a man.

His gasp was the only sound in the room as he watched her rise from the water. Sarah could see first the shock, then the hunger, the need, the delight register in his eyes. She stepped unaided from the tub and moved toward him. Her long hair slipped from its knot at the touch of her fingers, spreading in a golden brown cape around her sho———— nervously.

"You said to come to yo——

"At last," he answered, ——

D1399710

THE BEST IN HISTORICAL ROMANCES

TIME-KEPT PROMISES   (2422, $3.95)
by Constance O'Day Flannery
Sean O'Mara froze when he saw his wife Christina standing before him. She had vanished and the news had been written about in all of the papers — he had even been charged with her murder! But now he had living proof of his innocence, and Sean was not about to let her get away. No matter that the woman was claiming to be someone named Kristine; she still caused his blood to boil.

PASSION'S PRISONER   (2573, $3.95)
by Casey Stewart
When Cassandra Lansing put on men's clothing and entered the Rawlings saloon she didn't expect to lose anything — in fact she was sure that she would win back her prized horse Rapscallion that her grandfather lost in a card game. She almost got a smug satisfaction at the thought of fooling the gamblers into believing that she was a man. But once she caught a glimpse of the virile Josh Rawlings, Cassandra wanted to be the woman in his embrace!

ANGEL HEART   (2426, $3.95)
by Victoria Thompson
Ever since Angelica's father died, Harlan Snyder had been angling to get his hands on her ranch, the Diamond R. And now, just when she had an important government contract to fulfill, she couldn't find a single cowhand to hire — all because of Snyder's threats. It was only a matter of time before the legendary gunfighter Kid Collins turned up on her doorstep, badly wounded. Angelica assessed his firmly muscled physique and stared into his startling blue eyes. Beneath all that blood and dirt he was the handsomest man she had ever seen, and the one person who could help beat Snyder at his own game.

Available wherever paperbacks are sold, or order direct from the Publisher. Send cover price plus 50¢ per copy for mailing and handling to Zebra Books, Dept. 3534, 475 Park Avenue South, New York, N.Y. 10016. Residents of New York, New Jersey and Pennsylvania must include sales tax. DO NOT SEND CASH.

PATRICIA PELLICANE

FIRE'S TENDER KISS

ZEBRA BOOKS
KENSINGTON PUBLISHING CORP.

*To Patty and Gerry Croce, with love and
appreciation, for being there
when I needed you most.*

*And to Maureen O'Connell, for the phone calls
that added laughter to days of hard work.
I'm going to miss you.
Thanks for the bear.*

ZEBRA BOOKS

are published by

Kensington Publishing Corp.
475 Park Avenue South
New York, NY 10016

First printing: October, 1991

Printed in the United States of America

Chapter One

"Oh, God, noooo!" Sarah gave an agonizing gut-tural cry as another pain, this one stronger than any she'd so far suffered, tore into her back. It tightened her extended belly into rocklike hardness. It bent her in half and stole her breath, reaching deep with excru-ciating torment into her soul. It seemed to tear her asunder. Idly, she wondered if it would. Amazingly, she knew she didn't care.

She cared only that this would soon be over. She couldn't take much more.

It wasn't until the worst of the agony began to ease that she could gasp for air. Her weakened legs shook, barely holding her slight form.

Lord, she couldn't stay out here in the open. Her gaze wandered over the breathtaking beauty of the endless snow-ladened woods around her. She didn't notice their majesty. All she felt right now was her complete isolation from all humanity. A frown creased her smooth forehead. She had to find help, and if there was no help, at least some kind of shelter. Sarah eyed the low brush that surrounded her and wondered if she had the strength or the time to gather a few of the larger, thicker branches together. Perhaps with that large tree at her back, they might be made into something that would vaguely resemble a lean-to.

Her body strained forward. It bent into an unrelenting wind that sliced like knives above her woolen scarf and into her exposed skin. She breathed deeply through the fabric, trying to detect a wood fire, but the wind was too strong. If a fire existed, the wind had diluted the scent.

A sudden, powerful gust pushed at Sarah catching her off guard. She wobbled dangerously, then her foot slipped out from beneath her and she toppled back. Her arms were swinging wildly, uselessly, and quite ineffectually as she struggled to regain her balance. Her feet created a cloud of dusty white as they became visible from beneath more than a foot of snow. A cry was torn from her throat as she landed with a bone-jarring thud. The sound mingled pain with horror as she hit the hard ground, her breath knocked from her lungs. Helplessly, she began to slide down a steep, slick incline. She cried out again and grasped at the small frozen hill, desperate to gain a hold, all to no avail.

Despite her best efforts, Sarah's awkward body began to roll. A thick cloud of powder followed close upon her descent and soon engulfed her petite form. Her dark clothes coated in white, her vision was blurred as snow covered her from head to booted foot.

As graceful as a bloated calf, she came to a stop at last. Her woolen scarf had been knocked askew, and her nostrils, eyes, and mouth were filled with snow.

A low groan slipped from frozen stiff lips, while her hands, deep inside thick woolen gloves, moved automatically to protect and comfort her extended belly and the baby within. She pulled her legs up into a fetal position, subconsciously preparing herself for the next painful assault.

She had scarcely come to a stop than she clutched at her belly in earnest. A sharp gasp burned her lungs as she inhaled icy cold air, but that sensation barely registered as white-hot searing pain invaded her body and left her momentarily uncaring of her precarious position. She'd never known pain to equal this torment. Had she been able to think, she might have wondered why any woman would be foolish enough to birth more than one child.

She gasped for air, willing her body to rest between the periodic onslaughts of agony. Terror clutched her heart when the pain eased enough to allow her a moment to think. She tried to push the worst of the emotion aside, lest she lose the last of her reason and run screaming like a wild banshee into the forest, never to be seen again.

Sarah was a strong, brave woman, able to withstand the hardships of life and take them in stride, but nothing had ever prepared her for the pain and fear of birthing a child alone in the midst of a blizzard.

How in the world could she have been so thoughtless? What had possessed her to ignore the low, insistent backache she'd suffered throughout all of yesterday? And then last night. She'd hardly slept for the discomfort. Granted she'd suffered no real pain, but why hadn't she imagined it was the beginning of her time? And why was it all so perfectly clear now that it was too late?

Granted, Thomas would have been no help to her,

7

ill as he was with fever, but had she stayed at their wagon, she would have been warm and dry. And the knowledge that he lay by her side would have brought her a degree of comfort.

Her soul cried out for the feel of his warm hand in hers. *Please God,* she prayed, *I can't do this alone. I don't know how!*

Another contraction ripped into her back. For a long moment Sarah forgot her dire situation, her entire world centering around an agony that had no equal. She moaned in anguish, a guttural sound that was foreign to her ears. For a second she thought another had made the sound. Perhaps she wasn't alone after all. Was it possible another suffered as well? She almost smiled despite the anguish. Of course, there was no one else. Who would be foolish enough to brave the elements on a day such as this?

The pain began to ease at last. Sarah knew she had but a few moments before another one would come. She had to get up. Perhaps just over the next rise she'd find help. How horrible to think she might have been within yards of safety, only to die because she couldn't gather the strength to walk over this last hill.

The wind eased momentarily. And with its easing came a thick curtain of soft puffy white. It drifted prettily from a sky so low it looked as if it touched the treetops. In seconds the flakes covered her where her fall had not. Sarah's skin was damp, caused, no doubt, by the suffering she'd so far withstood and the effort of plodding through knee-deep drifts of ever-deepening snow. She gave a violent shiver as the wet cold began to seep through the many layers of her clothing.

She tried to get up, but her heavy clothes and rounded, awkward body weighed her down and caused her to roll helplessly like a turtle on its back. Lying in the shallow gully, Sarah couldn't imagine how she'd gain her footing again. A silent prayer slipped past her lips, that the snow would ease, and that somehow, miraculously, help would come. But God appeared of a mind to ignore her prayers on this particular day.

The small stone cabin, built into the side of a gently sloping mountain, looked inviting. Unadorned and rough, it seemed to boast of no luxuries, yet made a pretty, cozy picture as snow collected upon its flat slate roof. Wind swirled the cold white powder into high drifts along one side. One could easily imagine its comfort and warmth as smoke drifted from a tall chimney and soft light glowed from the cracks in its wooden shutters.

Despite the heavy snow and bitter cold, Thaddeus Payne, a huge dark, bearded man, with eyes that mirrored a soul containing no joy, left the warmth of his cabin. On long, muscular legs he headed for the base of his mountain. The downgrade was so gradual that an incline could not be easily determined, especially since it was impossible to see more than ten feet through the trees and wild underbrush that Thaddeus preferred to surround his home, rather than the smooth stretches of land that constituted most ranches.

With gloved hands, he pushed his hat more securely upon his head, digging his chin nearly to his chest and into the high collar of a heavy sheepskin coat. The woolen scarf that circled his head and covered his ears hardly mattered against a wind so biting it felt razor-sharp on unprotected skin. He cursed the foul weather. But foul or not, he had little choice but to brave the elements. He couldn't leave his traps unattended. He might hunt and trap for his food, but it still went against everything he believed in to allow an animal to suffer needlessly. And an abandoned trap would ensure just that.

The harsh climate appeared to have no effect on his dog, however. Tiger, appropriately named because of his orange and brown striped coat, barked out his enjoyment as he ran ahead of Thaddeus, only to disappear into a deep drift and come out a blur of speeding white. He raced back to his master and stood for a moment, shaking himself free of the cold particles that clung to his coat while Thaddeus cursed. "Jesus Christ! Do you have to stand here and shake?"

Suddenly, Tiger grew very still and gave a low growl, which turned oddly into a whine.

"What is it, boy?" Thaddeus asked, instantly down on one knee as he absentmindedly stroked the animal. His gaze narrowed against the blinding snow as it moved over the silent, apparently empty landscape. He eased the butt of his rifle to his shoulder, his finger on the trigger, ready to fire. The Cheyenne hadn't been too happy of late. Not since that fool Custer had found gold in the Black Hills and told the whole goddamned world. It wasn't bad enough that the Sioux were on the warpath, now the Cheyenne had to go and join them.

The few that lived and hunted in these mountains

10

hadn't bothered him much. 'Cept for an occasional stolen animal, he wouldn't have known they were around at all. Thaddeus shrugged. As long as they didn't bother him none, he didn't care what they did.

Those damn greedy fools who dared to search for gold that wasn't theirs to take deserved what they got.

Tiger made a soft high-pitched whining sound.

Thaddeus breathed a sigh of relief as he stood tall again. He knew what that meant. He'd heard the sound often enough of late. The wild bitches that ran in packs over his mountain had been in heat for a week, and their scent had driven Tiger half crazy as he tried to get out of the house. "Get it out of your mind. You ain't goin' nowhere."

Thaddeus imagined he spoke the words for his own satisfaction in this instance. Any second he expected Tiger to take off, not to be seen again until he finished his business and then some. Not that his dog often disobeyed. Except for an apparently uncontrollable mating instinct, he was the best companion any man could want.

Tiger turned his head and looked at his master. Another whine, distinctly eerie in tone, came from a tightly muscled throat. His head tipped slightly to one side and his eyes appeared to grow dark. If Thaddeus didn't know better, he could imagine them filled with sympathy.

"Jesus! What the hell is the matter with you? You're giving me the shivers."

The whining was growing in volume now, while he barked here and there, as if to emphasize whatever he was trying to say. "Damn," Thaddeus groaned. "If you want my opinion, no bitch is worth all that trou-

11

ble, but if you have to have her, go on. I won't stop you."

Tiger took off, bounding over the loose snow, creating a cloud of white powder in his wake.

Thaddeus walked in the opposite direction, a frown causing his rugged, weathered features to grow more harsh than usual. He shook his head as he bemoaned the helplessness of the male animal. And that went for all species. His poor dog didn't have a chance against the urges that plagued. And it wasn't much different as far as a man was concerned. All a man needed was to make the mistake of getting under a woman's skirts and the moment he did, his life wasn't worth two bits. He'd been that route before, and he knew from personal experience the pain and helplessness a man suffered when he let a woman into his life.

Mostly, he didn't take to women. Far as he could tell, they weren't good for much 'cept maybe for one thing. And he sure as hell didn't need to keep one around here for that. When the need struck him, he took himself off to town. After a few days, he'd make his way back home, knowing the time spent between a pair of white thighs would hold him for a spell, and his home as well as his life were his to do with as he pleased.

Halfway down the slope Thaddeus stopped in his tracks. Tiger's almost jovial barking had suddenly become fierce and interspersed with deep growls and mournful whines. What the hell was going on? Was there a Cheyenne brave or two out there after all? He shook his head. No. Indians weren't stupid. They wouldn't be out in weather like this.

A moment later Thaddeus watched as Tiger ran,

hell-bent, in his direction. Thaddeus grinned and realized the problem. No doubt the bitch already had a male escort. "She wasn't worth it after all, was she, boy?" he asked as he leaned down and gave his dog a few less than gentle pats. But if Thaddeus thought that was the end of the episode, he was mistaken. Tiger kept up his barking, whining and acting altogether loco as he spun in circles, started to run off again, then raced back to whine once more. Not expecting an answer but as most owners of animals are prone to do, Thaddeus asked, "What? What the hell's the matter with you?"

The dog simply kept up his wild antics.

Thaddeus ignored him and proceeded down the gentle slope, only to find his way blocked by a dog who grew wilder and apparently more anxious with every passing moment. "Goddamn it! What do ya want?"

Again the animal barked and spun and ran, only to return and run again.

It was obvious the dog wanted him to follow. Thaddeus shook his head, cursed again, and did just that, figuring if he didn't, he wasn't apt to get a minute's peace.

Tiger ran on ahead, barking all the while as Thaddeus made his way over the eastern slope and down its more vertical incline. He had almost reached the bottom when his feet slid out from under him and he began to roll. A stream of curses filled the silent forest. He lost his rifle in the tumble and knew he'd be freezing by the time he returned to his cabin, now that snow had found its way beneath his coat and dampened almost every part of his buckskins.

A second later Thaddeus forgot about his wet state and stared, stupefied, at the tiny ball of dark material that had somehow sprouted what looked like a human face.

Ridiculous, he thought as the momentum of his fall caused him to roll right on by. There was no one out here on his mountain. No one would be foolish enough to brave these elements. Not even a starving Indian could be found outside his hut in weather like this. Besides, even if someone had been wandering on his land, it wouldn't be a lone white woman. And from the quick glance he had had, Thaddeus imagined the vision to definitely be a woman.

He rolled to a stop at last and cursed again. "Damn." He was going to have a time of it finding his rifle in snow more than a foot deep.

Determinedly, Thaddeus made his way back up the slope. He had to find his rifle, but most of all, he wanted to see again whatever the hell it was that he'd taken for a woman.

He came upon her sooner than expected. In an instant he threw his weight to one side, trying to avoid stepping on her. The movement caused him to fall again. "Damn," he groaned as best as his stiff lips allowed. On his back, his face aimed at the sky while snow seeped into his collar, Thaddeus wondered if he wasn't losing his mind.

What was a woman doing here, miles from town and obviously ill, if her soft moans meant anything? Suddenly, her soft moans intensified. Thaddeus scrambled to his feet, his rifle forgotten as he stared in amazement at a woman who had rolled herself into a tight ball and looked to be caught in the throes of some horrifying, gut-wrenching agony.

"What's the matter?" he asked as he leaned over her body. "Who are you? What are you doing here?"

Between contractions, Sarah faded in and out of reality. Unable to bear the present torment and the fear of being alone, her mind reverted to her childhood, to the happiness and security of her family home. To the love and safety she had known then.

She laughed as she chased Ethan around the kitchen table. The glutton had stolen her candy stick after finishing his own. "Mother!" she called. "Make him stop!"

But Ethan had only stuck out his tongue and laughed at his sister, just before he ran into his father as the unsuspecting man entered the warm, inviting kitchen.

Sarah giggled as she once again saw the candy stick being torn from her brother's fingers and held up, out of reach, while her gentle father listened to two of his children tell their story.

But something was wrong here. Her father didn't have a beard, nor eyes so dark they appeared to be without pupils. She must be dreaming. Suddenly, she realized the folly of her thoughts. It wasn't her father or a dream. It was a bear! A huge black bear was leaning over her, asking her questions.

A bear? A bear with the eyes of a man? Asking her questions? Sarah's laugh caught in her throat as another contraction crashed down upon her. She groaned out a sound that resembled that of a wounded animal, telling clearly of the agony she bore.

He leaned close and spoke again, but Sarah

couldn't understand the words. She watched his mouth move, but the words got mixed up in her mind and became one deep droning of sound.

Amazingly, she felt no fear. She knew she should have been afraid, but Sarah couldn't summon the emotion. It didn't matter who this bearlike man was. There was nothing he could do to her that could be worse than the agony she already suffered.

She thought he was lifting her. Perhaps it was only another dream. But she wouldn't have dreamt of anyone who could look like him, would she? She'd never imagined a man so big, so dark, with a beard that covered his jaw and cheeks and hung almost to his chest.

She was exhausted, her feet and hands numb from the cold. Sarah didn't know how long she'd lain there, but she knew she was dying. All she wanted was for it to be over. She didn't care anymore. She was just too tired to care.

Thaddeus took her in his arms and blinked with surprise. She weighed hardly anything at all. What was a tiny woman like her doing out here all alone? Where was her man?

Carefully, he came to his feet, the treacherous ground offering little in the way of sure footing. It was going to take him some time before he managed to bring her to his cabin. Idly, he wondered if he'd make it in time. Judging by the looks and the sound of her, she was terribly sick. Even though he knew he would, Thaddeus felt no real urge to care for this woman. This was almost exactly how he'd come to meet his wife, except that that time it had been a rainstorm and it had been Annie who was pounding at his door. God, he didn't want another woman under his roof. He didn't want the pain again, and most of all he didn't want to remember. And caring for this woman was sure to cause him all kinds of memories. He almost hoped she wouldn't live long enough to see his cabin.

But she did.

Thaddeus laid her upon his bed. After seeing to his fire and taking off his own outerwear, he looked unhappily upon his soon-to-be patient. Gently, he unwrapped her stiff hands from their wet gloves and held them between his own, trying to bring some warmth and color back to flesh that had grown as white as the snow she'd lain in. Her boots were next, and this time he pressed her icy feet beneath his shirt and against his naked stomach. Holding them there, he listened to her cries of pain and watched as she tried to pull them back.

A puzzled look creased his brow. She looked to be in the throes of some agony. Would cold feet and hands cause such pain? He shrugged as he held her feet in place. No doubt she had low tolerance, that was all.

The pain eased and Sarah's mind cleared for a moment. Silently, she took in her surroundings. A man, the same one she'd dreamed of, was standing at the bottom of a narrow bed. He was watching her, waiting . . . waiting for what? What did he expect her to do? And why did he just stand there when she needed his help so badly?

"Help me!" she cried out as the pain came again, stealing her breath and perhaps her very life.

Tiger sat near the side of the bed, his head against

17

the mattress, his nose almost pressed to the woman's hip, giving soft whining sounds of sympathy that only served to annoy Thaddeus. He frowned at the dog and then spoke to the woman. "What, lady? What's the matter with you?"

"The baby," she gasped against the breath-stealing agony and rolled to her side, her hands rubbing over her clothes, over her stomach, as she tried to ease away the torment. "Oh, God, the baby's co—mi—n—ng!"

Her desperate plea rose in pitch, until the last word became nothing less than a scream. A scream that left Thaddeus in a state of shock. Baby! What baby? He stared at her for a long moment, until he realized the layers of clothes had disguised the fact that she was enormous with child. Jesus God, did she think he could help? Well, he couldn't. There was no way. She could just take herself out of here and try some other fool.

Despite her obvious chill, for she was shaking uncontrollably, her hair, which had come loose from its pins, clung in damp tendrils to her neck and face. Beads of sweat dotted her forehead and lip. She looked flushed, almost as if she suffered from fever. What the hell had he gotten himself into?

"I ain't a midwife. I ain't got no idea how—"

Sarah never heard the words. All she knew was unbearable pain. All she knew was this baby was coming at last.

She bore down with a long, hard grunt, her hands reaching instinctively toward the baby's exit. She couldn't stop the need to bear down as she raised her knees and pulled them toward her chin. Her face grew

18

red from the pressure, her eyes pleading as she gasped for a needed breath and then bore down again.

Thaddeus cursed as he watched her writhing in agony. There was no help for it. The damn fool woman was having her baby. It didn't matter that he wanted no part in it. She was doing it anyway.

Thaddeus tore at her clothes. Her coat and three heavy shirts were flung to the floor, just before he pulled her heavy stockings over her small feet. They fell unnoticed to the floor as he took a deep breath and raised her snow-encrusted skirt. She was wet, but besides the water that had soaked through her drawers and skirt into his feather mattress, there was blood everywhere. Jesus! Did all women bleed like this?

God, he hoped so. There was no way this one was going to drop a kid and then die. He didn't want no kids. He didn't have the first idea how to care for one. She wasn't going to die. Not if he could help it.

Thaddeus removed her drawers. He quickly washed his hands and found a soft blanket for the coming child.

Had she been in her usual frame of mind, Sarah might have found her present position most objectionable. But she was far from rational.

She groaned as the need to bear down came upon her again. She wasn't going to make it. No human being could suffer this torture and expect to live. Idly, she wondered why she felt no panic. In truth, she was just too tired to care.

She was gasping loudly for her every breath. "I—I c—can't . . ."

"Lady, don't give me that bull. You can and you will," Thaddeus ordered without the least bit of pity or concern. If there was a sense of real panic in his voice, neither seemed to notice.

"Go to hell," she gasped weakly, never realizing she spoke her thoughts aloud. She was so tired between contractions that she barely had the strength or will to breathe, let alone carry on a conversation with this heartless monster. All she wanted was for this to be over. All she wanted was sleep. She had to sleep.

"Push!" Thaddeus insisted, leaning over her, almost yelling it in her face. And then imagining the words to give her some encouragement, he went on. "I can see his head."

Sarah felt an overwhelming sense of anger. How dare he stand there telling her what to do? He wasn't besieged by agony. It wasn't his body being torn asunder. He didn't know the torture she suffered. "How wonderful for you," she gasped nastily as she glared at him over her raised knees. "I don't care if you can see North America. I'm telling you, I can't do this. It's killing me. Can't you understand I'm dying?"

Thaddeus grunted. "The hell you say. You ain't leavin' me with no squallin' brat, lady. I ain't lettin' you die."

Sarah moaned. She needed someone to speak sweet, encouraging words to her. She didn't need to be aggravated on top of this pain. "Get away from me. I don't need this. I don't want this. I've changed my mind."

Thaddeus chuckled at her anger. "Go ahead. Stop then. I'd like to see how you manage that."

Her lips curled into a snarl and she was about to bestow upon him a few well-chosen pieces from her father's extensive vocabulary, when the need for verbal retaliation was suddenly sucked away. Another contraction crashed into her belly.

Sarah gave a mighty guttural cry as she reached for the iron bedpost behind her head and held on, pushing with the last of her strength.

The baby slipped suddenly from her body and lay red-faced and squalling upon the bed, the smallest human he'd ever seen, covered with blood and slime.

Thaddeus shook his head and grunted. This woman was a hell of a lot stronger than she appeared. It was a miracle someone as tiny and as slim-hipped as she could birth a child at all.

Thaddeus got to work caring for the infant and her mother. He might never have assisted in birthing a child, but he'd had enough experience helping animals foal their young to know pretty much what to do next. Sarah never realized what he was about as she fell into the most exhausted sleep she'd ever known.

A soft bundle was placed in her arms, but already more than half asleep, she never noticed. "You'd best be feedin' your baby, lady."

"What?" she murmured, too tired to keep her eyes open for more than a second or two at a time.

"Your daughter," Thaddeus nodded at the infant. "She's fussin'. She needs to be put to your—" Thaddeus felt the heat suddenly warm his cheeks, then he cursed this fool woman for making him grow red with embarrassment and tongue-tied like an adolescent. "Feed your kid, lady!" he almost yelled as he turned his back on the woman and child in his bed and went about the chore of gathering up her soiled clothes.

Chapter Two

Sarah never felt him tug the bedding from beneath her. She didn't know he rolled her to her side and replaced the wet blankets and sheets with dry ones. She didn't hear his disgruntled murmurings, nor did she realize that he had taken away her blood-stained clothes and covered her nakedness with one of his shirts.

It was two hours before she awoke to the tantalizing scent of fresh coffee and hearty stew. Sarah's stomach growled, reminding her of her hunger. She tried to remember when she'd eaten last, then closed her eyes again unable to summon even that much energy.

Another hour passed before Sarah looked around in some surprise, to find herself in a small cabin. The walls were covered with a rough mixture of what looked to be white sand. Heavy dark beams crisscrossed the ceiling. A dresser sat against one wall, opposite the bed. Upon it a mantel clock ticked bringing the only sound into the room.

For a long moment she couldn't imagine where

she was. A man stood at the stove across the small room, mixing something in a huge pot. She smiled. Apparently, it hadn't been a dream. A man had taken her up in his arms and carried her to the safety of his home. He'd helped to birth her daughter. Would she ever be able to show him the depth of her gratitude?

Something stirred at her side and Sarah looked down at the tiny form. A soft smile lit up her face. Her baby. Her very own baby. And she was the most beautiful thing Sarah had ever seen.

Mother and daughter were snuggled beneath two heavy quilts. Her body was filled with renewed energy at the thrill of seeing her baby at last. "Oh!" she breathed with no little amazement as she studied the tiny human being who lay so comfortably warm against her. "Look at her," she said to no one in particular as a trembling fingertip came to stroke a sweet, perfect face.

The words caused Thaddeus to turn from mixing the stew. Sarah's eyes glistened with tears and beamed with pride and love as she gazed down at her baby. For some reason, the look caused a scowl to twist at Thaddeus's features and he heard himself saying, "Looks like a puny chicken if you ask me."

With a sudden surge of motherly love and protection, Sarah glared at the man who'd dared to insult her child. "She doesn't! She's beautiful. And I didn't ask you."

Thaddeus turned from the sight of her. He couldn't see the baby, for the covers were drawn almost to the woman's shoulders. But from the sounds that carried across the small room, it was obvious mother and daughter were taking a special moment to get acquainted. He couldn't say why, but the soft cooing sounds brought an empty ache to his chest. A second later, that emptiness was filled to overflowing with anger. Damn, he didn't want her here. He didn't want any woman here. He didn't need a woman in his life, with her soft way of talkin' and sweet way of smellin'. Thaddeus forced his mind from dangerous thoughts and cursed. Where the hell had that come from? It wasn't as if he found her appealing. And even if he did, she was obviously taken. His tone was harder than he'd intended, when he finally answered, "No accountin' for taste, I expect."

"And that from a hairy ape," Sarah said, almost but not quite under her breath. Despite the low tone, the words carried easy enough through his silent cabin to his ears.

Well, he could forget about her soft way of talkin', Thaddeus almost smiled with relief. This one was sharp-tongued and sure to keep his mind off things that could only lead to trouble. And for that he would have thanked God . . . if he believed in God.

Still, he couldn't help the feeling of resentment that filled his being. Thaddeus glared at the woman who had the gall to insult him while she lay in his bed. "And that's the thanks I get for taking you in and saving your scrawny neck? The next time I come across anyone in a blizzard, they can damn well die before I'd lift a finger." His hands were on his hips, his feet set apart as his lips—at least what she could see of his lips beneath a thick black mustache and beard—twisted into a snarl. "I didn't ask you here, lady. If you don't like what you see, you can take yourself and that brat and get out."

Sarah, who until now had never in her life met a man—or a woman, for that matter—whom she instantly disliked, suddenly realized how very sheltered her life had been. She struggled to come to a sitting position, the effort taking a good deal more strength than she had to spare. She turned her back from the man's dark, angry gaze and wrapped the small blanketed form securely beneath the covers. Obviously, she wasn't wanted here, and Sarah Carlton would never impose herself on anyone. "Fine. I wouldn't want to put you to any trouble."

"A bit late, wouldn't you say? You've already brought me a passel of it."

"I'll pay you for your care, sir. No matter that it was grudgingly given."

"With what?" he asked, knowing she carried no purse. And judging from the quality of her clothes, her pockets would more than likely be empty.

"Tell me how much I owe you. I'll send it."

Thaddeus snorted his disbelief.

Sarah wasn't about to swear to the truth of her words. She'd pay him all right. She wasn't about to be indebted to a man like him. Her arms shook, but she managed to inch herself to the edge of the bed.

The ugliest dog she'd ever seen in her life lay

25

alongside the bed. At her movement, he raised his head. A moment later he whined a soft sound, raised his head, and licked her hand.

Thaddeus uttered a sharp command and the dog moved away. With a deceptive, loose-hipped saunter, Thaddeus covered the less than fifteen feet separating his bed and stove in a matter of seconds. The fact that he'd obviously reached his destination didn't seem to stop his momentum at all. His body continued forward until he was leaning over her, denying her her personal space. In order to keep any distance between them at all, Sarah found her back pressed once again to his pillow.

If the truth be told, Sarah felt awful. Stiff, aching at almost every joint, she couldn't muster the needed strength to even try pushing him aside. He scowled as he leaned closer still. "Look, lady, I'll tell you clear. I want you here about as much as you want to stay, but neither of us has much of a choice. We're stuck together till the snow melts. I ain't chancin' the safety of my horses to bring you to town."

A dull headache joined her other ills. "How long will that take?"

"What?" he asked as a dazed look entered his eyes. Inadvertently, he'd breathed in her woman's scent. Thaddeus felt a horrifying jolt. He swallowed and then blinked as he tried to deny the powerful, almost overwhelming lust that suddenly filled his gut. He'd been too busy before, too caught up in a chaotic moment to think of her as a woman. But that was before. Jesus! He couldn't live with her for months. That was too much to ask of any man.

"Before the snow melts. How long?"

Thaddeus's laugh sounded hollow as he moved back a bit, allowing a more respectable distance between them. Far enough at least so her scent no longer filled his mind and brought a glazed look to his eyes. "Well, let's see. This is October." He shrugged. "I'd say somewhere around April, if we're lucky."

"What?!" Sarah's whole body stiffened. "You can't be serious!" There was no way on earth that she was staying with this evil-tempered inhospitable oaf for six months.

"Oh, I reckon I'm serious, all right." Thaddeus grinned happily, upon seeing she disliked the notion easily as much as he did. "Believe me, lady, I wouldn't keep you here if I had another choice." His sigh was weary indeed as he imagined the chaos a woman and her baby were sure to bring to his home over the next few months. "I guess we're stuck with each other."

"I'm afraid that is totally out of the question," Sarah returned primly as a deep flush of mortification colored her pale cheeks. She couldn't remember a time when she'd felt as insulted. She wouldn't stay here under conditions that were at best intolerable. Her voice trembled with emotion, embarrassment being the most prevalent. "If you'll let me up, I'll be on my way."

"You think so?" he almost sneered, so close to her again that puffs of his breath hit her in the face. "And how do you figure you'll manage that?"

"I walked here, didn't I? I'll walk back."

"And where is back? What were you doin' out in a goddamned blizzard alone? And where the hell is your man?"

Her eyes widened with horror. "Thomas! Oh my God!" she said so softly, he wouldn't have heard had his face not been inches from her mouth.

"I take it this Thomas fella is your man?"

"He's my husband." Her hands reached for his shirt. Holding on in desperation, she tugged him closer as she spoke. "Please!" Her eyes were wild with fear and her voice rose with panic. "He's ill with fever. I left him to find help."

"Husband eh? And you've only just remembered you have one?" Thaddeus chuckled a sound of disgust. "Spoken like a truly carin' wife."

Sarah's cheeks burned again, this time with the shame that she could have forgotten. How could she have been so caught up in her own dilemma that she hadn't remembered her husband and his illness? It was this man's fault. He'd aggravated her from the moment she'd opened her eyes. How was she expected to remember, when all she could think of was her need to leave this house forever? She tried to think. How long? How long had she been gone? Her eyes glistened with desperate tears. "Please! Oh God, please. You have to help him!"

"You can turn off the tears, lady," he sneered his dislike. "They don't work with me. Never had, never will. And get this straight. I don't have to do a damn thing." His coal-black gaze bore into her

28

soul, leaving nothing in its wake but despair. "And I especially don't have to go out in that storm again."

Tears were streaming down her face as she shoved him away. Where she got the strength from she never knew, but Sarah was out of the bed, standing unassisted. Her headache had grown in strength, and her face was suddenly as white as the snow outside. She swayed but, through sheer force of will, put aside her dizziness as she held onto the bed for balance.

A second later Sarah realized she wore nothing but a man's shirt. She gasped with shock. Too weak to stand on her own, she leaned against the bed and moved her hands in a protective fashion to cover herself, as if that would somehow keep her near nakedness from this man's gaze. "Where are my clothes?" Sarah didn't want to think this man was obviously responsible for taking them away. She didn't want to know it was his shirt she wore.

A second later she was almost thrown back upon the bed, an action that did little to relieve the pain in her head. Her eyes widened as she realized she'd almost landed on the baby. Thaddeus's dark, threatening look grew darker still as he loomed above her. "If you get out of that bed again, I'm going to break your damn neck."

The words, in and of themselves, were menacing enough, but his deep growl alone would have terrified any rational-thinking woman. After all, a man who was at least twice her size and probably outweighed her by a hundred or more pounds was clearly promising physical abuse. But Sarah was as far from being rational as she was ever likely to get. She felt not the slightest flicker of fear. What she felt was outrage that a man, that any man, could ignore another's desperate plea. And then have the unmitigated gall to think that simply because he'd said so, she would obey his command. Her blue eyes darkened to an almost violet shade as rage overcame her guilt. "You won't be keeping me here."

"Won't I?" Thaddeus asked, wondering why he bothered to argue. She couldn't leave. She didn't have the strength to dress and make it to the door. And if by some superhuman effort she accomplished that feat, there wasn't a doubt she'd die ten minutes into the storm. Absently, he wondered why he cared. Why didn't he just let her go and be done with it? He nodded. "I reckon you might be right." Thaddeus shrugged a massive shoulder and continued. "Don't worry. I'll bury you and the kid come spring." His smile was wicked and filled with glee as her eyes widened with fear. "That's if the wild animals leave anything to bury."

Sarah would have dearly loved to have laughed off his dire warning but she dared not. She couldn't chance the life of her baby by taking her into an icy world of probable death. But if she left her behind, wouldn't the risk be as great? Would this man care for her as only she could? She had to believe he would. She couldn't leave Thomas to die. There was no one else. She had to go back for him. Sarah took a deep breath, forcing aside the need to moan

30

as she grit her teeth and flung back the covers. She didn't care that she exposed more leg to this stranger than any decent woman would. In truth, she never gave it a thought. All she knew was she couldn't just sit here, knowing her husband was sure to die. "You don't understand," she stated as calmly as she could, sliding to the edge of the bed again. "I left my husband at our wagon. I have to go back. He was terribly ill."

Thaddeus was far from immune to the sight of a woman's legs, and this one's were a damn sight better than most. It having been a spell since he'd last been in town didn't help matters any. He found himself clearing the huskiness from his throat as he asked, "Why'd ya leave him, then?"

Sarah took yet another deep breath and sighed. "The snow. The horses couldn't pull the wagon any further."

"And you walked on foot instead of taking one of these horses?"

Sarah's expression told so clearly the folly of her actions that Thaddeus couldn't prevent a short, unkind snort, which might have been a laugh. She ignored as best she could the sound. "I never thought . . ."

Thaddeus's grunt cut her off. "Never knowed a woman who could."

His bulk prevented her from leaving the bed. "Are you going to let me up?"

"Why? So you can fall on your face?"

Sarah knew the truth of those words. The last time she stood, the room had spun around her and

31

she'd had to hold onto the bed to keep from falling. "Will you go for him, then?" She bit at her lip, not knowing whom she hated more—herself for begging or this man for forcing her into such an untenable position. Almost blinded by a pounding headache, she nevertheless knew the time for talking was over. Either this man was going to help her or she was going after her husband herself, no matter her weakened state. It didn't matter that he imagined he could easily stop her. She was going!

Thaddeus could barely think, what with the sight of her bare legs taunting him. Quickly, he pulled the covers over her again. His gaze lingered for a long moment on the blanket and the obvious form beneath it. His voice was low, scratchy when he finally asked, "Which way am I supposed to go?"

"I don't know."

He shot her a disdainful glare. "How long were you walking?"

She shrugged. "Two or three hours, I think."

"Yeah. That's just great, lady. You *think* you were walking two or three hours, but you don't remember where you were comin' from? Reckon we should flip a coin? That way we'd know which direction to start lookin' first."

Sarah bit her lip, miraculously forcing back the nasty retort that had almost slipped out. "We were coming from the southeast. There was a narrow road that was full of sharp turns. We passed a large boulder on our right just before the snow got so deep the horses could no longer pull the wagon."

Thaddeus grunted. By her description, he knew

32

where the wagon was, and he wasn't the least bit happy about the fact. Now he'd have to go. He couldn't knowingly let a man die any more than he could a helpless animal. He cursed beneath his breath. Now he'd have two of them to care for. The day was getting worse with every passing minute.

He was pulling on his heaviest outerwear when he glared over his shoulder. "I won't be gone more than an hour or two." His dark eyes hardened as he whispered with menace, "If you know what's good for you, you'll stay where you are."

Thaddeus's curses were so powerful they might have been heard over the ragings of the storm. Might have, that is, if the man he leaned over was capable of hearing anything. The poor bastard was dead, and as far as Thaddeus could tell, he'd been that way for some time.

He shivered against another gust of wind that caught him under his coat as he jumped from the wagon and moved to check on the horses. They were in bad shape, almost frozen from the cold. Thaddeus wondered how long it had been since they were last fed. He threw a sack of oats over each head and wondered if either horse would live long enough to make it back to his place.

He shook his head as his gaze moved over the small wagon. What the hell had ever possessed the man to travel into unknown territory with winter approaching and his wife obviously so near her time? Hadn't he given a thought to what disasters might befall them? Hadn't he cared about his wife's health? Or their baby's?

Despite heavy gloves, Thaddeus's hands were nearly frozen by the time he unhitched the two horses and mounted his own. Slowly, he guided the three animals through the knee-deep snow. He shook his head again, knowing he'd never understand what drove some people to do the most god-awful ridiculous things. If she'd been his wife . . . Thaddeus forced aside the thought. She wasn't and she never was going to be. He was as simpleminded as the fool he'd left behind if he imagined anything else.

Still, no matter his insistence that he would not think on it, Thaddeus couldn't get one thought out of his mind. The woman, who was right now lying warm and comfortable in his bed, was free.

Thaddeus put it off for as long as he could, wondering how a man told a woman that her husband was dead. Did he just say it? "Lady, your husband's dead." Or did he ease into it, gentle like? "Lady . . . ah . . . it's like this . . ." He shook his head with disgust. What the hell was he supposed to do? Thaddeus was so cold, that he couldn't stop the shivers that racked his body. He'd been in the barn for close to an hour, seeing to the care of the horses, and still had come up with no clear-cut plan.

Maybe if he just went into the house and said nothing. Maybe she'd get the message. And what if she didn't? What if she asked him what happened?

Thaddeus's curses were the most vile yet. What the hell was he feeling so guilty about? He wasn't the fool of a husband who had dragged his wife into the wilderness to have her baby, with no one to help but an inept stranger. It wasn't his problem, was it? It sure as hell was, he instantly corrected. Who was going to take care of her now? Thaddeus didn't bother to answer his own silently asked question. He already knew the answer. "Damn. Damn. Damn!" he muttered as he walked with obvious reluctance toward his own house.

The door opened with a burst of wind as Thaddeus's snow-covered form almost fell into the room. Sarah gasped at the sight of him. His collar was up, his hat pulled low beneath a scarf that circled his head and covered his ears. He made directly for the stove as he tore away gloves that had grown less than useless the lower the temperature dropped. His fingers were stiff, his toes numb. He shivered as he leaned close to the stove's warmth, wondering if perhaps he hadn't waited a bit too long. He'd never felt this cold before. His hands and feet had never hurt so bad.

If he had frostbite, it was all her fault. Damn her for coming into his life. God, he didn't need this. He didn't need this at all.

"Where is he?" Sarah asked, her eyes large, her voice small with fear. "Couldn't you find him?"

"I found him" was all he had to say, and she knew. A soft sob sounded behind him as Thaddeus turned to see dry blue eyes so huge they

35

threatened to swallow her white face.

"It was too late?"

Thaddeus's nod said all there was to say. He cursed at the sight of her sitting in his bed, holding her baby to her breast. The shirt she wore was open at her throat. He could see too much of the soft globe of her breast as the baby suckled contentedly. Thaddeus forgot for a minute, his painful extremities as other parts of his body reacted.

Tormented by guilt, Sarah never noticed that the blanket had fallen to her waist. She never looked at the man, staring blindly at her daughter instead. If only she'd moved faster. Or remembered sooner. "Did you bury him?" she asked, unable to stop thinking about the wild animals he had mentioned earlier.

"Jesus Christ, lady!" he snapped. His guilt, no matter that it was unfounded—for he'd done nothing wrong except maybe lust after a woman who was in no shape mentally or physically to respond— caused the nastiest words possible to tumble from his mouth. "What the hell do you think I am? Was I supposed to come back for a shovel and return to the wagon, dig through I don't know how many feet of snow, and then tackle a ground frozen as hard as rock?" The stunned look of horror that entered her eyes only caused him more discomfort and thereby increased the flow of words. "Is it my fault you two were simpleminded enough to travel this time of year? Where the hell were you off to anyway?"

"French Creek."

36

"In the middle of a goddamned war?" Sarah's gaze moved to his stunned expression. "You were lookin' to find gold in the Black Hills? With the Sioux on the warpath?" He couldn't believe anyone could be that stupid. "What kind of a husband would bring his wife into that?" He nodded toward the baby. "Especially in your condition?"

"We didn't have a choice. I had to go. We sold everything to get enough money for the supplies."

Thaddeus shook his head. It was too much to believe. Nobody was that stupid.

"You're about a hundred miles west of where you're supposed to be."

Sarah nodded. "Thomas knew he'd lost the trail. We were trying to find it again when the storm hit."

"Of all the goddamned fool things to do, this one tops the list. And now you look at me like I gotta take care of all your mistakes."

He was right, of course, Sarah reasoned through her sorrow. It wasn't his fault. She and Thomas had brought this on themselves.

Thaddeus sneered as he watched the tears roll softly down her cheeks. "I hate it when women cry," he said, the words almost a snarl. "They use their tears to bend a man to their will. Well, it ain't goin' to work this time. I ain't goin' out again till the weather clears." And at her soft sniffle, he snapped with disgust, "You don't ask for much, do you, lady?"

Sarah said nothing as she lay down again and closed her eyes. Slowly, she turned to her side and cuddled her baby close against her. Her heart ached. True, she and Thomas had shared no great passion, but Sarah believed passion to be only in a poet's imaginings. They had had more than passion. Something better. They had had a gentle love, a tender fondness, and best of all, a friendship that Sarah had considered herself lucky to find. She was going to miss him terribly. She'd miss his sense of humor, his willingness to listen to her point of view, the gentle way he treated her. She tried to stifle the sob that rose to her throat.

Chapter Three

The brilliance of the sun shone through the oil-cloth-covered windows, lighting the inside of the cabin to a soft glow when Sarah next awoke. The silence that surrounded the small cabin was almost deafening in its intensity. A moment or so later, she realized the silence was less complete than she'd first thought. From far off, she heard a distinct thudding. Someone was chopping wood.

Her gaze circled the room, making sure she was alone before she dared to venture from the bed. She didn't want to be found again in only a shirt. Caught up in emotion at the time, she might not have noticed it, but on thinking back, she realized her host had seen more than she would have preferred. And from the way his gaze had constantly returned to her legs, it was obvious he'd liked what he'd seen.

If she was forced to stay here for the next few months, Sarah was determined to be careful, very careful indeed. Certainly, she had enough problems. She didn't need what could only lead to disaster should this strange man lose his control. And a stranger man she'd never known. She wasn't about to flaunt her nakedness . . . or near nakedness, as the case may be.

Quickly, she tiptoed to the window, lifted the oilcloth, and gazed out upon a winter wonderland. It was blindingly white and exquisite in its cold beauty. The sun glared off thick, sparkling white snow. It covered every tree and bush, stretching on for as far as the eye could see. It was hard to imagine that the very same snowfall that had created this lovely setting had nearly caused her demise and had in fact hastened the death of her husband. Her brow creased with pain as sorrow filled her being. She prayed Thomas hadn't suffered.

The cabin, built into the wall of a mountain, faced south. A wide covered porch had protected its front wall from the worst of yesterday's storm. A small yard was sectioned off by thick split rail fencing. Beyond the yard, a dense forest surrounded the small spread. The line of heavy snow-covered trees was broken only by what appeared to be a narrow, winding road. Sarah sighed unhappily. A road that promised to be impassable for the next few months.

She moved to another window. Snow lay thick upon the roofs and had drifted up against each of the small outbuildings that dotted the clearing. A corral made of snow-covered split rails stood empty. Some little distance from the corral stood a weathered, unpainted barn. The building appeared many times larger than the house.

To the left of the barn stood her inhospitable host. His coat hung on a hook or nail that projected from the barn wall. Despite weather that was no doubt bitterly cold, he stood clothed only in a shirt, buckskin trousers, and boots. Even from this distance Sarah noted the dark patches that stained his shirt as he swung the axe high over his head, then down to the log that lay between widespread feet. In moments, he'd reduced an enormous tree stump to small irregular chunks that would fit into his stove.

Sarah studied the ill-humored man for a long moment. The sun shone upon his dark head, bringing out red highlights amid its black, wavy thickness. His muscles bunched with every rhythmic swing of the axe, hinting all too clearly of the manly strength that lay beneath his shirt. Again and again, the axe flew through the air and landed with a sharp crack. His muscles tightened, sinewy forearms bunched with the force of each blow smoothed and then bunched again as the axe lifted once more.

How beautiful the movement, she thought, then stiffened, silently proclaiming her denial. Beautiful? How odd that she should connect beauty to a man so male, so very rugged. Surely this particular man was as far from beautiful as one was likely to get.

As if sensing her presence at his window, he turned and faced the house. For a long moment he stood with the axe hanging loosely in his big hand, his legs widespread, his hips jutting forward. His trousers hugged tightly muscled thighs.

Sarah's face turned red as she realized where her straying gaze had settled. Darn the man. It was indecent to wear trousers so tight. Didn't he realize that his exertion had caused his trousers to cling immodestly upon damp skin? Didn't he know how his stance flaunted his manhood? She shook her head and tried to muster a revulsion she somehow didn't feel.

She should have felt a measure of disgust but instead knew only an odd sense of unfaithfulness. The idea of not being true to her husband had never entered her mind. She shivered with disgust that, no matter how unbidden, these thoughts should have suddenly come upon her. She was only one day a widow. Most certainly it was too soon to entertain such thoughts. And to entertain them about a man so hostile and undesirable was horrifying to say the least.

No doubt her most unlikely daydreaming was merely the effect of yesterday's trauma. She imagined the comfort and care Thomas would no doubt have bestowed during and after the birthing was something that she desperately needed. She bit her lip as she turned from the window and watched her daughter kick off the small blanket. Thomas would never see her now, and for that she felt immeasurably saddened.

A moment later, Sarah was searching the cabin

for her clothes. What in the world had he done with them? She had to get dressed. It was impossible that she'd be expected to remain indefinitely clothed only in the man's shirt. Sarah realized for the first time that she didn't even know his name. She gave a soft laugh. She had never been so exposed, not even to her own husband. She remembered, almost as if it had been a dream how he had, because of Sarah's exhaustion, opened this very shirt and put Emily to her breast. Her body held not a secret for him, and yet they had never told one another their names.

Sarah felt her stomach rumble. She was starving and thirsty. She moved to the sink and lifted the handle of the pump. She didn't have the strength to pull it down. Her breath came in quick, short pants. She was dying of thirst and unable to find a drop of water. No clothes. No water. Was he trying to keep her a prisoner here? Did he want her to die so he might rid himself of a nuisance?

She was so weak, that she suddenly wondered if she could make it back to the bed without falling. Her knees wobbled and she leaned against the sink. Suddenly, the door crashed open. Amid a gust of icy wind, the giant that had taken her into his home came inside, his arms holding an enormous stack of wood.

The scowl that crossed his features told clearly of his displeasure. He needn't have bothered to shout, "What the hell are you doing up? Do you have the sense of a jackass?"

Sarah gasped at the thunderous denunciation and then sneered her own comment. "I don't appreciate being compared to animals, sir. I got up because I was thirsty."

Thaddeus dropped the wood into a bin near the stove. He hardly glanced at her. "Get back into bed," he said, his voice lower but no less ruthless in its command. "I'll get you something."

Sarah had almost made it to the edge of the bed, when she suddenly found herself sitting on the cold, wet floor. She'd slipped on melted snow, and the knowledge that it was this man's fault didn't help her sense of humor any. Behind her, a round of curses filled the cabin. "Damn fool woman," he grunted as he picked her up and placed her on the bed. "Don't have the sense you were born with."

"I fell because you didn't wipe your feet. There's melted snow all over your floor."

"You got that right." Thaddeus pointed with his thumb to his chest. "It's my floor, and if I don't want to wipe my feet, that's none of your business."

"It is when I fall because of it."

"You ain't supposed to be out of bed in the first place. So don't go puttin' the blame on me, lady."

"Oh my, aren't we going to have fun?" Sarah remarked sarcastically as she quickly pulled the covers over herself. A weak sweat covered her body and her arms trembled, feeling no stronger than wet wax. With a weary sigh, she lay down beside her baby. "Imagine staying here for the winter with such a cheery soul."

Thaddeus returned from his sink with a cup of cold water. He glared at her when he saw her trembling and held the cup to her lips himself. "If you were looking for cheery, lady, you shouldn't have come here."

"I didn't come here," she snapped angrily, almost choking on a mouthful of water. "You brought me."

"Would you rather I left you in a blizzard?"

"I'd rather, since we're stuck here together, you spoke civilly and treated me with a measure of kindness."

"Yeah . . . well, we all want things we can't have."

"Oh, God," Sarah breathed in disgust as she cuddled the baby close to her.

After glaring at her for a long, silent moment, Thaddeus moved to the kitchen area of his cabin. He took off his coat and set about preparing a meal. His hands stilled at the sound of her voice. "What is it you want that you can't have?"

"To live in peace, for one thing. Not to have to listen to nagging, nosy females, for another."

"Lord, you are touchy, aren't you?"

"Why? 'Cause I like living alone?"

"What's your name?"

Thaddeus shot her a long, hard look. For a minute, he was tempted not to tell her. For some reason, he didn't want even that familiarity between them. He didn't want to know her name. It was going to be hard enough as it was. A moment later, he cursed his stupidity. Knowing her name wasn't the problem. Her being here was the problem, and he couldn't do a damn thing about that. It was impossible to hope that they could live together for months and never find the need to address one another. "Thaddeus Payne."

Sarah nodded at the reluctant answer and returned, "I'm Sarah Carlton." He refused to look at her, so he didn't see her tentative smile. Sarah sighed. Just because the man was obnoxious, she wasn't about to allow him to bring her to his level. Her voice was soft and filled with gratitude as she continued, "I want to thank you for everything you did, Mr. Payne."

Thaddeus shrugged and mumbled something unintelligible.

"If it weren't for you, Emily and I would have died yesterday. We owe you our lives."

Thaddeus eyed the baby in her arms. So her name was Emily. He shrugged aside the thought that it was a pretty name. It didn't matter what her mother named her. "You don't owe me nuthin', lady. I didn't do it out of the kindness of my heart."

"Of course, you did."

"I didn't!" he insisted, his voice rising again. "You might as well get this into your head, lady. I ain't got any kindness left." His eyes pinned hers, forcing her to listen. "I'm the meanest son of a bitch you're ever likely to meet. And one more thing. I don't like women. Far as I can tell, they're good for only one thing." Heavily laced with disgust, his dark gaze ran the length of her. "And you ain't in no shape even for that."

"Nor will I ever be, as far as you're concerned," Sarah returned, her cheeks pink, her mouth set in a prim line as she turned away and stared at the wall.

It was easy enough to see she felt uncomfortable at the sudden turn in conversation. If she wished herself gone from here, she wasn't wishing any harder than he was.

Thaddeus shrugged at her comment as he started slicing into a chunk of meat. His voice was a low grumble. "Don't make no never mind to me, lady. One woman's the same as another." He laughed at her obvious fear, even though she'd covered it well. "You ain't got no cause to be scared. I can wait till I get to town."

"Why?" The word slipped out before Sarah realized she was going to ask.

"Why what?"

She turned to face him again. "Why don't you like women?"

Thaddeus stiffened and he shot her a murderous glare. "I reckon that ain't none of your business."

"Perhaps not, but since I expect I'll be the one to suffer for that hatred, I should at least know why."

"You should at least shut up and give a man's ears a rest." He eyed her reddened face and grinned at the anger she just barely held in check. "I ain't got all that much patience.

"Do tell," she returned, forcing her voice to remain low and calm, although it cost her some. "I was under the impression you had none."

Thaddeus grinned. He liked the idea of her answering him back. He might not be happy about losing the peace and quiet he liked, but arguing with this particular woman was the first real entertainment he'd known in months. "I told you I was a mean son of a bitch."

"Mr. Payne, I wouldn't dream of disagreeing with you. After all, I am a guest in your home."

He chuckled. "Smart mouth too, eh?" He nodded at her furious expression. Her anger had caused her cheeks to burn pink and her blue eyes to grow almost purple in color. Her hair was long and medium brown, with heavy streaks of gold. She sure was a mighty good-looking woman. "You're apt to find yourself another husband, even with your sharp tongue."

Sarah gasped at the very idea. "Another . . . Mr. Payne, I haven't been widowed twenty-four hours!"

Thaddeus grunted. "And I can see you're mighty broken up about it, too.

Sarah wasn't about to describe to this man the depth of her sorrow. That she felt a deep sadness, an aching loss, wasn't any of his concern and certainly none of his business. She was a private person and expected she always would be. Still, the man was waiting on her answer. "Everyone feels sorrow, Mr. Payne. We all show it in different ways."

Thaddeus nodded. "Yeah, when there's sorrow to feel."

Her eyes widened with surprise. "And you believe I feel none?"

"Lady, I've seen women lose their men before. Some put on a good show but marry again inside of a year, while others say right out, "I'm glad the old bastard's dead." He shrugged a heavy shoulder at her look of shock. "At least they're honest."

Sarah shook her head. "You've obviously associated yourself with people who were shallow and unfeeling."

Thaddeus gave a harsh laugh. "You talk a good story, lady, but I haven't seen you shed a tear for your man."

Both of them ignored the fact that she *had* cried at hearing Thomas was dead. Silently perhaps, but there had been tears.

"And you won't." Her words were soft, heavy with pain, but proud. "What I feel is personal and private."

Thaddeus cursed himself for every kind of fool. He hotly denied it was her words that left a deep void inside his chest. He wasn't feeling jealous. The hollow sensation was hunger, that was all. How could he be jealous of a man who was dead and a woman he barely knew? He didn't care that she'd lived with a man, shared his bed, had his child. He didn't want to know her private memories. He didn't want to know her at all.

Sarah awakened to a loud crash. She turned to her side and watched Thaddeus as he picked up the cast-iron pot and cover.

Thaddeus grunted as he turned to see her awake. He hadn't meant to drop the pot, but he wasn't going to apologize for waking her.

Sarah glanced to her right, then stifled a groan. But her would-be groan wasn't because of the noise he'd made. Her milk had come in. Lord, her breasts felt feverish and so achy she could barely stand to touch them. "I'm sleeping too much, anyway," she said, as if the man had offered a word of apology.

"You need it. You lost a lot of blood." Thaddeus had no way of knowing how much blood a woman usually lost when birthing a child, but it seemed to him she'd lost a goodly amount.

Sarah's face turned pink at being reminded of their intimate introduction. Thank God, he hadn't felt it necessary to continue on in that vein. This morning, after he'd fixed them something to eat, he'd brought her a small bowl of water so she might wash up. Along with the bowl, he'd left her enough cloth to make her own paddings. She wore a clean shirt, but wished she had her own clothes back.

"Emily, sweetheart, wake up," Sarah whispered to the sleeping child as she brought the baby's mouth to her aching breast. "You have to eat, honey. Mommy's hurting."

Sarah might have whispered the words in her softest tone possible, but considering the size of the cabin, Thaddeus had no choice but to listen. And listen he did. With every gasping breath she made, with every softly uttered moan of relief, he felt his body grow tighter and more aroused. He couldn't stand much more. Her sighs filled his brain. Her moans sounded like a woman in the midst of having the best sex she'd ever known. She had to stop. He had to shut her up!

But Sarah was in real distress. She didn't think of the sounds she made. She didn't imagine what they were doing to the man across the room. It never occurred to her that they sounded decidedly sexual. "That's better," came on another sigh of relief. "Oh, sweetheart, you're such a good girl."

"Shut the hell up, lady," came a startling roar from across the room.

Sarah's eyes opened wide with surprise. What had she done this time? The man was prowling the cabin like a pent-up beast. "I wasn't talking to you."

"I know who you're talking to. And I don't want to hear it."

Anger flashed in blue eyes. "Now, there's a lovely thought. I don't want to talk to you, and I haven't your permission to talk to my own daughter?"

"Talk if you want, but not about things like that."

"Like what?" Sarah asked, her brow drawn into a frown of confusion, for she couldn't imagine what she'd said that had caused this man to grow so upset.

"That." Thaddeus nodded toward her, his gaze upon the swollen flesh beneath the shirt she wore.

Sarah felt her cheeks burn. Lord, but this man was easily the most obnoxious beast she'd ever been unfortunate enough to come across. She turned her back to him, promising both herself and her baby that they were getting out of here at the very first opportunity.

"Are you going back to the wagon soon?"

"Why?"

"I need clothes for myself and Emily." Having, of course, anticipated the baby's arrival, Sarah had added enough blankets and bunting to their supplies to see this child through her first year. She longed to dress her daughter in the tiny clothes she'd spent so many hours working on.

"You won't be getting out of bed anytime soon. You don't need much."

Sarah's cheeks grew pink, her gaze refusing to meet his. Her voice was low when she spoke again. "Mr. Payne, I need to take a trip to the outhouse. If you won't give me my clothes, how am I to go?"

"Use the pot in the corner," he said as he nodded over his shoulder.

"Not likely," she instantly returned, her voice

sharp, her face flaming at the thought of answering nature's call without the privacy she needed. From the look in her eyes, Thaddeus imagined this woman would burst before she'd allow what she no doubt considered an appalling indignity.

Thaddeus chuckled as he read her expression. He'd like to have told her it didn't matter . . . that she didn't have anything he hadn't already seen. But Thaddeus figured saying that would be a bit much for any lady to handle. He might call her *lady,* using the word in the most derogatory sense possible, but still there was no doubt in his mind that this woman was a lady. Not like . . . Thaddeus muttered a gutter word as he denied the thought. What the hell was he thinking? She wasn't no different. None of them were any different. Once they had a man panting after their skirts, the poor bastard wasn't worth a damn. His voice was hard again, filled with all the loathing he felt for her sex. "You'll have to use it at night." She remained silent, never glancing in his direction. "I'll take you outside now, but—"

"I won't need it at night," she said, refusing to meet the hard, angry look in his eyes.

This was no good, no good at all. There was no way he could hold her in his arms and keep his body from reacting. He didn't want to feel this. It should disgust him, considering the condition she was in, but he had no control over it. He'd been too long without a woman. All he had to do was breathe her scent to stir his loins. Damn! She was just going to have to use the pot inside or make this trip on her own . . . starting right now.

Inside the house again, Thaddeus deposited her on the floor near the edge of the bed. Within seconds, her coat was hung up, her boots discarded, and she was shoved almost roughly under the covers. "You don't need to do this," she said. "I can . . ."

"I'll fix you somethin' to hang around the pot," he interrupted, " 'cause I ain't doin' it again." He walked toward the door. It slammed shut behind him.

Sarah sighed at the sound and automatically reached for Emily. Had she ever met a more surly, wretched grouch? What in the world was the matter with that man? Why did he hate her? But it wasn't her, was it? He hated all women. He'd told her as much and his actions certainly proved his words. Sarah couldn't help but wonder why.

She sighed again, wondering what the months ahead would bring. Would they eventually establish a truce of sorts? Would the day come when they'd be able to at least tolerate one another? Lord, how was she going to live through a winter of his disagreeable temper?

Sarah changed Emily's damp clothes. Gently, she wrapped her in the clean coarse bunting that Thaddeus had supplied. She tucked in the end around the baby's middle and pulled the huge shirt back into place. All the annoyance she felt toward her short-tempered host disappeared at the sight of her tiny daughter almost lost in the folds of one of Thaddeus's long-sleeved muslin shirts. Sarah smiled and watched as Emily appeared to listen to her mother's soft cooing words. Mother and daughter played for some time before Emily's chin suddenly began to quiver. An instant later, her tiny features squeezed into a scowl and a high-pitched quivering cry filled the otherwise silent cabin.

Sarah's lips curved into a gentle smile as she asked with tender concern, "Do you have a bubble, darling?" She took Emily into her arms and held her to her shoulder. Gently, she ran her hand over the baby's back in small soothing circles as her lips smoothed the sparse brown hair over her perfectly shaped head. "We'll be out of here soon, sweetheart," she murmured as if the child understood her feelings and shared them. "Come spring, I'm going to take you to see Grandma and Grandpa. Lord, but they're going to love you to pieces."

Sarah and Emily were asleep again by the time Thaddeus returned. He'd collected her wagon and stored it in his barn for now. It had taken him two hours of exhausting work, but he'd managed to bury her husband in a shallow grave. He'd covered the body with rocks, thereby prevented any wild animals from digging it out again. He hoped to hell she was satisfied, because his hands and feet hurt like the blazes and his back ached something awful.

His entrance had again awakened her. Thaddeus shot her a long, evil look, silently blaming her for his pains and aches. And who the hell should he blame? He wouldn't have been outside at all if it weren't for her nagging. Thaddeus refused to acknowledge the fact that she hadn't nagged at all but had only once asked if he'd buried her husband.

Sarah looked at the giant walking toward her, his arms filled with bundles. Did the man never enter his home without slamming the door into the wall behind it? "Every time you do that, you make the baby jump."

"Do what?"

"Slam the door into the wall."

Thaddeus scowled his dislike. "Lady, it's my door and my wall. I'll slam it if I damn well please." He dumped the parcels on the foot of the bed and muttered clear enough so she might hear, "I don't need no woman around here, telling me what I can and can't do."

Sarah's soft lips tightened into a straight line. "Mr. Payne, my one and only hope is that someday I'll have the opportunity to return your Christian hospitality."

Thaddeus laughed, the sound short, sharp, and definitely without humor. "No chance on that score, lady. I don't travel much."

"What a shame," her voice dripped with sarcasm. "You realize, of course, that you're denying the world a glimpse of your bubbling personality and excellent sense of humor."

Thaddeus ignored her snide comment and pointed to the bundles at her feet. "Here's your clothes." He nodded toward the door. "You don't like my personality, you can leave whenever you're ready."

"If I didn't have Emily to think about, I'd do it in a minute."

"But you do, so shut up and leave off your complainin'." He was taking off his outer clothing as he muttered, "A man can't think with the naggin' in this place."

Sarah gritted her teeth in an effort to keep her nasty retort from being uttered. How was she complaining? Just because she mentioned that slamming the door made the baby jump? Well, maybe it was a complaint, but it certainly was a small one. He had no right to take on like a wounded bear just because she'd said something about it. Lord, it was impossible here. She'd never make it through a whole winter in his company. She'd never be able to hold her temper that long. In the end, one of them was sure to kill the other.

"You hungry?"

Sarah shook her head, refusing to look in his direction.

Thaddeus heaved a long, weary sigh. "I ain't apologizin'. You might as well get that into your head."

57

"I never expected you would."

"Then stop sulkin'. It ain't goin' to get you anythin'."

Sarah shot him an exasperated look. "Why are you always accusing me of wanting something? Have I ever asked you for anything?"

Thaddeus laughed a mean, hard sound, then mimicked nastily, "No, you ain't never asked for anything." His voice lowered to its usual rough, scratchy pitch, " 'Cept my help in birthin' your baby, and then to go after your man, and then bury his body when I found him dead, and get you clothes, and feed and keep you here till spring. Other than that, I reckon you ain't asked for a thing."

Sarah bit her lip. He was right. She had asked a lot of him. Through no fault of his, she'd been thrust upon him. Granted, the man lived like a hermit and didn't much take to this intrusion into his solitary life, but he needn't constantly remind her of her helplessness or the things he'd done to help her. Anything done with that begrudging attitude could never be appreciated. "Believe me, had I an alternative, I wouldn't be here."

"Right," he agreed with a nod. "Now you ready to eat?"

Sarah gave a weary sigh. She was starving and thirsty as well. Acting like a spoiled child would get her exactly nowhere, especially with a man who couldn't care less if she starved herself to death.

Dressed at last in a heavy robe and her own

thick cotton nightdress, Sarah felt a bit more at ease in the man's company. Without his help she came to the table, only to receive a glare for her efforts. What was the matter now? Granted, he didn't want her here. He'd made that clear enough. But when Sarah tried to do anything on her own, he sneered his silent objection. Well, he could sneer all night long as far as she was concerned. She didn't care what the man thought or said. She wasn't about to lie in bed and wait to be carried to the table, simply so he could berate her for having done so.

The thickness of the newly fallen snow muffled the sounds of the two horses. Sarah never heard them come to a stop just outside the cabin door. She watched in some amazement as Thaddeus rose from his chair, took down his rifle from a shelf, pulled the door open, and asked, "You two be lookin' for somethin'?"

From the bed, Sarah couldn't hear much of their conversation, but what she did hear shocked her into silence.

"No. My wife and I ain't seen nobody with that description. Fact a' the matter is, we ain't seen nobody at all since September."

Wife? What wife? Was he married? If so, where was he keeping her and why hadn't she seen a feminine article in this entire place?

Someone spoke again. Sarah couldn't hear anything but the lowest murmurings.

"Twenty miles," Thaddeus returned. "He pointed to the snow-covered road that stopped at his front yard. "If you follow that road, it'll take you right into town."

A moment later, he closed the door and leaned his shoulder against it as he glared across the room, his face twisted into a sneer. "Where'd you hide it?"

Sarah, who had been ready to ask about his wife, was momentarily surprised at the odd question and obvious anger. It drove the words from her mind.

"What?" Having had the opportunity to hear only Thaddeus's side of the conversation, she couldn't imagine what his anger was about.

"Those two were Pinkertons. They're lookin' for a Mr. Carlton and his wife."

Sarah sat up in bed. Her expression couldn't have told more clearly her astonishment. "Why?"

"Appears like Mr. Carlton helped himself to what was in the safe at the bank just before he left town."

"Nonsense," Sarah breathed as a smile teased her lips. For a moment there, she'd actually felt a twinge of fear. But the idea that Thomas could have been a thief was simply too ridiculous to imagine. "There's been a mistake."

"Did your husband work for a bank?"

"As a matter of fact, he did."

Thaddeus snorted a disgustingly smug sound. The look in his eyes told clearly his disbelief.

"What does that mean?"

Thaddeus's mouth twisted with annoyance. There was no sense arguing with her. The truth of the matter was staring him in the face, no matter her denials. "Lady, I saved your hide. I figure that's worth half of the take."

"Half of what?"

Thaddeus's eyes narrowed with anger. "So you want it all, is that it? You figure my takin' you in should come free, while you hold on to the three thousand dollars in gold.

Sarah gave a sudden hoot of a laugh, the sound more of surprise than of merriment. But when she realized this man actually believed her to have three thousand dollars, her laughing became real and didn't stop for some moments. As a matter of fact, she couldn't stop at all. She laughed until tears streamed down her face. "If I had three . . ." another bout of laughter had to be overcome before she could go on, "thousand dollars, would I be here? Would I allow myself to be beholding to a man like you?"

He shook his head. "You might as well give it up. It won't work."

Sarah giggled. This was surely the most ridiculous thing she'd ever heard. It was some minutes before she realized his remark. She wiped her eyes with the backs of her hands. "What won't work?"

"This act. You figure I'll believe you if you laugh it off. But I don't."

Sarah's eyes grew wide with incredulity. Her lips

quivered, threatening laughter again. "You don't?"

Thaddeus simply shook his head. "I don't."

Sarah started laughing all over again. She couldn't help it. It was just too much. He thought she had all kinds of money, when she was dirt poor. Lord, this was just about the most hilarious thing she'd ever heard. Sarah wiped again at the tears her laughter had brought about, and she breathed a long quivering sigh. She hadn't laughed like that in weeks. It took some effort now to control another rush of merriment. "Well, that really is too bad, isn't it?" She giggled and bit her lip lest she start laughing again. "What can I do to convince you?"

"Nothin'," he said as he slid his arms into his coat and moved toward her.

"I assure you, Mr. Payne" — she tried to back up, when there was really nowhere to go but deeper into the mattress — "no amount of threats or physical abuse will suffice. I cannot give up what I don't have."

"We'll see," he said as he lifted her from the bed, baby, quilt, and all.

"What are you doing?"

"The money wasn't in the bags I already brought inside. Three thousand dollars in gold weighs a bit. I would have noticed."

"So, why accuse me . . ."

"I said it wasn't in the bags. So, that leaves the wagon."

"Mr. Payne, I assure you . . ."

"Lady, I assure you," he glared down at her, his eyes hard with dislike. "I'm goin' to find it. You might as well tell me now where it is."

"Be careful of that! It's all I have left of my grandmother."

Thaddeus grunted as he lowered the huge grand-father clock to the barn floor. He shot her a suspicious look as he ran his hand over the smooth surface, "Can't rightly remember a clock bein' so heavy. Could it be—?"

"It's heavy because it's made of solid mahogany."

"If I take it apart . . ."

"If you take it apart, you'll ruin it," Sarah finished for him. "If you must continue with this ridiculous sport, look somewhere else."

But of course he didn't, no doubt because she'd asked him to.

Sarah could hardly contain her fury by the time he was done. "I expect that makes us about even. You ruined my clock. It was an heirloom. It can't be replaced."

Thaddeus shrugged. "I'll put it back together later."

Sarah wondered if he could and if the clock would ever work once he did. She was sitting wrapped in the quilt upon a wooden barrel, pondering how much longer she was going to be forced to watch this madman tear her meager possessions apart. "I told you there is no gold. Those men made a mistake."

63

Thaddeus grinned. "How many Thomas Carltons you figure worked for the bank in St. Joseph, Missouri?"

"They made a mistake," she insisted, knowing her husband would never have done such a thing. He was an honest man. Yes, he'd been anxious to leave St. Joseph and find gold in the Black Hills, but he'd never have stolen in order to do it. "If there's money missing, someone else took it."

Thaddeus was rummaging through a box that held momentos, things Sarah couldn't bear to part with. One earring from a set given to her by her father on her sixteenth birthday. Her marriage papers. A crushed flower from her first bouquet. A string that had at one time no doubt wrapped something important. She couldn't remember now what that was. One comb and old hair ribbons, a cracked mirror. Idly, she wondered why she'd kept most of this stuff.

Sarah fought back the urge to tell him not to look through these things. She knew she only had to say the words and he'd have dumped the entire contents on the ground. She breathed an audible sigh of relief when the last trunk and dresser drawer had been searched. "Are you satisfied? I told you there is no gold."

Thaddeus ignored her gloating comment, took a hammer, and began pulling up the wagon's floorboards.

"Now what are you doing?"

"What does it look like?" he grunted as the first board came loose.

"Oh, God," Sarah groaned as she rolled her eyes toward the roof of the barn. "I don't think I've ever met a more obnoxious, ridiculous man in my life."

"Maybe," he grunted as another board came loose. Without another word, he simply reached into the cavity and came out with a canvas bag. The gloating look on his face showed his obvious satisfaction. "But I'm probably one of the richest.

Sarah's mouth hung open with surprise. It couldn't be. It absolutely couldn't be! Thomas would never have taken the bank's money. Never!

Thaddeus laughed at her expression. "Does this belong to you?" He spilled part of the bag's contents into the palm of his hand. The dimness of the barn couldn't hide the golden glitter.

"I've never seen it before," Sarah said, her eyes wide, her voice soft with amazement.

"Fine, since it ain't yours, then I reckon it's mine."

"It belongs to the bank, Mr. Payne."

Thaddeus laughed. "So, you finally admit to it?"

"I admit to nothing except that the bank's name is written on the bag," she said as she came to her feet.

Thaddeus was reloading her wagon. Sarah didn't stay to watch. A moment later she was outside. Barefoot, she walked the short distance through the snow back to the cabin. Tears streamed down her

65

face as she held her baby in her arms and snuggled under the covers. Thomas had been a thief. Sarah couldn't fathom the idea. It was impossible and yet sadly true.

Thaddeus soon followed her inside. Neither of them spoke again for the rest of the day and night.

A week passed in much the same fashion. The gold was never mentioned. Sarah wanted above all to forget its very existence. She spent most of her days and nights in bed. The results were that she recuperated from Emily's birth with amazing speed. She felt physically fit, but it wasn't enough. The constant strain of living with a man who rarely spoke and, when he did, never had a kind word to say was wearing on her. Sarah, who had come from a talkative family, felt lonelier than she could have dreamed possible. Surely it was better to be alone than suffer being ignored or, when noticed, growled at. She needed someone besides the baby to speak to.

Sarah was determined to bring Mr. Payne around. She couldn't stand months of living like this.

The evening meal began, as usual, in silence.

"Tonight I'll do the dishes," she said. "I've been inactive too long."

"Tomorrow."

Sarah nodded her acceptance. Tomorrow would be soon enough. She wouldn't start the conversation with an argument. Instead, she asked, "Have you lived here long?"

Thaddeus grunted a response.

"Does that mean you have?"

He gave her a hard, steely look, which she ignored. "I imagine you like living here," she said, her gaze moving around the small, cozy cabin.

Thaddeus watched her, wondering what she was leading up to now.

Sarah smiled. "Silly question. You wouldn't be here if you didn't, right?"

Thaddeus didn't want to think what that smile did to his stomach. His gaze moved from lips that had kept him awake for more than a week to her eyes. They were bright, cheerful, and as blue as the summer sky. He didn't like it a bit.

"You don't get lonely, though. That takes a special kind of man, don't you think?"

And when he didn't answer, she asked again, "Don't you think?"

"I reckon you can answer that for yourself. You've been doin' fine so far."

Sarah took a deep breath. His animosity was almost unbearable. It took every bit of her self-control not to lash out. She breathed a calming sigh. "Mr. Payne, would it be asking too much for us to converse at meals?" She smiled again. "Some people think it aids the digestion."

"Do you?"

Sarah shrugged. "I only know that it would be much more pleasant if we could speak to one another."

His eyes narrowed with undisguised interest. In

67

the light from the lantern, they seemed to glow with an almost hidden fire. Sarah only wished she knew what he was thinking. "How pleasant you aimin' on gettin'?"

"Excuse me?" Sarah blinked in confusion.

"I said . . ."

"I know what you said, Mr. Payne," she interrupted. "What I don't know is what you meant."

"My meanin's simple, lady. I can see you're kissin' up to me." He watched her eyes grow wide with shock. She was good, but not good enough. She didn't fool him any. "I'm thinkin' you're after the gold. And wonderin' how far you'll go to get it."

Sarah came instantly to her feet. Surely the man wasn't insinuating . . . He couldn't be that low. She shivered with disgust but honestly couldn't think which was the more horrifying thought—that he imagined her to want the gold, or that he assumed she'd do anything to get it. Her lips were pinched into a tight line of disapproval. "I meant only to add to our meal with conversation. I can see I was wasting my time."

Sarah couldn't know that the animosity she sensed was, in fact, only pure unadulterated fear. Thaddeus refused to converse or to even look at her, true, but Sarah couldn't know it was simply because every time he did, she looked more beautiful than any woman had a right to be. Her sitting across from him, cheeks pink from the heat of the oven, hair flowing in soft curls over her shoulders and down her back, just about drove him crazy with the need to touch her. It didn't matter none to him that she'd tried to hide the money. She stirred his blood like no woman had ever done before. Day and night, damn, but most especially the nights, he tried to fight it. And he had everything under control until she started talking. He wasn't going to make it if he had to listen to the sweet sound of her voice.

Anxious to leave this ogre's company, Sarah washed down the last of her meal with her coffee. "Thank you, it was delicious," she said as she moved toward the bed.

Thaddeus made a snorting sound that was clearly meant as an answer. Her lips twisted into a scowl. The man had the manners of a pig. Everything he did only made that glaring fact more obvious.

Her robe was laid neatly across the foot of the bed and she was just about to slide beneath its covers, when she heard a sharp popping sound outside. At almost the same instant, the shutters that closed over the oilcloth-covered windows shattered splinters of wood everywhere.

Sarah gasped with astonishment. What was happening? Later, she'd swear she'd heard a bullet buzz past her ear, just before it lodged itself in the wall behind her. At the moment, though, she had no time to think at all.

Chapter Four

The sound of Tiger's ferocious barking filled the night as the cabin instantly became as black as pitch. Sarah stood for a moment in silent confusion. Her brain had yet to comprehend what was happening, when the wind was suddenly knocked from her as a heavy weight struck against her back. The force of the attack buckled her knees and sent her crashing against the unyielding stone floor. Sarah groaned as she hit the flat surface with a bone-jarring thud.

It took her a moment to realize that Thaddeus was the culprit here . . . that even now his heavy weight lay full length upon her. She might have railed at being so sorely abused and surely she would have, but his stream of angry gutter curses were so vicious that they startled her into silence.

Tiger was nearly beside himself as he barked, howled, then jumped against the door, almost hysterical in his need to meet their attackers head-on. His barking startled Emily awake and filled the cabin with her cries. Sarah struggled to get out from under his body. Every instinct called out to protect her baby.

"Stay still, damn it!" Thaddeus warned, his mouth close to her ear. Suddenly, he spun her to her back and pulled her more tightly, more protectively, more fully against him.

"Emily!" Sarah grunted as she tried to fight him off. "I've got to get her."

Thaddeus swore again, pushing her back when she would have sat up. "Stay here," he said, his voice although a whisper promising dire consequences if she didn't obey. He crawled on his stomach toward the bed. Emily cried all the harder at his less than gentle handling, but moments later the crying eased to soft whimperings as she was placed in her mother's familiar arms.

He took Sarah against him again. His rifle was ready to fire as he half lay over her body. The baby was squashed tightly between them. Dragging her and the baby with him, as if he dared not leave them for a moment, Thaddeus brought them to the wall of the cabin. Slowly, he raised himself so he might peer out of the splintered shutters and oilcloth-covered window. Through the slivered opening, his eyes scanned the landscape. Nothing moved. He called out a sharp command, and Tiger fell quiet but for an occasional low growl. He needed to hear, but the baby whimpered still. "Shut her up, can't you?" he asked, glancing down at a face gone white with fright.

"She can't help it. She's afraid," Sarah shot back the obvious fact.

Her back was propped up against the wall, her hips bracketed between his knees as he loomed darkly above her. Instinctively, he tightened his hold and pulled her against him with his free arm, knowing she spoke for herself as well as for the baby. "Yeah . . . well, so am I. Let her have some," he nodded toward Sarah's breasts. "I expect that would quiet anyone down."

Their eyes had adjusted to the dark. They could see one another clear enough. Still, Sarah didn't hesitate to open her gown and bare her breast to the child's tiny quivering mouth. She was too shaken to think beyond quieting her baby.

But Thaddeus wasn't. He muttered a low groan and felt himself grow hard at the unbelievably erotic sight. The baby did as expected and quieted as she suckled, breaking the sudden silence with only an occasional soft hiccuping sob.

"What's happening?" Sarah asked before she noticed the direction of his gaze. There was no way she could cover herself. He was kneeling on her gown, trapping it between himself and the floor. There wasn't any extra material to cover her breast.

Thaddeus never heard her. He couldn't take his eyes from the sight of her creamy white breast. He wanted to touch it . . . to rub his entire body over it . . . to bury his face against it . . . to breathe in the warm scent of her milk . . . to take his turn at the sweet, sweet nourishment.

His breathing grew harsh, labored, stilted, almost as if he had to concentrate on bringing air into and out of his lungs. But he wasn't thinking of breathing. It was this woman that filled his mind . . . the feel of her softness against his body. He took a shaky breath and her scent filled his senses. He felt himself tremble as the familiar ache came again to plague.

He might not want her here, but he sure as hell wanted her in his bed. It didn't matter that she was temporarily incapable of giving him what he needed. He'd tried, but he couldn't stop himself from wanting her. Wanting her enough, in fact, to have momentarily forgotten that they were under attack.

He never thought to resist the temptation she posed. His finger reached out and stroked the plump exposed flesh, sliding slowly and with tantalizing accuracy to where the child's mouth met her mother. He felt the baby's lips and shivered. As if in a trance, Thaddeus brought his damp finger to his tongue. His eyes closed and a soft moan was torn from his throat at the pleasure of tasting her.

Sarah watched his movements as if spellbound. Nothing she'd ever known had affected her so profoundly. She couldn't believe she hadn't objected to his unbelievable daring. Worst of all, she couldn't believe she wanted him to do it again. This grizzly mountain of a man was foul-tempered and lacking in any Christian charity, yet she trembled for him to touch her. Pinned as she was, she couldn't move. But the fearful truth of it was, she was afraid she'd never want to move again.

His eyes found hers through the near darkness and held. Each drank in the sight of the other, as if they'd never truly seen before. "Sarah," he whis-

73

pered, the name sounding much like a prayer in a night gone suddenly still. His mouth was slowly descending, about to cover hers. Her lips parted to more easily breathe. She felt his warm breath hit against her lips and took his scent deep into her lungs; her entire being ached to sample his taste. And then, amazingly, they both heard the sound of singing.

Sarah's head spun dizzily as she suddenly found herself on the bed. In an instant, the covers were brought up to her chin. Her eyes were wide, filled with confusion and anger. His quick movements might have resulted in catastrophe. It was a miracle she hadn't dropped the baby. "Are you mad? What do you think—?"

Thaddeus leaned over her, his mouth close to her own. In his eyes she detected her own sense of confusion mingled with anxiousness, and most definitely anger. "Don't give me a hard time, lady," he snapped, his tone abrupt. "We have company." He was already on his way to the door as he spoke the last few words.

"What are you do—?" Sarah's words were cut off by the sudden appearance of two laughing, obviously drunk snow-covered men.

"Damn fool sonofabitch! I could have shot you dead," Thaddeus growled at one man who staggered into the cabin and nearly fell over the table. Miraculously, he landed on one of the chairs. Upon impact, the chair rocked wildly and then somehow, to the man's obvious surprise and delight, it righted itself. He howled his laughter at the accomplishment.

Emily jumped and then whimpered at the unusual sound.

"I thought you might be a Cheyenne raiding party."

Joe shook his head. "Indians wouldn't likely find themselves out in a storm like this."

Thaddeus shrugged. "No tellin' what an Indian might do."

"It was Joe's idea," the man who stood at the door explained with a nod toward his drunken friend. "Wanted to see if we could catch our old Sergeant off guard."

Thaddeus grumbled a retort so vile Sarah hadn't a notion as to what it meant. It appeared her ignorance was one-sided, though, for the two men laughed uproariously. Joe slapped the table in his hilarity. Emily stirred again at the sharp sound, but she soon quieted at her mother's soft cooing and gentle touch. The man standing at the still-opened door slapped Thaddeus on his back and, uninvited, walked inside. "Damn, it's as cold as hell out there. Starting to snow again, too," he said as he stood before the stove and reached his hands out to its warmth.

The lamp was relit. "Last I heard hell was a bit warmer than a Colorado winter," Thaddeus remarked as he emptied the last of the coffee into the sink and began to pump clean water into the pot.

The men chuckled.

"Where are your horses?"

"In the barn."

Thaddeus's eyes widened slightly. "You figure on

stayin' a spell?" He didn't sound overjoyed with the prospect, but these men were apparently used to his rough, unfriendly manner. Both seemed to shrug it aside. "Reckon we'll have to. At least till it clears again. The wind's blowin' every which way. Can't see a damn thing."

Joe, the man who had almost fallen upon entering the cabin, shook his head and grinned foolishly as he watched Thaddeus at the sink. "Johnny and me, we don't want no coffee. Got somethin' better than that." He reached into the sack that hung over his shoulder and pulled out three bottles. "Let's celebrate the end of the war."

Thaddeus frowned. "The war's been over for some ten years now. Besides, this ain't the time for celebratin'."

"Why?" Joe asked simply.

"My wife had a baby a few days ago."

"Your wife!" Joe suddenly stood on wobbling legs. His face expressed clearly his shock. "You mean you took her back?"

"My second wife," Thaddeus corrected the misunderstanding and lied without the slightest hesitation. His gaze moved toward the bed and a white-faced Sarah, who couldn't believe what she was hearing. His wife! Was the man insane? God in Heaven, what had she stumbled into?

The two men followed Thaddeus's gaze. Suddenly, both were on their feet, standing as if at attention, their wide-brimmed hats, sodden from hours of collecting snow, held at their sides. Joe licked the fingertips of one hand and smoothed down already-

76

matted hair, while Johnny eyed her with astonishment. The trouble was, his astonishment didn't last for long. His expression soon grew speculative. The hard glitter in his eyes brought shivers up Sarah's spine.

"Jesus," the man said, almost under his breath, "ain't you a lucky sonofabitch!" Immediately, he seemed to realize he'd spoken his thoughts aloud and continued with, "Excuse me ma'am. Ain't used to seein' womenfolk this far out of town." He cleared his throat. "And I ain't never seen one half as pretty."

Sarah might have thanked him for the compliment, but Thaddeus was suddenly blocking her view and pushing the man toward the table. Because of Thaddeus's shove, he too almost toppled a chair. "Ain't you gonna introduce your two best friends?"

"No," he said, not caring in the least what anyone thought of his rudeness. He didn't want these two near her. He didn't want them here at all.

Johnny chuckled a decidedly wicked and knowing laugh, while the other almost whined, "Aw, come on, Thad. Jesus, it ain't like we're gonna steal her away or anythin'. We only —"

His words were brought to an abrupt halt as Thaddeus's fist contacted with the man's jaw. "Damn!" Joe groaned as he tried to pick himself up from the floor, gave up on the idea, and rubbed his jaw instead. "What'd you go and hit me for?"

Thaddeus flexed his fingers and purposely placed his bulk between the two men and his bed. His intent was obvious, even to the most dim-witted soul.

He didn't want them looking at her. "Watch what you're sayin'." He gave a long, weary sigh and then added, hoping this would end the subject, "Sarah's tired. No need to bother her."

Sarah turned her back to the three men and brought Emily tighter to her body. God Almighty, but she'd never seen a rougher, more motley specimen of manhood. And these were Mr. Payne's best friends? She shivered, imagining that it might have been one or both of these men who had found her instead of Thaddeus. Granted, he didn't want her here, but at least he offered her a measure of safety. Somehow she doubted she would have felt the same had she been found by either of these two men.

The conversation across the room grew lower as the night wore on, obviously in deference to Sarah and the baby. She gathered, before their voices grew too soft to hear, that the two men worked a claim not too far from Mr. Payne's place. They were on their way back to it from town when it had started snowing again.

Sarah knew silver had been rumored to have been found in the San Juan Mountains. Is that where they were now? Had Thomas wandered so far from the trail that would have taken them north?

Thomas had dreamed of one day striking it rich. She wondered if these men were rich, then decided they probably weren't. A man who had money was apt to dress a sight better than these two.

Just before she drifted off to sleep, Sarah's thoughts returned to the moment when she and Mr. Payne had huddled against each other beneath his window. How he had touched her, whispered her name, his sudden gentleness. The moment hadn't lasted more than half a minute, but in her mind, it seemed to have gone on forever.

In the few short moments that came between wakefulness and sleep, Sarah wondered what it would have been like if he had kissed her. Would she ever know the touch of his mouth?

Hours later she awakened to find Thaddeus draping a sheet from an overhead beam, thereby separating the bed from the rest of the cabin. Her eyes fluttered shut and she brought the baby closer to her side, falling immediately into a deep sleep again. When Sarah next awoke she gave a soft gasp, finding herself cuddled warmly against Mr. Payne. Her entire body stiffened with dread. His hand was instantly there to cover her mouth. "Don't cry out!"

Had she not been terrified, Sarah might have laughed at his ridiculous command. Did he expect her to obey his order simply because he said so? Her eyes widened with fright. What did he think he was doing in this bed? Surely this man wasn't the kind to abuse a lady. Of course he was, a small voice answered her silent thought. Sarah grew instantly enraged. Granted, the man had been obnoxious from their first meeting, but she had never suspected him of this. She kicked him as hard as she could with the heel of her foot and listened with satisfaction to his grunt.

Heavy legs pinned hers to the bed as he rolled toward her, trapping a sleeping Emily between them. His eyes were hard as he hovered threateningly above her. "You goin' to let me explain?" he asked, his voice barely a whisper.

Eyes wider than ever, Sarah nodded as she tried to shrink away from his touch. Her heart pounded so loud she could barely hear the low spoken words.

Thaddeus felt her pull away and sighed unhappily. It had felt so good with her in his arms. Maybe better than it had ever felt before. He shook his head, determined to put aside the thought. He couldn't think about that now. They had to come to an understanding, no matter her obvious objections. "They think we're married. We'll have to share this bed till they leave."

"Why?" she spoke the word aloud the moment he released her mouth. At the stiffening of his body and his glaring look, she softened her tone to a whisper. "Why did you tell them we're married?"

"Lady, did you see the way they looked at you?"

"So?"

"So," he sneered in return, "if they thought you meant nothing to me, I wouldn't be able to stop them from taking you with them." Thaddeus knew that for the lie it was. He didn't much want her here, but there was no way he was going to allow anyone to take her, especially against her will, and he was almost positive she wouldn't have gone willingly.

"Don't be ridiculous," she dismissed his statement with a shake of her head. "Of course, they wouldn't take me. I simply wouldn't go."

"Oh, you wouldn't? Suppose they didn't ask your permission?"

"You mean they might take me against my will?"

80

Sarah couldn't believe any man would do something so dreadfully evil.

He nodded his agreement. "You're a mighty good-lookin' woman. Hard for any man to resist. Especially a man who has to go for months without."

Despite the terror his words had instilled, Sarah couldn't deny the warmth that invaded her chest. He thought she was good-looking, and for some insane reason the knowledge made her feel wonderful.

Sarah shook her head again. She didn't want to hear his ominous warnings. The thought of being taken against her will was repugnant. She'd never allow it. "It would never happen."

"And how could you stop it?"

"I'd notify the sheriff, of course."

It took some effort for Thaddeus to control the need to laugh. Was this woman as naive as she sounded? "Of course. Not accountin' for the fact that you'd be stranded atop a mountain, you would have notified the sheriff. Would that be before or after you shared their beds?"

"What?"

"Maybe they share the same bed. I reckon they would have themselves a mighty good time with you snuggled between them."

The mental picture he painted was beyond Sarah's realm of understanding and Thaddeus knew it. Even in the semidarkness, he could see the incomprehension in her eyes.

"Do you think they'd take you because you're such a good cook?"

Sarah shot him a look of annoyance and shook

her head. "They don't know if I can cook."

Thaddeus nodded. "Right. And they don't care none, either."

"Mr. Payne, if what you say is true, how can you count men like these among your friends?" she asked, her eyes trying to see his expression as he loomed over her.

"I don't got no friends, lady. Especially not those two."

"They said . . ."

Thaddeus heaved a heavy sigh. The sound interrupted her words. He laid down at her side again and stared up at the dark ceiling. "I've known them a long time, is all. We were in the same company during the war."

"And they were the kind of men who might take a woman against her will?"

"I've seen them do worse."

"And still you welcome them into your home?"

"Did I have a choice? If I had my way, you wouldn't be here, either. When the weather clears, they'll be gone."

"You mean they're still here? Sleeping in the same house?" Her whisper grew so soft as to be almost nonexistent.

"Why do you think we're whisperin'? Now go to sleep."

"Suppose they try to take me?"

"They won't."

"Suppose they sneak up on you while you're sleeping—and—and—" Sarah couldn't finish. The thought was too horrible to bear. "Emily would die if they took me away from her."

"Tiger's sleepin' alongside this bed. He's been protecting you since you got here. Nobody's goin' to take you nowhere. Go to sleep."

The thought of the dog being nearby brought a measure of relief, but it wasn't enough. Sarah more than welcomed the comfort of his arms and eagerly cuddled against him as he turned to his side. "Ain't much room here. Gonna have to make due." She was trembling. It never occurred to her to push him away. She needed the comfort and safety she felt in his arms. She needed to feel his strength, his protection.

He felt her shiver and almost smiled as his face buried itself in her thick hair. Silently, he hoped it would snow for another week. Thaddeus was destined to curse the thought.

Light was just creeping its soft glow over the horizon when he heard the men stir. Thaddeus groaned. He'd never felt so damn comfortable in his life. The last thing he wanted to do was get up.

Sarah lay with Emily against her breast, her back to his chest, her bottom to his front. Her head lay directly below his, her soft hair tickled his throat. Thaddeus held her tightly to him with an arm thrown over her waist, while his hand had somehow found its way inside her unbuttoned gown. He blinked with surprise as he realized his palm was damp with her milk as he cupped a naked breast.

Every nerve in his body came instantly awake.

83

Damn. He hadn't meant to touch her like this. No doubt he had unknowingly reached for her in his sleep. The thing was, she was never going to believe it. He had to bring his hand back to his side and do it before she awoke.

But her right arm lay over his, trapping it in place. Any movement was sure to awaken her. And the worst of it was, his body was responding against her backside like it never had before. She was going to think he was as bad or worse than the two who slept across the room.

Thaddeus scowled. What the hell did he care what she thought. She was a damn sight better off staying with him, but he sure as hell wasn't going to force her. If she wanted to leave, she wasn't going to get an argument from him.

Thaddeus took his hand from her warmth, came up on his elbow, and watched as her eyes blinked open with confusion. He waited for the anger to set in, but what he saw instead almost stole the last of his breath. Her gaze was soft, gentle, filled with an emotion he couldn't fathom as she rolled to her back and met his fierce, dark glare. Her hand came up to his bearded jaw and she smiled. "You're so handsome. Why do you hide it beneath all that hair?"

He could tell from the sudden widening of her eyes that the words had shocked her, perhaps even more than they had him. It was just coming from sleep that had caused her to speak her thoughts aloud. She'd never have otherwise blurted them out. Her hand pulled back as if burned. Her face grew pink with embarrassment at what she'd said. "I—I what I meant was—" Her words faltered. It was clear she didn't know what to say next.

"Why would you think I'm handsome?" Thaddeus couldn't stop his lips from curving into a smile.

Sarah shook her head, at a loss to explain her lapse of common sense. She couldn't understand why she had spoken so foolishly. "I didn't—"

"But you did." His voice was low, thick with sleep, and something more that sent shivers of excitement down her spine. "Tell me why." His head dipped until his lips were almost touching hers. "Tell me," he insisted, then never allowed her the chance as he gave in to the temptation of her beautiful mouth.

His kiss was gentle, his lips brushing against her own tentatively, pulling back and then touching her again as if testing her softness, her response. He heard her short gasp of surprise and smiled. She never thought to refuse him this pleasure. And Thaddeus was determined to show her just how pleasurable it could be.

Again, again, and yet again his mouth brushed hers, so softly, so gently, she might not have known if she hadn't watched. His beard and mustache tantalized her skin and sent chills down her spine. She marveled that it could be so soft, so tempting. Her fingers itched to touch it. She never thought to stop them from sinking into the black silkiness of his beard as her hands discovered the shape of his jaw, the hollowness of his cheeks. She shivered at the feel of him. Lord, but the crisp texture was a delight to the senses.

Thaddeus felt her lips grow softer, malleable, pliant, and he deepened the kiss. He felt her moan, absorbed its sound into his mouth, and growled at the growing urgency that exploded into pure lust in the pit of his belly.

His mouth grew heavy, hotter, sweeter than anything she'd ever known. He ravaged her mouth and then gently sucked at her lips, grunting his approval as they moved further apart. He savored her taste, breathed her scent, and felt his world tip crazily out of control. His arms tightened around her and his breath came in short, jerking hot pants.

Helpless but to give what he demanded, her lips parted on a whimper. A low buzzing sound filled his brain as his marauding tongue found no obstacle to the deep, hot wetness of her mouth. He groaned again, absorbing her taste, feeling her shy response as his tongue imitated the movements his body so desperately longed for.

She was warm, soft, so very much a woman and God, he wanted her so badly he wondered if he'd survive the needed wait. Thaddeus wasn't a patient man. He knew it wasn't going to be long before he took her. But it wouldn't be today. He knew this moment couldn't go further than a kiss. Nothing could happen between them, not with two men sleeping across the room. Besides, she'd yet to heal from the birthing. And her husband had only just died.

Thaddeus pulled sharply back at the thought, then scowled into passion-softened features. Her husband had just died, and here she was lying all soft and cuddly in his arms. A look of pure contempt settled over his features. He didn't think that this aching need she'd brought about was his own damn fault . . . that he never should have kissed her . . . that her responses were at first tentative and sweet, almost virginal. All he could think was that she was a woman and, like all women, deceitful, untrustworthy, and void of any real, lasting emotion. Hadn't her actions proven that? His mouth twisted into a sneer and he couldn't stop the sharp words from spilling out. "The grievin' widow," he ridiculed in disgust. "What has it been? Eight whole days? I guess that's time enough to wait for a little screwin'."

Had he slapped her, Sarah couldn't have come more sharply to her senses. Her eyes widened with shock at what she'd done. At what she'd allowed him to do. That he thought her despicable was obvious, but he couldn't have felt the emotion stronger than she.

Mortified by her actions, her face grew bright red. In her embarrassment, Sarah never thought that he should shoulder at least half the blame. Her eyes were huge, her expression pure confusion. She cleared her throat twice before she could find the courage to speak, and when she did, she couldn't imagine what to say. "I—I—" her words faltered.

Thaddeus chuckled. "No need to flash those beautiful eyes at me, lady. If you're thinkin' I'll believe your little innocent act, think again." His grin was mean, as if he delighted in her suffering. "You're good, I'll give you that, but not good enough."

"For what?"

Thaddeus turned his back to her and reached for

his buckskins. He was pulling them up his legs when he turned to face her. "To fool me."

Anger filled her blue eyes, causing them to grow almost violet in color. A long, silent moment passed as she watched him pull on his boots. Just before he was ready to leave their sectioned-off area, she remarked, "Mr. Payne, to my knowledge, it's not possible to fool a fool."

Chapter Five

She wouldn't think about it. She couldn't think about it. Every time she remembered her disgraceful actions this morning, her face flooded with color. The heat in her cheeks grew so intense as to threaten to flame, while a dull ache filled her heart. Thomas had died just eight days ago. How could she even think of another man so soon? And if she did, how could it possibly be that wretched ogre?

It couldn't. She never thought of him. He was just a man, a foul-mouthed brute, nothing more. If the day ever came when she looked seriously at another man, it certainly wouldn't be anyone like him.

How dare he accuse her, when it was his actions that had started it? She hadn't asked for his kiss, and she had certainly not cooperated in his debauchery. The next time he felt a need to kiss someone, she'd . . . she'd . . . Well it just better not be her, or he'd curse the day.

Lord, but it felt good to wear a dress again. Sarah grinned. Even her new and slightly tight button-down shoes felt wonderful hugging her feet. She was sick of nightdresses and robes. She was sick of staying in bed, sick of feeling weak and just about useless. And the longer she stayed in bed, the weaker and more useless she did feel.

She wasn't wanted here, but as long as she was forced to stay, she was going to pull her own weight. Searching through the dresser, she found a drawer holding two blankets. Sarah used the blankets to cushion its hard bottom and sides. After feeding and dressing Emily, she placed the baby in her new bed and brought her into the kitchen, where she was determined to make the best breakfast these men had ever tasted.

On the table, Emily was close enough to the stove's heat not to need an extra blanket. After a few minutes of kicking and making soft baby sounds, she fell into a contented sleep.

The cabin was filled with the delicious smells of freshly brewed coffee and frying bacon, but upon entering, Thaddeus only glared at the sight of her standing before his stove. He didn't like the idea of a woman making herself at home in his kitchen, or in any part of his house for that matter. But he couldn't order her out, not with Joe and Johnny standing almost directly behind him.

Sarah noticed his scowl. It would have been hard not to notice, since this one was more threatening than most. She merely sighed her relief at his near

90

noiseless entrance and then shot him an amused, victorious glance. For once, he had made nary a sound, for she had taken one of her bags, stuffed it with two petticoats, and placed it where the door usually crashed against the wall.

"Breakfast is ready," she said cheerfully, purposely ignoring her host while centering her attentions on his two guests.

Thaddeus eyed her for a long moment. She wore a gray cotton dress that buttoned up to her throat and was covered with a long white apron. Her cheeks were pink from the heat of the stove, and her long hair had been parted in the middle and combed sleekly back from her face. Loosely pinned to the nape of her neck, tendrils of honey-brown and gold had already fallen to curl against her cheeks.

He knew it was a mistake the minute his dark gaze traveled the length of her. He muttered an unconscious, almost unheard curse as he felt his body's involuntary reaction to her luscious curves. She was a fine figure of a woman. Did having a baby only add to that fact? Thaddeus shrugged. There was no way he could know. A second later he found himself mumbling furious curses that he should wonder about it at all.

He didn't like it. He didn't like it one bit. He didn't want any woman taking over his kitchen. Besides, she shouldn't have gotten out of bed, not while these two were here. No telling what evil thoughts were nagging at them, what with a woman as beautiful as Sarah. Damn her for standing there and letting them look their fill.

Thaddeus glanced at the two men. Hell, their eyes were just about ready to pop. He'd bet his last dollar they'd never seen anything half so pretty. Thaddeus felt his entire body stiffen when Johnny licked his lips, his gaze fastened on Sarah's breasts. Absently, he wondered how he'd managed to control the urge to ram his fist into the man's face. No, he didn't have to think much about it. One look at the lust shining in their eyes and he sure as hell knew their thoughts.

In full view of his guests, Thaddeus closed the short distance that separated him from the stove, took a startled Sarah into his arms, bent her back just a bit, and staked his claim with a kiss that left her breathless. "Good mornin', darlin'," he said, for his audience's sake, then grinned down into Sarah's astonished but angry expression.

The sudden tightening of the hand at her side told her clearly enough that he was expecting a wifely response. "Thaddeus, we have guests," she reminded demurely as she managed to gracefully free herself of his hold, her cheeks aflame at being so familiarly handled. She was going to get him for that. She didn't know how, but she would.

The two men chuckled at her clear embarrassment. Each held out their hand as Thaddeus, with obvious reluctance, performed the introductions. Sarah, half blocked from view by her "husband," shyly accepted their enthusiastic handshakes. A

92

moment later she decided Mr. Payne was mistaken. They might present a picture of hard, dirty, almost uncivilized men, but these two harbored no menacing intent. Why, they were as nice and as pleasant as a person could be.

Sarah's smile was radiant. "Sit down, gentlemen," she nodded toward the table. "I have coffee ready and enough bacon and flapjacks to soothe the biggest appetites."

Sarah couldn't know that at that particular moment the two men were thinking on a decidedly different fare, involving appetites of quite another order. Their belly's might growl, for breakfast smelled delicious, but it was the hunger just below their bellies they longed to appease. Thaddeus frowned, noticing the men couldn't keep their eyes off her. Sarah seemed not to notice at all.

Emily's little bed was placed on a chair and positioned at Sarah's side, as they sat around the table. All three men ate as if this were their last meal on earth. Their plates were emptied of stacks of flapjacks before Sarah had even finished her two.

"I'm stuffed. This is the best meal I ever ate," Johnny remarked.

"And the best coffee I've ever drunk," Joe said as he finished what was left in his cup and smacked his lips.

Sarah glowed at their compliments. Thaddeus only scowled. "Would you care for more?"

"If it wouldn't trouble you none, ma'am."

"No trouble at all, Mr. . . ."

"Joe's just fine, ma'am. We're neighbors, after all."

Sarah smiled and refilled all their cups. In doing so, she brushed against Thaddeus. For just a second he could feel her breasts soft against his back as she leaned over. Carefully, he watched as she went about pouring coffee for their guests. He nodded his approval that she kept her distance from the men.

Sarah was feeding the baby behind the curtain when the door burst open again. Almost immediately, the hanging sheet was brushed aside. "I only got a minute," Thaddeus said, as an inch or more of snow fell from his hat and boots, forming a small white mound at his feet. Sarah scowled at the mess he was making and made a mental note to wipe it up before she slipped and fell again.

Thaddeus ignored as best he could the gentle, delicious sight of this woman feeding her child, a sight that caused an ache to twist at his inners. His gaze remained on her face as he spoke. "Weather looks like it might be clearin'. If so, they'll be leavin' in the mornin'. Till then, I want you to keep yourself behind this curtain."

Sarah glared her resentment. So, she was to be banished from sight simply because this man insisted on having the most evil thoughts. Well, she didn't believe Joe and Johnny were the villains he imagined. Not for a minute. They treated her po-

94

litely and as pleasantly as any decent man would. Far more decent, in fact, than did her host.

Sarah was of a mind to tell him exactly her thoughts on the matter, when she realized coming to his guests' defense was just about the worst thing she could do. Instead, she countered with, "And what would that accomplish but to remind them I'm in bed? If they're thinking along the lines you imagine, wouldn't that be the worst thing I could do?"

Thaddeus cursed. For a woman, she knew how to use her head. He knew that having her stay behind the curtain might only entice them, but damn it, he couldn't stand the thought of them looking at her! He knew the things they were imagining they could do to her . . . the things they'd be doing right now if it weren't for him.

Thaddeus didn't respond to her remarks. He knew from experience that there was no sense in arguing with a woman. Once they set their minds to something, you couldn't sway them under the threat of death. And this one was no different. She was sure to give him a hard time.

"I told them we met at the beginning of last year. That your family lives just outside of town. That your father owns a small spread." He stopped to take a breath of air. His voice took on a slightly breathless quality, which brought Sarah's gaze to meet his. "They'll think twice about taking you off if they know help is close by."

He stood silently before her for a long moment.

Sarah noticed a pulse pounding in his throat. Her gaze moved again to his and was captured by a look so dark, so filled with emotion, that it brought shivers up her spine. She felt her breath catch in her throat. Her pulse began to throb. She could feel it, hear it. Sarah leaned back a fraction, unsure of what to expect. What was he waiting for? Did he want a response?

Sarah was about to ask him for some privacy, when he uttered a low sound that rivaled pain, then dropped his gaze to Emily and the exact point where her lips suckled her mother. Sarah could have reached for the blanket. She could have covered herself, but for some reason she couldn't understand, she did nothing. Did she want him to watch? Had she wanted him to notice what she was doing from the moment he had moved the sheet aside? Lord, what was happening here? What was this heat that was slowly spreading throughout her body?

A second later he disappeared. Sarah couldn't rightly say if it was relief or disappointment she felt as the door slammed behind him.

Of course it wasn't disappointment, she silently berated. What a ridiculous notion. Sarah dismissed the man from her mind. This was her and Emily's time. He had no right to interfere, no right to barge in unannounced. She'd noticed the flush that had spread up his cheeks just before he'd left. Good. She hoped he was uncomfortable. Maybe the next time he'd call out before moving behind the curtain.

But the flush hadn't been embarrassment. Thaddeus had entered the cabin to find the room empty. Obviously, Sarah was behind the curtain. There could only be one reason why she'd seek privacy. He knew what he'd find there, and yet, like a fool, he moved aside the sheet anyway. Damn! He'd tried not to look, knowing what would happen if he did, but in the end he couldn't resist. His mouth had gone dry and his heart hammered in his throat. Jesus! He couldn't believe how badly he longed to be held to her breast.

He closed his eyes as memories of the sweet, warm taste of her came to assault him. He ached to sample just a moment of the tenderness she showered on her child. Thaddeus uttered a round of the most vile curses he could think of as he vehemently denied the thought. That would be the day. That would be the *goddamned* day! Just let her show him a moment's tenderness and he'd kick her out on her sweet little butt, storm or no storm.

Besides, it wasn't her. Any woman who bared her breast was sure to set him on fire. He was a man, after all. What the hell was the matter with her? Why hadn't she covered herself like she usually did?

Sarah smiled as she watched all three men rub their stomachs with varying degrees of satisfaction, Thaddeus, of course, being the least obvious. The apple pie had finished off a delicious meal of pot roast, potatoes, and gravy. Sarah had every right to be proud of her accomplishments. Earlier that day she'd been delighted to find a sack of apples, almost hidden behind the barrel of flour in the corner. The pleasurable smiles she received at the first mouth-watering bite was worth all the hours of work.

Sarah sliced three more pieces of pie and placed a second piece before each man. "If you keep her, she'll only make you fat," Johnny said as he swallowed an enormous chunk of pie, his expression as innocent as a newborn babe's.

But Thaddeus wasn't fooled by the man's play at innocence. His hand inched slowly from the table to caress the gun that hugged his hip. "Meanin'?"

"I'd be happy to take her off your hands. Then you wouldn't have to go buy all new clothes."

Everyone laughed. Everyone except Thaddeus.

" 'Course, you don't have to get fat. Not if you exercise," Joe said, dragging out the last word until it sounded strange to Sarah's ears.

"And how would I do that?" Thaddeus never moved his lips. His voice was deep, the words almost whispered. His eyes were hard and threatening.

Sarah felt a chill race up her spine.

"Aw, I don't know." Joe's eyes twinkled as he looked from Thaddeus to Sarah and back again. "But I'll bet you could think of something."

"I'd be right careful of what I said next." Thaddeus didn't have to tell him why. There was murder in the man's eyes.

"I only meant that now that you have yourself a family, you'll probably make this place bigger."

Sarah didn't breathe for a long moment. She could actually feel the tension as if it were a thick, unbreathable substance in the air. She heard Thaddeus take a deep breath, but beyond that not a sound came to her ears save the solitary ticking of the clock on the dresser. She waited for some kind of an explosion but none came. A moment later all three men smiled, and if their smiles weren't exactly friendly, Sarah nevertheless breathed a sigh of relief. She finished clearing away the dishes and, after wishing the men good night, took the baby behind the hanging sheet.

Sarah could hear the men making up their pallets before the stove. Hurriedly she undressed, positive that Thaddeus would step behind the curtain at any moment. She wasn't wrong. She'd just pulled her nightdress over her head, when she felt a draft created by moving the sheet and her lantern went out.

"What are you—?"

Thaddeus stood directly before her, so angry he could hardly contain himself. His entire body trembled and his voice was almost nonexistent as he pushed his bearded face within an inch of hers. "If you want to give them a real show, why not take down the curtain?"

"What are you talking about?"

"Your body is silhouetted on that," he nodded at the sheet. "There's nothing they can't see 'cept maybe exact color."

Sarah gasped with shock and a hand instantly covered her mouth. "Quiet," came his low whisper, "If you make those kind of noises, they'll think we're doin' somethin' . . . somethin' they want a hell of a lot more than apple pie." He shrugged. "Could be they'd be tempted to join us." He grinned, but the smile wasn't meant to portray merriment and it didn't. "Maybe you'd like that."

"You're disgusting," Sarah returned as she freed her mouth with a sharp shake of her head.

Thaddeus snorted a sound that was obviously meant to be a laugh. It didn't quite make it. "Am I?" he asked, his mouth hovering close to hers. "Maybe, but not half as disgusting as those two." His hands took hold of her shoulders and gave her a slight shake. "You know what they want, don't you? That's why you lit the lamp. You wanted them to see you, didn't you?"

"I'm going to bed, Mr. Payne." She wrenched herself from his hold, thoroughly disgusted that he could accuse her of something so horrible. The man was demented. There was no other excuse for his actions. "And I'd appreciate it if you kept your evil thoughts to yourself."

"It wouldn't matter none, lady. Those two"—he nodded again at the hanging sheet—"are thinkin' plenty enough for all of us."

* * *

Sarah tried to create some room between their bodies, but she soon realized she had only two choices — either lie there in his arms, as she had last night, or fall on the floor.

"Satisfied?" he asked, only barely holding back his laughter as she settled at last into place.

"I'll be satisfied when I leave here forever," she said into the warmth of his neck, while silently cursing the fact that he had to lie on his side lest his width knock her off the bed. Why hadn't this brute bought a larger bed? It was hardly big enough to hold him, never mind give her an inch of space. Lord, it was downright disgraceful being forced to sleep this close.

"Don't like me much, do you?"

"Now, there's an understatement, Mr. Payne. The truth of the matter is, I don't like you at all."

Thaddeus chuckled. "Maybe Johnny could give you a ride back to town. I reckon he would, if you asked him real nice like. Only problem is, you might not get there for a few years."

Sarah shrugged. "He seems pleasant enough."

"Not like me, you mean?"

"Definitely not like you, Mr. Payne."

"You figure it's better for a man to seem pleasant and later show you his evil side?"

"Taking for granted, of course, that he has one?"

"Don't all men?"

"No," Sarah said. "My husband was a good man. He treated me kindly. There was no evil in him."

"A paragon of virtue, hiding a fortune of stolen gold in his wagon," Thaddeus returned snidely, then silently cursed his stupidity. Didn't he have sense enough to know better than to argue over a dead man? What was it to him how she thought of her late husband? He knew the truth well enough. If she refused to believe her husband a thief, what matter was that to him?

If she wanted to believe he was the best, she could just keep her opinion to herself. He didn't want to hear it. It wasn't any of his business, anyway. Thaddeus noticed an annoying little ache that had settled near his heart. Damn. He knew he shouldn't have eaten two helpings of pie.

"There's been some kind of mistake. I can't explain what happened, I simply don't know. I only know Thomas was a good man."

Thaddeus felt no little amazement as he heard himself say, "It's easy enough to forget a man's faults once he's dead."

"Good night, Mr. Payne," Sarah returned. There was no way she was going to discuss her husband with this beast. He couldn't begin to compare, and she wasn't about to listen to any snide comments directed at her husband's character.

"It must be hard on a woman, out here by her lonesome." Johnny watched the lady of the house reach into the oven for a tray of biscuits.

He'd come back to the cabin, leaving Joe and

Thaddeus with the impression that he'd had to use the outhouse.

Sarah smiled as she placed the hot biscuits on a plate. "Sometimes," she said, knowing it prudent to go along with Thaddeus's claim that she was his wife. She might not like the man, nor the thought of pretending to be his wife, but she wouldn't go against him. These men wouldn't know Thaddeus had lied. She owed him that much. "The snows came early this year. I expect spring will be a long time coming."

"You got that right. There are winters when I think I'll never see spring again."

"And yet you stay."

Johnny shrugged. "Don't know much but minin'. Wouldn't know what else to do."

"You must be lonely at times yourself."

Johnny licked his lips as he watched her move around the kitchen. She had the kind of rounded shape that made a man forget she belonged to another. Johnny figured it would take just one bullet between the man's eyes and she would be his for the taking. "I wouldn't be if I found myself a woman."

"Have you looked?"

"I'm lookin' now."

Sarah smiled. "You mean when you were in town? And you didn't find a suitable lady?"

Lady, my ass. What he wanted was a woman who knew how to spread her legs, and if she could cook a bit, that was all to the better. "Not yet."

"I'm sure you will," Sarah said with a smile which almost caused Johnny to rise from the chair and take her in his arms. Probably would have, too, if Thaddeus didn't pick just that moment to come crashing inside.

The fact that she'd just had a baby didn't matter much to him. He didn't mind a little blood. But he had to be careful of his host. The man looked ready to tear his heart out just for talking to her.

That stupid bastard Joe was supposed to have kept him busy for a bit. How the hell was he going to make any time with her with her husband breathing down his neck?

The storm raged for three more days. Now and then the men went to the barn to see to the horses, but mostly they stayed inside. Thaddeus never left her alone with either of the two. Even a trip to the outhouse meant both of them had to go.

Their confinement caused tempers to flare, but they were quickly brought under control. It was obvious to Thaddeus that Sarah's presence made a difference. He knew from experience that his house would have been in shambles by now if there hadn't been a lady present. In all the years he'd known them, Thaddeus had never seen either Joe or Johnny show such a marked degree of discipline.

Too bad their discipline didn't extend to their thoughts. That they both wanted Sarah was becoming more clear as each day went by. And after four nights of sleeping together, Thaddeus couldn't think of much else himself.

This morning they'd awakened with their legs entwined, his hand possessively cupping her bottom. Her nightdress had slid up during the night and the silken, warm smoothness of her legs had rubbed deliciously against his thighs.

He'd been fully aroused, a fact he could neither deny nor hide. The bed was narrow. There was no way she couldn't know his condition. No way she couldn't feel him hard against her. And yet she never let on for a moment.

Sarah silently left the bed the moment Emily made the slightest sound. After feeding her daughter at the foot of the bed, while modestly turning her back to Thaddeus, she dressed the baby. Somehow, with a little ingenuity, she managed to dress herself without allowing him the pleasure of seeing an inch of skin, for it was all done under the cover of her nightdress. All the while she was about this chore, Sarah pretended he was asleep. It wasn't until she was finished that she turned toward him and made some remark about getting breakfast ready. When alone with him, she was cool, neither pleasant nor nasty. It wasn't till they were among the others that she became a shy but loving wife.

Thaddeus watched her place the baby in the drawer. "Let me hold her while you start breakfast."

Sarah's head snapped up. Her dark blue eyes opened wide with surprise. "Why?"

Thaddeus shrugged. "I want to hold her, is all. I won't drop her."

Thaddeus hadn't an inkling, till that moment, the extent of a mother's pride. He couldn't have complimented her more than to want to hold her child. It put him in an entirely different light. Sarah reached across the bed and handed him the tiny, tightly bound bundle. "Put your hand under her head. She can't always hold it by herself."

Thaddeus nodded at her instructions, then smiled as the baby looked him fully in his face. "She looks like she's surprised. She's not afraid of me, is she?"

Sarah laughed, the sound somehow filling his chest with pleasure. He hadn't heard her laugh before. The closest she'd come was soft, tender chuckles as she played with the child. "No. She's too little to be afraid of anything yet. The only thing that scares her is loud noises."

Thaddeus looked up from the baby and asked, "Like when I slam the door?"

Sarah nodded and Thaddeus had the grace to blush. She'd never have believed it if she hadn't seen it with her own eyes, but the man looked shamed at his ill manners.

She left him a moment later, her heart filled with an odd sense of contentment. It was ridiculous, she knew, to feel like this simply because the man had asked to hold her baby, but she couldn't help it. She loved Emily so much that Sarah wanted everyone to see her as she did.

Later, after breakfast, when the men went outside, Thaddeus warned them to close the door softly. Sarah smiled as their eyes met and held for a long moment after the others left.

Thaddeus grew more steadily silent as the evening progressed. It didn't make for easy conversation having this man glare at her from across the table. Still, Sarah was determined to ignore him as much as she possibly could and enjoy these rare moments when she could converse with adults. Thaddeus's grunts and growls could never be considered as such, and after weeks spent in his disagreeable company, she was starved for conversation.

"You are a pretty lady, Sarah. Thaddeus is a lucky man." Sarah smiled at Johnny, feeling her cheeks flush at his compliments. It was impossible to resist a man so charming and pleasant. Impossible not to react in kind. "Thank you, sir," she said shyly, her manner above reproach.

She wasn't flirting, but was merely thanking another for a compliment. He could clearly see that. Why then did he feel this need to grab her and shake her till she begged him to stop? No, that wasn't true. He didn't want to shake her. He wanted to kiss her to stake his claim, to show Johnny he was wasting his time trying to sweet-talk her.

Sarah glanced at Thaddeus and sighed. What in

107

the world was the matter with the man? Why did he sit there and sulk? Granted, his guests had come uninvited to disturb his solitary life, but no one was to blame for that. Surely, he could understand the imposition was unintentional. Surely, he could see neither Sarah nor his friends had a choice, but that the weather prohibited traveling. Lord, but he wasn't dense enough to imagine she enjoyed his company, his silence, his evil glares. Why then was it necessary to make his displeasure so obviously known with a scowl at every remark? His attitude certainly helped no one. All it did, in fact, was to make Sarah uncomfortable. And in her unease, she turned her smiles on one who greedily accepted her attentions.

Sarah and Johnny talked for a long time as they sat at the table drinking coffee.

"How is it you were educated in Missouri?"

Sarah hesitated, knowing she'd made an error here in telling him so. Thaddeus had warned her, and if she didn't want to be the object of his rage, she had no alternative but to go along with her "husband's" previous statements. She felt her cheeks darken at the lie. "My family only moved here a few years ago."

"Do you like it here?"

"It suits me very well. The country is beautiful."

"But the company leaves much to be desired."

Sarah tipped her head to one side, eyes wide with uncertainty as she waited for the man to explain himself.

108

"He means me, Sarah. Johnny figures I ain't good enough for the likes of you." The words were said with such disgust that no one could have misunderstood his anger.

"Surely not," Sarah shook her head, knowing it impossible that a guest might so insult his host. "Surely you mean our lack of neighbors."

"Of course," Johnny quickly returned, knowing he was close to seeing his host's temper in full bloom. It wasn't something Johnny was eager to witness, for he would never face a man like Thaddeus. Cutting barbs and innuendoes or maybe a bullet in the back were more his style.

Sarah smiled at his eagerness to set things aright. "I do miss my friends and family. But —"

"She'll get to see them when spring comes. It's only during the winter that she's stuck here with me."

"I do not consider myself stuck, Thaddeus," she said, speaking before she realized, then blushing furiously at her unexpected outburst. What in the world had caused her to speak out? What could she possibly mean by it? Of course, she was stuck here. They all were.

Joe chose that moment to inquire, "You got any of that whiskey left, Sarge?"

Thaddeus shot the man a humorous look. He had whiskey, but he sure as hell wasn't going to share it with either of these two. "If you wanted it to last, you should have taken it easy the other night."

It was with some relief that Sarah heard Emily begin to fuss. Thaddeus had not once lifted his gaze from her person since her unthinking statement, and Sarah was decidedly uneasy beneath his gaze. She bid the men good night. It was time to attend to the baby's needs.

Not long after her disappearance behind the sheet the cabin grew quiet, except for the snores that came from opposite the curtain. Sarah had long since fallen asleep. She never knew when Thaddeus had joined her in bed. She didn't feel the tightening of his arms as he pulled her closer. She never knew he'd brushed back the soft wisps of her hair from her face so he might watch her gentle features in sleep. She didn't know of the fierce moment of possessiveness that suddenly filled his chest.

They'd be leaving in the morning. The snow had finally stopped after supper, and the two men were anxious to get going. They were already a week late getting back to their claim and they didn't dare stay away much longer, no matter the weather conditions.

Thaddeus shook her awake. "It could be tonight."

Sarah moaned, more than half asleep, and instinctively cuddled closer to his heat. She came sharply awake when he repeated his whisper near her ear. "What could be tonight?" she asked, feeling herself once again pressed close to his body as they lay in bed.

"If they're going to try anything. They'll have to do it soon."

"I don't think . . ."

"I do," he interrupted. "Put Emily in her box and slide it under the bed. I don't want her hurt."

Sarah could hear the snores coming from beyond the curtain. She didn't believe anything would happen but nevertheless did as he asked. She wasn't about to risk Emily should the man prove himself right. "Are you sure?"

"No, I ain't sure," his tone mocked. "I'm just not taking any chances."

It took her longer than she might have imagined to fall back to sleep. She'd had Emily for so short a time and yet she felt oddly alone, almost uncomfortable without the baby pressed close to her breast. Besides, with Emily in her own bed, she was alone with Thaddeus. And even though neither were inclined to take advantage of their intimate positioning, she felt ill at ease without the baby between them.

Thaddeus only dozed on and off. An hour or so before dawn he came sharply awake at the sudden sound. What was it? What had awakened him? Thaddeus's lips twisted into a mean grin. It wasn't what he'd heard, it was what he hadn't heard. The cabin was still and silent, but for the ticking of the clock and the soft, even sounds of Sarah's breathing. His heart pounded as he strained to see through the blackness. Nothing. He eased himself gently from Sarah's side and reached for his gun beneath his pillow. Without a sound, he pulled on his pants, moved to the lamp, and waited.

The curtain fluttered. Tiger growled and then, with a muffled roar, was instantly upon one of the two dark figures that had suddenly appeared on this side of the curtain.

Joe cried out in pain and dropped his gun. "Get 'im off me," he yelled as the dog dragged him to the floor. His jaws were opened wide. The man's neck was held between razor-sharp teeth that had only just broken the skin. Joe knew the slightest movement would ensure his throat being ripped out.

The sound of Joe's cry brought Sarah awake. She sat up in bed, for a second unable to understand what was happening. Thaddeus cursed. Why hadn't he awakened her? Why hadn't he insisted she move beneath the bed with her daughter?

Johnny took the opportunity offered and dragged her from the bed, her body held as a shield before his. In his other hand a gun was aimed at the empty bed.

Thaddeus ran a match down his rough wall and lit the lantern, his gun held ready to fire the moment he found the opportunity. "I figured you for a visit tonight."

Johnny's eyes widened with surprise to find Thaddeus up and partly dressed. Still, he only laughed.

"I reckon you wasn't walkin' in your sleep, then,"

Thaddeus continued, his voice hard, filled with menace.

Johnny laughed again as he tightened his hold on Sarah. "She's a beautiful woman. You can't blame me for—"

"Can't I?" The grin that twisted at Thaddeus's mouth cause gooseflesh to race up Sarah's back. She couldn't imagine the devil looking meaner. Johnny only laughed. "You forgot one real important thing. She belongs to me."

"Why don't we let her choose?"

"The choosin's done. She's my wife."

"But she didn't have a chance to get to know me." Johnny purposely ran his hand up her chest, squeezing playfully at her breasts. Sarah could have probably broken free at that moment, but she was paralyzed with fear. She trembled with revulsion but she didn't move. His arm came around her waist again. "I think she likes me some," he said to Thaddeus, smiling at the man's obvious rage.

"I think you're a dead son of a bitch."

Thaddeus cocked his pistol. He was an excellent shot. There was no way he could miss at this distance . . . not even with Sarah half blocking the bastard's body.

At the same moment, Johnny raised his gun. Sarah felt the movement and in a split second knew Thaddeus was going to die. "Noooo!" she cried out, and jammed her elbow into Johnny's midsection. The man gave a soft grunt of surprise and pain. He instantly released her and stumbled slightly. The reason he kept falling was because a bullet had gone clear through his side.

The cabin was silent for one short moment. And then Emily began to scream. For the first time since she was born, Sarah didn't hear her.

Thaddeus came around the bed and tore down the sheet. Standing at Sarah's side, his arm around her waist, he hugged her gently, possessively to his chest. "Are you all right?"

Sarah couldn't answer, her body wracked with sobs as tears streamed down her face. She'd never seen anything like this in her life. She simply couldn't comprehend anyone taking another's life.

He was a killer. Sarah shivered at the thought. She'd forever see his cold-blooded, dark-as-night eyes as he aimed his gun and sent a man to his death.

But Sarah was wrong. Johnny wasn't dead. If she hadn't been so upset, she'd have heard his low moans.

Thaddeus spoke a command and Tiger left his prisoner. "Put your boots on and get your friend out of here."

Sarah couldn't stop trembling. "Get on the bed," Thaddeus said. She never heard him nor did she move.

Joe was shaking so bad he could hardly stand. Even counting all the years he'd spent fighting the war, he'd never been so helpless or so close to death. He felt his neck wet with a mixture of his blood and the dog's saliva, and he shivered again.

114

It took him some time but he finally managed to dress. When he was finished, he helped Johnny into his clothes. It wasn't until the men were at the door that Thaddeus warned, "Don't stop by here again. The next time I see either of you, I'll put a bullet between your eyes."

The door closed behind them and Thaddeus left Sarah for the time it took to slide the wooden bar into place, extinguish the lights, and check the rawhide that secured the shutters closed. He glanced at the wall and nodded. The two men had no weapons. Their rifles were still in place. Their handguns lay on the floor. Still, he wasn't taking any chances.

"What's the matter with you?" he asked upon finding Sarah standing exactly where he'd left her. "Why are you letting Emily scream like that?"

"Sarah?" he asked as he looked closer into blank eyes and a face as white as the snow outside. "Jesus! Are you all right?"

Thaddeus didn't wait for an answer. He picked her up, placed her in the bed again, and took Emily from the drawer beneath the bed. The poor little thing was crying so hard, that her entire body shook with the force of it. Gently, he placed the baby in Sarah's arms. But Sarah still suffered from the shock of seeing someone shot. She didn't know the bullet had only wounded Johnny. She thought she'd witnessed death. A death so violent she couldn't stop seeing it repeated again and again in her mind's eye.

Thaddeus stripped off his clothes and slid beneath the covers. It took some doing, but he finally managed to open Sarah's nightdress and put the baby to her mother's breast.

Emily quieted almost instantly, and Thaddeus smiled at the soft shuddering sobs that often choked her as she tried to nurse. "Little glutton," he said so gently it might have been an endearment, "can't you wait till you calm down before you eat?" He smiled again as he rubbed the baby's back, then blinked with surprise as she did just that.

His arms went around Sarah and pulled her close into a comforting embrace. "It's all right, darlin'," he whispered into the darkness. "You just go to sleep. Everything will be all right in the morning."

But it wasn't.

Chapter Six

Sarah lay in bed staring at the ceiling, listening to the soft whistling sounds that Thaddeus made while working in the kitchen. Water was pumped into a pot. The stove rattled as wood was added to a fire that was never allowed to go out.

Her world was encased in gloom. How could he whistle? What did he find cheerful? She sighed in despair. If his sudden and, as far as she was concerned, ill-timed good humor was anything to go by, he'd enjoyed himself last night. The thought alone was ghastly, almost as horrifying as the actual deed itself.

Coming from a small town in Missouri, she'd known only peace in her life. Gunslingers did not walk the streets. People simply did not shoot one another over a disagreement. She'd read, of course, of the wild West . . . of the killings, the total disregard for law and order. But she'd never before been unfortunate enough to witness, firsthand, the horror of violent death.

He was a murderer. Sarah shivered at the thought.

She couldn't possibly stay with a man so ruthless, so lacking in human compassion as to cold-bloodedly kill another and never give it a thought. Surely if he killed once, he'd kill again. No doubt, if she gave him enough trouble, he'd turn his murderous intent upon her next. She had to get out of here. No matter what she might face alone on the snow-covered road to town, she couldn't chance Emily's safety by staying. She was leaving today.

Thaddeus smiled as he glanced toward the bed and saw she was awake. The warmth that had filled his chest since last night grew in intensity. He couldn't wait for the moment when she'd turn to him and thank him for saving her again. Certainly, he would have done as much for any woman in trouble, but to do it for her made him feel ten feet tall, able to conquer the world and lay it at her feet. He couldn't stop smiling.

He hadn't consciously intended to move toward her. Still, he wasn't surprised to find himself suddenly leaning over her. His eyes were filled with concern as he asked, "How are you feeling?"

"Very well, thank you," Sarah returned without a flicker of her usual warmth.

"What's the matter?"

"Nothing," she answered, never meeting his eyes. "Would you move aside? I'd like to get up."

Thaddeus shrugged away his disappointment at finding her less than exuberant this morning and moved back to the stove. Maybe she was a bit ornery in the mornings. He hadn't noticed it before, but then he hadn't talked much himself.

Maybe she just needed a cup of coffee to cheer her up. Coffee and a little food had been known to soothe the most cantankerous soul. Thaddeus grinned as he plopped a double serving of bacon and then some into the pan. The small room was suddenly filled with its mouth-watering aroma.

Thaddeus listened to Sarah as she spoke to the baby. His brow furrowed as he realized what he was doing. When had things begun to change? When had the empty ache in his chest been replaced by a deep, soothing feeling of contentment? When had he started listening for the sound of her voice, looking for her presence?

What was happening? Thaddeus shook his head. He didn't know. He didn't want to know. He wasn't thinking of the future. She was here and the knowledge made him almost happy. He couldn't think beyond today.

"You want to take a bath today?" he called over his shoulder.

"No, thank you," Sarah returned as she began to gather up her belongings.

Thaddeus never noticed what she was about. "Why not? You are able to bathe, aren't you? I mean, the baby . . ."

"Yes, Mr. Payne, I'm able but unwilling. I'd rather bathe in town, if you don't mind."

"First thing, I reckon you know me well enough to call me by my first name." Thaddeus grinned. Sarah denied the sight of his smile brought a weakness to her knees. The man was a killer. She couldn't allow herself to forget that.

His smile widened as he studied her tight expression. Was she embarrassed? Did she imagine he wasn't going to give her the privacy she needed? "I'll wait outside till you're done," he said, hoping to ease away her worry.

His warm gaze caused her to feel suddenly self-conscious and oddly nervous.

He chuckled softly. "You might be a bit potent if you wait till spring before you bathe."

Sarah ignored his teasing comment. "You don't understand. I'm leaving. If you could direct me, Emily and I will be on our way to town."

Thaddeus laughed, then scowled when he realized she was perfectly serious. "Why?"

"Why what?" she asked, and for the first time he noticed she was pushing her clothes into a bag.

"Why do you suddenly want to leave?"

Sarah sighed, wondering how to best handle a sticky situation. She didn't want to upset him. There was no telling what the man might do next. "Mr. Payne, we both knew I'd be leaving at the first opportunity." And at his obvious look of surprise, she added, "You didn't imagine I'd be staying on indefinitely?"

Actually, Thaddeus had been thinking exactly that, even if he had only just now admitted it to himself. One thing was for damn sure. He wasn't about to admit it to her. His tone was hard. Obviously, he wasn't pleased by her intent. "Lady, I imagined you'd stay till spring."

"Joe and Johnny made it from town. I should be able to make it back."

"That was two men, not a woman and a baby. Besides, it's snowed for four days since then." And when she appeared not to have heard, his hand pushed through his hair in frustration and he raised his voice just enough to bring her to face him. "It's twenty miles. You'll never make it."

"I'll make it."

"No, you won't, 'cause you ain't goin'," Thaddeus snapped, losing what little patience he possessed. There was no sense trying to reason with women. They didn't know up from down. The damn fool didn't even realize that if it hadn't been for him, both she and Emily would have been a meal for wild animals. Now she was eager to put herself back in the very danger he'd only just rescued her from.

"Do you mean to keep me a prisoner here?"

"I reckon."

"Why?" she asked, exasperated at his insistence that she stay. "You've wanted to get rid of me since you first found me in the storm."

"I still want to get rid of you," Thaddeus shouted, then winced as his bellow made Emily whimper. Again, he ran a hand through his hair and lowered his voice. "Only it will have to wait till spring. Now sit and eat." He slammed a frying pan filled with greasy, half-cooked bacon on the table. Leftover biscuits from last night's dinner were added to the fare.

Goddamned woman! She'd gone and ruined his whole day. He'd been thinking on spending some time together. Maybe getting to know one another. Maybe doing some serious talking. Maybe finding out where she came from, what her life had been

121

like till now. And what did she do? He slammed the coffeepot on the table, unconcerned that boiling liquid spilled over the clean surface. She'd ruined everything.

"Or what?" Sarah taunted, amazed that she felt no fear. Shouldn't she be afraid? Wasn't it sensible to fear this man? "Will you kill me, too?"

"Kill?" Sarah couldn't prevent the shiver she felt as his eyes bore deep into her own. Thaddeus came to a complete stop and asked, in a deceptively soft voice, "What are you talking about?"

Sarah shook her head. "I'm not staying here. I couldn't share a house with a murderer. I wouldn't be able to sleep with the fear that you would . . . that you . . ." She couldn't say the words.

He finally understood what was going on here. So she thought he'd killed Johnny last night. Well, since she'd never bothered to even ask what had happened, he'd just let her go on thinking that. Wouldn't want to shake up her mind once she'd set it on something. "Might put you out of your misery?" Thaddeus asked, finishing the sentence for her. He grinned, only this time his smile was far from gentle. His dark eyes narrowed menacingly. "Then don't push me, lady."

Sarah's spine stiffened. She raised her chin and glared. "Are you threatening me?" Sarah tried to keep the tremor from her voice. She almost made it.

Thaddeus ignored her question. He didn't like it. Not one bit. She was mad at him because he'd shot Johnny. It didn't seem to bother her none that the coyote had had a gun pointed at his belly. Maybe she'd wanted Johnny to kill him. Maybe she'd wanted to go off with the bastard after all.

Jesus, how could he have been such a fool? Of course! He'd ruined her plans. That's why she was so upset. Thaddeus ignored the ache that suddenly settled deep in his gut. His stomach had been acting up lately. He'd have to eat a little slower and a lot less.

"Kinda sweet on him, were you?"

"Don't be ridiculous."

Thaddeus laughed, the sound hard and cruel. "If you wanted to go with him, why didn't you just say so?"

"Because I most certainly did not want to go with him!" Sarah couldn't have been more emphatic. Thaddeus had no choice but to believe her.

"Then what the hell's got up your butt?"

Sarah's lips thinned into a disapproving line. "There's no need for gutter talk, Mr. Payne. I cannot abide violence. It's as simple as that."

"I was protectin' you, damn it!"

"And now it's all my fault?" she gasped, clearly aghast at the thought.

"You're goddamned right it's your fault. Women bring nothin' but trouble, and you ain't no different. If you weren't here, temptin' him with come-and get-it smiles and wide blue eyes, nothin' would have happened." His dark eyes narrowed to almost slits as he allowed them to move insultingly up the length of her. "And the way you sashay around this place." His gaze grew darker than ever as it lingered upon her breasts. His voice was suddenly lower, more gravelly, as if he were having some trouble speaking. "Not countin' the sounds that came from behind that curtain," he nodded toward the bed. "Didn't you figure we knew what you were doing?"

In her fury, Sarah's eyes darkened to purple. Her back stiffened, and her shoulders squared, all of which brought into further prominence her full, lush form. "What I was doing behind that curtain was taking care of my baby. If your evil mind chose to interpret the most precious, sweet, and innocent moments possible between a mother and her child as tempting, then your imagination is beyond disgust."

"Lady, it don't take much imaginin' when Emily is slurpin' and sighin' with pleasure at every taste of you. A man can't help what those sounds do to his body."

"Lord," Sarah groaned as her eyes rolled toward the heavens. What kind of man would think such nonsense? Her gaze fell to the floor and she breathed a sigh. "I don't believe this." Suddenly, she was facing him again, her hands on her hips, her eyes flashing their anger. "And what's the matter with the way I walk?"

"Your hips move." Thaddeus wasn't the least bit pleased with the conversation. He could feel his body stirring just talking this way. In another minute, he was going to embarrass both of them. Damn. If her gaze lowered to below his belt, she'd be embarrassed right now.

Sarah looked momentarily confused. "Aren't they supposed to? How else could I walk?"

Thaddeus glared at her for a long moment.

124

Thinking they'd both be better off if they dropped this particular subject, he ignored her question, reached into his pocket, and snapped open his watch. "Lady, I ain't killed anyone in eight hours. If I was you, I'd stop tryin' to rile me."

"Exactly my point. How do I know that Emily and I won't be your next victims?"

"You don't." Thaddeus left his greasy breakfast untasted, all the while cursing her and the sorry day she'd come into his life. He put on his coat and reached for his hat. Just before he walked outside, he said, "If you change your mind about the bath, let me know. I'll be in the barn." He gave her one last angry glare, then softly closed the door.

Sarah watched him from the window over the sink. He was digging a path through waist-high snow, from the front steps to the outhouse at the side of the cabin. Absently, she wondered if he'd have bothered digging if he'd been alone. Was he doing this for her?

She shook her head, denying the thought. The man had never seen fit to welcome her in his home. There was no reason to suspect he'd suddenly had a change of heart.

No. He might not be willing to let her leave, but he certainly wasn't about to make her life pleasant during her stay. She shrugged. It hardly mattered. The day wasn't far off when they'd see the last of each other.

Sarah gave a weary sigh as she turned from the

sight of thick muscles bunching together beneath his shirt, for he'd again taken off his coat. She shouldn't be watching him. It did something odd to her stomach when she saw him like that. Something she didn't recognize, something she instinctively knew she shouldn't be feeling.

Moments later, Sarah was laughing at Emily's soft sounds of pleasure as the baby splashed in her bath. Clean, pink, and fresh from her bath, her little body was soon dry and wrapped in a long cotton dress. Sarah was smiling at the baby's gurgling sounds when she suddenly realized what had happened last night.

She gasped with surprise as the action played again in her mind's eye. At the time, she'd been so shocked at the discharging of a gun that she'd closed off her mind to everything but the sound and the cry it had brought from Johnny.

Now she remembered that Joe had helped Johnny with his coat and boots. She remembered hearing their struggles, particularly Johnny's moans. Dead men did not moan in pain.

Why had Thaddeus allowed her to believe the worst? Why hadn't he defended himself against her accusations? Was he satisfied knowing she saw him in a lesser light? Surely not. Then why hadn't he explained? Why hadn't he told her the truth?

Sarah could find no answers to her silent questions. She knew only that this man could boast of no simple personality. Whatever it was that plagued Thaddeus Payne went deep. Sarah wondered if she'd ever know what lurked behind his dark

126

gaze. What were the secrets that haunted his soul?

Blood was dripping all over the floor. The cabin was warm, but Thaddeus felt his entire body begin to shake uncontrollably as his frozen limbs met what felt like searing heat.

Sarah gasped with horror at the sight of him. His darkly tanned skin held a sickly gray hue. His beard and mustache were covered in ice. "What happened?"

"I cut myself."

Sarah muttered aloud that she could see that much from the tear in his coat sleeve and the blood that was running down his hand, splashing on the floor.

"Why did you stay out so long?" Sarah asked as she pulled off his jacket, dropped it to the floor, and ran to the bed. A moment later, with the quilt draped over his shoulders, she pushed him into a chair before the stove.

"I was working," he said, never acknowledging her attentions. She placed a hot cup of coffee into his stiff hand and, with her hands over his, guided the cup to his lips.

"You look like you're frozen solid."

"I think I am," Thaddeus returned between violent tremors. He might not have acknowledged her care; he might not even want it, but despite his wants, he sure was finding it right nice to be fussed over.

"How did you cut yourself?" she asked as she tried to roll up a blood-soaked sleeve to see to the injury. The cut was too high on his arm. The shirt would have to come off.

"Knife slipped," Thaddeus explained, offering her no further information.

"You'll have to take your shirt off. I can't . . ." Sarah shrugged helplessly.

Thaddeus nodded, but his fingers were too stiff to do her bidding. "I can't. Forget about it."

"Thaddeus," she spoke his name gently and for the first time easily, no longer pretending to be his wife, and he wondered at the odd sensation the sound caused in his chest. "You're bleeding. I can't just forget about it."

"I can't take my shirt off. My fingers are too stiff."

Sarah nodded, then swallowed. It wasn't that she'd never seen a man's bare chest before. She'd been a married woman, after all. The problem was, she hadn't seen *his* chest, and she wasn't all that sure that she wanted to. Still, there was no hope for it. The shirt had to come off, and despite her reluctance, she would just have to do it. "I'll take care of it. You just concentrate on getting warm."

Sarah unbuttoned his shirt and gently pulled his arms from the sleeves. Next came the muscle-clinging long john shirt. That was harder to get off since it was tighter and more form-fitting. She unbuttoned it to his waist and pulled his arms out of the sleeves.

Sarah made a small sound upon spying the deep, jagged gash. "How did you do this?"

"My knife. It slipped."

Sarah poured hot water into a shallow pan and

128

knelt before him. The wound was on the inside of his upper arm. She didn't think anything of it as she positioned herself between his thighs; her total concentration was on the horribly jagged injury.

Thaddeus only wished he could claim the same degree of ignorance. His body felt instantly flushed. His frozen fingers and feet were forgotten as she leaned forward, her waist between his thighs, her breasts occasionally brushing against his belly, her stomach against his groin.

He had to put the cup down. In another minute he was going to spill the damn coffee all over himself and her.

Thaddeus groaned as she leaned forward again. Instantly, her gaze moved to his face. "Does it hurt?" Thaddeus could only manage a nod. She'd never know exactly how much. Her face was within inches of his. All he had to do was to lean down just a bit and their lips would touch.

"Do you have any whiskey?" she asked softly, her tender expression causing an unreasonable thunder in his chest.

"In the top drawer," he said, his gaze lost in hers.

"Don't move," she said as she came to her feet. Thaddeus groaned again because her hand had fallen to his thigh. And it was his thigh she used for balance as she came to her feet.

Sarah found the bottle in the dresser and quickly returned. "I'm afraid this is going to hurt a bit."

Thaddeus almost smiled at her inaccurate phrasing. "Sarah, it's going to hurt more than a bit. It's going to hurt like hell," he corrected.

At his nod of consent, Sarah poured a goodly amount over the wound. Instantly, Thaddeus was on his feet, the chair knocked to the floor behind him as he groaned a whispery, "Jesus, God!"

Sarah said nothing as he paced for a moment, waiting for the worst of the sting to abate. She straightened the chair and waited. "I have to wrap it, or it'll start bleeding again."

Thaddeus nodded, feeling ridiculously satisfied at her look of concern. A moment later he was sitting again, while Sarah positioned herself once more between his legs and began to wrap the wound. Her total concentration was on what she was doing. She never realized how precarious her position was. She never imagined that the man she was administering to was studying her face and the loose tendrils of hair that had fallen from the knot at her nape to her cheeks . . . the delicate length and slenderness of her neck . . . the sweet lush curve of her breasts.

"There," she said as she secured the bandage into place. "I think that will be all right."

She turned to face him, concern in her eyes and a soft smile on her lips. The smile instantly vanished as she noticed his pained expression. His skin was flushed and spread tightly over his features as if he suffered some great pain. His breathing was uneven, his eyes glazed. "Are you all right?" she asked as she unthinkingly cupped his bearded face in her hands and brought it down so her lips were pressed to his forehead, testing its warmth. Sarah never realized what she'd done. Her mother had always checked the children's temperature in just that fashion.

"You feel a little warm," she went on as her hands left his face and touched his chest. Thaddeus groaned, and Sarah whispered at his obvious pain, "Oh, God, you're ill. Why did you stay outside so long?"

She hurried for a towel. The ice coating his mustache and beard had melted. Water was dripping down his chest. Between his thighs again, she wiped at the dampness and remarked with an oddly anxious voice, "Why didn't you tell me you weren't well?"

"I'm—I'm all right." Jesus God, he was better than all right. If he felt any healthier . . . "It's not what you think," Thaddeus managed through a tight throat. The words were like a dousing in cold water. She became instantly still, for she recognized the signs at last.

"Oh, dear," she gave a soft gasp, knowing he had to have heard the soft quiver in her voice as she realized her position. "I'm sorry," she muttered as she came quickly to her feet, careful this time not to touch him at all. "I didn't think. I . . ." Sarah let the words falter, loath to offer an excuse for her actions. He'd known she hadn't realized where she'd knelt or what she'd inadvertently touched as she had gone about caring for his wound. To say more on the subject would only embarrass her further. "Are you hungry?" she asked, purposely and quickly changing the subject.

Thaddeus smiled as he slowly looked over her delicious form. "Starving."

"Good," she nodded, deliberately misinterpreting

the obviously sexual response. She turned from him and began to put supper on the table.

Thaddeus was struggling to put his long johns and shirt back on. The house was warm enough. He didn't need both for extra warmth, but he couldn't sit at a table with a lady in his underwear.

Sarah heard his grunts and turned from the stove. "Do you need some help?"

Thaddeus only nodded. He didn't dare speak, for he didn't trust the sound of his voice. Just knowing she was going to touch him again left him weak and shaky.

Sarah's hands moved quickly. Within seconds, she had him buttoned into both shirts, taking care not to touch his skin. Thaddeus almost sighed his disappointment.

"I brought the tub from the shed. It's on the porch. If you want to take a bath, just let me know and I'll drag it in."

Sarah nodded. "Tomorrow."

"Why not tonight?" Thaddeus knew it was his own fault if he suffered. Still, he was unable to stop the words. He wouldn't look, but just knowing she'd be naked, warm, her skin slippery wet, and in the same room with him would be an agonizing experience.

Sarah grinned. "Are you giving me subtle hints, Mr. Payne? That's the second time today you mentioned a bath."

Thaddeus scowled. "You called me Thaddeus before."

"Did I?" Sarah asked while her cheeks grew pink,

remembering how upset she'd felt at seeing him injured.

"Does it always upset you to see blood?"

She shook her head and lied . . . badly. "I wasn't upset."

"I saw your hands shake."

"I was nervous. I didn't want to hurt you."

"Is that all?"

"What else could it be?"

"You could have been afraid to touch me."

Sarah purposely blinked, praying the slow, measured movement would portray an innocence she wasn't sure she possessed. Was he right? Had she, in the back of her mind, thought about what it would feel like to touch him? "Whatever for?"

"Maybe you thought you'd like it too much."

Sarah closed her eyes and only at the last second stifled her groan. "That's ridiculous. I'm not afraid to touch you, Mr. Payne."

"I think you are."

"Well, I can't help what you think, can I?"

"I think you're scared spitless." He grinned at her look of annoyance. " 'Cause once you do, you won't be able to stop."

"Total nonsense."

"There's one way you can prove me wrong."

"You needn't bother to try goading me into touching you." Sarah laughed as she realized that was exactly what he was trying to do. "I promise you I'm not so easily manipulated."

Thaddeus shot her an evil grin. "Shall I try another tactic, then?"

Sarah grinned. "Shame on you, Mr. Payne. That was uncalled for."

"If you don't call me by my first name, I'll be tempted to do something even worse."

"I won't ask what, so you might as well take that silly expression off your face," Sarah returned primly, but her eyes sparkled with laughter.

Thaddeus laughed. Probably for the first time in years. Damn, it felt good. "All right. If you won't take a bath, I will."

Chapter Seven

An unspoken truce settled between them as they shared the evening meal. Neither had exactly apologized for the harsh words that had previously passed between them, but the mood was decidedly more relaxed.

They might not as yet be comfortable enough with each other to carry on anything but polite and slightly stilted conversation. Still, polite conversation was certainly preferable to the silent animosity that had earlier existed between them. Sarah felt herself able to relax, at least to some degree, in his company, while Thaddeus appeared to have accepted her presence at last.

If asked, he would have denied it. He would have vehemently insisted there was nothing he liked better than living alone. And yet if he were made to think on it, he might have admitted this enforced cohabitation wasn't as bad as it could have been.

It probably wasn't the worst thing in the world having a woman share his home. At least not this particular woman. Coming in from the cold to a warm, fragrant home wasn't so bad. He could live with having his meals prepared for him. Maybe he even liked it a bit. But what he liked most of all was looking at her. He liked the idea that he could tease her into a smile. And when she laughed . . . well, he couldn't rightly say what the sound did to him, but he guessed he liked it well enough.

Sarah finished cleaning up after supper and left the small kitchen area, bringing Emily with her to the bed. This was their special time, a moment for both mother and daughter to play before Emily fell asleep for a good part of the night.

While they played, Thaddeus dragged one half of a large wooden barrel from the porch and into the cabin. He was sitting at the table rubbing an oily solution into the leather saddle he'd brought in earlier, while he waited for pots of water to heat.

Sarah lay on her stomach, her feet at the top, her head at the bottom of the bed. Propped on her elbows, she leaned over the baby and made soft cooing sounds. "Do you like that, sweetheart?" she asked as she rubbed Emily's belly and chest. Her lips touched against the baby's forehead. "Does that feel good?"

"What's the matter?"

Sarah turned to her side, bracing her weight on one elbow, and looked up at Thaddeus, who hovered suddenly at the side of the bed. His eyes were filled with concern as he leaned forward, his attention solely on Emily. "Nothing. Why?"

"You put your lips on her forehead. I thought she might be hot."

Sarah laughed softly. "I put my lips on her forehead to kiss her." She glanced down at the child, her eyes shining with pride. "Her skin's so soft, she's hard to resist."

"You like playing with her, don't you?"

"Very much."

"And you don't feel silly talking to her even though she can't understand you?"

"She understands I love her from the tone of my voice. It doesn't matter what I say."

Thaddeus leaned closer, his dark shoulder-length hair falling forward as he watched the baby.

"I think she likes me," he said, with not a little awe.

Sarah smiled, knowing the baby neither liked nor disliked. It would be a while before she knew more than to selfishly seek her own comforts. Still, it seemed important that he believe the child favored him, and Sarah hadn't the heart to tell him otherwise. "It's hard not to like someone who treats you kindly."

Sarah had twice found him leaning over the baby's tiny bed, staring at her, his expression filled with tenderness. She smiled as Thaddeus reached a tentative finger toward the baby's cheek. Gently, he ran it over the soft, plump surface, then glanced at Sarah. The two adults smiled as Emily turned her mouth toward his finger. "She thinks you're—" Sarah grew suddenly red, unable to finish what she'd started.

"You?" Thaddeus asked as he watched her cheeks stain a most becoming color. He smiled at her obvious embarrassment. This woman was no innocent.

137

She'd been married. She'd shared a man's bed. And yet he could bring her cheeks to flaming color with just a few words. He couldn't understand why, but having that ability brought the oddest sensations to his chest. "Doesn't she know the difference?"

"She would if you tried to—" She stopped again. *Oh, Lord, you've simply got to stop this.* When was she going to learn to think before she spoke? Besides, they weren't talking about anything shameful. It was an act that was natural and correct. Why in the world did the subject constantly cause her to grow upset?

Thaddeus laughed, knowing what she was about to say. "I imagine she would." His gaze was dark, warm, and altogether too gentle. She wasn't used to gentle looks from this man. They caused a fluttering in her chest. Her mouth went dry, while a trembling invaded her entire body. "Maybe we should talk about something else. Your cheeks need a rest."

"It's mean of you to tease." Sarah sat up on the bed, feeling suddenly all too vulnerable in this prone position. "I'm new at mothering and unused to talking about such matters."

Thaddeus nodded his understanding of her dilemma. "Maybe you need another baby. It might relax you some." And as Sarah's mouth simply hung open in astonishment, he grinned and went back to the kitchen to check his bathwater.

Sarah sat with her back to him as she played with Emily and listened to the sounds of pouring water. Soon after, she heard him curse. "What's the matter?"

138

"The water's too hot."

But the heated water didn't stop him any. She heard more curses and then a blissful sigh as he settled himself in the tub.

Thaddeus didn't speak again for some time. He washed, while Sarah cooed softly to the baby. The only sound above her voice was the splashing of water, until he asked, "How long were you married?"

"Three years," she returned without looking in his direction.

"And after three years, you're still shy with men?"

"I'm not shy."

"Aren't you?" Sarah never looked his way, therefore she missed his grin. "Your cheeks grow pink every time we talk."

"That's because you seem always to talk about matters better left unsaid."

"Like feeding your baby?"

"Exactly."

"Does it embarrass you to do it?"

"Of course not. It's the natural way of things."

"Then why does it embarrass you to talk about it?"

"Because we're not talking about feeding Emily when we're talking about feeding Emily."

Thaddeus laughed at a statement that should have made no sense. But both knew it did. "Then what are we talking about?" Thaddeus asked playfully.

Sarah sighed. "Mr. Payne, I imagine if we tried, we could find another subject to discuss."

"What about your husband?"

"What about him?"

"Were you shy with him?"

"Is that any of your business?"

"No." Sarah imagined he shrugged. "Just curious."

She listened to the sound of running water and imagined him getting out of the tub. "You sure you don't want a bath. Water's hardly dirty at all"

Without thinking, Sarah shot him a look of amazement. Did he imagine she'd use the same water? Good Lord, she'd never do anything so . . . so . . . intimate. Sarah's eyes widened to find him standing beside the tub with nothing but a towel—and a skimpy one at that—wrapped around his middle. His face was buried in another towel as he rubbed it over his head. She must have made a small sound, for the towel was suddenly brought from his face and hung around his neck. He grinned as he watched her gaze move over his near nakedness. "Not that I mind, but I thought we made a deal not to look."

"I—I thought you were dressed."

Thaddeus grinned. "Did you? Or were you just trying to get a little peek."

This had to stop. She was going to incinerate if her cheeks got any hotter. Sarah decided it best to ignore his question. She turned to play with Emily again, only to find the baby already asleep.

How had he managed to talk her into this? She should have lied. If he'd never found out she'd cut Thomas's hair, then he wouldn't be sitting here waiting for her to begin.

Thaddeus sat in a chair near the table, while Sarah hovered nearby. She looked less than pleased, while he was having a time of it hiding his grin. She was obviously nervous, a fact easy enough to realize by the way she kept biting at her lower lip.

Thaddeus almost groaned aloud, imagining it was his teeth holding that lip, his tongue running along its softness. Damn, but it didn't take much for his thoughts to run toward bedding this woman. She only needed to stand near him. Thaddeus gave a silent curse and reluctantly admitted it took less than that. This woman called to a man with no more than a gentle look and, with that gentle look, caused an ache that threatened his very sanity, not to be lessened until the day he took her for his own.

Thaddeus wasn't happy about the fact, but he couldn't deny it. No matter how much he hadn't wanted to get involved, he wanted her. And he was going to have her. For at least as long as she was forced to stay.

His voice was hard, abrupt, and filled with annoyance at his own thoughts. "Well? Do you know how or don't ya?" Thaddeus almost laughed aloud, for the sharp words startled her so she nearly jumped across the room.

"I said I did, didn't I?" Sarah came back, her tone every bit as angry as the man's sitting before her. She picked up both the scissors and her comb and warned, "If I were you, I'd keep your bellowing down to a roar, unless you don't mind my getting nervous and cutting something I shouldn't."

Thaddeus chuckled. The squint lines around his

141

eyes deepened with his merriment. "What can you do that would make any difference?"

"You wouldn't look like much minus an ear."

Thaddeus laughed again. "I'd just grow my hair to cover it."

Sarah grasped a handful of thick black hair and tugged harder than necessary.

"Ow! You sure you know what you're doin'?"

"I told you I did, didn't I?"

"When Connery cuts my hair he don't pull it."

"Who's Connery?" Sarah cut a chunk of hair from the back of his head.

"Barber in town."

"He's gentle, I take it?"

"Sure is."

"Why not wait till you get to town, then?"

Thaddeus suddenly reached for her hand. Despite her obvious reluctance, he brought it and her around to face him. "Are you afraid?"

Thaddeus didn't bother explaining his question and Sarah never asked him to. She knew what he was talking about. "Certainly not!" she snapped, but both knew the words to be a lie. She was afraid. She didn't want to be this close. She didn't want to touch him.

"You're actin' mighty jittery."

"I just don't want to make a mistake."

Thaddeus shrugged a massive shoulder. "Nobody here to see me but you. I reckon it won't matter much if a chunk or two of hair is missing."

They didn't speak again as Sarah brought her shaking hands under control and went about the task of shearing the shoulder-length hair. The texture of it was wonderfully thick and vibrant. Soft and silky, its shorter length began to curl into soft waves beneath her fingers.

Sarah wasn't unaware of the fact that she'd more than once leaned too close and touched her breast to his shoulder. Each time she'd see him stiffen and knew he felt it as well. That was bad enough, but when she stood between his legs to cut the front of his hair, Sarah almost dropped the scissors in his lap.

His gaze was level with her breasts and he didn't for a second think to look elsewhere. She could feel her flesh swelling, almost as if she needed Emily to feed, but it wasn't her daughter's mouth she wanted against her breast. It was this man's.

Sarah felt no little astonishment at the sudden realization. She'd never known passion before, and because she hadn't, she couldn't put a name to the disgraceful emotions that suddenly caused her breathing to grow choppy and harsh. She'd never known what it was to want a man's touch, to ache with the need to touch him herself.

Yes, she'd been married, and both Thomas and she had loved, but that love was born of a sweet, tender friendship. There had been no great passion between them. She'd never wanted it, never looked for it, never felt its loss, but had been happily content in what they had together. Never in her life had she once felt this overwhelming desire to touch. She hadn't ever needed to feel his lips against her own.

Jesus, he could smell her! Thaddeus closed his

143

eyes against the unbearable ache that ripped into his gut and yet, despite the pain, breathed deeply of this lusciously sweet, clean female. The scent brought a weakness he'd never known before. Every breath became an effort as he fought to gain control of this need. Her sweet breath floated over his face as she leaned closer. Thaddeus's knuckles turned white with the effort it took not to reach out and touch her. He couldn't think but to take hold of her hips and guide her closer. To bury his face against the softness of her breasts. To nuzzle the delightful sweetness, to breathe in more deeply the delicious scent of her.

He couldn't prevent the tremor that shook him. Sarah had no need to ask if he were chilled. His skin burned her fingers as she went about her business. She didn't want to know why he shivered. She didn't want to hear put to words what she could read in his eyes.

"Finished," she said at last, her voice telling clearly her relief. But when she tried to move away, his hand caught her wrist and held her in place.

"My beard," he said, his voice low, the words said on a shudder.

Their eyes met again. Her voice was soft, almost a whisper. "What about it?"

"It needs to be trimmed." Thaddeus knew he was close to losing his mind. He was purposely causing himself the greatest pain he'd ever known, and yet he was helpless but to allow it. He couldn't let her go.

Her eyes silently pleaded. She didn't want to do this. She didn't want to touch him anymore. "You can do that yourself."

"I can't." His dark eyes held hers captive. "Trim it."

Sarah hadn't the strength to argue. She might say she didn't want to touch him, but it was a lie. She wanted to touch him more than she'd ever wanted anything in her life. The touch of his hand on her wrist was causing her pulse to jump wildly out of control. He had to release her and quickly lest she do something insane, something she'd forever regret.

Sarah breathed a long sigh, straining for a weariness she was far from feeling. "How short?"

Thaddeus grinned. Sarah could have sworn his eyes actually twinkled at the victory. "I'll leave that up to you."

Sarah felt a moment's anger as she set about her task. But the anger soon faded as she concentrated on cleaning up his straggly beard. By the time she was done, his beard and mustache were neat and his curling hair barely reached his collar.

She stifled a groan. What had she done? How was it possible that a grizzly mountain of a man could be suddenly transformed into one so handsome it nearly took her breath away? Lord, the tension had been bad enough when it was only his compelling gaze and enormous size that taunted. How could she be expected to resist this?

Sarah said nothing but took a step back. She dared not utter a sound lest her voice give away the unnamed emotion that rocked her to her very core.

"Don't," he said as he gave in at last to the need that had brought no peace since finding her. His

145

hands reached for her hips and gently brought her back.

"No," she said, but the low, breathy sound of her voice made little difference in this instance. In truth, it only seemed to add to a need that could no longer be ignored. "Thaddeus, don't," she said as she was helplessly guided closer. She couldn't do this. She couldn't allow this. A hand slid around the back of her neck, and she closed her eyes and gave a soft whimper as she leaned forward.

"Kiss me, Sarah," he breathed against her lips.

Sarah had never known that a heart could beat so fast. She couldn't form rational thoughts, not standing so close, not when her body touched against his. All she could do, all she could think, was to run for her life. "Thaddeus, please," she moaned. "I can't."

"Yes, you can," he countered. "Kiss me."

"What's happening to me?" she asked, never realizing she'd spoken aloud.

"Don't you know?" Thaddeus asked, his dark eyes growing black, his large hands cupping her face, holding it for the teasing brush of a dozen kisses. No part of her face was left untouched. Breezy light kisses feathered her cheeks, her jaw, her nose, her closed eyes. And then he stopped.

Her eyes opened wide and she stared into the depth of black magic. It had to be magic. Nothing else could have so easily taken her under its spell.

Thaddeus read the fear in her eyes. "Don't be afraid, darlin'," he breathed, his breath teasing lips that were suddenly sensitive and aching for his touch. "I'd never hurt you. You know that, don't you?"

She did. No matter his tremendous size, his wild rages, or evil scowls, she knew he'd never hurt her. "Yes, I know."

"And still you won't kiss me." His mouth curved into a tender smile as he made his plea.

Sarah couldn't bring herself to take the final step. No doubt, he read as much in her eyes.

"Then I'll have to do the kissin', won't I?"

Sarah sighed in defeat. There was no hope. She couldn't win out against his allure. Against her own wicked response.

He brought her closer, settling her within the warm confines of his thighs, forcing her to her knees. Sarah felt a moment's gratitude that she was thus positioned, for once he brought his lips to hers, she knew she no longer had the power to stand on her own.

He breathed heavily against her mouth, and Sarah's mind swam with the combined scent of his clean breath and the gentle pressure of his lips. The pulse in her throat almost choked her. She couldn't bear his teasing lips a moment longer.

"Thaddeus, please," she murmured as his mouth moved away from hers to tantalize the smooth line of her throat.

"Please, what?" he asked, unsure of her meaning. All he could hear was the yearning in the words. He wanted to be sure. He had to be sure. "What, Sarah?" he asked again when it became clear she couldn't do more than moan a response.

"Kiss me, Thaddeus. I want you to kiss me," she whispered, for the first time in her life uncaring of the consequences. Her eyes closed; her head was thrown back. She never saw his smile, never realized his victory.

He pulled her tightly against him, then groaned as his mouth lowered to ravage hers. At her moan he gentled the kiss, but at the taste of her he soon lost what little there was of his control.

"It's not enough," he gasped as he broke apart for air, then like a man starving for his next meal took her mouth again. He ate at her, delighting in her taste. He groaned his pleasure at the delicious texture of lips, teeth, and then at last the dark, wondrous heat he found deep in her mouth.

His hands trembled as they moved from her face to her waist, holding her against him as he gently slid his hands up, up, until they rested just below her breasts.

She tried to talk. She tried to tell him to go on, that she wanted more, that she needed more, that her entire body strained for his touch, that she'd surely die if he didn't continue, but his mouth absorbed every sweet sound she uttered.

Mouths opened wider, each seeking to discover the other, reveling in shared tastes, hungering for more of this exquisite pleasure.

And still it wasn't enough.

Sarah's hands moved over his chest, delighting in his strength, glorying in the freedom to touch him at last.

Thaddeus ripped open his shirts. Neither noticed

the sound of tearing fabric or the buttons that hit and rolled to a stop upon a stone floor.

They groaned in unison as her hands found his naked, muscled flesh and smoothed over hair-smattered skin. Her fingers slid into his hair, his beard, down his throat to the swelling of a massive chest. And she trembled with the ache of wanting more. Her hands moved to his waist and stopped at the feel of his belt. Thaddeus raised his hips, his hunger for her to go on knowing no bounds. But Sarah was a lady of untried passions. Even caught up as she was in this exhilarating moment, she dared not go further.

Again her searching fingers returned to his chest and shoulders, and Thaddeus pulled her closer, locking her tighter between his thighs.

She was sitting on his lap. Sarah couldn't have said how she got there. She didn't care. All she knew was his mouth was like fire, burning her flesh as it slid from her lips and nuzzled the skin beneath her ear.

Sarah leaned back against his supporting arm and eagerly awaited his caress. It wasn't right. Later, she'd no doubt suffer the most horrifying degree of embarrassment, but she couldn't stop. She never wanted to stop.

"Do you want me to touch you?" Thaddeus asked, knowing he was going to, no matter her wants.

"Yes," she gasped. "Oh, God, yes," she managed, just before his mouth closed over hers again.

"I'm going to taste you, Sarah." His eyes were

darker than pitch and glowed with the reflected light from a nearby lamp.

She trembled at his promise, wanting desperately to urge him on, but the words wouldn't come. Instead, she reached shaking fingers to the bodice of her dress and slowly parted the fabric.

His breath was rougher than ever as he watched her. His eyes filled with a tenderness she'd never seen before.

Thaddeus knew well enough that she was new to passion. Her shy, unknowledgeable responses to his kisses had told him of her inexperience from the first. That she was a lady of some morals was also apparent, since even caught in the throes of passion, she was unable to say the words he needed to hear, but to see this was almost more than he could stand. Her cheeks already flushed from passion, flamed at her daring. Thaddeus felt something squeeze at his chest as her gaze proclaimed her shyness as no words could.

Broken and choppy, their breaths mingled as hungry eyes clung to one another. Thaddeus had never known such passion, such need. It had never been this way before. He knew he'd never want a woman as badly again. He wouldn't allow the thought that he'd never want another . . . that even though they had yet to come together, he'd never find another to compare.

Her bodice was opened. She couldn't go further. Thaddeus smiled and, with one finger, brought both the dress and chemise to each shoulder and down her arms.

He groaned a low sound that mingled torment with pleasure. "Beautiful," he managed, although he couldn't say how. His blood was throbbing so hard he could hardly breathe, never mind speak. "Sarah, God, you're so beautiful," he choked.

Thaddeus ran a long finger from the base of her throat down, slowly, achingly slow, to the soft plumpness of her breasts. It never stopped until it brushed over straining moist nipples, brushing again and again, back and forth, until she felt the sensation throughout her entire body.

Sarah groaned, her eyes closed against the pleasure, her head falling back on a neck too weak to support it.

"Watch me," he said. "Sarah, open your eyes and watch me touch you."

Sarah felt without a will of her own. She couldn't refuse. Her eyes opened, her gaze captured by his, then slowly his head lowered until his breath fanned the hard budded tip of her breast. Her back arched as she silently begged him closer. Without thinking, she lifted the heavy globe and rubbed the milky tip over his lips.

Thaddeus smiled, then brought his mouth to her hungry flesh. Sarah cried out her pleasure while Thaddeus growled a sound of relish.

"God, oh, God," she groaned as his mouth moved over her. He bit her and then soothed the tiny injury with his tongue. His lips plucked, teasing her straining flesh, then his mouth opened wider and, with a hungry growl, took what he could of her deep into flaming heat. He suckled, and Sarah wondered if

151

she wouldn't die from the pleasure. Nothing could be better than this. Even the exquisite pleasure of Emily's sweet sucking dimmed in comparison. Sarah had never known such ecstasy to exist.

Her hands caught his head and pressed him closer, all the while tiny whimpering sounds escaping her throat. She had to have more or she would die from this yearning.

Thaddeus chuckled as he felt her sweet acquiescence dissolve into an aching hunger that easily matched his own. He knew what she wanted. She didn't have to say the words.

Thaddeus's mouth suddenly hovered over her own. "Taste me, Sarah. It's you on my tongue."

Everything he did drove her closer to insanity. One thrill overtook yet another, and this was probably the best yet. She tasted the sweet warmth of her milk in his mouth. How had it become so sensual a tasting? When had her breasts forgotten their original purpose to seek another's mouth, another's pleasure?

He couldn't touch her, kiss her, speak to her, that she didn't crave more. Her arms discovered a strength she hadn't known as she pulled him closer, eager for all he could give.

Her mouth gave and demanded equally, and Thaddeus thrilled with the knowledge that he had brought about this wild hunger. His hand dipped beneath her skirt, up the long length of her leg and beneath her drawers.

Sarah felt the movement and found herself capable only of arching her hips so he might touch what they both craved most.

Thaddeus groaned at finding his way blocked and then he remembered. A low whispered curse escaped his lips, but the sound was lost in Sarah's passion. She groaned a soft sound of loss as he pulled his lips from hers and wrapped her tightly against his chest.

Her head was cradled in the hollow of his throat as he waited for his passions to ease. It wasn't easy, considering Sarah was mindlessly kissing his throat while whispering the most delightful approval of what she'd found.

"Sarah," he managed through a tight throat that told of his aching need. "We have to stop."

Sarah murmured a sound of disagreement. She didn't want to stop. She never wanted to stop.

"Sarah, darlin', listen to me. It's too soon."

His words, combined with a tiny shake, penetrated the mindless fog of desire like a splash of cold water. Sarah blinked her surprise to find herself in his arms. How? Lord in Heaven, how had she let this happen? She'd heard his words but imagined he spoke of her husband's death, rather than of the birth of her baby. How had she managed to forget so soon her sorrow, her decorum, her modesty? What must he think of her? It was hardly more than a few weeks since her husband had died. What in God's name was she doing?

Chapter Eight

Lord in Heaven! What was happening here? How could she have lived twenty-three years and never suspected that she so lacked in character as to succumb yet again to such depravity? Barely a few weeks had passed since her husband's death. Why was it necessary to remind herself of that fact? Sarah shivered her disgust. She could understand his need, for he lived for months without female companionship, but what was her excuse? She was a woman. Anyone could tell you that a woman, a good woman, didn't crave a man's touch, didn't ache for the feel of his lips against hers.

The only answer then was that she was anything but good, for she craved and ached like never before. Odd that she'd never known this wanting. Why, she wondered, did it happen now? Why with this man?

She wanted him, and the knowledge that he had twice called to a halt their lovemaking was a horror not to be borne. Her actions had been nothing less than deplorable, and Thaddeus had every right to think what he would.

Would he snarl again his contempt, his disgust? Sarah sighed her dismay, knowing his repugnance couldn't compare to her own.

Tears filled her eyes. She couldn't look at him. She wasn't brave enough to chance seeing again the distaste in his eyes. Never had she known this wretchedness, this shame, this confusion. If only she could understand what was happening to her . . . why she acted like she did once this man touched her.

Sarah might not have understood what was happening between them, but Thaddeus knew well enough the sexual attraction. Older and more worldly, he'd recognized from the first the emotion and yet honestly admitted to never having known a longing to equal this. He'd never have believed a man could want so desperately. Before Sarah, he wouldn't have believed any woman could bring to his life this odd mixture of excitement and a deep sense of contentment. He couldn't have explained why it felt so good knowing she was in his home, why her smile brought a tender ache to his soul. All he knew was that this particular woman was everything a man could want.

He'd denied it for as long as he could. But there was no longer room for denial. He didn't love her, of course. Thaddeus didn't believe in the existence of the emotion, except perhaps between parent and child. No, love was only a word used by men to get what they wanted from a woman.

Women contented themselves with believing they were loved and believing they loved in return, when

155

in truth they sought only a man who would care for their needs and comfort. He gave a slight shrug. In most cases, it worked out well enough. What difference did it make what they called it? All he knew was that he wanted this woman. Wanted her like he'd never wanted another.

"You're so isolated out here," she said, imagining the harsh loneliness he'd chosen for his way of life. "Don't you miss the company of others?"

"Nope."

"What about supplies? Suppose you need something?"

"During the spring and summer, I get to town once a month. And then I stock up in the fall." He shrugged. "If I run out before spring, I do without."

"What about church? It's impossible to attend regularly. Doesn't that—?"

He cut her off. "Don't go to church, regularly or otherwise."

"Why?" she asked, her blue eyes puzzled as she poured coffee into his cup.

"Can't think of one good reason why I should," he answered, never taking his eyes from Tiger as he rubbed his hands over the animal's thick coat.

"Well, thanking God for all he's given you would be a good start."

"Don't believe in God."

"Of course, you believe in God." Sarah smiled at

the impossible notion that one might deny the Lord's existence.

"Sarah," he said softly, his dark eyes growing darker still as he leveled a hard gaze at her, "don't tell me what I believe."

Her mouth fell open with surprise as she realized he meant every word he said. "How could you not believe in God? How do you imagine you got here?"

Thaddeus raised one brow and shot her a knowing look. "Much the same way you did, I expect."

Sarah's withering glance told clearly she wasn't pleased by his attempt at teasing. "If you don't believe in God, then you don't believe man has a soul, am I right?"

Thaddeus shrugged. "I reckon."

"Then what makes you better than any animal?"

"Nothin'." Thaddeus stretched and then sighed. "Most men I know ain't any better than animals." He shrugged and then grinned. "No, that ain't fair. Animals are mostly a damn sight better. They never hurt for the simple pleasure of watching another's pain."

"And men do?"

He nodded.

"You don't."

"What makes you think I don't?"

"Because you're not like that. You're . . ." Sarah's words came to a sudden stop. She was unsure how to go on. Her cheeks grew pink with embarrassment, knowing he was waiting for her to finish and that she'd already said too much.

157

Thaddeus grinned as he watched her cheeks gain in color. "What? What am I?"

"You're kind."

Kind wasn't a word that Thaddeus freely or happily associated with himself. "I ain't." He obviously didn't appreciate her opinion.

"You might not want to be, but you are."

He shook his head. "Ain't."

"You saved my life. Twice," she reminded. "Wasn't that kind?"

"Nope. I saved your life 'cause I didn't have a choice." He held up his fingers as if to count. "I never wanted you here, but I didn't want Johnny to have you, either."

"All right." Sarah nodded, knowing the truth of that statement. Her gaze moved to the dog at his side. "What about Tiger? You're kind to him."

Thaddeus shook his head again. "Not kind, smart. Any animal responds better to a gentle touch."

Sarah sighed and watched as he sipped at his coffee. It was obvious to her that the man had a real problem with the word. She wondered why and didn't hesitate to ask. "Do you equate kindness with being weak?"

Thaddeus met her inquisitive gaze with annoyance. "That's a damn fool thing to say."

"I don't think so."

Thaddeus opened his mouth to argue further, but Sarah cut him off. "Let's talk about something else.

158

Tell me why you don't believe in God," she said as she sat facing him.

" 'Cause there ain't no such thing."

"But the Bible—"

"—is a pack of old wives' tales, superstitions, and outright lies written just to keep people like you in line."

Sarah's mouth hung open in shock. She'd never heard anyone spout such utter nonsense. Thaddeus's lips twisted into a scowl; his eyes darkened as he leaned toward her. "What kind of God lets babies die and wives cheat and men kill each other? Where's your God when a Gatlin' gun nearly cuts a man in half and you see his guts laying on the ground, while he begs somebody to push his inners back in where they belong? What kind of God—"

"Enough!" Sarah snapped, coming instantly to her feet. "I won't listen to this."

His mouth twisted into an evil, knowing smile. "Oh, you won't, eh? Why? 'Cause you know I'm right?"

"No, Mr. Payne. Because you couldn't be more wrong. God isn't going to stop men from killing each other. We all have a free will."

"Yeah . . . well, I'll take my free will and believe what I want. If it's all right with you, lady."

Sarah's eyes were bright with intelligence and her lips curved into a smile as she silently laughed at her surprising spurt of anger. Surely that emotion wouldn't go far toward convincing him to her way of

159

thinking. She eased herself into her seat again. "It's perfectly all right with me, Mr. Payne." Sarah grinned as she tried one more time. "I've only one question, if you don't mind." He gave a careless shrug. "What have you got to lose by believing? If you're right, then nothing we do, say, or believe can matter, but if you're wrong, what then?"

Thaddeus grinned, never expecting so logical a statement from a woman. "Then I expect I'm facin' a pack o' trouble."

Sarah gave a soft gut-twisting chuckle that caused Thaddeus to squirm uncomfortably. "Then I expect you are, Mr. Payne." And without missing a beat, she changed the subject. "More coffee?" she asked as she reached for the pot.

"No." He moved quickly to her side, caught her hand, and pulled her to her feet. "Let's go outside. I need some fresh air."

Sarah glanced at Emily, sleeping comfortably in her makeshift bed.

"We won't go far. You'll hear her if she cries."

It was dark, nearly time to retire for the night, but Sarah gladly accepted his offer. She hadn't left the cabin since he'd brought her to the barn when he'd found out about the gold. With the exception of her daily visits to the outhouse, she hadn't stepped foot outside for weeks. She, too, needed a few moments of fresh air.

"Lord, but this is beautiful," she said, her gaze taking in the forest that surrounded three sides of his home. Trees of varying sizes, some almost as tall as mountains, their branches heavy with snow, were simply majestic bathed as they were in silver moonlight. Snow crunched beneath her boots. Soon the cold would penetrate and her feet would grow wet and uncomfortable. But for now it was wonderful. Sarah breathed lustily, filling her lungs with still, cold night air, as she silently reveled in the beauty that surrounded her.

Thaddeus kept to himself his opinion on the Lord having anything to do with it. He glanced down at the woman at his side and grinned. The moon was full, its light on the snow-covered ground enabling him to see her almost as clearly as he had inside. The cold air had brought roses to her cheeks and a sparkle to her blue eyes. Thaddeus watched her for a long moment before he managed to control a need unlike anything he'd ever known before. He ached to take this woman in his arms, to feel her warmth, her softness, to breathe again her scent.

Sarah raised her gaze to his shadowed face, then laughed as he tried to ease the moment with a teasing remark lest he lose all control and pounce upon her unsuspecting form. "Your nose is red."

Her eyes danced with merriment. "How unkind of you to point that out, Mr. Payne."

Thaddeus laughed. "Told you I wasn't—" He never finished, ducking instead as a snowball came flying in his direction.

An instant later Sarah was running. Her intent was obvious as she made for the huge tree at the center of the front yard. She'd almost reached her destination when a snowball smacked against the back of her head. Sarah turned, her eyes dark with the promise of retaliation.

Thaddeus laughed as she calmly went about the business of arming herself with a pile of snowballs, placing them neatly at her feet. "Where's your Christian spirit?" he taunted as he dodged an occasional throw. "Aren't you supposed to turn the other cheek?"

"You didn't hit me on the cheek, Mr. Payne." Her eyes sparkled as she prepared her arsenal. "You hit the back of my head, and none too gently I might add." She had to bite her lips lest her laughter come bubbling forth. "I'm afraid I can't, in all good conscience, let you get away with that."

"Oh, I see. An eye for an eye, or in this case," he gasped as he shifted away from a snowball that nearly caught him smack on his nose, "a head for a head, is that it?" The next snowball knocked his hat clear off his head.

Thaddeus grinned as he bent to pick up his hat, inadvertently offering her yet another target, which Sarah didn't hesitate to bombard. He chuckled, his eyes gleaming with laughter as he dusted both his hat and the seat of his pants until they were free of snow. It was then, with a wicked, menacing promise of retribution in his eye, that he began moving toward her, his body crouched and weaving as he dodged his way through a constant barrage of snowballs. Her aim, although amazingly accurate, didn't deter him one iota. He kept up his advance. Kept it up, in fact, until his boots squashed her supply of weapons to useless white powder.

"Beast!" Sarah couldn't keep the laughter from her voice, even as a shiver of excitement overtook her. She turned on her heel and ran as fast as her legs could carry her, the second before he reached for her. Her laughter carried upon the silent night and invaded his soul. He had to capture the sound and to do that he had to take this woman.

Sarah gasped to find herself suddenly flung to the ground. An instant later, she was flipped to her back as if she weighed no more than a feather. Thaddeus settled himself comfortably upon her, his arms supporting most of his weight.

He was looking down at her, his expression a strange combination of laughter and something she couldn't quite identify as he loomed threateningly above her. She felt so tiny, so helpless, when he looked down at her like this, and yet she faced him bravely, desperately trying to put aside the odd tingling sensations that tightened her stomach. Her voice was light, denying the trembling he caused inside her. "Look what you've done," she sputtered as she blew already-melting snow from her lips. "I'm covered with snow."

"Better yet, look at what I'm going to do," he said as his hot mouth descended upon hers.

"Thaddeus, you shouldn't do this," she said on a soft sigh as he parted his lips from hers at last. His mouth grazed the exposed moist flesh of her face with a hundred tiny, sipping kisses and the warm,

163

sensual whisper of silky beard and mustache, until the snow that had bathed her face was gone.

"I know. I should have waited till we went back inside."

"That's not what I mean," she murmured thickly, finding it an almost impossible task to keep her mind on what she'd intended to say. "You shouldn't do this at all."

"Why? Are you going to tell me you don't like it?"

"Thaddeus, it's not right. I'm not supposed to feel—to feel—" She moaned as his lips found the sensitive area just beneath her ear. "Oh, God, I don't know what I feel."

He chuckled softly, gaining confidence at the whispery, almost dreamy softness in her voice. "Am I confusing you?"

Sarah shook her head. "No. Yes." And then she finished with an honest, "I don't know."

Thaddeus gave a low rumbling laugh at her indecision, the sound sending chills up her spine. "A woman who knows her own mind," he teased. "Tell me what you feel."

It took her a long moment, but Sarah finally garnered the strength to answer. "I'm embarrassed that I've allowed you such liberties." She shivered and made a small sound, much like a groan, when his lips nuzzled again the tender spot just below her ear. "I've never—"

He stole her words from her mouth with another long, hot, eating kiss, which seemed to draw the strength from her entire body. "You've never what?"

164

"Felt this way before," she breathed against his throat.

"What way?" His arms tightened around her as he silently urged her to tell him all.

Unskilled in the art of the games men and women play, Sarah never thought to be anything but honest. She told him her feelings never realizing the effect her words were bound to have on this man. "Like I'm floating and weak. When you kiss me, I feel helpless. I can't fight against you and me at the same time."

Thaddeus closed his eyes and groaned as erotic pictures of them together flashed in his mind. "You're supposed to feel like that."

"No, I'm not. It's unseemly."

Thaddeus's smile was tender, his gaze lost to her, for in her shyness she couldn't look him in the eye. He switched their positions. Now he lay in the snow while she was supported above him. His hands guided her hips until she was pressed against him, held in place between hard thighs. "Do you want to touch me?"

She shook her head, denying the truth even as her fingers itched to slide inside his coat. "You do. I can see it in your eyes."

"It's wicked."

"It's not."

Sarah continued to shake her head in denial.

"Remember last week when you cut my hair? Remember what it felt like when I kissed you, when I touched you? You touched me then. Did you like

165

it?"

She couldn't answer him. She couldn't admit that she more than liked it, that she'd thought of little else since. "What's happening to me?" she almost wailed, never realizing her cry answered clearly his question. Her body slumped forward, leaning heavily, helplessly upon him. "I don't understand. This is so wrong. Why am I—?"

"Sarah, it's not wrong for us to want each other. It's normal to feel this need."

"It can't be. I've never felt it before."

"Haven't you? Didn't you want your husband?"

Thaddeus was instantly sorry he'd asked. He didn't want to know. He didn't want to think of her in another man's arms. He didn't want to imagine her wild and hot and hungry with need, unless that need was for him.

Sarah couldn't, wouldn't, answer him. Somehow she felt it disloyal to discuss so personal a subject. If she hadn't felt this almost overpowering desire in Thomas's arms, no one but she had the right to know. "Emily," she breathed as if the name were the answer to all her questions.

"What about her?" His hand ran up and down the length of her back in gentle, soothing strokes.

"Women have been known to act strangely after birthing a child. No doubt—"

Thaddeus chuckled and cut her off. "No doubt you could find a hundred excuses, if you put your mind to it. But only one would be the truth. You want me as I want you."

166

Sarah gave a soft, wordless murmur of denial.

"Nothing is stopping you from—"

"Thomas—"

"—is dead."

Sarah made a soft choking sound, obviously distraught as she pressed her face into the shoulder of his coat.

Thaddeus realized her distress and held her gently against him. "I won't push you, Sarah. You have to understand that what we feel is right. You have to come to know you won't find peace until you lose control in my arms."

Her troubled gaze raised to his and slowly brightened, until he recognized sparks of burgeoning laughter in her eyes. "Lose control in order to find peace, Thaddeus?"

Thaddeus's grin was deliciously wicked, his lips so tempting Sarah would never know how she found the strength to resist. "I could show you exactly what I mean."

"I think I hear Emily," she said a bit breathlessly as she disengaged herself from his warmth and came to her feet.

Thaddeus nodded, silently accepting her decision. Instantly, a plan formed. Judging from her responses to his kisses, he imagined it wouldn't take much to tease this woman until she grew mindless with need. Thaddeus smiled at the thought. No, he needn't push just now. He wouldn't have to wait for long.

* * *

They were experiencing an unseasonable stretch of springlike weather. The last of the snow, all four feet of it, had melted two days ago and, to Sarah's delight, Thaddeus hadn't once mentioned the possibility of taking her and Emily to town. Her eyes danced with happiness. A smile was never far from her lips. Secretly, although she'd deny the thought if asked, she hoped he never mentioned it.

Since that night almost two weeks ago, when they'd played like children in the snow, Thaddeus hadn't pressed his advantage. He'd grown free with his touchings and even shared an occasional kiss, but was careful to take it no further. Oddly enough, he always left her wanting more. And want she did. Her hands itched to touch him. Her body ached to feel him close to her, to be held in the warmth of his arms.

That he wanted her was obvious. Sarah realized the need he experienced must certainly cause him a degree of discomfort. Still he didn't press her and for that she was grateful. Or was she? Should he take her in his arms, would she fight off his advances or moan her acceptance of a desire she could no longer deny?

Sarah shook her head. It wouldn't do to allow these wicked thoughts. They caused her only to grow more unsettled by the day.

Sarah took the sweet-smelling apple pie from the oven and placed it on the window ledge to cool. Both the door and windows were open on this springlike day, in order to take advantage of the warm, clean air.

As always, Thaddeus had left early that morning. He had promised a fish dinner tonight. After seeing to the herd that roamed the pastures on the mountain's western slope, he'd gone off to the river to see what he could do about fulfilling that promise.

Thaddeus had been talking lately of increasing the size of his herd and perhaps hiring on a few hands to help out. Sarah wondered how he could convince a man to work this far from town. How could anyone be satisfied never to see another human being for months at a time? Even as she wondered, she never thought how completely satisfied she was to share only this man's company.

Standing at the table rolling pie crust dough into even, thin ovals, Sarah thought she saw movement from the corner of her eye. "Oh!" she cried. Her pie was no longer sitting on the windowsill.

In an instant, she was outside and running around the side of the house. What she saw when she turned the corner brought her to an abrupt stop. A giant black bear was standing as calm as could be over the dish, eating her pie. "Stop that!" she ordered. And if her voice wasn't as strong as she'd have liked, she couldn't be held to task, for Sarah had never in her life seen a bear. And to find herself suddenly this close to the huge beast would have been enough to shake the bravest soul.

Sarah ran to the porch, grabbed the broom, and

moved quickly back to confront the animal. "Go away," she demanded as she prodded the animal. Why she bothered she couldn't have said, for the pie was lost to her. Even if he left a bite, which was apparently not his intent, she wasn't about to eat from the pan after he had slobbered all over it. Angry to see her morning's efforts gone to waste, she snapped, "Get out!"

The bear, having been fooled by the unusual break in the long winter and awakening early from his hibernation, was not at all happy about having his first meal of the season interrupted. He didn't take kindly to this human poking him with a stick. His straight nose wrinkled in objection, while a huge growl erupted from his throat. His brown face split as he showed her a perfect set of the most horrifying teeth she'd ever seen.

"Get away from him, Sarah," Thaddeus said, standing suddenly across from her, the bear between them.

"He stole my pie."

Thaddeus grinned at the annoyance he heard in her voice. "I figure, if he's brave enough to go up against you, he's due the prize. Now back off."

The bear growled again. Thaddeus lifted his gun from his holster, knowing, even as he did, that it would take more than the six bullets the gun held to stop this hungry beast. "Get inside and bar the door."

"And leave you out here?" she asked incredulously.

Thaddeus nodded, his gaze never leaving the huge animal as the bear licked the pie plate clean. "If you have another pie, throw it out the window."

"I will not!"

"Sarah, he's hungry. Do it."

Thaddeus threw the line of fish he'd caught toward the animal. He sighed with a measure of relief that the bear turned his attentions from Sarah to the next course of his meal. "Get me the honey pot."

"Thaddeus, if you give him that, we won't have but half a pot left."

"If I don't, he just might take it anyway."

Sarah's expression spoke clearly her reluctance, but at Thaddeus's hard look she did as she was told. Thaddeus walked toward the corner of the cabin and waited for Sarah's return. It wasn't until the bear finished his meal that Thaddeus took the honey and started away from the house. As he moved, he trailed a narrow stream of the thick, heavy fluid behind him, purposely drawing the animal away from Sarah and his house.

It worked for a time, but the bear soon tired of licking sweet dirt. He hurried his pace, trying to get to the origins of one of his favorite flavors.

He growled his frustration and moved even faster. Suddenly, he stood on his hind legs, looming over Thaddeus. Sarah screamed and ran inside. Within seconds, she returned with Thaddeus's rifle. She put it to her shoulder and pulled the trigger. A second later she gasped with shock, finding herself thrown back upon the ground. She landed with a bone-jarring thud.

A moment later she was up again. This time braced for the rifle's kick, she pulled the trigger again. Amazingly enough, considering the trembling that wracked her body, the bullet hit the bear in his shoulder. Sarah blinked her astonishment. She hadn't known until then that a wounded bear was like no other animal she'd ever seen before or was likely to see again. He roared his pain and instantly turned his attentions upon his attacker.

Sarah could hear Thaddeus bellow out orders for her to shoot again, but she was frozen with shock and fear. She couldn't move. She couldn't make her finger squeeze the trigger.

All she could do was stare. Her gaze centered upon the huge black figure and his opened mouth, filled with knife-sharp teeth. The animal raced toward her, blocking her vision of all else. He wasn't six feet from her when she realized Thaddeus was shooting. Somehow the sound brought her from her dazed state and she managed to pull the trigger again. And she didn't stop pulling it until the gun was empty.

The animal lay dead at her feet. Her body trembled as she stared at its huge black coat and the blotches of blood that stained its shiny fur.

Thaddeus was shaking at least as badly as she when he came to her side. "Sonofabitch! Are you out of your mind? Why'd you wait so long? He almost got you."

Sarah turned a white face toward the man who railed. She never heard his condemning words. Never realized his anger. Her eyes were dull, blank with the horror of what she'd seen, what she'd done. She made a tiny sound and then suddenly, silently, without any warning at all, collapsed at his feet.

The baby was screaming, the sounds of gunfire having frightened her from a sound sleep. Thaddeus brought Sarah inside and laid her on the bed, before he took Emily into his arms and soothed her cries with gentle pattings and soft, tender words. Moments later, the baby quieted. Thaddeus grinned, filled with no little pride that he'd been able to calm her. He scowled at the woman lying on the bed as he put the baby down to play in her little drawer. Damn fool woman! What the hell was the matter with her to chance her life like that? God, he'd never known such terror as when watching the bear charge at her. What the hell did she think she was doing? What the hell would he have done if she'd missed at the last minute? If the bear had gotten to her? He pushed aside the pain that clutched at his chest, refusing to recognize or name its cause as he shuddered, all the while imagining what might have happened.

Sarah opened her eyes to a glaring Thaddeus leaning over her prone form. "I hope to hell you're satisfied," he snapped, his words biting and cruel. "You didn't listen to a damn word I said. I should warm your goddamn ass."

It was the threat that did it. The moment she'd

opened her eyes, Sarah had felt the self-pitying need to cry. His harsh words did little to ease the need, but his threat instantly dispelled the notion and caused anger to fill her to overflowing. She sat up and glared at his hard expression. "Oh, you should, should you? I just saved your life, and that's the thanks I get? Threats?"

"Lady, you almost got yourself killed. What the hell did you think you were doing?"

"I didn't think at all. I did what I had to do." No matter that her entire body trembled like a leaf in a windstorm, she shoved him aside with sudden and amazing strength as she came to her feet. "You needed my help."

"The hell, I did."

"Oh really? Do you often wrestle bears?"

"Lady, I was about to drop the honey and run. He wouldn't have come after me. He was too interested in what was inside that pot."

Sarah blinked her astonishment as his reasoning made itself known. There was a moment of silence before she countered. "How was I supposed to know that? All I could see was this giant beast hovering over you. What was I supposed to do?"

Thaddeus couldn't think beyond the horror of her being mauled by the bear. He'd suffered untold fear for her safety and now to find her yelling at him was enough to push him to the limit of his control. His nose was almost against hers. He grabbed her shoulders and snarled, "You were supposed to obey my orders. I told you to get into the house." He gave her a none-too-gentle shake, then threw her on the bed. "The next time I tell you to do something, lady, you'd better do it."

Somewhere along the line, her pins had fallen from her hair. Sarah brushed the heavy golden-brown mass from her eyes and glared her resentment. She was smart enough to keep her mouth shut, but she couldn't keep the anger from her eyes.

"You can give me all the evil looks you want. Just do it. You hear?"

"I hear," she said as sullen as a child when he looked as if he were coming at her again.

"Fine," Thaddeus remarked as he turned for the door. "I hope you like bear. We'll be having it for a spell." He swung the door shut behind him, grabbing it just before it slammed.

"Not hungry?" Thaddeus asked, a gleam of laughter in his eyes.

"Not particularly," Sarah returned, avoiding his gaze as she moved the glaringly obnoxious piece of meat around in her dish.

"Too bad. It's good," Thaddeus said as he reached for yet another slice of bear roast.

Sarah nodded but said no more on the subject. She might not have admitted it, but there was no way she was going to eat this meat. Just the thought alone disgusted her. Granted, she'd had no choice but to kill the bear, but she knew now the whole episode was her fault. The bear would have gone away

175

unharmed if she'd only obeyed Thaddeus's orders. Because of her, the bear was dead. Sarah had never killed anything larger than a fly in her life. She'd never known such guilt.

Thaddeus got up and refilled his coffee cup. Standing behind her, he allowed his gaze to move over her slender frame and felt a twinge of guilt at the slump of her shoulders. Maybe he'd been too hard on her. She'd thought she was saving his life. Damn! Why hadn't he taken that into consideration before he let his temper get the best of him?

Because he couldn't stand the thought of her being in danger. Just imagining what that bear could have done to her caused a pain the likes of which he'd never known to grab at his gut.

Thaddeus sat himself across from her again. He wasn't much for apologizing. Far as he could remember, he'd never done it before. He tried to figure out how he should go about it, what words he should say. Finally, he just blurted out, "Look, I reckon I was a bit hard on you today. Why don't we forget about it?"

If only she could. Sarah raised tear-filled eyes to Thaddeus's amazed gaze.

Thaddeus hadn't often seen this woman cry. And to see it now caused his heart to squeeze in his chest. Silently, a tear slid slowly down a rounded cheek and Thaddeus cursed himself soundly for causing her this pain. In an instant he was on his feet, pulling her to stand in the warmth of his arms. "I'm sorry, Sarah."

"For what?" she asked, clearly surprised to hear the words.

"For making you cry."

"I'm not crying," she said as still more tears came.

"You aren't?" he asked as a small, tender smile touched the corners of his mouth. "Then what's the matter?"

"I can't eat."

"Why? Are you feelin' poorly?"

Sarah shook her head. "I've never killed anything before, Thaddeus. The smell . . ." She shuddered with horror. "I think I'm going to be sick."

Thaddeus smiled again as he sat and pulled her into his lap. He tucked her head beneath his jaw as he faced her away from the table. This lady sure had an aversion to killing. He'd never seen anyone so sensitive. Where did she think they got the food they ate every night? Thaddeus figured it best he didn't mention it. "We won't eat it again. I'll give it away or feed it to Tiger." And when his words brought no immediate response, he lowered his head, trying to see her expression. "All right?"

Sarah nodded as she wiped her tears on the back of her hand.

Thaddeus pulled back a bit and asked, "Don't they eat meat in St. Joseph, Missouri?"

"Of course, they do. But I don't have to kill it."

There was a long moment of silence before Sarah asked, "You think I'm acting like a fool, don't you?" She wouldn't meet his gaze. She didn't want to see the mockery she knew she'd find there.

Thaddeus felt his heart squeeze with tenderness. The emotion scared him, but not like it might have a month ago. His voice was lower than usual and filled with a huskiness that caused him to clear it twice before he could say, "Sarah, I think you're the bravest woman I've ever known. You risked your life to save mine today and I haven't even thanked you yet."

Chapter Nine

Thaddeus pulled the wide evergreen through the doorway and listened with nothing less than delight as Sarah laughed. "It's too big. We won't have enough space to move with something that large."

Thaddeus grinned and pulled her into his arms. He planted a long, hungry kiss on her mouth, just before he laughed at her struggles.

"You're wet!"

"That's probably 'cause it's rainin' outside."

Sarah laughed again and smacked his shoulder. She leaned into his strength as she brushed water from his beard and mustache in a decidedly wifely manner. Her eyes glowed with pleasure, her body soft against his. She didn't fight the embrace. Still, she knew better than to linger overlong. "You'd better let me go."

Thaddeus did as she asked, to the disappointment of them both.

Sarah chuckled as she watched him place the large tree in the corner of the small room. "Couldn't you find anything smaller?"

Thaddeus stood back a bit and eyed the tree. "You really don't like it?"

Sarah smiled. It often amazed her how this rough man could be so sensitive. She could see the need for her praise in his expression. Sarah didn't have to lie. The tree was beautiful. "I love it."

Her eyes were shining with delight as she gazed up at him and marveled that this was the same man she'd met only two months ago. At first they had hardly spoken, except perhaps to insult one another. She would often sulk while he would growl his annoyance. Slowly, their enforced cohabitation had evolved to a mutual acceptance of a situation neither could change. And then somehow they had become friends. Now friendship wasn't enough. Both of them wanted more. They hadn't as yet made love, but the thought of coming together was never far from either of their minds.

It had taken some time before Sarah was physically able, and by then they had come to some sort of silent, mutual agreement not to rush into this relationship. Thaddeus might lie beside his stove at night aching for her soft warmth beside him, but he did nothing to hurry them together.

Sarah was happy. She laughed often and felt a measure of pride that she could bring a smile to Thaddeus's once-grim lips. Amazingly, they'd been less grim of late.

Emily thrived and glowed with health. Her tiny body had almost doubled in size. She was a good baby and a delight to her mother. Oddly enough, even though he'd never before made the acquaintance of a newborn, Thaddeus fell completely under her spell. He marveled at her smile, especially when he was the reason behind it. Frequently, it was Thaddeus who went to the child upon her first murmur. "You'll spoil her," Sarah would warn. "You're not giving her a chance to ask before you answer her needs."

"A little spoilin' won't matter much," Thaddeus would answer as he shrugged away her concern.

For Thaddeus was of a mind to do just that. He'd never before felt this tenderness for another human. He'd never known he had it in him to feel this need to protect her from the evil that lurked in the world beyond his small cabin.

He'd made her a crib that boasted of elaborately carved, beautifully intricate scrolls. The night his knife had slipped he'd been carving the headboard. The crib was finally finished and sitting in the barn waiting until tomorrow to be brought inside. His eyes glowed with happiness as he imagined how delighted Sarah would be. How might she show her appreciation? Thaddeus grinned at the scenario that played again in his mind. He'd imagined it often enough since he'd first started the project.

She'd come to him. Her eyes would be wide with delight and then filled with longing, her lips parted in a tender smile. A smile that would grow to laughter and then to moans of pleasure.

"What are you grinning at?" she asked suspiciously.

"I'm wondering what we can find to decorate this tree."

181

"Candles? Do you have any?"

"None small enough."

"What about popcorn. We've often strung—"

"Nope."

"What about ribbons?"

Thaddeus laughed and shot her a look of incredulity. "Do I look like the sort to wear ribbons?"

"I meant my ribbons," Sarah said as she poked him with an elbow.

Thaddeus chuckled as he went outside again and pulled in a mountain of white pine. He removed his outer clothing, sat at the table, and began to string the pine together into a long rope.

When he was finished, he hung it in great loops about the cabin walls. "What?" he asked as he moved up behind her, his voice low and gravelly as his mouth took tiny nips at her neck. "Is that all you've done?" he asked as he watched Sarah tie one ribbon after another into bows and place them on the branches of the tree.

The multicolored streamers gave the tree a festive air, but it still needed more. Sarah shot him a glare, then smiled at his low laughter. "It's going to need something more." She sighed as she remembered all the pretty decorations she'd left back in St. Joseph. "I'll bake cookies and we'll hang them."

"And I'll find some berries. That should do the trick."

Emily had been bathed, fed, and was now down for her morning nap. The bird was in the oven. Sarah wondered how Thaddeus had ever found anything as big and what in the world they were going to do with it after they'd eaten it for a week.

It was Christmas, but Christmas or not, the ranch's animals had to be cared for. Thaddeus had gone to check on his herd up the western slope of his mountain. Sarah smiled as she slid beneath the warm water. She never bathed till Thaddeus had left the cabin. She knew it prudent to be careful, since the forced intimacy they shared was already fraught with danger. She didn't want to end up in his arms in a wild moment of crazed passion. If they were to make love, it had to be a mutual decision arrived at with logic and reason. Each had to know what the results of their actions would entail.

Sarah knew she was falling in love. Only this love was nothing at all like the love she'd shared with Thomas. This love encompassed a passion so rare, so bold, so intense, as to sweep her away into a time of mindlessness whenever in his arms. It had to mean as much to him. She couldn't bear it if it didn't.

How often had she lain awake at night wishing she had the courage to ask him to come to her? How much longer could she hold out? How many more of his lusty kisses and hugs could she endure before her control snapped and she begged him to take her to bed?

Sarah sighed as the last of the soap disintegrated between her fingers. She had only one bar left and she doubted it would last till spring. Spring. What would happen then? Would Thaddeus take her to town and leave her there as previously planned? Or would he ask her to stay? Did he care for her just a little? Did his kisses mean he cared, or was it simply the fact that he'd been so long without a woman?

Sarah was lost in her thoughts. She never heard the door open. It wasn't until she shivered from the cold draft that she realized she wasn't alone. Sarah never looked his way. She could feel his presence, could feel his gaze upon her nakedness. She could imagine his astonishment at finding her like this. "I thought you'd be longer."

"The . . ." He cleared his throat as his gaze took in the sight of her. Her breasts were just visible as they bobbed gently upon the surface of soapy water. He could hardly think with the lust that had suddenly exploded in his gut. It took him a long moment before he realized she'd spoken. "It's snowing again. The snow brings the herd closer to the base, where it's easier to find food."

Sarah nodded, then raised her gaze to his. Her cheeks were warm with color upon finding him staring. Suddenly, she realized it didn't matter what he felt. She knew what she wanted. And she knew what she'd have to do to get it.

Her hands reached slowly for the side of the tub for balance. Her entire body trembled at her daring. Never had she stood naked before a man. Not even before her husband had she been so bold. At the last second, she realized she couldn't go through with it. Her hand snatched at the towel she'd placed nearby. She wrapped it clumsily around her as she came to her feet.

Thaddeus was taking off his woolen scarf, his hat,

his coat. His eyes were on her. Automatically, his hand reached out to place the discarded articles on the hooks behind the door. All fell unnoticed to the floor.

His gasp was the only sound in the room as he watched her rise from the water. He couldn't tear his gaze from the lusciously pink sight of her skin. Never in his life had he seen anything half as lovely. Dripping wet, she stood there, mere seconds before she hastily covered herself. But Thaddeus knew he'd never forget. If he lived a hundred years, he'd never see anything that might compare. She seemed to be waiting for him to make the next move, but Thaddeus suddenly felt unable to breathe, much less move. His legs threatened to buckle beneath him and he gave a silent curse as he tried to clear his brain. *Don't make her stand there. Don't make her think you don't want her.*

But Sarah thought nothing of the kind. She could see first the shock, the hunger, the need, and then the delight register one after the other in his eyes. She adjusted the towel, stepped unaided from the tub, and moved toward him. Her long hair slipped from its knot at a touch of her fingers. It spread in a golden-brown cape around her shoulders as she stood before him. Her eyes were soft and grew as purple as violets as her desire rose to meet his. She licked at her lips nervously. "You said . . ." She swallowed, closed her eyes as if gathering her strength, then forced herself to go on. "You said to come to you when I was ready."

All his dreams were coming true. It was happen-

185

ing now. At last. He groaned again, never realizing he said the words aloud. "At last."

Sarah smiled into eyes gone black as pitch and gleaming with hunger. "It hasn't been so long."

"It's been years." He was opening his shirt. A moment later the heavy long john shirt hung loosely at his waist. He stood before her naked to his waist, waiting for her to make the next move.

Her blue gaze focused on the golden smoothness of his chest. Dark hair curled over smooth skin, its crispness silently imploring investigation. Sarah felt a shiver of delight as she ventured to touch him. Clearheaded this time, she reached out a tentative hand and smiled as she slid her palm upon a wide chest. "I love the way you feel."

"Do you?" Thaddeus choked, not at all sure he had the strength to carry on a conversation at this moment. Would he be able to control the lust, the need that had filled his being almost from the first? He was half afraid to touch her and told her as much.

Sarah smiled again. "Are you? Why?"

"I don't want to hurt you."

"You won't."

"I've waited so long." He gasped, filling his lungs with the delicious scent of her. He tried to steady his breathing, then groaned at the impossibility. As long as she touched him, he'd never breathe normally again. A pulse pounded in his throat. His voice vibrated with the exquisite agony her touch brought about. "I've needed you forever," he warned. "This won't be gentle."

Sarah had never felt so bold, so desired, so sure of her own worth. "I don't care," she said as she dared to brush her mouth upon his chest.

Thaddeus swallowed. "No." His hands came to hold her from him. "Give me a minute." Jesus, he didn't want to attack her, to throw her on the bed and have his way with her, and yet he was close to doing exactly that. Closer than he'd ever been in his life.

"Don't touch me. Not yet. I won't be able to—"

Sarah chuckled her response, having just the opposite intent in mind. She was going to touch him . . . touch him like she'd never touched a man before. Her towel dropped to the floor. Her damp cool skin contacted with his scorching nakedness, while her hands boldly reached for his aching thick arousal.

Thaddeus closed his eyes and moaned, knowing himself lost to her seduction. There wasn't a damn thing he could do about it. He couldn't resist. Somehow, he'd known from the first he'd never be able to resist.

His arms reached around her and pulled her tightly against him, while his hips moved deliciously against her cupped palm. "Sarah," he choked, unable to say more than her name. "Sarah," he said again and again as his mouth buried itself in sweetly scented hair.

Her arms circled his neck as her mouth rained openedmouth kisses over his chest. She delighted in the feel of crisp curling hair and hard muscular strength. "I want you to make love to me, Thaddeus.

I can't remember wanting anything half so much."

Thaddeus muttered a vicious curse as he fought against the madness her words instilled. His arms lifted her and held her close against his chest, supporting her legs and back as he walked quickly to the bed. "I'm sorry, darlin'," he whispered brokenly as he nearly ripped his clothes to shreds. He never realized the destruction as they fell from his body. He positioned himself above her and gazed down into a face as tight with passion as his own. "This should be slow and easy, but I . . . can't."

His thrust was powerful, swift, and mindless, almost vicious, in fact, as his body desperately sought to claim hers. Caution and tenderness were thrown aside and forgotten, his mind knowing only overwhelming need, his body bent on satisfying that need, a need she had teased to near insanity.

Enclosed within the folds of her body at last, he suffered almost diabolical pleasure. Heated muscles tightened and clutched around his sex, squeezing him tighter than anything he'd ever known before. He groaned with the torment, but the sound wasn't his alone. Beyond his pleasure, he felt her stiffen. He heard her gasp, watching as her back arched, her head fell back, and a guttural sound of anguish was torn from her lips. In that one moment, Thaddeus lost every trace of the lust he'd suffered these last two months.

"Damn it!" He pulled instantly back, but Sarah prevented his full escape with arms stronger than either had suspected. His body locked against hers, he snapped, "I told you. Sarah, why didn't you listen?" Thaddeus ran a frustrated hand through his hair as he raised himself up on his elbows. "Christ, I should have known. It was too soon, wasn't it? I was too rough, wasn't I?"

Sarah smiled as she reached up and left a lingering trail of openedmouth kisses on his throat and shoulder. But Thaddeus was too engulfed in misery to notice the movement of her lips, the teasing of her tongue. "No. You weren't too rough."

"I hurt you."

"You didn't," she reassured, still caught up in the wild moment of passion that had exploded between them.

"I did, damn it! Why else would you groan like that?"

It was plain to see this man had little experience with a woman of deep passion. Sarah hadn't realized until this moment that she possessed such emotion. She was almost ashamed to admit that the sound she'd made was due solely to pleasure. . . . that he hadn't hurt her in the least. She wondered how she might go about explaining her feelings without sounding like a woman of little virtue.

He tried to pull away again, but her arms and now her legs held him secure. She couldn't explain if she was made to face him. "Thaddeus, don't move away," Sarah said softly. Her face was hidden in the curve of his throat, her cheeks growing in color as she forced the words, lest he leave her side never to return. "I can't tell you the things I feel if—"

"Tell me, then," he said as he rolled to his side. Holding her still in his arms, he tucked her head beneath his chin. "Tell me what you feel."

"Would you have me speak boldly my most secret thoughts?"

"I would," he said as he nuzzled his face in the silkiness of her hair.

Sarah breathed a long sigh as she searched for the right way to explain. "Wasn't it enough that I came to you?"

"Tell me," he insisted.

"I never realized men came in different sizes. I was surprised, is all," she blurted out quickly, lest she lose this moment to cowardice.

Thaddeus was at first confused and then astonished. A moment later, he grinned. His body moved in an odd jerking fashion as he strained to hold back his laughter.

"Are you laughing at me?"

"Who, me?" he asked, holding her in place when she might have pulled back to study his expression. Still, his voice was obviously strangled with merriment.

"No," she snapped sarcastically, "the man standing in that corner." She was angry now. Angry that he'd found something to laugh at while she still suffered a degree of embarrassment at being forced to speak her thoughts.

"Hold on," he said as she tried to wiggle her way out of his arms. "Where do you think you're goin'?"

"Let me go."

He ignored her wishes and held her firmly against him. "Are you tellin' me you didn't imagine that I'd be so big? And that it felt good?"

"I'm not telling you anything, except to let me up!"

Again Thaddeus ignored her demand. His voice filled with amazement. "I didn't hurt you?"

"I told you you didn't!" She was really angry now, and Thaddeus pinning her to the bed with the weight of his body wasn't helping her temper any.

"So, if I didn't hurt you, then it was pleasure I heard in that groan?"

Sarah struggled in earnest. She wasn't about to lay here and watch this grinning fool gloat. "Get off me, you big oaf."

Thaddeus laughed aloud, then groaned at her squirmings. "You bein' once married should know what happens when you move against a man like this."

Sarah might have told him that she couldn't have known. That she'd never squirmed against a man before. That Thomas and she had never made love in the light of day. That he'd always come to her under the cover of darkness. That she'd never lain next to him, or beneath him, naked. But she said nothing. She didn't have to. The look in her eyes said it all.

"Oh, God," Thaddeus moaned as her most secret thoughts made themselves known. He caught her chin and peered deeply into clear blue eyes. With a helpless groan, he brought his mouth to hers.

At his look, Sarah felt an instant tightening somewhere deep in her stomach. The world spun away as his lips and beard teased her mouth with feather-light touchings. She found herself suddenly breathless, her lips aching for him to complete the kiss.

She groaned again, never realizing the sound. And Thaddeus answered the groan with a hungry growl that sucked at pliant lips, forcing them farther apart.

His heart pounded as he fought back the urge to appease this need, to take her quickly with all the passion that trembled through his body.

A thought came suddenly to haunt. Silently, he tried to deny the truth of it, but he suddenly knew he'd never be satisfied with another. He didn't believe in love, but this feeling came as close as he was ever likely to get. He'd never known happiness like this existed in a woman's arms and he knew damn well he'd never find it again. This one was the one for him. He wasn't about to let her go.

His caresses grew bolder, less gentle, as he staked his claim. She wouldn't be leaving come spring. Absently, he wondered how she'd take to the news.

His mouth held hers in a long drugging kiss as his hand skimmed the length of her. He grunted his approval at her soft purrings. She couldn't hide her delight at his touch, and Thaddeus wasn't fooled again into thinking these low moans meant anything but pleasure.

Her back arched and her breath caught in her throat as his palm cupped her breast. She groaned again as his fingers brought the tips to hard aching buds. His tongue ravaged her mouth. He couldn't get enough of her taste, her scent, her feel. The soft whimpering sounds she made left him crazed for more and yet filled his soul with sweet contentment. It was almost enough to witness her response, almost enough to watch her pleasure.

His hand slid over her smooth stomach to nestle in the sweet curls at the juncture of her thighs. He felt her hips arch into his hand and delighted in yet more groans of pleasure as he discovered the warmth, the slippery wet sweetness offered to him.

Heavy-lidded with arousal, she looked up at him. "Thaddeus, what are you doing?" she asked, her voice hardly more than a whisper and suddenly tight, as two of his fingers slid gently into the moist folds of her body. She groaned in mindless pleasure.

"Pleasurin' you, darlin'. Does this feel good?" he asked as his fingers began to move in a gentle, yet earth-shattering tempo that threatened to drive her out of her mind.

"Ohhh," she breathed on a long sigh as she strained toward the movement, her heart beating wildly, pounding in her throat, shutting off her ability to breathe.

Her hand clutched at his shoulders, holding on to the only security in a world gone mad. "Don't, oh please, don't," she cried, even as her hips strained away from the bed and closer to the magic of his touch.

"Yes, Sarah," he growled, then smiled at the exquisite tenderness that filled him. He watched in awe as she lost the last of her restraint and gave herself over to the sensations that wracked her body.

Turning greedy now, her nails bit into his shoulders. And when he deliberately slowed his pace, drawing out her agony, she cried, "Don't stop."

Thaddeus smiled, knowing nothing could stop

him now. He had to bring this moment to its rightful end. He had to witness the ecstasy.

The muscles in her belly tightened. It was too much. She couldn't survive this. She couldn't stand the pressure. "I can't," she cried out, her voice breaking, clearly telling of her suffering.

"You can. You will," he returned as he increased the pace, the movement tearing from her throat an agonizing groan of mingled pain and pleasure.

Her hips were off the bed now. The lower half of her body balanced on the balls of her feet, she strained toward the elusive pleasure. Gasping for her every breath, she hungered toward the release. And then it was there, within her grasp at last. Her breathing shut down. She didn't fight the coming pleasure but greedily accepted the wrenching waves of tormented ecstasy, as tremor after exquisite tremor shuddered throughout her body.

She fell back on the bed, exhausted, capable only of uttering a long, blissful sigh. Moments later, she opened her eyes to his oh-so-smug grin. "Take that smile off your face, Mr. Payne. It wasn't that good." But her voice was breathless, weak from the trauma she'd just suffered. It easily belied her words.

Thaddeus laughed aloud. "Wasn't it? It looked pretty good to me."

"I'm a consummate actress. I didn't want to disappoint you."

"I can tell you right now that you didn't."

Sarah couldn't hold back the grin that curved her lips. Her eyes closed again. "You wretch," she whispered woefully, then shot him a soft, tender glance.

"I suppose you'll nag at me now. I'll be forced to forever expound on your mastery."

Thaddeus chuckled at her glum prediction. "Only if you believe it."

Sarah's grin was undeniably and deliciously wicked. "Right now I'd believe the world was flat if you could do that again."

"Greedy wench." Thaddeus's voice was filled with soft, gentle laughter as he slid slow openedmouth kisses along the length of her neck.

Sarah shot a glance his way and then groaned. It shouldn't have been possible, but his smug grin had only grown in strength. One thing this man didn't need, on top of everything else, was confidence in her reaction to him. It was apt to make him totally obnoxious. If she hadn't felt so exhausted, she might have been tempted to bring him down a peg or two. As it was, she figured he had a right to look pleased with himself. She couldn't deny she'd never been more pleased herself.

Thaddeus lowered his head to nibble at the dark pointed tips of her breasts. "How much longer before we eat?"

"Hours," Sarah said on a long breathy sigh, her back arching unconsciously toward his mouth.

"Good."

"Good?" she asked as she pushed him to his back. Propped up on her elbows, she awarded him with the most enticing display of swaying breasts but refused him anything more as he reached for her. "You're not hungry?" she asked, moving away from his greedy hands. Her eyes gleamed with a wicked light as she came to her knees. Her hands slid down the length of his chest, over his flat hard stomach, and boldly cupped his sex.

Thaddeus gasped at her daring. His heart, his mind, his soul, delighted in the boldness of her touch. He grinned at the devilish laughter that sounded above him. He tried to control the need to ravish her and submit instead to her erotic handling. It was the hardest thing he'd ever done in his life. Through sheer force of will, he put aside his passion and managed a slightly strangled, "I reckon I am, now that you mention it."

"Would you like a little something to hold you over?" she asked, her voice shaking with the laughter she tried to hold at bay.

Sarah couldn't believe it. Where had her inhibitions gone? Where was her natural sense of modesty? She was like a different person in this man's arms. She'd never known such freedom, such power as she watched his reaction to her touch. That he was obviously pleased was a given. His low groans and gasping breaths only served to spur her on to more delicious, erotic discoveries.

Thaddeus knew nothing existed to compare to this. He could hardly speak from the pleasure that filled his being. "My thoughts exactly, ma'am," he finally managed as he gave up the last of his control. He rolled her to her back, buried himself deep into her warmth, then proceeded to make the most deliciously slow love either of them were ever likely to suffer.

Chapter Ten

"Damn! I'll have to build another room," Thaddeus groaned, his tone telling clearly the idea was far from appealing. He collapsed upon her, gasping for his every breath. A moment later he rolled to his side, bringing her pliant body along with him.

"What?" She frowned and then asked, "Why?" unable at the moment to understand the reason behind his words or why he should choose to talk about additions to his home at this particular moment.

"You're a screamer, darlin'."

"A what?"

Thaddeus chuckled as he pulled her tighter against him. "A screamer. We can't let the young'in's hear their momma cry out, now, can we?"

"I assume you believe you're making sense, but—" Sarah shook her head, completely baffled and much too tired to worry over what the man was about.

"Emily." He grinned as he pulled back just enough to see her expression. "Emily and our young'in's. They'll hear you when we—" He grinned and pressed his hips suggestively against hers. "You know."

Sarah felt a wave of pure happiness fill her to overflowing. He was asking her, in the most outlandish way possible, to stay. She arched a brow and shot him a disparaging look. "And your roaring wouldn't be noticed, I take it?"

"Did I roar?" he asked innocently, while wondering how Emily had remained asleep through their moaning and groaning.

"In my ear."

"Well, that explains it then. It only sounded like a roar 'cause my mouth was so close."

Sarah smiled. "Clever." She sighed as she moved against him, snuggling at last into a comfortable position.

Thaddeus held her tighter against him, closed his eyes, and breathed a contented sigh. "Yeah, I reckon I'm stuck with you, all right."

"Are you? I wonder why?"

" 'Cause come spring, you'll be rounded out real nice like with the first of the batch."

"The batch? I assume you mean children."

"Sure do."

"Is there a particular number you're aiming for?"

Thaddeus grinned. "I kind a' had my heart set on six, all told."

"Six!" she repeated, while a grin teased her lips. "That's quite a lot, don't you think?"

He shrugged. "Well, it doesn't have to be six."

"Thank God," she breathed in obvious relief.

"We could have eight."

"Eight!" Sarah gave a shout of a laugh. "What

happened to the man who liked living alone? Eight children are apt to put a cramp in his privacy."

"As long as he can take you into his bedroom, he can have all the privacy he needs."

Sarah smiled. "You are taking quite a bit for granted, don't you think?"

"Like what?"

"Like, I'll be staying. You don't know that I will. Actually, you haven't once asked."

"Sure I did."

She shook her head. "I don't think so. I'm sure I would have remembered."

"Well, I must've. I ain't the kind to leave loose ends like that danglin'."

Sarah simply shook her head.

Thaddeus opened one eye and peered down at her, his expression far from happy. "You're gonna make me ask, ain't ya?"

Sarah laughed at his evil look. "If you want me to stay, I'm afraid you must."

Thaddeus smiled at the sound of her laughter. "Marry me, Sarah?"

"Now that wasn't so terribly hard, was it?"

"Hard enough. And you didn't answer me."

"Will you promise not to ever again give me an evil look and always be of good cheer?"

"Can't rightly promise the impossible, darlin'."

"All right, then, I'll marry you."

Thaddeus laughed with amazement. "You mean you like me grumpy?"

"I mean I like honesty. If you would have promised, you would have lied."

199

"Why? Don't you think I can be nice?"

"You've had your moments, but all the time?" she asked, the look in her eye telling clearly the impossibility of the notion. "Even I can't be nice all the time. And I'm ve—e—ery nice." She dragged out and emphasized the word, ending her statement with a giggle.

"You surely are," Thaddeus chuckled as he brought her hips to rub against his. "Should I show you where you're the nicest?"

Sarah grinned as she came up on one elbow "We shouldn't be doing this until we marry."

Thaddeus shot her a puzzled look, then remarked sarcastically, "Oh, I reckon not. It was all right to do it, but if I want to marry you, I should wait." It was obvious Thaddeus wasn't taking to the idea. "What the hell for?"

"Because I'd be so embarrassed if I stood before the preacher all rounded and—"

"Spring will be here in four months. No one's apt to notice." And if they do, they won't care, he silently added. There was no way he was going to wait four months to feel this pleasure again. The truth of it being, he wasn't about to wait another minute.

"You don't play fair," Sarah cried as he nibbled gently on the tip of her breast.

"And I ain't never gonna, either." He smiled at her soft groan, then asked, "Emily gonna wake up soon?"

"I think so."

"Then I'd better leave her some supper."

200

Thaddeus rolled until his hips lay nestled in the hollow of hers. Propped up on his elbows, he looked down at her. His eyes were dark, hungry, as he watched her blue eyes grow to purple. Her hands moved to his chest, her fingers spreading, enjoying fully the texture of crisp hair over smooth skin. She smiled at the feel of his body stiffening above hers. Her eyes sparkled with laughter and a hunger that easily matched his own, as she slowly followed the hair as it formed a thin line that bisected his stomach. "She's only a tiny baby."

Thaddeus moaned at the erotic invitation as he lowered his mouth to her breast.

He couldn't get enough. Absently, he wondered if a day would come when he would. They'd romped and played most of the morning and afternoon away. And still he wanted more. He'd always want more. Like in a trance, he'd come from the barn, leaving the chores half finished.

"I don't know what it is, but I can't get enough of you. I think about you and I'm suddenly here. I don't remember how I got here."

Sarah laughed as she tried—not too hard—to swat away his hands. "You were only gone ten minutes." Thaddeus had his hands under her skirt. She didn't argue as he rid her of her drawers but instead suggested, "We could be more comfortable on the bed."

"Later," he groaned as his body moved into her delicious heat. "I have things to finish outside."

He'd come silently into the house only moments before and asked, "Is Emily asleep?"

Sarah had only the time it took to nod her head, before she found herself in his arms, pressed up against the door. His coat was still buttoned, her clothes in place, all but for her drawers, which lay discarded on the floor.

Some minutes passed before Sarah's cry was cut off by the pressure of his mouth. She was gasping for breath, her body covered with a fine sheen of sweat as she leaned her damp head against his shoulder. "Supper is almost ready. I hope the gravy hasn't burned."

His hand supported her butt, never releasing his hold as he walked them both to the stove and moved the pan to the table.

"You should put me down."

Thaddeus sat and then grinned. "There, you're down."

"Thaddeus," she warned as a grin teased her lips, "you'd better come to your senses soon, or you're apt to lose a bit of weight. Maybe you'll even take sick."

"You're right. I need food to keep up my strength, or I'll never be able to do this," he grunted as he pushed his hips up from the chair.

"I give up," Sarah moaned at the pleasure. As impossible as it was to believe, the man was anxious to again sample this wonder. "It's too bad about the horses, though."

"What about them?" he asked absently, his mind only half on their conversation as he reveled in the

202

delicious warmth of her body. "Damn," he grunted again as he lifted her from him and adjusted his clothes. "I gotta go. Stop temptin' me, will you, woman?"

"Me?" Sarah pressed her hand to her heart, her eyes wide with indignation as she bent down and pocketed her drawers. "How have I tempted you? You haven't given me the chance."

Thaddeus, on his way to the door, stopped in mid stride and turned to face her. "You mean you want to?"

"You're never going to find out. Not if every time you see me you rip off my clothes and—"

Thaddeus grinned. "I can't help it." He nodded toward the barn. "I have to go." His head lowered until his mouth was planted solidly, heavily, wonderfully, against hers. "I'll be back in a few minutes."

At least they managed to get through most of their meal before Thaddeus reached for her again. She was refilling his coffee cup when he pulled her onto his lap. "I'm gonna like havin' you here."

"You think so?" Sarah asked as she settled herself more comfortably. "Why?"

"For one thing, you make a damn good apple pie."

Sarah grinned as she felt his hand slide under her skirt. "You're not apt to find apple pie there, Mr. Payne."

She giggled as he growled, "No, but it's something just as sweet."

"Don't start. It's almost time for Emily's bath."

Thaddeus smiled and removed his hand, cupping

her waist he pulled her closer. "When you're finished, we'll have Christmas. I want to give you your present."

Sarah shot him a suspicious glance, not sure what he meant by that. What present could he possibly have for her? He hadn't gone to town. Had he made something for her?

Thaddeus chuckled as he read clearly her confusion. Without offering an answer to her silent questions, he helped her to her feet as the baby started to fuss. "I'll hold her while you get her bath ready."

Thaddeus assisted with the chore, happy to be included. In actuality, Sarah would have been finished at least twenty minutes sooner had he not insisted on helping. Still, she didn't mind. Fussing over the baby together brought a special warmth to her heart.

"Does she always fight like this when you dress her?" he asked as Sarah finally managed to put her arms through the tiny sleeves.

"She feels better, I think, with no clothes." Sarah shot him a glare at his low, wicked snicker. "Yes, she's much like you in that respect."

"What did I say?" he asked, trying for an innocence he couldn't begin to feel.

"You don't have to say a thing. You get a naughty gleam in your eyes when you think of certain things."

"Do I?" he asked as he moved to take her in his arms. The baby was between them, but Thaddeus didn't mind. It felt good holding them both. "Do you know what I'm thinking now?"

Sarah nodded her head. "You're thinking, 'Sarah

204

has to feed Emily, so I'll be a good boy and drink my coffee while I wait.' "

"Is there something in particular that I'm waiting for?" he asked, the words suggestive as he added a slight movement of his hips.

"You said you wanted to exchange presents."

Thaddeus chuckled, his mind obviously on matters other than presents. "Do you have something special for me?"

Sarah nodded. "I hope you'll like it."

"I can tell you right now, I love it."

She looked momentarily puzzled. "How do you know? You haven't seen it yet, have you?" Sarah sighed her disappointment. "Thaddeus, you didn't peek?"

Thaddeus blinked his surprise. "You mean, you really have somethin' for me?"

"Of course. What did you think we were talking about?" Sarah suddenly realized exactly what he was talking about and laughed at his wicked grin. "Oh, see. If that's the case, then you've already given me my present, haven't you?"

"Part of it," he said softly as he watched Sarah move to the table. He sat opposite her as she opened her dress and began to feed her baby.

His eyes were gentle as they watched the baby suckle. Sarah smiled as she realized she had his full attention. "You are a wicked man, Mr. Payne. No doubt, you'll soon thoroughly corrupt me with your evil ways."

"God," he whispered on a groan, "I hope so."

* * *

"Oh, Lord, it's beautiful!" Sarah eyes were shining with unshed tears as they searched out his gaze. "Thaddeus, I can't believe you did this. It must have taken hours of carving," she said, her voice low and filled with awe. She ran her hand over the intricately carved headboard.

Thaddeus sat as she'd left him, stunned as he unwrapped the scarf and socks from the sheet of brown paper. She'd tied it with one of her red ribbons. He hadn't wanted to disturb the package. It had looked so beautiful. If she hadn't prodded, he might still be staring at it. Again and again, he wrapped the woolen articles around his hands, his heart swelling in his chest as he realized she'd actually taken the time to do this for him. He couldn't remember when anyone had ever given him anything. Certainly, never something they'd taken the time to make.

"I don't know what to say. You're so talented."

"I figured Emily needed a bed of her own," he said, then cleared his voice of its sudden huskiness. "She'll be too big for the drawer soon."

Sarah laughed. "She won't outgrow this any time soon." The cradle was big enough for Emily to use until she was old enough to have her first real bed.

"Put her in it. See if she fits."

Emily was snuggled comfortably in her cradle, already asleep. Thaddeus stood at the opened door of the cabin and watched as the gentle falling flakes added inches to what already covered the ground.

206

Winter was back, gentle for now, but soon in all its fury. He knew they wouldn't see another soul for months. Would this marriage end as had the last? Was Sarah the kind that could bear the loneliness? Would she be content with her life here, or was he bound to suffer the agony of her leaving? Could he go through it again?

Dare he try? He wondered, if she left, how he'd survive.

"Is something wrong?" Sarah asked as she put her arms around his waist and hugged his back to her.

Thaddeus turned her so she stood before him. His arms around her middle held her back against his chest. The heavy cloud of snow had moved off. The sky was dark, but the setting sun lit the white caps of the mountains before them with an ethereal glow. "It's lovely. I've never seen such beauty till I came here."

Thaddeus lowered his head and rubbed his face against her hair. "Sarah, are you sure? Tell me now if you think you'll be too lonely."

"What? You mean staying here?"

He nodded and pulled her tighter against him. "Well . . ." She seemed to hesitate, and Thaddeus thought his world was about to end. Think what he might, he couldn't keep her a prisoner here. She had to stay because she wanted to. "You're staying, too, aren't you?"

Thaddeus grinned at the teasing light in her eyes as she tipped her face to his. "Far as I know."

"For a minute, I thought you planned to leave me here."

Thaddeus chuckled.

"Well, then, except when you're a grouch or when you give me that obnoxiously smug look of yours, I expect I'll be happy to stay."

"And you won't be lonely?"

"At times, probably. But you'll be here." Her eyes shone with happiness. "I expect we'll find something to keep us busy."

"You think so? I wonder what?"

"Well, for one thing, I can knit."

Thaddeus shook his head and laughed. "And I can whittle."

"There you go," she grinned as she turned and slid her arms around his neck. "I told you we'd find something to keep busy."

"Suppose I hire on a few men. If cabins are built, some might bring their women."

Sarah narrowed one eye as she experimented with a mean glare. It only looked hilarious. "Women, eh? You wouldn't be thinking of—"

Thaddeus laughed and hugged her tightly against him. "You little witch. You know I meant them to keep you company."

"I'm telling you right off, I don't take to a man with a wandering eye." She poked his chest. "Just so you don't go getting any ideas."

"Ideas? Me?" he asked as he moved them away from the draft, closed the door, and locked it. His eyes were filled with laughter even if he did a remarkable job of keeping a straight face. "Now, what kind of ideas could I get?"

* * *

"Lord, you surely are taken with that scarf." Thaddeus had thanked her about a hundred times and in at least a dozen deliciously different ways for making it. "I'm terrified to think what you would do if I knitted you a sweater?"

Thaddeus's eyes glowed with laughter. "Why don't you knit me one and I'll show you?"

"I don't think I have the strength," she said as she allowed him to pull her exhausted form over his.

Sarah snuggled her face in his hairy chest, too tired to care that it tickled her nose. "Hasn't anyone given you anything before?"

"No."

Sarah chuckled at that absurd remark. "Not even your mother?"

"No."

"Thaddeus, be serious. Of course, she gave you something."

"If you say so."

Her head lifted so she could see his face. She pushed a mass of golden curls from her eyes. "Well, didn't she?"

"My mother ran off with one of her clients when I was eight. I can't remember her ever giving me a thing."

Sarah blinked, suddenly silent with shock, all trace of exhaustion gone as she stared into his dark eyes. "What? What kind of client? What do you mean?"

"I mean my mother was a who—a lady of the night," he quickly amended.

"Thaddeus, that's a terrible thing to say," Sarah grumbled, obviously annoyed that he should besmirch his mother's character. She crawled off him and yanked the covers into place.

He shrugged. "It's a terrible thing to be."

With a start, Sarah realized he wasn't teasing. She didn't know what to say. Her eyes were wide with shock, her voice husky and low. "Where did she go?"

He shrugged again. "Who knows."

"What happened to you? Where did you go? What did you do?"

He smiled at her obvious concern. "I stayed with my father."

"Your father? Your mother was a—a—and your father lived with you?"

"Sounds like your everyday average family, doesn't it?"

"Tell me," she insisted, her voice soft with pain for the suffering he'd known.

"Not much to tell. It's over now, anyway." He turned her back to him and cuddled her comfortably against him. "She left when I was a kid. I never saw her again. When I was old enough, I left, too. Joined the army. After the war, I settled here.

"Annie, she was my wife." Sarah felt a moment of dread at the mention of the woman's name. She knew there had to have been something or someone in his life to turn him into a man satisfied to live alone. There had to have been pain, or he'd never have locked himself away on this mountain. She hardly had a chance to think how his wife might

210

have added to his woes when he continued, "She didn't like it much here, so she left for the excitement of the city."

Sarah almost moaned aloud. The man certainly hadn't been blessed with fidelity in the women in his life. Well, he could put aside the old hurts. He'd never have to worry about that again.

"Both my mother and my wife left me. Does that give you second thoughts?"

"About what?"

"About staying."

"Don't be stupid."

"You told me, only this morning, that I was clever."

"It appears you have the capacity to be both."

"You might consider the possibility that they had cause."

"You're making me angry," she warned.

Thaddeus chuckled. "Am I? Now, I wouldn't want to go and rile you any, especially since you're the kind of woman who'll go up against a bear, just to save her apple pie."

Sarah smiled and snuggled her rump closer to the warmth of his body. "Don't tease." Her voice was heavy with sleep. "You know it was you I was saving. He'd already eaten the pie."

"Did I thank you properly for saving my life?" he whispered against her ear.

"Oh, Thaddeus," she said on a yawn, "do you think you could wait till later to thank me? I need just a few minutes sleep."

Sarah was more than half asleep when she heard

Thaddeus's deep, rumbling laugh.

The blanket was laid smooth upon the floor. Sarah leaned upon a pillow and laughed at the baby, who was trying to catch her left foot and bring it to her mouth. A moment later the deed was done, and Emily's mouth curved down in a pout of pain. Sarah laughed as she rolled her daughter onto her stomach and rubbed her back.

At the sound of Emily's cry, Thaddeus brought his gaze from the book lying open before him. "What's the matter?"

"She bit herself."

"But she hasn't any teeth."

"Believe me, she doesn't need teeth."

Thaddeus's gaze was drawn instantly to her breasts. "You mean she bites you?"

"Now and again," Sarah said as she swung the baby playfully over her head and down again.

The cabin was filled with the sharp, quick squeals of Emily's laughter. The indrawn gasping sounds delighted the two adults. They smiled at one another. A moment later, Thaddeus joined them on the blanket. "There's a river not far from here. We'll picnic there this summer.

"And while Emily takes a nap, you and I will swim."

"Will we?" Sarah laughed at the wicked gleam she saw in his eyes. "But I don't know how."

"I reckon I can teach you, only you'd have to take some of this stuff off." Thaddeus nodded at her dress and petticoat.

"How shocking! Surely, you wouldn't expect me to completely disrobe out in the open."

"You'd drown otherwise."

"Not everything? I'd be so embarrassed."

"I'll keep my eyes shut."

Sarah had to laugh at that. "And your hands?" she asked as she watched him play with her breast.

"Now, that's a different story. If I don't hold you, you might drown."

"And you'd have to hold me there, am I right?"

"Has anyone tried to teach you before?"

"No. Why?"

"You sound like you already know what learning to swim is about."

Sarah laughed. "I'm afraid I do. It seems to me, you have a one-track mind, Mr. Payne."

"You wear too many clothes," Thaddeus complained.

Sarah grinned as he tried to get her bodice open while she held the baby. It wasn't easy, but he managed at last to dip his hand inside.

"As a matter of fact, even though it's mighty interestin' watchin' your skirts move up your legs, while you roll around on this floor, I can't figure on why you bother to dress every morning.

"I've been thinking, it would be more convenient if you wore only your robe."

"All day?" she asked in amazement.

He nodded his head.

"Suppose someone should come to the door?"

Thaddeus grinned. "Like a neighbor?"

Sarah laughed, knowing they weren't about to get

213

visitors for months, not with the weather as foul as it was.

Emily grabbed a handful of her mother's hair. "Ow!" Sarah said, then gently dislodged the baby's fingers. A moment later, her hair was free from its pins. It fell beautifully in soft curls around her face.

"You're a mighty good-lookin' woman, Sarah," Thaddeus said as he leaned over both mother and child. "Isn't it Emily's bedtime, yet?"

"Almost," she said as she smiled up to him. "Do you have anything in particular in mind to do tonight?"

Thaddeus grinned. "I was thinkin' on maybe a little whittlin'."

"Really? I would have thought you had something else entirely in mind."

"Like what?"

"Like thanking me for the sweater."

"I'd be happy to thank you, but you didn't knit it yet."

"Mmmm," Sarah murmured as she gave his comment some thought, then finally suggested, "Well, you could show me your appreciation for the thought."

"You got a mighty interestin' notion there," he agreed as he laid upon his back, his hands propped under his head.

Sarah brought Emily to her cradle and covered her for the night. Without a word spoken, she moved back to the blanket. Standing at its edge, she started peeling off her clothes.

Thaddeus's eyes gleamed with fire as her movements slowly exposed her nakedness to his view. When she was finished, she knelt down beside him, her hands reaching for his belt. Moments later, he was as naked as she. Sarah smiled as she straddled his hips. "In the meantime, why don't you thank me for saving your life?"

Chapter Eleven

Spring at last! Now and then, Sarah had cause to wonder if it would ever come. A tiny grin touched the corners of her mouth as she remembered the countless nights of intimate sharing spent in the luscious warmth of Thaddeus's arms. Without a doubt, winter had had its moments. But the long, cold days had left her aching for a renewal that only spring could bring. She smiled with delight as her gaze scanned the edges of thick, dark forest, burgeoning with new life, ready to burst free. She breathed deeply of the gentle, fragrant breeze, marveling in the scent of fresh pine and the delicious warmth of the sun.

Sarah smiled again, her gaze on Thaddeus, her heart beating with excitement as he finished the chore. The horses were hitched to his wagon. She was going to town. Lord, but she'd never imagined feeling such excitement over so simple an affair. Her newest bonnet covered her hair and protected her fair skin from most of the sun's rays, while her one and only Sunday dress was ironed free of wrinkles. It looked almost new. She felt wonderful.

"You ready to get married?" Thaddeus asked as he brought the wagon to a stop before the porch.

Sarah grinned as she teased. "Married?!" she asked in feigned astonishment. "Is that what you have in mind?"

Thaddeus jumped to the ground. "You didn't change your mind, did you?"

Standing before her, his expression so wary, so unsure, Sarah hadn't the heart to keep up her teasing. She laughed, her happiness not to be borne as she stepped into the warmth of his arms. "Thaddeus, you will simply have to resign yourself to the fact that I'm staying. Ogre that you are, you cannot scare me away."

She felt him relax against her. His arms tightened as he held her in an almost desperate embrace, and Sarah wondered if he'd ever get used to the idea that she was here forever. He couldn't seem to put aside the notion that she might take it into her head to leave him. Sarah knew he was haunted by the fact that it had happened before. Despite her protests, it seemed she alone knew it would never happen again. "I know I'm not always as gentle as I could be and I have one god-awful temper, but I don't mean to scare you."

Sarah's soft laughter echoed over the silent surrounding forest. "I think you're a bit disappointed that this is one woman who doesn't scare easily."

Thaddeus chuckled. "Reckon you're right about that. A man likes to think he's the boss."

Sarah shot him an innocent glance, her gaze sweetly consoling. "Darling, don't I let you think that?"

He laughed at her teasing, feeling once again that strange, unnamed twisting that tore at his heart. His gaze softened with emotion, his voice lowering to a husky drawl as he crushed Emily between their bodies. "If you call me darlin' again, we might never get to town."

The baby began to fuss at the suddenly tight quarters. "She doesn't appreciate my hugs."

Sarah's grin was almost enough to cause him to carry her back inside. Her face tipped to accept his descending mouth and she moaned her pleasure as, with lips parted, their tongues meshed in sweet delight.

Emily was trying to get her face between the two adults. She was babbling some foreign-sounding words, known only to herself, as she poked them both in the eye and knocked Thaddeus's hat to the ground.

"Shame on you, woman. You shouldn't kiss me like that in front of your own daughter."

"If you don't want my kisses, you shouldn't hold me so close."

Thaddeus sighed as he raised his eyes to the clear blue sky. "How about we go tomorrow instead?"

"Why?" Sarah couldn't hide her disappointment. She knew Thaddeus could hear it in her voice.

" 'Cause then we could go inside and get buck naked."

Sarah grinned. "And then what?"

"I reckon we could think of somethin'."

Sarah laughed and pulled herself free of his embrace. She tried to match her expression to her stern voice. "Thaddeus Payne. Do you want to marry me or not?" She didn't quite make it.

Thaddeus knew he was grinning like a fool, but it was beyond his power to stop. "I surely do, ma'am."

"Then let's stop this dillydallying and get on with it."

Thaddeus murmured a low, "Yes, ma'am," and placed both mother and baby upon the wagon's seat. A moment later he joined her there, snapped the reins against the horses' backs, and they were off.

The monotonous swaying and bouncing of the wagon over the rough ground soon had Emily sleeping, cradled in the comfort of her mother's arms. The sun was getting stronger as the day progressed and the dust kicked up by the two horses left a film of dirt over all three faces. Perspiration trickled in tiny rivulets down her back and from under her arms. Her perfectly pressed gown was streaked with dirt and wrinkled beyond repair. Sarah had cause to wonder why she'd spent hours ironing it in the first place.

It was harder now to detect the scent of pine, for sitting directly behind the animals only horseflesh permeated the air. Still, the beauty and majesty of her surroundings could not be overlooked. Dark lustrous pines stood straight and tall, their gently curved branches lifted toward the sky. Thick underbrush housed thousands of small animals, while beautifully colored birds flitted from branch to branch. "Oh look! How pretty," Sarah whispered as she spotted a deer some distance ahead alongside the road.

A moment later, the animal dashed into the thicket away from the intruders. "Mule deer," Thaddeus explained.

Sarah smiled, "I've never seen country more beautiful. Was that the reason you settled here?"

Thaddeus grinned. "Not exactly."

Sarah turned to watch him. He was concentrating on avoiding the worst of the holes and rocks that dotted the dirt road. The effort it took often left little room for conversation. Sarah didn't care. "Not exactly" was hardly an answer.

"Well? Are you going to tell me or not?"

"What?" he asked, clearly puzzled that she should suddenly sound annoyed.

"Why did you settle here?"

"I won the place in a poker game."

"Did you?" she asked, clearly surprised. "How amazing."

"Not really. Goddamn it!" he grunted as his wagon hit a hole, jarring them both and momentarily bringing Emily awake. "I'm going to lose an axle if that keeps up." And then in reference to her statement, he remarked, "It happens all the time."

"I can't imagine it happening at all."

Thaddeus grinned at her innocence. "I once saw a man lose his wife."

"He lost her? Where? In the forest? Did he ever find her again?" Sarah shuddered, imagining the poor woman's plight, knowing the terror she'd feel at being lost.

"He lost her to a winning hand. And he only said she was his wife. I doubt it was the truth."

"I don't . . ."

It was easy enough to see Sarah didn't have the vaguest notion what he was talking about.

"He was playing cards and he put the woman up for collateral . . . much like the man with the deed to my place."

Flabbergasted, Sarah asked, in a high-pitched voice, "You mean he used her as if she were coin?"

Thaddeus nodded.

"I don't believe you." Sarah smiled weakly. "You're teasing me. If she was his wife, how could he—?"

"My point exactly," Thaddeus agreed. "That's why I figure she probably wasn't." He shrugged. "She didn't seem to mind none. Went along with the winner like it happened every day." He shrugged. "Maybe it did."

"Lord, the goings-on," Sarah mused, her voice filled with astonishment.

"She was a looker, too." Thaddeus glanced at the woman beside him and then forced back the threatening grin, his gaze on the road ahead.

"Are you sorry you didn't win her?" Sarah asked, feeling just the thread of growing annoyance.

"Well, I did think about her now and again. I couldn't help wondering . . ." Purposely, he left the sentence unfinished.

Her eyes narrowed; her displeasure was obvious. "Are you trying to make me jealous?"

"Yeah. Is it workin'?"

"Amazingly well," Sarah admitted honestly and not without some real surprise.

Thaddeus laughed and, taking both reins into one hand, hugged her to his side.

"You have no cause. You're the only woman I'll ever want."

Tall Pines, Colorado much resembled many of the towns that dotted the West. Except for the surrounding rocky canyons and the majestic peaks of the San Juan Mountains, it looked no different from a hundred others. Two sides of a wide dusty street boasted a long line of rough, uneven sidewalks butting against weather-beaten wooden buildings. Unpainted, they stood undistinguished one from another but for the signs above their doors. Most of the buildings were of the simplest design and consisted of one floor. Dotted among these were a few onto which the owners had added an extra story. These taller buildings were the boarding house and saloons.

Sarah felt some surprise to find a town of this size holding two drinking establishments. One could only surmise there had to be need or the businesses couldn't thrive. Idly, she wondered what kind of people lived in these parts.

"There's two of them 'cause of the hands that come in from the ranches around here on Saturday nights. Usually too many come for one place to hold."

Sarah looked at him with some amazement. "How did—?"

"I saw you staring at them."

"Where will we be staying?" she asked, knowing, of course, that they'd be spending the night. They couldn't stay longer because the livestock needing tending.

"You can bet it won't be there."

Sarah laughed at the steely determination in his voice. "Why not? I think it would be interesting to see—"

"Forget it. No wife of mine is ever going inside one of those places."

"Not even with you?"

"I won't be going in, either."

Thaddeus pulled his wagon to a stop before the boarding house. Moments later, he had Sarah and their bags settled in a room, with the promise that Mrs. Stanley's daughter, Amy, would sit the baby so her parents might shop.

"Tell me what they're like," Sarah said after throwing aside her soiled dress and changing into a brown skirt and white blouse. The outfit wasn't nearly as pretty, but at least it was clean and neat. She smoothed her hair and wiped the dust from her face and hands with a wet cloth.

"What what's like?" He played innocent, knowing exactly what was on her mind. Sarah had looked too long and appeared far too interested for him to hear the end of this anytime soon. She had stared in

223

shock when the lady stepped out onto her balcony wearing little more than her corset and drawers. At the time, he'd laughed at Sarah's expression and pressed his finger to her jaw to close a mouth hanging open with astonishment.

Sarah glared at his image through the mirror. "The saloons. Tell me."

Thaddeus was lying on the bed, his hands propped under his head as he watched Sarah neaten her appearance. He breathed a long, weary sigh. "Loud music, louder voices, rooms filled with smoke, men cursing, loose women, dirty jokes. The stink of stale whiskey and smoke, cheap perfume and unwashed bodies."

Sarah laughed. "Sounds appealing, indeed. No wonder so many men visit these places."

"Darlin', they don't visit for the sight and smells."

"No?" Her grin answered his. "Why do they go there, then?"

"For a drink and a woman."

"In that order?"

He shrugged. "Usually."

"Did you go there for that reason?"

"Who said I ever went there?"

Sarah only smiled, realizing, of course, that he couldn't know what it was like inside unless he had been there. She didn't answer his question but asked instead, "Did you?

"Sarah, don't ask a man about his past. You might not like the answers you get."

"I'm sure I wouldn't," she said as she crawled on the bed and leaned over him. A grin teased her

4 FREE BOOKS

FREE BOOKS

TO GET YOUR 4 FREE BOOKS WORTH $18.00 — MAIL IN THE FREE BOOK CERTIFICATE T O D A Y

Fill in the Free Book Certificate below, and we'll send your FREE BOOKS to you as soon as we receive it.

If the certificate is missing below, write to: Zebra Home Subscription Service, Inc., P.O. Box 5214, 120 Brighton Road, Clifton, New Jersey 07015-5214.

FREE BOOK CERTIFICATE

4 FREE BOOKS

ZEBRA HOME SUBSCRIPTION SERVICE, INC.

YES! Please start my subscription to Zebra Historical Romances and send me my first 4 books absolutely FREE. I understand that each month I may preview four new Zebra Historical Romances free for 10 days. If I'm not satisfied with them, I may return the four books within 10 days and owe nothing. Otherwise, I will pay the low preferred subscriber's price of just $3.75 each; a total of $15.00, *a savings off the publisher's price of $3.00.* I may return any shipment and I may cancel this subscription at any time. There is no obligation to buy any shipment and there are no shipping, handling or other hidden charges. Regardless of what I decide, the four free books are mine to keep.

NAME

ADDRESS _____ APT

CITY _____ STATE _____ ZIP

TELEPHONE ( )

SIGNATURE _____ (if under 18, parent or guardian must sign)

Terms, offer and prices subject to change without notice. Subscription subject to acceptance by Zebra Books. Zebra Books reserves the right to reject any order or cancel any subscription.　ZBMS02

GET
FOUR
FREE
BOOKS
(AN $18.00 VALUE)

ZEBRA HOME SUBSCRIPTION
SERVICE, INC.
P.O. Box 5214
120 BRIGHTON ROAD
CLIFTON, NEW JERSEY 07015-5214

mouth as she tried to hold her lips in a prim fashion. "For this time only, you have my permission to lie to me."

Thaddeus laughed as he grabbed her and flung her to her back. He was leaning over her, coal-black eyes dancing with laughter. "I only went there once and that was to find a man who owed me money."

Sarah laughed in obvious disbelief. "But you won't be going again, am I right?"

"Absolutely right, ma'am," he growled. "There ain't no reason for me to go near the place again."

"Are you sure? I told you, I don't take to a man with a wandering eye."

Thaddeus grinned his delight. He couldn't be happier than when she showed her jealousy. His gaze softened and Sarah was sorry now that Amy was due to arrive in a few minutes. "You got no call to be jealous. I ain't never gonna look at another woman."

"Where do you want to go first?"

Sarah laughed with excitement. "I can't decide." She looked longingly across the street at the sign that read "Seamstress," then quickly down the street toward the general store, lest Thaddeus think she was hinting at a need for clothes. "I imagine the first thing we should do is get our supplies."

Thaddeus shook his head. "We can order them and pick them up tomorrow before we leave. The first thing we should do is return the gold, and then I'm going to buy you a new dress to get

225

married in. I reckon you'll be needin' a ring, too."

Sarah was astonished. "What?"

He grinned at her wide-eyed look. "Which part didn't you hear?"

"Thaddeus? Are you giving back the gold?" she asked, her eyes glowing with pleasure.

"Of course, I'm giving it back. It doesn't belong to either one of us, does it?" His shrug was obviously meant to dismiss the subject. "I'll tell the sheriff I found it somewhere along the road."

"But I thought—"

He shook his head. "I know I said some bad things, but I only said them 'cause I was piss—mad," he instantly amended.

"At me?"

He nodded. "I was mad 'cause you were beautiful and I was wantin' you like I've never wanted a woman before. Your husband had just died and you'd just had a baby. I knew there wasn't a chance in hell that I could have you, so I—" He shrugged, not entirely happy that he'd revealed so much.

"—vented your frustrations on me?" she asked.

He shrugged. "I reckon."

Sarah grinned, delighted that he'd thought her beautiful. "And if I'd been ugly?"

"If you were ugly, I wouldn't have been half as horny."

Sarah gasped, then colored prettily at the indelicate word.

Thaddeus grinned. "It would have been better if you were, I can tell you that. You probably would

226

have looked prettier by the day, anyway, but I wouldn't have been afraid."

"Afraid? Of me?"

"Of course, of you. I know what happens when a woman casts her spell."

Sarah smiled. "What happens?"

His voice lowered to a gentle husk. "A man gets caught, that's what. There ain't no help for it. He don't have a mind of his own no more."

"Is that what happened to you?"

Thaddeus eyed her, not at all sure he was willing to hand over such power. Suddenly, he shrugged, knowing there was no sense in fighting what had already occurred. "Oh, I'm caught, all right."

Sarah laughed her delight, realizing for the first time the reason behind much of his anger. Her gaze was gentle as she looked up at this big, rough man. Her heart twisted with the love she felt for him. He loved her, she knew, but he hadn't said it yet. She couldn't wait to hear the words. "After we bring the money back, why don't we get married? Then you can buy me a dress."

Sarah smiled at her reflection. The dress plunged low, exposing an almost indecent amount of breast. It pinched tightly at her waist and flared wide above three petticoats to the floor. It was just about the prettiest dress she'd ever seen and much too fancy for her life on a mountaintop. She should be looking at plain dresses, not this confection of lace and blue satin.

"It's lovely, Mrs. Simon, but I don't think I'll have use for something this fancy."

"Your husband told me he 'specially wanted you to try it on. He's waitin' to see you in it right now."

Sarah stepped beyond the hanging curtain and watched as Thaddeus's gaze widened with astonishment. He wouldn't have believed she could be prettier, but she was. She was the most beautiful woman he'd ever laid eyes on. He could hardly find his voice. "Buy it," he said, in a tone husky and low, his dark gaze promising her secret delights at their very first opportunity.

"Thaddeus, it's too fancy. When would I use it?"

"To get married in, and later we'll have dinner at the restaurant."

"Spend all this money for one wearing?"

Thaddeus looked past Sarah at the beaming shop-keeper. "She'll take it," he said, closing the subject. "Show her a few things for everyday."

Thaddeus was gathering all kinds of apparel, from nightgowns—which he knew Sarah would seldom wear for more than a few minutes at a time—to petticoats, stockings, and drawers, as Sarah tried on the dresses Mrs. Simon had brought into the small room.

"Fancy meeting you here," came a female voice from behind him.

"Hello, Annie," Thaddeus said, his voice tight as he turned at the sound and then glared his disgust.

She looked different, cheaper, more flashy, but he would have recognized her anywhere. She wore makeup now. Her cheeks were painted as were her

228

lips, and her eyes were darkly lined with kohl. Her hair, although naturally red when they'd been married, was now bright with color that he knew came from a bottle. She wore a tightly fitted satin dress of wide diagonal green and white stripes. The garment left nothing to the imagination. Her breasts, which he knew to be small, appeared large, for they bulged above a tightly corseted waist and were almost completely exposed by a neckline no decent woman would wear.

"You buyin' ladies' clothes now, Thad?"

"My lady is tryin' on a few things." He nodded toward the curtained-off room.

"Your lady?!" Annie never thought to hide her shock. She couldn't believe another woman would willingly stick herself on a mountain with this rough man.

He nodded. "Gettin' married in a few minutes," he couldn't help but boast.

"She's inside?" Annie asked unnecessarily, for there was nowhere else she could have been. And there was no way Annie was leaving this shop without seeing for herself this woman.

"Annie," he began, but a moment later she disappeared behind the curtain.

"So, you're the one," Annie said, her hands planted on her hips as she glared at the woman who'd dared to take her man. The fact that she didn't want him herself hardly mattered. No one else had the right to him.

"Excuse me?" Sarah asked as Mrs. Simon unbuttoned the back of her shirtwaist. Sarah stepped out of her skirt and immediately pulled the blue gown over her head again.

"You marryin' Thad?"

Sarah grinned, her happiness not to be held at bay at the thought of being his wife. "I am."

"I was his first."

Sarah fought to keep her good cheer from fading. This wasn't exactly the one woman in the world that Sarah was anxious to meet. "Thaddeus told me you lived in San Francisco."

"I do, but I figured maybe it was time to visit with old friends." She laughed at Sarah's look of alarm. It didn't take a fortune-teller for Sarah to know this woman was going to cause trouble and that she was just itching to start right now. "Maybe I could make a few new ones while I'm at it. What do you think?"

"I think that would be very nice," Sarah said non-committally.

"You figure you're gonna be happy up there on that mountain?"

"I've spent the winter there." She shrugged. "Don't see why anything should change."

"Aw, honey, things change all the time." Annie's darkly painted eyes narrowed with accusation. "If you figure on takin' him for some of that silver, you'd better forget it. The man's tighter with a dollar than a school marm's ass."

Sarah's eyes widened at the coarse language. She blushed in embarrassment for Annie's sake, knowing a lady never spoke so foul. "If you're talking about Thaddeus, you're wrong. He's buying me clothes right now. Expensive clothes, as a matter of fact."

230

Annie's laugh told clearly of skepticism. "There ain't anything expensive in this town." She sighed and her eyes took on a far-off look of remembered pleasure. "You should see the city. Now, that's where you can find expensive clothes. Tell Thad to take you to San Francisco and spend some of that silver he hoards."

"What silver?"

"The silver he mines."

Sarah shook her head. "He's a rancher, not a miner." Obviously, the woman had him confused with someone else. "Is it Thaddeus Payne you're talking about?"

"Sure is, honey."

"I have to go," Sarah said, anxious to get away from this woman's offensive company. She might be stunning, but her manner and speech left much to be desired.

"Wait." Annie took her arm, stopping her from moving out of the room. "I should warn you first. You're an innocent and don't know his kind. He's usin' you. He doesn't care for nobody but himself. You could do a hell of a lot better."

Thaddeus felt almost overcome by blinding rage. In another minute, he was going to walk behind that curtain and take Sarah by the hand. If he had to drag her away from that witch, he was going to do it. He took two steps toward the curtain but came to a sudden stop at the sound of Sarah's laughter.

"You couldn't be more wrong. I'm far from an innocent, having been once married and widowed. I know well enough when a man cares for me.

And he's the most generous, loving man I know."

"Maybe," Annie conceded the point, having had no choice since it was so vehemently professed, "but what about bed?"

Sarah frowned, positive she wasn't going to like her next statement. Still, she was unable to resist this woman's tauntings. "What about it?"

"He's not as well endowed as some." A spiteful look entered her eyes. "A woman . . . well, she needs certain things."

Thaddeus never realized his soft groan. For a second, he wished only that the ground would open up and allow him to disappear forever. Why hadn't he walked into that room and taken Sarah out like he'd first intended? He couldn't look at the woman who was browsing through a stack of lace shawls or the man who had entered the store with her.

Suddenly from behind the curtain came a loud exclamation that told clearly of Sarah's shock. "Good Lord! I pray you're not talking about what I think you're talking about!" Her voice lowered a fraction, but not enough so everyone in the shop couldn't hear perfectly. Her tone was harder now, more certain and obviously angry. "You should know we couldn't possibly be talking about the same man. Thaddeus couldn't be more . . ." She faltered, obviously unsure as to how to proceed. "I'm convinced I couldn't stand it if he were more . . ." She faltered again, then realized with no little horror that she was telling this woman her personal business. "I really can't stay. Good-bye."

Sarah's cheeks were bright red as she pushed the

232

curtain aside and moved out of the room. Her eyes widened at Thaddeus's astonished look. Why, the man looked almost dumbfounded, as if he'd received a shock or perhaps a blow to the head. It took only a moment to realize his dazed expression was slowly turning into the most ridiculously smug grin of male satisfaction that Sarah had ever been unfortunate enough to witness. Her mortification knew no bounds. She was never going to talk to him again for the rest of her life. She wanted to curl up in a corner and die. He'd heard her. Of that she had no doubt. Oh, Lord. How was she ever going to face him again?

But that wasn't the worst of it. Sarah gave a silent groan and felt her cheeks burn with heat. Her coloring was, no doubt, as red as the lady's face who was pretending not to have heard a thing. A moment later the woman's husband, having held back as long as he could, laughed out loud. "You hear the damndest things in dress shops, wouldn't you say? Never sorry that Emma drags me along." He thumped Thaddeus on the back, as if the man had performed some great deed. Sarah wouldn't think until later about this disgusting display of male camaraderie. All she knew at this moment was pure mortification. She'd never known a time when she'd felt so horribly embarrassed. She couldn't look at the man and woman. Most of all, she couldn't look at Thaddeus. "I ain't seen you in town for a spell, Payne." The man grinned as Thaddeus took a stiff, obviously unwilling Sarah against his side, his arm circling her waist in a highly possessive manner.

233

"Reckon I can see why."

"I'd give it less than half an hour."

"Oh, God," Sarah groaned.

They were walking along the sidewalk, Sarah's newly acquired purchases having been sent on to their room, their direction momentarily unnoticed as they spoke of the last few minutes.

"If you had to defend the size of my . . . physical endowments," Thaddeus could hardly hold back his laughter, "why'd you do it with Emma Turnbolt listenin'? She's got the biggest mouth from here to the Rockies."

"How was I supposed to know she was listening? Or that anyone could hear our conversation?"

"The way you was yellin', no curtain was gonna stop our hearin'."

"Oh, God," she groaned again, while wondering how she'd ever lost all control. What in God's name had ever possessed her to speak on so intimate a subject?

Thaddeus gave up trying to hold off his laughter. People turned and smiled at the deep, rich sound.

Sarah wasn't the least bit amused by the last few minute's happenings, nor did she appreciate his laughter. She poked him in the side with her elbow. "Stop laughing, you oaf. I'll never be able to face these people again."

"Why not?"

"Oh, Thaddeus," she said on a groan, "don't you know that a lady doesn't speak of such things?"

"It wasn't you that brought the subject up." His mouth twisted with disgust, his eyes hardening with hatred as he thought of his first wife and the evil words she'd used trying to hurt him again.

Sarah came to a stop. The fact that Thaddeus had obviously enjoyed her encounter only added to her fury. "It doesn't matter. By the time the last one hears the story, they'll have forgotten about Annie. And what is she doing here, anyway? I thought you told me she was in San Francisco? And what is this about silver? Do you really have a mine? Are you rich? Why didn't you tell me? Why did I have to hear it from her?" Sarah's chest heaved. Her eyes glittered with frustration and rage as she realized just how much this man had kept from her.

Thaddeus's lips tightened at her outburst. "Are you finished? First I couldn't get you to say anything more than 'Oh, God,' and now you won't shut up long enough for me to get a word in."

Sarah was fast losing any trace of embarrassment as anger took over. She glared at him, her hands on her hips, her stance all belligerence. "Is this the kind of treatment I can expect as your wife? Will I forever be held in the dark, hearing from others your personal business?"

Thaddeus felt unjustly accused. He knew she wouldn't have been half this upset if she hadn't been embarrassed. But that wasn't his fault. He hadn't done a damn thing. Still, she blamed him anyway. He couldn't prevent the sneer in his voice as he angrily counted off on fingers that were shoved within inches of her face. "Number one, I didn't know she was in town. And yeah, I have a silver mine. It brings in some, but nothin' like Annie thinks, even if I worked it regularly, which I don't. No, I'm not rich, but I reckon we won't have to worry about where our next meal comes from. And I didn't tell you, 'cause ranchin' is more important and I didn't think of it." He leaned close, their noses almost touching as he growled, "Guess you could say I had other things on my mind this winter."

They glared at each other for a long moment before Thaddeus grabbed her hand and said, "Let's go."

"Where?" Sarah returned, pulling her hand back, her expression easily as angry as his.

"We're gettin' married."

"Why?"

Despite her objections and the kick he took in his shin, he grabbed her and pulled her close, so none other could hear but she. " 'Cause we've been sleepin' together for months. I reckon that's reason enough as any to marry."

Sarah gasped, suddenly realizing that a small crowd had gathered around them. She could only pray they hadn't heard his last words or she'd never recover from her humiliation.

"Marry me, Sarah?" Thaddeus asked with a certain dramatic flair, obviously for his audience's sake.

"Aw, go on. Marry him, Sarah," someone in the crowd took up his cause. "He loves you, girl," another remarked, assuming it to be a fact even though Thaddeus had said no such thing. And still another, "Put the poor man out of his misery."

236

Thaddeus was laughing as he hugged her to him. He practically dragged her into the general store, leaving the small crowd behind to go about their business. Thaddeus might have found the situation amusing, but Sarah was far from pleased. She'd never been so embarrassed in her life. "Aw, don't be mad, darlin'."

"I'm going to kill you for this," she whispered, her lips never moving.

Thaddeus chuckled as he directed her toward the counter where Mr. Pike displayed a few pieces of jewelry. "Which one do you like?"

"This strikes my fancy at the moment," she said, for only his ears, while pointing to an ivory-handled derringer.

Thaddeus grinned. "If you don't stop teasin' me, I won't be accountable for what might happen."

Sarah's brow creased into a frown as she looked up into fiery dark eyes that danced with laughter. "Like what?"

His arm tightened at her waist. "Like kissin' you senseless, right here for anyone to see."

"I like this one," she said, pointing to a simple gold band, without a moment's hesitation.

There wasn't a man alive who could lay claim to this kind of happiness. Who would have thought that being married would have made such a difference? If he'd had his way, he would have carried her back to their room. He couldn't wait to get her there. He wanted to see her try on a few of the gowns he'd ordered, especially that black lacy thing. He almost groaned at the thought of seeing her, really seeing her, through that thin material.

"You're not still mad at me, are ya?"

Sarah refused to speak to him. She looked straight ahead, pretending that she was alone. No, she wasn't angry, but he didn't have to know that. The man deserved all manner of suffering for the embarrassment he'd caused her today.

"Sarah, answer me."

"Do you think we could discuss this when we get back to our room?"

"Well," he dragged out the word a bit, "I was thinkin' on doin' somethin' other than talkin' when we got there."

Sarah couldn't prevent the tiny smile from curving her lips. "Were you?" She shot a glance his way. "And what might that be?"

"I was thinkin' you could try on one of those lacy nightgowns we got today."

Sarah's eyes widened with feigned innocence. "But it's not time for bed."

Thaddeus grinned. Even though it wasn't yet three in the afternoon, he said, "Sure looks like it's gettin' dark to me."

Their plans had to be postponed. When they returned to their room, they found Mrs. Stanley in need of her daughter's help in the kitchen. Having no sitter, they decided instead to go to the restaurant to eat. The one and only restaurant in town wasn't fancy. Sarah felt terribly overdressed in her satin and

238

lace gown, but Thaddeus's obvious appreciation made up for any uncomfortable feelings she might have had. The food was delicious. More so perhaps because she didn't have to cook it. The couple lingered over coffee until Emily grew bored playing with the flatware and started to fuss.

By the time they returned to their room, Emily was cranky and in real need of her mother's care. Soon she was fed and changed, but for some reason, perhaps because of the long nap she'd taken earlier, the child refused to settle down.

"This is probably why they don't take babies on honeymoons."

Sarah laughed at her husband's obvious anxiety. "Calm down. You're making me nervous with all that pacing. Emily's bound to feel it, too."

Thaddeus watched the baby with frustration. "Looks to me like she's ready to play the night away."

"If she is, it's only your own fault. I've told you often enough that you spoil her."

Sarah put the baby down on a smoothly spread blanket to play, knowing she'd soon grow sleepy. "Leave her for a bit."

Emily immediately started to fuss.

"Give her some," he nodded toward Sarah's breasts. "That always quiets her down."

"She's not hungry."

Sarah was stripping off her clothes as she longingly eyed the screen that hid the deep tub brought in earlier and filled with steaming water. She knew a bar of lavender soap sat upon a folded white towel, waiting for her use. Sarah couldn't wait to slide beneath the water's surface.

"Untie me?" she asked as she turned her back to him and waited.

"Why do you have to wear this stuff?" Thaddeus asked as his fingers fumbled with the knot he'd made this morning.

"Because I can't walk around town like I do on a mountain."

"Why not? You don't need this thing," he said as the corset parted and fell to her feet. "It doesn't do anything."

Sarah sighed with relief as she pulled her chemise over her head and flung it upon a chair. She was standing before him, bare to her waist, rubbing the marks the corset had made around her waist and midriff. Thaddeus was loving every minute of it.

"I want to take a bath first."

"Did I say anything?" he asked as innocently as he knew how, which wasn't innocent at all.

Sarah gave him a knowing look, which was accompanied by a saucy grin. "You didn't have to." She glanced at a still-fussing Emily. "Play with the baby while you wait."

"I'd rather play with you."

Sarah shook her head and laughed again. "I know you would and I'd prefer that myself, but if Emily won't quiet down . . ." Sarah didn't need to finish. They both knew that unless the baby slept, neither of them would get their wish.

Sarah was half asleep. The water felt deliciously warm against her skin. Totally relaxed, she entertained the thought of never getting up. She heard the knock on the door, listened as Thaddeus spoke to someone, and then heard the door close again.

A moment later a tray holding a bottle of wine and two glasses was set upon the chair near the tub. Sarah opened one eye to find Thaddeus naked, one leg already in the tub. "Where's Emily?"

"I gave her to a band of gypsies."

"Is she sleeping?" Sarah asked unnecessarily, knowing, of course, that she was, for she'd listened as Thaddeus cooed gentle soothing words and paced the floor until the room grew silent.

"Nope. I told her if she couldn't settle down, to get herself someone else to look after her." He shrugged, "So she left."

Sarah smiled. "You're getting as good as I am at putting her to sleep."

"I'm learning, but I don't have the equipment you do, so I can't do certain things."

Sarah chuckled and then gasped as water spilled over the tub's edge as he joined her. "You're soaking the floor!"

"I'll wipe it up later." He parted her legs, on the pretext of finding enough space, and placed them on either side of his. "Why didn't you tell me this felt this good?"

Sarah hadn't moved. Her head was still resting against the tub's rim, her eyes closed. "Because you would have gotten here first, and I would have had to put Emily to sleep."

Thaddeus grinned as he reached beneath the water. His hands ran along the inside of her thighs, his

241

destination obvious. "Do you like that?"

"What?" she asked dreamily as she raised her hips a fraction, awaiting his touch.

"What I'm doing to you."

"Oh." She gave a long "ahhh" of pleasure. "Is that you doing that?"

Thaddeus grinned. "Who did you think it was?"

"My eyes are closed. I didn't know for sure." Her breathing was growing a bit unsteady as his fingers moved masterfully over her.

"But you didn't say anything."

"Because I didn't want whoever it was to stop."

Thaddeus gave her a threatening growl. "I'm going to drive you crazy for that remark."

Sarah grinned and opened one eye. "I already am crazy. Why else would I have married a man who would give my baby to gypsies?

Chapter Twelve

Their bodies were slick with sweat. Thaddeus had brought her three times to release, only to tease her senses until the passion rose wildly out of control again. He smiled, knowing he needed only to touch her and she craved more, to kiss her and she grew hot and pliant beneath him.

Thaddeus had never known such a night. The months they'd spent together had never been like this. He hadn't known she could be so open, so greedy. He'd never seen her so lost in the throes of passion. She held nothing back, but gave all she could and demanded her needs met in return. He loved every minute of it.

His mouth, wild, wet, and hot, held to hers as he gave in at last to her desperate urgings. His body slid deep into her warmth and he felt her pleasure in the sound of her broken sob. Belly to belly, thigh to thigh, they raced madly toward that one fleeting moment of blinding white-hot ecstasy. "I can't . . . Oh, please, I can't!" she choked as her hips strained desperately beneath his, her movements belying her words.

Their bodies slid together and then apart. Hot! She was burning up. Crazed with the need he'd instilled. Her fingers gripped his shoulders, her nails biting deep. Neither noticed. He had to give her this. This one final time, she had to find the pleasure or die.

He wouldn't release her mouth. Thick, hot, and delicious, his tongue imitated the movements of his hips, hungry, devouring. It didn't matter. She couldn't find the will or strength to breathe, anyway. All she could think, all she could want, was more of this exquisite torment.

"Oh, God, yes," she groaned into his mouth, for it was coming at last. She strained into the feeling, the overpowering need, hungry to taste the moment when the rest of the world would fade into oblivion.

He pulled her hair, yanking her head back hard so her mouth couldn't break free of his. Taking unto himself the last of her choice, her control, as he loved her with near ferocious madness.

And when she cried out as he knew she must, his mouth was there, greedily absorbing her cry into a growl of frenzied pleasure. Breathing life back into a body gone almost lifeless, as aching uncontrollable waves of pleasure came to squeeze with agonizing delight around his body. She suffered what could have been a terrifying second when her body felt incapable of going on . . . when she could neither breathe in nor out . . . when blackness danced around the edges of her consciousness . . . when blinding ecstasy filled all of her being, and she might have wondered, had she the power to form the thought, if she'd died.

But no, Sarah was alive, more alive than she'd ever realized. Exhausted perhaps, but filled with a rich sense of contentment, of satisfaction, of power, and best of all, of knowledge, for she knew a man's love as only a chosen few are ever likely to know.

"You're a mighty fine woman, Sarah," he said on a gasping, breathless sigh, his bearded chin brushing her damp hair back from her face. His body slumped heavily upon hers.

Sarah smiled, her eyes closed as she delighted in the feel of him against her. "Am I? Why?"

Thaddeus laughed. " 'Cause I ain't never seen or felt anything like this before."

Sarah grinned. "Am I supposed to return the compliment?"

"I reckon," he said as he rolled them both to their sides. His hand came to hold her hips to his, refusing to allow their bodies to part. "If you want to play by the rules."

Sarah shot him a wicked, teasing look. "What kind of rules are we working with here?"

"I say somethin' like, 'Darlin', you're mighty fine,' and then you say somethin' back."

"Is that how other women do it?"

Thaddeus didn't want to talk about other women. There were none. Not for him, anyway. Besides, that kind of talk was sure to rile her up some. He didn't want to lose the peace and contentment of this moment.

Sarah laughed, feeling him stiffen. She teased, "Do you tell them all—"

"Sarah," he said, his voice gruff as he jerked her hard against him. "Don't compare yourself with others. There ain't any that can hold a candle to you. Besides, there haven't been all that many."

"I don't believe you."

Thaddeus's sigh was decidedly unhappy as he allowed her to push him to his back. Damn! This was exactly what he didn't want. Why did women insist on spoiling moments like this? Sarah leaned over him, her breasts brushing tantalizingly against his chest. Thaddeus thought that with a little effort, he might be able to take her mind from its present course, but no. She'd only bring it up later. It was best to get it out in the open now and be done with it. Thaddeus's unhappy look turned to one of surprise and then delight as he heard her say, "No one can do the things you do without some practice."

He grinned at the compliment. It was clear he'd been worrying for nothing. A thick eyebrow raised in inquiry. "Was it that good?"

Sarah chuckled, knowing she had his complete attention. "Well, I wouldn't exactly say good. The word doesn't somehow tell all. I'd say it was interesting."

"Was it?" Sarah could almost see the puffing out of his chest. "It wouldn't swell my head none if you told me exactly how interestin'."

"Wouldn't it?" she asked as her hand drifted in an apparent aimless direction down his chest and over his belly. She felt him stiffen as her fingers boldly inched closer to his sex. "What would it swell, then?"

"God," he groaned, unconsciously raising his hips to her wandering fingers. "You shouldn't talk like that."

"You're right. A lady shouldn't talk about those kind of things."

"But you liked them?"

Sarah laughed at his hopeful expression. "I imagine you could say that. You could even say I loved them. Almost as much as I love you."

There was a moment of total silence. For some reason, Thaddeus felt a wave of intense disappointment as the easily spoken words spilled from her lips. If she'd wanted to destroy his playful mood, she'd chosen just the right method. Something like pain, or panic, or both gripped his inners. He didn't want to hear this. He didn't ever want to hear this. They had that special something, all right, but it sure as hell wasn't love. He knew from personal experience that love was a lie. He felt a spurt of anger that she'd gone and ruined this intimate teasing. His voice was hard, his eyes black and dull when he asked, "Do you?"

"Do I what?"

"Love me."

"Would I have married you if I didn't?"

"I reckon."

"Really?" she asked with some surprise. Wondering how he'd come to that conclusion, she continued with, "Why?"

" 'Cause I can take care of you."

She pulled her hand back and stiffened. Thaddeus cursed, knowing she was upset. What the hell was the matter now?

Sarah was acquainted with a few women back in St. Joseph who had married solely for money. To her mind, these women were shallow, heartless fools who had used their charms to trap the men who loved them. Thaddeus couldn't know the disgust she felt for any who so desired monetary gains. And she felt deeply hurt that he considered her no better than those awful, greedy creatures. "You know, of course, you've just insulted me.

"I didn't!" He came up to his elbow; their faces were almost even. "Women marry all the time for security. Who else would take care of them 'cept a husband?"

"You believe a woman's only alternative is to use a man?"

He shrugged. "What else can they do?"

"They could go to work. In St. Joseph, women get jobs as clerks and servants. Two worked in the bank. I was a schoolteacher."

"And you were all just waitin' for the right man to come along."

Sarah thought it was best to ignore his scathing comment, for most did give up their work once married. And most believed to marry for security no

248

great crime. Instead she asked, "Why do men marry?"

Thaddeus knew she was upset. Her voice was soft, but not soft enough to disguise her anger. He wished now he'd ignored her comment, but he answered her question as honestly as he knew how. "For a woman to warm their beds and a family." He cursed as his words brought a flush of anger to her cheeks.

Her voice was tight and low when she wanted to scream. "Is that all? What about love?"

"Love?" he asked, as if he weren't sure he'd ever heard the word. "Love ain't real. It's just stuff poets write about."

"What about people who think they're in love."

"You got it right, darlin'. They *think* they're in love." He shrugged. " 'Course, they can't be, 'cause love don't exist." He smiled, obviously hoping to soften his words. When his smile brought about no apparent reaction, he asked, "What's the matter?"

Sarah stared at him, absolutely stunned. Why in the world hadn't they spoken of this before? What in heaven's name had she gotten herself involved in? She grimaced as she realized how ridiculous her surprise. A man who refused to believe in God wouldn't have a qualm about denying the existence of love. "Nothing," she answered momentarily, dropping her gaze to his chest. Her cheeks flushed as she dared, "I was already warming your bed. You didn't need to marry me." Suddenly, her gaze caught his again. The depth of need in it caused an odd trembling to squeeze around his heart. "Why did you?"

Thaddeus frowned. Something was happening here. Something he didn't understand. Something in her eyes was scaring him spitless. He didn't know how to handle it except with anger. "Don't start sounding like a wife."

"Meaning?"

"Meaning that was a dumb thing to say."

"How lovely. Now wives are dumb. Let me tell you, mister," she poked him hard with her finger, "as far as I can see, husbands aren't all that great, either."

He pushed her to her back and scowled. "Don't go getting yourself all riled. I married you 'cause I want kids. I told you that months ago. There ain't no reason for you to be mad."

He was right, of course. It was ridiculous and probably irrational to feel anger. Just because she'd been foolish enough to have fallen in love with the man, it didn't mean he had to love her back. After all, one couldn't force another to love. Sarah's mind raced back to the months they'd lived together. And she knew without a doubt that he did love her. He did! Why was he afraid to admit it?

"You didn't mean all that love talk, did you?" he asked warily, his voice filled with hope. Sarah could have sworn she saw real fear in his eyes. She watched him for a long moment before she shook her head. "No, I didn't mean it. It was just talk."

Sarah felt a wild need to laugh at the ridiculous position she'd suddenly found herself in, only she didn't. It was going to take calm, deliberate action on her part to break down the walls of protection he'd built around his emotions. She'd never accomplish anything with a bout of hysteria. Sarah almost felt sorry for the man and the suffering he was bound to know. Almost, but not quite.

"Did you find enough men?"

Sarah sat beside him atop his wagon, now filled almost to overflowing with enough supplies to last them for months. They'd woken up ready for a busy morning and hadn't lingered long in bed.

Once Sarah got up to care for Emily, she hadn't come back. It was just as well. They had shopping to do and supplies to pick up and bags to pack. He could wait till they got back home before he got her into bed again.

The wagon rolled over a rock. The swaying movement caused her to fall against his side. "Sorry," she said, and added a weak smile.

Thaddeus shot her a puzzled look. What the hell was the matter with her? He'd never seen her act so quiet. It was more than just not talking. Something was wrong.

"Is anything botherin' you?" he asked for about the hundredth time.

"I told you no. But there will be if you keep asking me that." Her eyes were clear but kind of distant. He didn't like it one bit.

"You ain't sick or nothin'?"

She shook her head. "Thaddeus, I'm fine."

"You ain't sulkin' over that love stuff, are ya?"

Sarah smiled. "I never sulk." She ignored the rest of his question and asked again, "Did you find enough men?"

Thaddeus sighed and then nodded. "I hired on six. Two of them are bringing their wives soon as we can build them a place to stay."

"Oh, good," Sarah said. The relief he heard in her voice couldn't be misunderstood. So she wasn't looking forward to spending another winter alone with him. Thaddeus shrugged. He couldn't blame her none. The solitude was hard on a woman. A man didn't yearn for company. At least he hadn't. He'd been satisfied for years with just his dog. But this winter with her had been as close to heaven as a man was ever likely to get. He felt a little disappointed that she didn't feel the same way.

It was different for women, he silently argued. They had to talk. Only Sarah didn't talk much, especially not since they'd woken up this morning. Was she already sorry that they'd married? Damn! What the hell had happened? How had she changed overnight?

Thaddeus had everything he'd ever wanted, everything any man could want and yet he couldn't find one damn thing to be happy about. Nothing was wrong. Nothing was right. Why? What had happened?

Three months had gone by since they'd married, and Thaddeus ached for the woman he'd lost somewhere between town and his home. Not that she wasn't pleasant. She was. As a matter of fact, she never raised her voice. She smiled all the time, but her smile was oddly empty, as if she could find no real reason for laughter, no joy. He'd asked her about a million times what was wrong, but she'd always told him nothing was bothering her. He couldn't keep asking. If she didn't want to tell him, he guessed it was her right.

Only problem was, the laughter was gone from his home, and for some reason, Thaddeus felt the loss so deep he ached.

He felt the loss even more when he took her in his arms. Not that she refused him. She never did. But something was missing. She was holding back. The wildness, the near-crazed feelings they'd once shared, were gone. Nothing was the same.

Thaddeus felt an ache that nearly stole his breath. She couldn't be nicer or sweeter, but down deep something was missing. A void had come between them, an emptiness he didn't know how to fill.

Sarah was laughing as she walked away from Joe Edwards. Thaddeus watched the man whose gaze had gotten stuck on the gentle movement of his wife's hips and felt anger bubble up in his chest. He was going to fire every goddamned one of them. What the hell did he need hands for, anyway? He didn't have to increase his herd.

"I don't like you out there talking to the men."

253

"Why?"

" 'Cause they ain't doin' their work if they're talkin' to you."

"I don't talk to them when they work. I talk to them when they stop to eat."

"You're my wife."

"Exactly! I'm your wife, not a slave. If I have to cook for them, the least I can get in return is a few minutes of conversation. There's nobody else around here to talk to."

"I suppose that means me."

"Yes, that means you. Why are you avoiding me?"

"I ain't. I've been workin', is all."

"Until all hours of the night?"

He couldn't meet her eyes, hadn't been able to, in fact, since the night they returned from town. He remembered the hopelessness he'd felt that night. He remembered how rough he'd been, how he had, in his desperation, almost viciously taken her body, hoping to absorb her into him and never let her go. Afterward, he couldn't look at her. He still couldn't. And he wasn't sure why. She hadn't complained that he'd been too rough, but he knew he had. He wondered why he was the one who hurt. What was happening here? Why weren't they together? It was guilt that kept him from looking at her. Was it guilt that kept them apart? "We had to build a shack on the western slope, in case someone wants to ride out there and has to stay the night."

"So? That only took two days. Why haven't you been home?"

Thaddeus's lips grew grim. "I didn't get a wife so she could nag at me, Sarah."

Sarah nodded her head. "You're right," she returned, just before she turned away from him. "It won't happen again."

Thaddeus cursed as he watched her move to the stove.

They'd been married three months and he could count on one hand the number of times they'd made love. He needed her so bad, but something was missing. Every time they came together, it was worse than not having her at all.

He was just about ready to climb the walls. His teasing had long since ceased to exist. They rarely managed to be in each other's company ten minutes before Thaddeus would start a fight. He knew he was at fault, but he couldn't do a damn thing to stop it, unless it was to find the root of their problem. They needed to talk. He couldn't stand much more of this. She was driving him out of his mind.

He'd washed up and sat at the table, waiting for her to serve him his dinner.

"Emily gettin' to be a handful?" he asked as she served him his meal. Outside, he could hear the men laughing as most of them began to drift off to sleep in their new bunkhouse. He'd been late getting in again, something that happened more often than not.

Sarah laughed as she joined him at the table and sipped from a mug of coffee. "She's getting into everything since she's learned to crawl. I shudder to think of her walking."

"Would you like me to get you some help?"

"What kind of help?"

"Well, when the women come, maybe I could get one of them to help out during the day."

Sarah shrugged. "What would I do with myself?"

"You could come with me."

"Where?"

"Anywhere. Just with me."

"Why?"

"What do you mean why? I want you to, is all."

"Why, Thaddeus?" she insisted on knowing and because he couldn't give her answer, couldn't give himself an answer, he growled, "Goddman it! Can't a man sit down and eat in his own home without being aggravated?" She was like a damn dog, gnawing at a bone, only the bone was him. "Forget it! Stay here. You can stay here forever for all I care." He was furious again. Damn this woman. When the hell was he going to learn they just couldn't talk anymore without fighting?

"I intend to, just like I intend for you to tell me why."

Thaddeus came to his feet in a flash. Glaring at her, he leaned over the table, his face inches from hers. "I don't take no orders from no woman. Not ever. You'd best remember that." A moment later, with his rifle in one hand, his coat in the other, Thaddeus slammed out of the house. For the first time in almost eight months, he forgot about the door.

256

Thaddeus walked toward his barn, grumbling most of the way. Son of a bitch! He should have known better than to come in off his pastures. He couldn't find any peace around here. The woman was just itching for a fight, he swore, knowing it to be a lie. He was the one with the temper, but damn it to hell, she was the one who caused it. Lately, they set each other off like a match to a stick of dynamite. And the wilder he grew, the calmer she became.

He saddled his horse. Might as well spend the night on the range. He sure as hell wasn't going to stay here. Damn, but he couldn't take much more of this. This wasn't what he'd planned when he'd married her. This wasn't it at all.

All he wanted was a little peace. Was that asking so much? He didn't need a relationship that involved any depth of emotion. Even if he had the emotion to give, which he didn't, he didn't want it. All he wanted was to see his needs met and in return he'd take care of this woman. But she wasn't fighting fair. She wanted more. A hell of a lot more than he was willing to give. A hell of a lot more than he'd give any woman.

Four days later, Thaddeus rode back to his ranch, a dejected set to his shoulders. He looked terrible. If he'd lacked sleep before, it was nothing compared to the endless nights he'd lain in his blanket watching the stars. His eyes were sunken and hollow. He needed about a week's worth of sleep. But thoughts of sleep were about as far as they could get from his mind. His mouth was set in a hard line when he took care of his horse and then walked inside the cabin. Sarah had just settled Emily for the night. She turned at the sound of footsteps, her eyes widening with surprise and a gentle smile touching her lips.

Thaddeus didn't say a word, but stared at her with eyes that feasted on her loveliness.

"Are you all right?" Her gaze was soft and gentle. He ached to feel the peace she knew. He couldn't take any more.

"Do you love me?" he asked, his back leaning against the door. His eyes were dark, almost haunted, as he awaited her answer.

"Yes," she said so softly he thought perhaps it was his own thoughts he heard.

He breathed a long sigh, only realizing then that he'd been holding his breath. "Do you?" he asked again.

"Yes," she repeated.

"I don't deserve it, you know."

"You do," she said softly, then grinned. "Sometimes."

"Tell me again," he said as he moved toward her, his dark eyes glowing with fire.

"I love you," she said as she was lifted by her waist and brought up to meet him eye to eye.

"Tell me again."

"I love you."

"Again! I can't hear it enough." It was a balm to his soul. He felt the ragged edges of his heart begin to heal. He felt peace fill him to overflowing. How had he done this to himself? Why had he denied for so long this need? Yes, a need for her body, but more than that. He needed this . . . this exquisite moment when she said those words. He needed her laughter, her joy, her peace, everything she could give.

Sarah smiled. Her hands came to frame his face, her fingers threading through his dark, silky beard. Her blue eyes darkened to violet. "I love you."

He shook his head. "I'll never hear it enough." He buried his face in the warmth of her neck. Savoring the feel of her, he crushed her against him for long aching moments. He groaned at the scent of her, the taste, when his open mouth touched against her skin. He couldn't believe the relief, the happiness that filled his soul. It left him weak, exhausted, and yet filled with the strength of ten. "I almost lost you."

"You didn't," she said as she held him tighter to her. "No, you didn't."

"I reckon you know by now that I love you."

Sarah made a small sound deep in her throat and simply nodded. Her eyes closed and a delicious smile of contentment curved her lips. Her voice was deeper than usual when she finally spoke, "It took you long enough to say it."

"I'd rather face a gang of rustlers than admit to it."

Sarah's laughter was soft and sweet. "It doesn't take away, darling. It only adds."

Thaddeus groaned at the endearment, knowing she was right. His face was buried still in the curve of her neck when he murmured, "I need a bath."

"Yes, you do."

Thaddeus pulled back and grinned. His eyes sparkled with laughter. A laughter he hadn't known in months. "Interested in washin' my back?"

Sarah laughed as she disengaged herself from his arms. "Bring in the tub and I'll start the water. Are you hungry?"

An hour later, Thaddeus sighed with pleasure as he lowered himself into the steaming water. After days of consuming little more than hardtack and water, he'd eaten until he could hardly move. His full stomach and the heat from the bath brought on a loud and lusty yawn.

"Tired?" she asked, coming up behind him.

"A little. Haven't had much sleep lately."

"Why?" she asked as her small hands came to his shoulders and began massaging the stiff muscles found there.

"Thinking of you, mostly, and why I was so mad all the time," he admitted freely, then groaned at the pleasure of her kneading fingers. "It took till last night before I finally figured out what the problem was."

"And what was it?"

"That I love you."

"Why should that be a problem?"

" 'Cause I didn't believe in love. I thought it was only a word men used to get what they wanted from a woman."

Sarah smiled. "And?" she prompted.

"And I didn't want to love you."

"Why?"

" 'Cause I was scared of what a woman like you could do to me."

"What could I do?"

"Destroy me."

Sarah's laughter sent chills down his spine. "You're giving me more credit than I deserve."

Thaddeus leaned back and glanced up at her. "No, I'm—What the hell are you wearing?"

Sarah grinned at his obvious interest, as he turned his head and body to look his full. "I never got a chance to wear it." She looked down the length of the see-through black lace. "Do you like it?"

"God," he groaned, never answering her question. He didn't have to. The look in his eyes told her everything she wanted to know. "Come closer. Let me see," he said and, without thinking, started to get up.

Sarah pushed at his shoulder. "Sit! You can see later." She was rubbing at his neck and shoulders again, determined to prolong this delicious expectation. "Your neck is stiff."

"Something else just got stiff. Maybe you could massage that, too."

"Does it hurt?" she whispered, her breath a tantalizing brush against his ear.

261

"What?" he asked, then wondered how he'd managed, for his heart thundered wildly, his pulse throbbing in his throat as his body reacted to her touch.

"Whatever it is that just got stiff," she reminded, her mouth taking tiny little nibbles from his neck and ear. "Does it hurt?"

"Yeah. I need you to make it better."

"If I massaged that, too, would it help?"

Thaddeus knew she wanted a night of loving. The only problem he had was he wasn't likely to last two minutes. He'd waited too long. He'd wanted her for too long. He groaned, while every muscle and nerve in his body responded to her gentle nibbling. Her hands were smoothing down his chest and back up again. "It just might kill me."

"Then I probably should stop."

"No! God, no," he said as her lips moved over his cheek and teased his mouth with light, airy almost kisses.

Sarah squealed, then laughed as she suddenly found herself sitting on his lap. Her hand wet, she gave his chest a stinging slap.

"Ow!"

"Look at what you've done?" A second later, her eyes hardened as she noticed the water still sloshing over the tub's rim. "You're cleaning up this water."

At that moment, Thaddeus would have done anything she asked. If she wanted him to wash the whole floor, or clean the entire house, or wrestle a mountain lion, he would have done it. The only problem was, he couldn't think beyond what faced him. He looked to be in some sort of trance, his dark, fiery gaze unable to move from the sight of her pink-tipped breasts peeking through the black lace. "Shhh," he said. "You'll wake up the baby."

Sarah grinned. "And you wouldn't want that."

"Not for ten hours, at least."

"Ten hours!" she said, as if shocked that he'd imagine such a thing. A second later, she eyed him wickedly. "Do you think that's enough time?"

"Not for what I want to do to you."

"I thought the plan was to scrub your back."

"Go ahead."

"Now? Like this? I can't reach your back."

His grin was growing more wicked by the moment. "Then scrub something else."

"Something like—" She waited for him to fill in the blank, and when he didn't, she asked, "What?"

"Take your pick. There's plenty to chose from."

"Do you mean I can only scrub one thing?"

Thaddeus swallowed. His mouth was suddenly dry. "No. Scrub anything you want."

He watched her eyes darken and knew without a word spoken that he was going to suffer for the dare he'd just issued. "I wouldn't be too slow about it, though."

Sarah watched him carefully. "Wouldn't you?" She grabbed the floating edges of her gown, pulled the sodden mess over her head, and dropped it on the floor. "It's a good thing then that I'm doing the scrubbing, because slow is exactly what I had in mind."

263

Some few moments had passed in silence before Sarah asked, "Are you awake?"

Thaddeus, his head resting against the rim of the tub, had kept his eyes closed. Her hands were beneath the water. On the pretext of massaging him, her wandering fingers hadn't missed an inch. Starting from his toes, she'd worked her way up to his stomach and then mercifully down again. He chuckled in amazement at her question. "Do you think a man could sleep through this?"

"I don't know, could he?"

Thaddeus only opened one eye. It was enough to see the fire. "Take my word for it. Sleep is the last thing on my mind."

"Then why are your eyes closed?"

" 'Cause every time I open them, I reach for you. You keep pushing my hands away, so it's easier if I don't look." Helpless to resist, his hands moved again to her bobbing breasts, but she was out of the tub and wrapping herself in a towel before he realized what she was doing.

"Lie on the bed. On your stomach," she said, when he came to his feet and started drying himself off.

Thaddeus grinned. "I think I like you bossy." He came to her and held her against his naked body. A long, low groan came from deep in his throat. "Thing is, I like you period."

"Thaddeus, darling," she grinned at another groan. "I've been thinking about this for hours. Let me—"

"All right, all right," he said as he released her and aimed his exhausted body toward the bed. "I hope you know what you're doing. Don't mind tellin' you I'm a mite tired."

"Maybe you'd like to take a nap first," she teased.

"No!" he answered instantly. His body had been stirred something fierce from her love-play. There was no way he was going to sleep in this condition.

Sarah chuckled at his vehement response. "Good."

He groaned again when he felt her straddle his hips.

"You sure do make a lot of noise. I thought you would enjoy this."

"Sarah," he said half in warning, half in pain.

But Sarah ignored his weak complaint. "Take advantage. This isn't about to happen all that often."

"My men are gonna give me some strange looks tomorrow," he murmured as she smoothed perfumed oil on her palm and began to massage it into his back and arms. "When I start to sweat, I'm going to smell like a whore hou—a garden of flowers," he quickly amended.

Sarah gave him a sultry laugh. "Maybe, but if you give them one of your evil glares, they won't say a word."

"My glares don't stop you none."

She leaned forward and purposely allowed her breasts to rub against his back. "That's because I'm your wife and you can't fire me," she whispered between openmouthed kisses across his neck.

"Sarah, no more," he said into the pillow.

265

"Turn over," she whispered, and Thaddeus knew he wasn't going to make it.

Still, he couldn't resist and obeyed her orders. She might be killing him, but a man could never find a better way to die.

Chapter Thirteen

Sarah smiled with delight as she watched Thaddeus come from the barn at the sound of the approaching wagon. With Emily held in her arms, the toddler balanced comfortably on her hip, she moved toward the empty cabin, while the heavy wagon lumbered up the slight incline, loaded nearly to overflowing with everything the Spencers owned. Moments later, it came to a stop before the second and most recently finished cabin.

The two wooden-framed buildings stood beyond the barn some distance from each other. Each house had a small, fairly private yard, separated from the other by a thick line of trees and undergrowth. Much of the property surrounding each cabin could be cultivated into a garden, which would provide all the vegetables needed for the families living there. Will Spencer had left almost immediately after the last nail had been hammered into place to retrieve his wife, Kate, from her family's place in Kansas. This made a total of two women, not including herself. Two! And if Joe Edwards had his way, his wife,

Emma, would be joining them before winter came. Sarah couldn't believe it. After months of isolation and then weeks of anticipation, she would finally have a small circle of friends. The long, hard months of a Colorado winter wouldn't seem nearly as harsh or lonely now.

Sarah watched Will help his wife from the wagon and smiled at the woman's rounded form. It was plain to see that Will was soon to be a father. Sarah couldn't have been happier. Kate was somewhere around her own age, and Sarah couldn't help but envision a long, friendly relationship with their children becoming close friends.

Kate stood at the wagon's side and smiled a shy greeting, while unconsciously rubbing at her aching back.

"Don't pick up a thing," Sarah ordered as Kate reached for a box sitting high upon the loaded wagon. "Let the men do that for you.

"And you won't be cooking tonight. I'll bring something over later."

Kate turned and smiled her pleasure at the small reprieve. "You don't have to tell me twice. My mamma didn't raise no fool," she said as she moved toward Sarah. The two women introduced themselves.

Sarah grinned, knowing immediately that she was going to like this woman, while Thaddeus raised his eyes toward the heavens. His groan was masterfully done holding just the right amount of despair, for it was his expert opinion that his small spread had more than enough smart-mouthed women.

Without a doubt Sarah headed that list, and she sure as hell didn't need another example of how a wife was not supposed to act.

Except for Zack, who had hired on as blacksmith and was now at work in the lean-to attached to the back of the barn, all the men were with the herd. This left Thaddeus and Will with the laborious chore of unloading the wagon. The many boxes could be unpacked later. For now, Kate was ordered to sit on a small ladies' rocker, one of the first items to be taken down, while the two men went about the chore.

By the time they were finished, three women gathered inside the cabin, each offering their opinion of what belonged where. Thaddeus made a quick escape on the pretext of finding everyone something cool to drink.

Sarah put Emily down for her nap some two hours later and gratefuly accepted Lottie Morgan's offer to listen for her daughter, while she went in search of her husband. She found him in the barn. He was in a stall, carefully checking a pregnant mare, when she approached. "Are you hiding out?"

Thaddeus laughed as he glanced over his shoulder. "Why should I hide?"

"I watched you sneak off. Very tricky. Did you think I wouldn't notice?"

"I thought with that gaggle of female voices you wouldn't give me a thought."

Sarah watched his hopeful expression but refused to give him the satisfaction of an answer. The man was far too full of himself as it was. "If you weren't

269

going to bring back a pitcher of lemonade, you should have said so."

Thaddeus chuckled. "Pretty smart, don't you think?"

Sarah shrugged. "Lottie brought enough for everyone. You weren't missed."

"Not even by you?"

"Especially not by me," she teased as she stood outside the stall, her eyes sparkling with humor.

Thaddeus walked toward her. He leaned his arms on the stall's half door. "I figure that this second female cuts our privacy down to nothing."

"Why?"

He shrugged. "When I'm workin' around here, I like to stop by for a little somethin' in the afternoons."

"A little something?" Sarah did a poor job of pretending innocence. "You mean like a drink of cool water?"

Thaddeus shot her a warning look but otherwise ignored her question. "I reckon that little habit is shot to hell."

"Why?"

" 'Cause you'll have the house full of females. Either that, or you'll be at one of their places, jabberin' the afternoon away."

Sarah didn't bother denying the obvious. She wasn't about to stay locked up in her cabin while two women were ready and willing to associate. Still, there were ways to see both their needs met. "Now that the ladies are here, I might find a free afternoon now and then. One of them could watch Emily and

270

we could meet somewhere."

Thaddeus seemed to take to that idea without a moment's hesitation. His eyes lit up with anticipation as he imagined an afternoon spent alone in her company. "The whole afternoon?" he asked, while erotic thoughts came suddenly to plague. He moved uncomfortably, wondering if she noticed the instant reaction her words had brought about. A reaction he seemed unable to control. Maybe it wouldn't be such a hardship having these women here after all. "Where?" he asked, his eagerness undeniable.

She grinned at the sudden glowing interest in his eyes. "It's your mountain."

Thaddeus appeared thoughtful for a moment. "We haven't had any trouble, but word in town has it that the Cheyenne ain't been too sweet on whites lately." He muttered a low curse. "What with that fool Custer turnin' the Black Hills into one giant gold field and puttin' the Sioux on the warpath." He breathed a long sigh of disgust. "We'll find a place tomorrow, but I don't want you ridin' out there alone. You can only go with me. Understand?"

Sarah nodded, and when it looked like she might be leaving, he caught her arm. With his free hand, he unlatched the door and silently led her to a clean, empty stall. Sarah didn't give much resistance, even though she did manage, "Thaddeus, this place offers less privacy than our cabin."

"There's no one around." He grinned as he guided her into a corner where they couldn't easily be seen by a passersby. "Besides, we ain't gonna do nothin'. I just want to kiss you some and maybe touch you a little."

He smiled at Sarah's low laughter. "Do you now?" Leaning up against a wall, her blue eyes danced with wicked lights as he pressed his hips against her belly, making her instantly aware of his arousal. "Only a little?"

"Now, don't go sulkin' on me, darlin'. I can't service you every time you snap your little finger, you know." His eyes were alive with mischievous laughter. His hands came to cup her breasts. "I do have one or two things to do occasionally."

Sarah laughed at his accusation, while wondering if she'd ever get the chance to snap her finger. "Of course not. So when can you?" she inquired wickedly.

Thaddeus closed his eyes and made a small sound. Sarah wasn't sure if it was in appreciation of her curves or her wicked question. "Damn, if you ain't the most brazen woman." His arms slid around her slender back and suddenly tugged her tightly against him. He groaned at the feel of her. His voice was lower and more gravelly than usual. "And soft, too. We sure are different, you and me."

Sarah ran her hand down his thigh and slowly backed up. He stiffened and made a sound deep in his throat as she boldly cupped his arousal. "I think you may be right. Do you think we should further investigate this phenomenon?"

"We could, but it might take some time."

"Are you busy right now?"

Thaddeus grinned. "Thinkin' those thoughts ain't going to get you much."

"No?" Sarah answered his grin with one of her own. "What will they get me?"

He couldn't hold back a shiver as she gently slid her palm up and down his bulging front. His forehead pressed against hers and he breathed a long sigh of delight. "I love it when you do that."

Sarah's free arm circled his neck and held him in place so she might take advantage of the nearness of his lips. Light, breezy kisses danced over his mouth, his bearded cheeks, and nearly drove him wild, until he could take no more. Holding her head still, he crushed her mouth beneath his and then groaned as she parted her lips.

Sarah was decidedly breathless when he tore his mouth from hers at last. "Are you terribly unhappy with the others here?"

His breathing was harsh, labored, his pulse beating in his throat as his hips tilted up for her further exploration. "I never said I was unhappy."

He might not have said it, but Sarah knew his feelings well enough. Thaddeus wasn't happy about having their privacy interrupted, their simple lives complicated by neighbors that promised, because of the distance from town, to be closer than the usual sort.

A long winter spent together hadn't lessened in the slightest his greediness for her total attentions. He cursed the jealousy he felt while watching mother and daughter play, knowing even as he felt it that it was wrong to want her all to himself. But she was the first human being to show him love. And he couldn't get enough. He had no right to demand more, but he couldn't help this almost obsessive need.

"You know that I'll always be here for you, don't you?"

Thaddeus groaned as she worked his buckskins open. "I know."

He filled her hand and then some, the heat of him burning against her palm. "I love you," she whispered, and Thaddeus was held motionless, speechless, his heart filled with unimaginable joy as she sank to her knees and showed him exactly how much.

Her breath was hot, burning, as she nuzzled her face deliciously against him. Soft lips kissed, while her tongue took the small dot of moisture she found at the tip. He wondered how his heart managed to continue beating when she drew him deep into the wet, exquisite heat of her mouth.

Thaddeus held to the wall. He hadn't the strength to do more than force his lungs to breathe in and out. His body was hers to do with as she would, and even had he the mind, he was unable to stop her.

Her hands were busy, touching even as her mouth refused to part from him. It was too much. He couldn't hold back much longer. His breath was coming in huge, unsteady gasps as he finally brought her to her feet.

Sarah's eyes were slightly dazed as she stared into coal-black eyes softened with raw, aching love.

"Too much. You have to stop," he gasped, then groaned as he crushed her against him. His hand, under her skirt, quickly disposed of her drawers.

Sarah hardly had a chance to help before she was lifted from the floor and pinned against the wall, his body pressed deep into her heat.

He cursed. It was over a lot sooner than either would have liked. "Too fast," he gasped. "Oh, Jesus, it's too fast," he breathed against her ear as his body shuddered uncontrollably against the spasms that held and squeezed, only to ease and grip him yet again, spinning them both into mindless ecstasy.

He held her for a long moment, wishing they had the time to start again, promising himself that he was going to love her long into the night.

"You're right. We are different," Sarah finally managed, once her breathing had returned to normal. "Lord, I hadn't imagined the difference to be quite so glaring."

Thaddeus chuckled, the sound muffled against her neck. He felt his gut tighten and his heart twist with the magnitude of love he knew for this woman. "Are we? How?"

Sarah grinned as he allowed her body to ease down his length. She adjusted her skirt and petticoat, he his trousers, as she primly replied, "Well, for one thing, you're very big."

"Am I?" Thaddeus grinned ridiculously.

"I meant tall," she corrected, noting instantly his smug look and how he purposely misunderstood her comment.

Thaddeus laughed. "And you're short."

"I'm not short," she quickly defended, as those of lesser stature are apt to do. "It's just that" — she reached her hand to the top of his head — "from up there, everything's bound to look short."

Thaddeus wasn't about to object. He was too interested in hearing what she'd say next.

"And for another, you're very hard."

"Mmmm." Laughter crinkled the corners of his eyes. "I reckon you might say that."

"I mean your chest and stomach, of course."

"Of course," he mimicked.

"While I'm much softer."

"Mmmmm." Thaddeus nodded his approval of her softness.

"I think it's probably a good idea that we're different."

Thaddeus grinned.

"It makes things much more interesting, don't you think?"

"Lately, I ain't been thinkin' of much else."

Thaddeus got a glimpse of the teacher she once was as she nodded and then replied in her best schoolmarm voice, "That's very good."

Thaddeus laughed and hugged her tightly against him. "Do I get an A?"

"You get anything you want."

"I already have everything I want."

She walked from the barn with a beautific smile curving her lips, while the remnants of the last hour replayed itself in her mind's eye. She shivered as the most intimate and delicious memories were forever imprinted on her mind. She'd been gone quite some time and Sarah hoped Emily was still sleeping. She hurried toward the cabin.

Lottie looked up from the book she was reading. "You found him, I take it."

"He was in the barn," Sarah said noncommittally as she bent to check on her sleeping daughter.

Lottie Morgan grinned but said nothing regarding the lovely flush that rose to Sarah's cheeks.

Sarah poured herself a cup of coffee from a pot that constantly simmered on her back burner, then grimaced at the taste. "You haven't been drinking this, have you?"

Lottie nodded toward her cup. "Tea."

Sarah made a fresh pot of coffee and served what was left of a batch of sugar cookies, while they talked for the next hour or so.

It wasn't until Lottie left that Sarah wondered at the gentle knowing smile she'd received upon entering her home. Had Lottie known what she'd been about? Of course, she did. The woman was, after all, a wife of some ten years. She knew well enough the happenings between a man and a woman.

But what of the others? Sarah had seen two hands riding back toward the ranch when she'd left the barn. She'd felt uneasy, wondering if her cheeks had been as flushed as they felt, her lips as swollen. Was she forever destined to worry over who suspected what? She imagined that to be the case, for it wasn't likely she could easily put aside the strict formality of her childhood.

Sarah had been raised in a home where intimacies were never referred to. Now that she thought about it, she couldn't remember ever seeing her mother and father kiss. They'd treated one another kindly but with enough formality to no doubt be horrified at the sensual creature their daughter had become.

Sarah smiled with relish as she remembered the hour spent in the barn. Before Thaddeus, she hadn't known a man could be so lusty, so at ease with intimacy, so accepting that their actions were right and natural. Sarah couldn't deny the joy she experienced when in her husband's arms. She only hoped that eventually she would be equally at ease and not worry that others might guess the reason behind flushed cheeks and swollen lips.

Jack Blackman groaned as he pumped against Annie's white flesh. Their body's were covered with sweat, for they'd just about pounded the mattress into the floor for the last half hour.

"No more. Jesus, you're killing me," Jack groaned as the shudders eased at last. A moment later, he rolled away from her greedy arms.

Annie sighed with pleasure. Damn, but this man was good. She almost hated to follow through with her plans. She gave a mental shrug, knowing they could have enjoyed a long, delightful relationship if he were anything but the greedy bastard she knew him to be.

But Jack would two-time her the first chance he got. She couldn't allow him the opportunity. She had to take care of Annie. No one else would.

* * *

"From what you're saying, he sure don't live like he's rich," Jack said as they sat in the sitting area of the large, over furnished room.

Annie nodded and took a sip of Kentucky bourbon. She sighed as the liquor's warmth slid down her throat and into her belly. "Hoards the stuff. Too damn cheap to spend a dollar. Made me wear rags when we were together."

Jake grinned, finding it impossible to believe this woman had ever worn anything but the finest silks and satins—if she ever got herself out of bed and wore anything at all. He'd been in town only twenty-four hours, and all of them had been spent in Annie's bed. He'd never known a woman half as greedy.

He eyed her lounging on the couch across from him. Damn, but he couldn't remember spending a more exhausting night. And it hadn't ended at dawn. She'd been damn hungry for him. Hungrier than she'd ever been before.

Annie didn't have the least bit of modesty. Normally, he liked that in a woman, but she carried it a little too far. Unconcerned as to who saw what, she'd sat naked across from him while the servants had brought them their food and whiskey. To their credit, they hadn't raised a brow at finding her sprawled naked on the small sofa.

Jake watched her with a cynical smile touching the corners of his handsome mouth. She sure wanted something awful bad. He wondered what it was.

"Annie, you ready to tell me what you have in mind? I know you didn't bring me all the way from San Francisco just to drain me dry with a twelve-hour session in your bed." He shrugged and swallowed the last of his steak, then finished off the meal with a long sip of red wine.

Annie laughed. "Are you sure you're dry, Jake?" she asked as she allowed her legs to part.

Jake sipped at his drink. His dark gaze moved over the creamy whiteness of her skin. Her breasts were small but perfectly shaped, her waist tiny, her hips wide. She was pretty in a course, rough way, and she sure as hell knew what to do in bed. He couldn't deny she'd stirred him, but after last night and most of this morning, he felt not at all interested.

"What do you want?"

"I want you to kill a man."

"Why?" he asked, not the least bit shocked, for Jake had killed more than his share and for as little a reason as a word sharply spoken.

"Because I want him dead."

Jake grinned. "Just like that?"

Annie nodded and came from the couch. She pushed aside the small low table and sat herself upon his lap, facing him. "I'll give you anything you want."

"What do you have that I want?"

Annie pouted. Jake imagined she thought herself pretty in doing so, but all she managed to do was look sulky and mean.

Her hands rubbed against his limp member. The caress had no effect. There was no way in hell she was going to get it up again. He'd had just about as much as he could take. She smelled of stale sweat, expensive perfume, and sex. From experience, Jake knew she wouldn't wash again for a day or so. The thought wasn't appealing.

He came to his feet and dumped her back on the couch. "Like I said, 'What do you have that I want?' "

"Money." Her eyes gleamed with satisfaction as she saw the light of interest enter his. "Money and a woman."

"How much and what woman?"

"She's his wife."

"Whose wife?"

"I want you to kill my ex-husband. Then you can have her and half the silver the bastard is hiding."

"How much you figure he has?"

"Thousands, at the very least."

"But you don't know that for sure. You've never seen it, right?"

"I've seen the vein. Damn it! It was at least a foot wide and the thing went on forever!"

It never entered either of their greedy minds that the ore might still be almost fully intact. They never imagined that a man, that any man, might give up his chance to be rich and settle instead for the comfortable living gained by trapping and running a horse ranch. Because they wanted money most of all and the things it could buy, they never considered a man might be satisfied with the simple things in life. They never imagined he might hate choking black holes. That he might savor the clean, pine-scented air of Colorado's San Juan Mountains. That he might prefer sunshine and riding to the slavery of his next big strike.

"And how am I supposed to get the silver if I don't know where it is? You said the mine is a big secret."

"I can tell you where the mine is. What I want you to do is find what he's already taken out."

Jake laughed. "It could be anywhere in those mountains. I could look for twenty years and not find it."

"Go to work for him. If you keep an eye out, you'll spot him hiding it eventually."

Jake sighed. "I could work there for months before I saw anything. I'd be better off at the tables downstairs. And I wouldn't have to break my ass for every dollar I made."

"You could occupy your time with the woman while you wait."

"What's she like?"

"Plain."

Jake laughed. "Coming from you, that has to mean she's a beauty."

"She's all right, I guess." Annie felt a twinge of jealousy but pushed the emotion aside. If she wanted this man's help, she couldn't let any emotion stand in the way. The son of a bitch that she'd married had done her dirty. He'd never given her a cent in all these years. Desperate to leave the isolation, monotony, and hard work of his mountain, she done it, with no more than the clothes on her back. She hated his guts for that. He had so much and she had nothing. But not for long. She was going to get her share. And soon. Now that she was getting on a bit and a few of her usual customers were starting to visit the younger girls, she knew she couldn't wait much longer. She wanted to set up her own house. A big, expensive brothel in San Francisco, and she needed money to do it. And this man was going to get it for her. "She comes into town once a month. You can see her tomorrow if you're interested."

Jake nodded and slid his arms into his jacket. Just before he left the room, he said, "I'll let you know my answer tomorrow, then."

Chapter Fourteen

The buckboard trailed a thick cloud of dust as it wove its way down the busy street. It was the beginning of the month and time again for a trip to town to load up on supplies. From the number of wagons waiting in the heat of the day outside the general store, it was obvious that many of owners of the outlying ranches were already in town and about their business.

Most had come to town, as had Sarah and Thaddeus, for dual purposes. It was July and the fourth was three days away. Festivities were planned for the entire weekend. Everything from shooting and riding contests to roping, racing, pie judging, barbecues, and dancing. The huge barn at the end of town was, at this very moment, being cleared of the stacks of hay and grain at its center so there might be room enough for tonight's dancing. A small group of men were setting up tables that would, no doubt, serve as a bar near the entrance.

Sarah smiled her delight. She couldn't wait for the

festivities to begin. Her eyes sparkled in anticipation. It had been more than a year since she'd danced. And her feet fairly itched to move to a snappy tune.

Sarah wasn't alone in her anticipation of a good time. Ranch hands, rowdy and loud, hungry for a good time after a month of hard work, had come in from neighboring spreads. They appeared anxious, almost desperate, in fact, to spend what there was of meager monthly earnings. The saloons and the ladies upstairs were, as always, doing a booming business. Many of the men, not at all happy with the confining, smoke-filled quarters inside, waited in the shade supplied by the building's overhang. With drinks in hand, they gathered in small boisterous groups, watching the traffic, eyeing the pretty ladies, and joking while they waited for their turn upstairs.

As Thaddeus and Sarah drove by, the men, their eyes widening with appreciation, looked their fill. Thaddeus grinned with smug, possessive satisfaction, knowing the reason for their looks. Sarah was the prettiest woman he'd seen since moving to these parts. And she belonged to him. He felt his chest puff up with pride.

"What are you smiling at?"

"Nothin'."

"You surely were," Sarah returned. "What's funny?"

"I'm just happy that you belong to me, is all."

Sarah smiled. "And you just realized that fact?"

"I was watching those cowhands look at you.

Their eyes just about fell out of their sockets."

Sarah shook her head. Possessing no false modesty, she knew she was far from ugly, but to suppose herself pretty enough to cause a man to stare was beyond her ability to imagine. She flushed at her husband's admiring look. "Don't be silly."

What Sarah didn't realize was that she, in the months since coming here, had grown from a young girl into a lovely, desirable woman. Pretty to begin with, her blue eyes now sparkled with happiness and her mouth was often curved into a devastating smile. Her skin was clear and glowed with a golden tan. Her brown hair was liberally streaked with gold, and the more time she spent outside the blonder it grew. She radiated health, contentment, and happiness. Emily's birth had added to her full, if petite form in the best ways possible. Curvy, soft, and oh so appealing, it was no wonder the sight of her often struck a man speechless.

"Reckon I'm as serious as I'm ever likely to be. There's not a woman in these parts that can compare to you."

"What about the ladies? . . ." Sarah grinned, then nodded over her shoulder as they passed the last saloon.

"Especially not them." Thaddeus frowned at the thought that this woman might compare herself to the likes of those whores.

She grinned and teased, "I don't know. From what I've seen, they look awfully pretty to me."

He shot her a glance from the corner of his eye.

"That's because you haven't seen them up close."

"And I suppose you have?"

"Nope." He shook his head, a gleam of laughter in his eyes. "Somebody told me they were ugly."

No matter Sarah's gentle probing, Thaddeus had continuously avoided answering questions regarding his relationship with any of those women. Sarah imagined she knew better than to believe his innocence in the matter. She knew her lusty husband wouldn't have gone for long without female companionship. She laughed at his professed ignorance of first-hand knowledge, the delicate sound carrying sweetly in the dry heat of the late afternoon. More than one man, still watching their progress, felt a distinct tightening in the general vicinity of his groin at the soft feminine sound.

One man in particular, even after a night spent in another's greedy arms, felt a need unlike anything he'd ever known twist at his inners.

His dark eyes narrowed with interest as he watched the wagon carrying the smiling lady pass by. Jake licked his lips as he remembered a flash of white teeth, the gentle slope of slender shoulders, the fullness of her breasts, the narrowness of her waist. Was she the one? he asked himself, knowing it didn't matter. She was the best thing he'd seen since coming to this hick town. And he knew, suddenly and as surely as he knew his own name, that he wasn't leaving here without her.

Children darted into the wide dirt street, oblivious to the danger of heavy wagons and horses' hooves.

They laughed at one another as they ran between moving vehicles and dashed around startled horses, while ignoring the shouts of riders and drivers to stay clear.

Thaddeus pulled his wagon to a stop before the boarding house. Sarah wiped the dust from her lips. It coated her face. She could feel its grittiness between her teeth. She looked forward to cleaning up. With this long dry spell, the dust was getting worse every time they came to town.

She sighed with relief upon reaching the cool and quiet of their room. "I'm so used to having Emily with me that I can't feel easy about being alone."

"You're not alone," Thaddeus reminded.

"I'm not?" Sarah blinked in feigned innocence, while the hint of a smile touched the corners of her mouth.

Thaddeus grinned at her playacting. "This is our time together, remember? Two whole days without anyone stopping by, or the baby's crying, or—"

Sarah looked up and made a face, pretending confusion. "Do I know you?"

Thaddeus laughed and moved toward the door. "I expect you'll know me a lot better after I order us a bath."

When he returned he glanced at her, a quizzical look in his dark eyes. "Why are you still dressed?"

"I'm hungry."

"Good, so am I. Take off your clothes. The water will be here in a few minutes."

"I meant for food."

"Damn!" he grunted as he shoved his shirt back into his buckskins. "I'll be right back."

"You certainly are agreeable today," Sarah sighed as she leaned back in the tub of lukewarm water, comfortably replete after a delicious meal of steak and buttered potatoes. She sipped from a glass of ruby-red wine. "One might wonder if you have ulterior motives."

"You don't have to wonder. Just ask me."

"All right." She sat up a little straighter and grinned as he pulled off the last of his clothes. "Do you have ulterior motives?" He was standing naked beside the tub. Her hand slid up the length of his naked thigh and lingered without conscious thought. She cupped the fullness of his sex for some moments before he tore himself away from her caress.

"Nope," he said, his voice noticeably lower as he eased himself into the tub and positioned her between his long legs. "My motives are clear enough. I want you, and the best way to get what I want is by bein' agreeable."

Sarah laughed, came up to her knees, and turned to face him. Her breasts bobbed along the water's surface, bringing his attention from her smile to the rosy, inviting tips. "Otherwise, you wouldn't think of it. Am I right?"

His arms resting upon the tub's rim, Thaddeus wondered what she was about. He eyed her suspiciously. "You tryin' to start a fight?"

Sarah leaned closer, her eyes shining with happiness, her arms wrapped around his neck, her breasts brushed teasingly against his chest as her lips grazed his mouth with brief unsatisfying touchings. "Not a fight, exactly." She gave him a look from beneath thick lashes, the wicked light in their depths undeniable. "But I am trying to start something."

Thaddeus's eyes crinkled at their corners. He flashed white teeth, the sight startling against his black beard and tanned skin. "Somethin'?" he asked. "You couldn't be a bit more—"

"—specific?" Sarah finished for him.

"Darlin', you're soundin' more like a wife every day. Now you've takin' to finishin' my sentences for me. You figure I don't know the words?"

"Sorry," she said, while biting at her lips, but the accompanying giggle told him clearly she wasn't sorry at all. "I wouldn't want to sound like a wife."

Except for a quick glare, Thaddeus ignored the last remark. "Like I was sayin', you couldn't be a bit more explicit, could you?"

Sarah laughed, her eyes widening with delight. "I know you're not an ignorant mountain man. Why do you pretend?"

"Answer my question first."

"You mean what I'm trying to start?"

He nodded and waited patiently . . . well, as patiently as any man who was sitting naked in a tub with his equally naked wife could.

"I was thinking that I wouldn't be terribly upset if you made love to me."

He grinned at her prim and proper expression. How the hell did she do it? Thaddeus was positive not another woman existed who could look so innocent while sitting naked between his thighs. "You wouldn't, eh?"

She shook her head.

"Why?"

"Why what?"

"Why wouldn't you be terribly upset?" he asked, mimicking perfectly her words.

"Because I love you, of course."

Thaddeus granted her another of his devastating smiles. "Then I'd best be gettin' at it, don't you think?" He paused a moment. "Turn around."

Sarah did as she was told, then sighed with delight as he pulled her against his chest and began a slow, delicious, almost torturous washing of her entire body. She took all she could without comment and then finally groaned out a sound that resembled pain. Her head, on a neck too weak to support it, fell back to his shoulder. She closed her eyes and sighed her pleasure.

"Do you like this?" he asked as his hands moved under the water, delving into hidden secrets, luxuriating in the warm silken folds of her body.

"I'm hating every minute of it," she breathed, the sound soft, the words slurred with obvious pleasure.

Thaddeus grinned. "Maybe I should stop, then."

"No, don't," she quickly returned.

"I wouldn't want to do anythin' you hate."

"It's all right. I'm strong enough to bear it."

He laughed and then growled, "Witch," as his mouth found her willing, pliant lips.

The water turned cold long before they moved from the tub to the comfort of the bed.

He rolled aside and brought her close against him, their bodies damp from the long afternoon of loving. His fingers were playing in the silky thickness of her golden-brown hair, as they each concentrated on bringing their breathing back to normal. "Do you know how beautiful this stuff is?"

Sarah glanced up. "What, my hair?"

He nodded.

She sighed and came up on her elbow. "You have a ways to go before anyone will ever call you a poet."

"If they know what's good for them, no one ever will."

Sarah giggled at his glare. "Why?"

"I don't say no sissy words."

"A big, rough, ignorant mountain man wouldn't even know those kind of words."

"That's right."

"Liar. I saw the book of love sonnets in your drawer. The edges are worn from reading it. And I know you're far from ignorant."

"It ain't mine."

Sarah's look told him clearly her disbelief.

"All right, so what if it is?" he snapped, reversing their positions. His look was fierce, daring her to make a further comment.

"There's no reason to get yourself worked up into a snit. I'm not asking for sweet words. Relax."

"You, the kind that likes 'em?"

"Only if they're freely given." She shot him a despairing look and breathed a long sigh. "Somehow it doesn't mean quite the same thing if I have to hold a gun to your head."

He gave her a long look and Sarah saw clearly the vulnerability he tried to hide. She instantly understood. "Annie didn't like them?"

His eyes shuttered, closing out all expression, but not before she saw the pain. His lips twisted with dislike. "I don't want to talk about Annie."

"Tell me," she said gently.

Thaddeus shook his head. He couldn't. It was too much to ask of any man.

"What did she do?"

"Nothin'."

"Didn't she like them?"

"She laughed," Thaddeus blurted out, then sighed with disgust that he had allowed the admission. The damn woman wasn't going to give him a minute's peace until he told her. He shrugged, forcing himself to act as unconcerned as he wished he felt. "No big deal. She laughed, is all. Matter of fact, she went on laughin' for days." His mouth twisted with hate. "Thought it was the funniest thing she'd ever heard."

Sarah knew Annie's tactless reaction had hurt him deeply. This man was a sight more sensitive than he liked to let on. Silently, she imagined most men were, only, like Thaddeus, they were no doubt loath to admit to what they considered a failing. "Then she was a fool."

"She was a bitch," he corrected. "If I wasn't so damn horny, I never would have married her."

"Didn't you love her?"

Thaddeus grinned down at his wife. "Never loved anyone 'cept you."

"Two lies in one conversation." Sarah shook her head and pointed a finger that tapped his nose. "Shame on you."

He chuckled. "What makes you think I'm lyin'?"

"Because you wouldn't have been so mean and grouchy when we first met if you hadn't been afraid of getting hurt again."

"Think you're pretty smart, don't ya?"

She pushed him to his back and grinned as her hands moved slowly, slyly, wickedly, down his body. "Smart enough to take care of you, mister."

And to his delight, she did just that.

"Hurry up. I want to dance."

"How can you think about dancin'?" he asked, still lying on the bed. "I'm dead tired."

Sarah threw his trousers and shirt over his prone form. "How can I not? Just listen to that music." The distant sounds of lively country music came easily to their ears through the open window. Sarah swayed her hips to the sound.

"We could dance here," he suggested. "We wouldn't even have to get dressed." His eyes took on a heated gleam as he obviously took to the notion. "I can't rightly remember dancin' with a naked lady before. It might be interestin'."

Sarah laughed at the ridiculous thought. "I imagine it would be that." She laughed again. "I'd be bouncing all around and—" She blushed at the thought, and her blush grew darker still as she realized she'd spoken aloud.

"I know."

"I thought you said you were exhausted?" she asked, recognizing correctly the renewed hunger in his gaze.

Thaddeus grinned, feeling a sudden new burst of energy. "If I hurry, could we do it later?"

She glared at his reflection through the mirror as she tried to work her hair into place. "We've been doing it all afternoon."

Thaddeus grinned. They had been at it all afternoon, but that was to be expected. He hadn't touched her in weeks. Each night he'd fallen into bed totally exhausted. He couldn't be held accountable for making up for lost time. "You know what I mean. Would you dance with me naked?"

"I'm not going to get a chance to dance at all, if you don't get out of that bed."

"Will you?" he asked again. His apparent intent was to go nowhere until she answered.

"Not a jig, Thaddeus." Her cheeks grew dark at the embarrassing thought. "A waltz, if you like."

* * *

295

It was a beautiful night. The stars glittered brilliantly against a black velvet sky. The temperature had cooled drastically and Sarah was thankful for the wrap she'd brought along.

Inside the barn, the music played loudly. Couples swirled in circles as their feet kept rhythm with the music. The crowd was large and loud. Many of the younger set had moved outside to either dance, flirt, or perhaps sneak off for a few minutes of privacy that the dark afforded.

Thaddeus kept a close eye on his wife, even if he didn't dance to every tune played. More than once, he warned off an approaching cowboy. After one of his fierce glares, none were brave enough to approach his lady for a dance.

Sarah smiled into his warm, possessive gaze as she sipped at a glass of lemonade. "Don't you think it's odd that the only men dancing are married or old enough to be my grandfather?"

He shrugged. "I don't see how that's odd. Just because a man is married don't mean he don't like—"

"What did you tell them, Thaddeus?" she interrupted, not for a minute believing him the innocent he portrayed.

"Tell who?"

"Anyone who wasn't old enough to need a cane to stand. How did you warn them away?"

"I don't know what you mean. I didn't say a word."

"Then you gave them one of your evil glares," she said with certainty.

He shrugged again. "Maybe one or two. I didn't mean anything by it."

"Except death to anyone who dared come near me."

"You belong to me," he stated, as if that cleared up any misunderstanding.

"So?"

"So, I don't want you dancin' with just any old cowboy."

"Especially not one that might be appealing." She laughed at his fierce expression.

He was about to ask which man she thought appealing, when the soft, sultry sound of her laughter caused all but the thoughts of her to leave his mind. All he could suddenly think about was the shape of her mouth and the sweet warmth he knew he'd find there. An afternoon of love-making had definitely not been enough. He couldn't wait to get her back to bed. "You're not supposed to laugh," he said, his voice sounding somewhat strangled.

"I'm sorry, but you were giving me one of those looks."

"And you think I'm funny?"

"No. As a matter of fact, I think you are the most attractive man here." She batted her eyelashes, feeling deliciously wicked as she allowed a soft, teasing smile. "Evil looks and all, there are none other to compare."

"Are you flirting with me, Sarah?" he asked, his eyes widening with surprise at the softly spoken words and the smile that teased the corners of her mouth.

"Of course, darling," she said simply. Her hand smoothed over the crisp material of his shirt, lingering with delight as she felt the hard, warm muscles beneath. "Why wouldn't I flirt with you?"

Thaddeus, whose confidence in her love was growing stronger each day, felt a moment of clear astonishment. He didn't know how to react. No one, as far as he could remember, had ever flirted with him before. He didn't know what to say.

He wished words came easy to him. Why couldn't he be glib and tease her in return? She was everything a man could want in a woman. Open, alluring, sweet, and so damn sexy. Just looking at her made his guts ache. He wanted her, even after all this time, like he'd never wanted another. He knew she was different. She wasn't anything at all like Annie. Still, the fear was there. It was something he couldn't control. He was terrified, even when he gave in to the glory she offered. She couldn't play him false. Somehow he knew this time he wouldn't survive the pain.

"Don't you think it's hot in here?"

Sarah's blue eyes met his, a skeptical look in their shimmering depths. She was obviously wondering why he had suddenly changed the subject. "A little. Why?"

"I thought we could step outside for a breath of air."

"Oh, no, you don't," she said as she neatly twisted out of the arm that suddenly circled her waist.

298

"Once you get me outside, you'll drag me back to our room. I want to dance."

Thaddeus laughed. "I won't. I promise. I just wanted a kiss."

"Is that all?"

Thaddeus nodded.

"Then go ahead and kiss me."

Thaddeus pulled at the collar of his shirt, uncomfortable with the stiff material so tight around his throat. He couldn't wait till it came off—the shirt along with everything else. "Well, the kind of kiss I was thinkin' on would be better had in some privacy."

"Now that sounds interesting." Sarah grinned and took his arm as they moved outside.

Sarah gasped for a lungful of air as Thaddeus released her lips at last. Her head was thrown back to allow his lips, tongue, and teeth greater access to the golden column of her throat.

Her head spun dizzily and she held on to his shoulders, pressing the lower part of her body tantalizingly against his. Her voice was no more than a soft murmur, "When I was a young girl, I sometimes thought about a romantic night like this."

"Did you?" His voice was muffled against her skin.

"As I got older, I figured they were only the dreams of a silly girl. Or the imagination of a writer. I didn't think it could ever happen."

Thaddeus raised his head to look into her eyes. "You mean, you never walked outside with a young man?" Her blue gaze glittered in the silvery moonlight, and it took all his concentration not to crush her in his arms.

"I did, but we never did anything like this." Sarah glanced down at Thaddeus's hands possessively cupping her breasts and she grinned.

"Never?" he asked, obviously surprised.

Sarah smiled. "Of course not." She pulled slightly away, but not far enough so his arms couldn't hold her at her waist. "You should know better than to think that a young lady would do something like this."

Thaddeus had lived long enough to know young ladies often did just this and more. But to tell her of it left himself open for a barrage of questions. Wisely, he realized he was better off accepting her answer without comment. "I reckon you're right, but what about your husband?"

"Thomas and I never . . . We didn't . . . Actually, it wasn't at all like . . ." Sarah sighed with dismay. She hadn't realized how hard it was to speak of her relationship with her first husband. She tried again. "I loved Thomas very much, only what I felt for him was very different."

Thaddeus's heart nearly burst through the walls of his chest. His arms tightened and he was greatly tempted to drag her back to their room, no matter her objections. "You felt no passion, is that it?"

She gave him a disapproving look. "I don't think it's fair to compare. It was different, is all."

"How much longer do you want to dance?" he

asked with an eager gleam in his eyes.

Sarah laughed and slapped his shoulder. "Don't go getting that look in your eye. The night is still young. Get me something to drink."

Thaddeus grumbled his displeasure, but at the promise shining in her eyes of a long night ahead, he went about her bidding. At the moment, he could think of better things to do than dance or drink.

This afternoon had been a delicious break from the hard work they both knew at the ranch. It had been long and pleasurable, but not nearly long enough. Right now it felt like forever since he'd last insisted on his husbandly rights. Thaddeus grinned at the knowledge that he never had to insist very hard. God, he couldn't wait to get this luscious woman back to their room.

Sarah joined Jill Cooper, whose husband owned the Emporium, Becky Smithston, the owner of the town's only restaurant, and Mrs. Stanley outside the barn as she waited for his return. Knowing them from previous visits to town, she felt comfortable in their presence. A few more visits to town and she knew they'd all become the best of friends. She was laughing at something one of them said, when a cowboy came up behind her and touched her shoulder.

"How about a dance, little lady?"

Sarah turned to face the man and smiled politely. "I'm sorry, but I'm waiting for my husband."

But the man didn't hear her words. The only thing that registered in his drunken mind was the smile she flashed his way. He staggered slightly. Even if the scent of whiskey hadn't permeated the air around him, it would have been easy enough to see the man was deep in his cups. "Come on, lady," he insisted as he grabbed her arm.

"Excuse me," Sarah said firmly as she pulled her arm from his grasp. "I said I'm waiting for my husband."

Becky Smithston glared at the young man. "She said she didn't want to dance."

The man stood towering over the women. He blinked slowly, as if he were trying to understand and couldn't quite grasp the meaning. Suddenly, his blank look turned hard as he glared at all four women. "Did she? I didn't hear her say that."

"I don't want to dance," Sarah said, hoping her direct statement would make her wishes clear.

"Sure you do." He took her arm once more, while ignoring or never noticing the fact that she was again trying to free herself from his hold. "Every lady likes to dance. That's what you're here for, ain't it?"

"If you don't mind . . ."

"Is this man bothering you, ma'am?" came a voice from behind her. Sarah turned and looked into the eyes of the most handsome man she'd ever seen. He was clean shaven, but unlike the other men in these parts, his skin was only slightly tanned. Obviously, he didn't spend the greater part of his time under the harsh western sun. His features were perfect, his hair dark, but his eyes were hard and cold. Sarah felt a

302

slight shiver of fear. A moment later she realized what she'd thought she saw in his eyes was simply a trick of the light that fell beyond the barn's doorway. She almost smiled at the absurd notion. What could this man do that might cause her to be afraid?

Sarah shook her head. "No," she said in answer to his question. "Thank you, anyway."

"Come on, lady," the cowboy said as he pulled her hard against him.

He didn't hurt her, but Sarah cried out with shock. She'd never been roughly treated and didn't at first know how to handle this situation. Actually, things happened so fast that Sarah had no time to think of much of anything.

She would never be sure she'd actually seen it. But before she knew what was happening, she was yanked from the man's arms and flung aside. Off balance, she staggered, almost falling to the ground. The stranger's hand moved faster than lightning. A shot was fired before the cowboy's hand touched his gun.

The amount of alcohol already consumed made the cowboy's reflexes absurdly slow. He fired his gun, but not until long after a bullet had already crashed into his chest. Too late, he realized a man in his condition shouldn't have been wearing a gun. He couldn't see clearly enough to hit anything, anyway. The man before him kept separating into two, then slowly floating back and reforming one image . . . a horrifying image holding a smoking gun.

Sarah cried out her shock. Amazingly, even

though he had started the trouble, her sympathies lay with the drunken cowboy. The poor man hadn't had a chance. For a long, silent moment, he looked with no little amazement from his killer to the hole in his chest and back again. He coughed. Sarah shivered, her stomach churning as blood came rushing from the man's nose and mouth. He was already dead before he hit the ground.

The three women standing nearby screamed and faded into the shadows. Everything seemed to be moving in slow motion. Sarah imagined it must be a dream, a nightmare. She wanted to run, but she couldn't seem to get her feet to move.

Her gaze moved about the slowing milling crowd and found Thaddeus's stunned expression. How was it he was suddenly and simply there when a moment ago he was not? She looked with some perplexity at his concerned expression. Why was he staring at her like that? What was the matter? Why did his arms seem to grow in length, his hands reaching out but never quite touching her? The drinks fell from his hands. Sarah frowned at the spilling. What was he doing throwing their drinks to the ground? What was the matter? His eyes were filled with fear. Why? And why were her knees suddenly threatening to buckle?

She moaned ever so slightly at the pain. Only it wasn't pain exactly, but more like a burning discomfort. Still, it nagged at her unreasonably. Odd, but even though she felt it, she couldn't discern its actual location. Where was it coming from? A wave of dizziness assaulted. Why? What was happening to her? Thaddeus reached her at last. She almost sighed her relief, but no, it wasn't Thaddeus who held her. She tried to see, but the man's face was in shadows. Who was he?

Thaddeus was standing over them both. She watched him lean down and blinked with surprise at his vicious, agonized curse. She knew a moment's terror at his cry, then nothing but the sublime peace of a black, empty void.

Chapter Fifteen

He was going to kill the bastard, Thaddeus thought wildly, then groaned with disgust as he paced the tiny room outside the doctor's office, remembering that the drunken cowboy who'd shot his wife was already dead. It didn't matter that the whole episode was nothing more than the worst bit of luck . . . a shot gone wild. Thaddeus was glad the man was dead. He only wished he'd been the one who had pulled the trigger.

But it had all been over before he'd returned to her side. Another had reacted before he'd gotten the chance. Later, he'd have to remember to thank the man.

He ran his fingers through his hair for the hundredth time. God Almighty, he couldn't stand this waiting another minute. The worst was not knowing. He had to know what was happening. She couldn't die. He wouldn't let her die. And how the hell was he going to stop it from way out here?

Thaddeus walked to the door that led to the doctor's small surgery. He couldn't stand this waiting another minute. Nothing could be worse than this terror, this not knowing.

"You can't go in there," said James Honeycut, the man who assisted Dr. Winslow, while learning first-hand doctoring at the same time. The man had chosen just that moment to open the door, run for a stack of toweling, and charge back into the room.

"The hell, I can't," Thaddeus said as he walked inside the small room.

The room was empty, but for the doctor and his one patient. Sarah lay on one of three narrow cots that stood against one wall. Dr. Winslow worked over her pale, unconscious form. He was digging a thin pick-like knife into the bleeding wound beneath her left shoulder. Thaddeus felt a wave of dizziness at the sight. He'd never seen her so pale, so helpless. He couldn't stand it. He couldn't bear to watch and yet he couldn't look away.

His stomach lurched at the sucking sound of a bullet being dislodged from flesh. The doctor muttered a low curse as blood pooled the wound and pumped over his hands. He worked quickly, with absorbent toweling and compresses to staunch the flow. After a few minutes of pressure, he dared to look again and then sighed his relief that the bleeding was beginning to ease.

A few drops of chloroform, the scent sickening and powerful even from where he stood, were sprinkled upon a pad of thin cotton that already covered Sarah's nose and mouth. With needle and thread, as if he were a seamstress, the doctor soon made neat stitches, bringing together the gaping hole in her upper chest.

"How is she?" Thaddeus asked, not recognizing the sound of his voice, so filled was it with the horror of watching this woman bleed.

Doc Winslow's head snapped toward the sound. "You shouldn't be in here."

"I'm stayin'." Thaddeus ignored the doctor's look of displeasure. "How is she?"

"She's a strong lady." The doctor nodded and then smiled. "She'll probably make it."

"Probably?!" Probably wasn't exactly the answer Thaddeus was looking for. "What the hell do you mean probably?"

"I mean an artery was nicked and she lost a fair amount of blood. I mean the wound will probably fester. If she makes it past that, then, with a little rest, she'll be fine."

"What if it festers?" Thaddeus asked, unable to believe she could go through this much suffering only to die from fever.

"If it does, I'll drain it. Quinine should help the fever."

Thaddeus nodded. He knew quinine was used mostly for malaria, but during the war he'd seen doctors use it, when it was available, to combat fever of any kind.

"She'll make it," Thaddeus said forcefully, the look in his eyes promising untold misery to any who dared dispute his statement. His voice held such fierce determination that neither the doctor nor his assistant felt it prudent to mention the distinct possibility that a dozen things might go wrong.

"When can she be moved?"

"Where?"

"I live twenty miles outside of town."

Doc Winslow shook his head. "Not for at least a week." He watched the man, unconcerned by the evil looks being directed his way. "If you cart her over rough countryside, she might start bleeding again."

Thaddeus swallowed, his skin growing a sickly gray as he imagined her bleeding like that again. He wouldn't know what to do. She'd die for sure. He couldn't chance it, no matter how much he might want her home. "What about moving her to the boarding house?"

Doc Winslow nodded. "Tomorrow. If there's no bleeding during the night, you can move her then."

Thaddeus leaned against the wall. He felt light-headed. It was the shock of seeing her shot and then the horror of watching blood pumping from her chest, he rightly reasoned. The room began to sway. He never realized what was happening, having never fainted before.

"If you're going to faint, sit down," the doctor ordered, noticing correctly the distinctly pasty pallor beneath Thaddeus's tanned skin and the glazing over of his eyes.

Thaddeus had seen his share of blood, especially during the war between the states, but he'd never seen someone he loved bleed. And the sight of it was more than he could take. "I'm not going to faint," was the last thing Thaddeus remembered saying. A moment later, he crumbled to the floor with a loud crash.

"Damn! Why can't we ever get a small one?" James Honeycut remarked with disgust. "You know what it's like lifting someone his size?"

Doc Winslow chuckled. "No need. He'll come around in a minute. Just leave him there." Turning back to his patient, he secured a clean bandage over her wound and remarked, "We'll have to watch her carefully. If she starts bleeding again, call me."

Thaddeus awakened a few minutes later with a splitting headache. He groaned at the discomfort, only realizing he'd hit his head on the floor when his big hand found a lump just inside his hairline. Momentarily confused, he asked no one in particular, "What happened?"

"You fainted," came a soft slurred voice from the bed.

Thaddeus came quickly to his feet and staggered as a wave of dizziness assaulted. He looked down at his wife. She was awake! His heart pounded with joy, and the relief he knew was so great that he thought he might yet again fall at her feet. His knees buckled and he held onto the wall for support.

"I didn't think you'd be awake so soon."

"Dr. Winslow tells me he used just enough chloroform to keep me asleep while he took care of my shoulder." She grinned at his dazed expression, noticing his wobbly stance. "If you're going to fall again, don't do it on me."

"I won't," he replied meekly, overwhelmed with embarrassment that he should have shown himself so weak in her presence. His dark brown skin showed signs of a deep blush.

Sarah forced aside the laughter that threatened at his sheepish look. "Dr. Winslow says this happens all the time. It isn't easy to watch someone you love in danger."

Thaddeus could testify to that. "Where is he?"

"With his family."

"Sonofabitch! You mean he left you alone?" Thaddeus pushed aside his fear for her and allowed a blinding burst of anger at what he believed was the worst case of incompetence he'd ever known.

"No, he didn't leave her alone. I'm here," came a voice from across the room. Thaddeus looked toward the sound and watched as James Honeycut mixed something in a glass. "If you want to stay, you'll have to be quiet. Your wife needs rest."

Thaddeus sat on the cot closest to hers. His elbows rested on his knees, his hands held his head as he tried to steady his heartbeat and clear away the weakness that refused to abate. "How do you feel?"

"Not so bad. Sore, of course." Sarah was glad he didn't mention the shooting. She couldn't think about it. A man had lost his life and it was her fault. She didn't want to remember the horror.

"You'll feel worse later," the assistant said as he put the glass with the concoction he'd been mixing to her mouth. "Drink this. It will help you sleep."

Sarah did as she was told, then smiled at her husband. "Will you stay with me?"

He reached for her hand, almost crushing it in his as he nodded. "I'll stay." Nothing could have taken him from her side. He'd never in his life known such fear, such terror, as when he'd found her shot. The sight of blood oozing from beneath her shoulder and staining her pink dress was more than he could bear.

He never remembered snatching her from the man into whose arms she had fallen. His first conscious recollection was finding her clutched tightly against him as he raced toward the doctor's office.

Thaddeus watched her throughout the night, dozing only now and then. His eyes were bloodshot from lack of sleep by the time the sun began its slow journey over the peak of a distant mountain and brought the birds outside the window awake.

A rooster crowed in the distance. Horses, tied to the hitching post outside, whinnied. A man, obviously drunk, was singing in the alley behind the doctor's office. His voice grew faint as he moved along. Another day was beginning, a day like a thousand others and yet as different as it was ever likely to be.

He breathed a deep, heavy sigh of relief. She'd made it through the night. There was no sign of bleeding. Sleeping soundly, she'd awakened only when made to take an occasional dose of medicine. Thaddeus had watched her breathe for hours, had watched her until the soft, even rhythm had teased him into joining her. But he wouldn't give in to the need, denying himself the luxury of more than a few seconds of rest at a time. He didn't dare sleep. If he stopped watching, stopped listening . . . Thaddeus refused to allow the words, not even in his mind. Everything would be all right. The doctor had said she was strong. She'd make it, all right. He was going to see to that.

"You look exhausted," Sarah said some hours later, as she reclined upon the fluffed pillows, back in their room at last. She had just awakened from a short afternoon nap. "Did you get any sleep last night?"

"The cot wasn't comfortable," he said, avoiding telling her that he'd sat up all night watching her.

"Did you bother to lie on it to find out?"

Again he didn't answer. "Would you like something?"

"An answer would suit me fine."

"An answer to what?"

Sarah grinned, knowing he wasn't about to admit to purposely staying awake all night. And he had. She'd seen him watching her the few times she'd awakened. Watching her like he expected her to disappear at any minute. Sarah slowly shook her head. "Nothing would have happened if you slept."

Thaddeus didn't verbally respond, but his dark, determined expression told clearly his thoughts on the matter.

"Come over here and kiss me."

Thaddeus sat on the very edge of the bed near her hip. She had never looked so slender, so delicate, so terribly pale. He was terrified to touch her.

"Come closer."

"I don't want to hurt you."

313

Sarah shot him a disgruntled look. "Thaddeus, I'm not going to fade into a cloud of mist if you touch me. And you needn't hover over me like I'm on my death bed." Her eyes grew suddenly wary, tinged with fear. "I'm not, am I?"

"What?"

"Would you stop acting like I'm at death's door? You're giving me the willies."

"You've been shot. How do you expect me to act?"

"I don't expect you to act like a dolt."

"Well, your mouth sure as hell hasn't taken any injury. It works just fine."

Sarah grinned. "If you kissed me, I could show you how fine."

"Don't be smart. You're in no condition for that kind of thing."

"What kind of thing?" she teased, her eyes just a little too shiny for his liking.

Thaddeus placed his hand on her forehead and cursed. His whole body stiffened with fear. Her skin was warm and dry. A hell of a lot warmer than he would have liked. "You're hot!"

"My gown is too heavy." She grinned wickedly. "Why don't you help me take it off?"

"Sarah, damn it, behave yourself," he muttered as he opened the buttons of her gown and peeked beneath the lightly secured bandage. The wound looked all right. Still, he couldn't be sure it wasn't beginning to fester. She shouldn't be feverish. The fact that she was had to mean something was wrong. "I'm going to call the doctor."

"No. Don't. I'll be fine. Just hold me for a little bit."

Thaddeus reluctantly gave in to her plea and moved to the top of the bed. Terrified of hurting her, he allowed her to snuggle against his half-reclining body. Careful, making sure not to touch anywhere near her wound, he kept his arms around her waist. Sarah sighed a soft sound of contentment. "This is better," she said as she nuzzled her cheek against his chest and breathed in his scent. A few moments later, she'd fallen asleep again.

Something was wrong, only he couldn't think for a moment what it could be. Slowly, he pulled himself from the depths of sleep at her low moan. She was moving restlessly against him. He grunted at a sudden kick, then her arms and legs were swinging wildly, kicking the covers off them both.

Held securely against him, she quieted for a moment; her eyes moved quickly behind their closed lids.

It was dark. So dark she couldn't see him, but she knew he was there. She could feel his presence, hear his breathing. He was close. Terribly close. She tried to run but her feet wouldn't move. Why couldn't she get them to move?

God, she was so scared. She could hear the pounding of her heart. Could he?

He pulled the gun from its holster. Moonlight glittered off the dark metal. Its barrel grew before her eyes. Longer, longer, it continued to grow until she wondered how one hand could hold it? Her eyes followed its pointed direction.

Thaddeus stood there bathed in light. Hide! She tried to tell him to hide, but the words wouldn't leave her mouth. She tried again. She heard the suppressed sound, but no matter her efforts, the words wouldn't come.

Annie laughed. She walked toward Thaddeus. Slowly, his arms moved around her and they kissed. No! Sarah's throat ached as she tried to scream. But no matter how she tried, all she could do was moan.

Annie moved out of his arms and laughed again. Something made her look toward the gun. Sarah screamed. The hammer was pulled back. It was going to fire! Get out of the way! She heard the explosive sound and watched the bullet leave the gun. She watched it move through the air and screamed again. Why didn't he move? Couldn't he see it coming? But he couldn't see it coming. He was watching Annie. Fool! Don't look at her! And then Thaddeus's face darkened with pain as he clutched his chest.

"Nooo!" came a wild scream of horror. "Don't! Don't kill him!"

"Sarah," he said as he forced her arms down lest she rip the wound open with her movement. Holding her tightly against his chest, he soothed, "Sarah, honey, listen to me. You're dreaming. Wake up."

She moaned. Still caught in the dream, Sarah struggled all the more.

Thaddeus reached a hand to her forehead. His whole body stiffened. Jesus! She was burning up!

316

"You kissed her," she mumbled. "I hate you." And then her thoughts went on to new directions. "Cold," she groaned, the word hardly distinguishable between her low moans. She shivered as though to emphasize her words. "I'm so cold."

Her eyes blinked open. She grew completely still and appeared quite lucid. "Thaddeus, could you please find us another blanket?" she asked, as if she weren't suffering more than a slight chill. A second later, her eyes closed and she groaned again.

Thaddeus felt a moment's terror as chills raced down his spine. How could she slip so easily in and out of rationality? One second she was a wildly thrusting being, striking out against him, fighting off his calming caresses, mumbling broken, unfinished phrases. The next she became still and spoke so clearly, appeared so normal, as if she weren't burning up with fever.

He moved from her side and spread the quilt over her. She curled herself into a tight, shivering ball. He could see the movement even beneath the two heavy blankets. He had to get help. That damn doctor should have given her something so this wouldn't have happened. Why hadn't he made sure of it?

Thaddeus called all manner of curses upon the man's head even as he quickly moved through the night toward his office. He pounded on the door like a person gone wild, not at all concerned about those sleeping within. He had to get help and it had to be now!

"She's burning with fever and talking crazy," were the first words he spoke to a befuddled, sleepy doc-

317

tor. "You've got to come," he said, his desperation clear in his voice.

Doc Winslow nodded in agreement, reached for his bag, and followed Thaddeus back to the boarding house without even taking the time to change into street clothes. Even if he'd thought on it, he somehow knew this man wouldn't have allowed him the time.

In sleeping gown, robe, and slippers, he followed Thaddeus into the room. A moment later he grunted his disapproval at finding Sarah twisted in her covers, her skin flushed, her arms and legs striking out in her delirium.

"Keep her still," he said as he reached into his bag and pulled out an array of medicines and a syringe. Sarah quieted a few minutes after swallowing a mixture of laudanum and water. Doc Winslow then administered the quinine.

The skin around her wound had grown tight, puffy, and red. The doctor shook his head, then punctured the skin with a knife, allowing the wound to drain. He spread some horrible-smelling concoction on a bandage and placed it against the oozing stitches.

Sarah cried out at the pain and reached for the injury, only to find her hands held firmly to her sides.

She glared at Thaddeus. As sick as she was, she knew him to be the culprit here. On her next breath, she snapped, "Let go of me, you sonofabitch!"

Thaddeus was too scared for his wife's well-being to even notice the inappropriate language. He wouldn't realize until later that he'd never heard her curse before.

But Doc Winslow had heard just about everything there was to hear in his many years of practice. He never blinked an eye. "She'll need this changed and the wound cleaned." He handed Thaddeus the jar of the foul-smelling cream and showed him how to apply it. "Cool rags will help keep the fever down. She'll fight you. Can you do it?"

"I can do it," Thaddeus returned, while wondering if he truly could.

The doctor was packing up his things when he remarked, "I'll be back in a couple of hours. Keep her as quiet as you can. And get her out of that flannel gown. If she complains of the cold, use another blanket."

Thaddeus worked for hours changing cool, wet rags and laying them over burning skin. An hour before dawn, her fever broke. Thaddeus's relief didn't last more than fifteen minutes, though, before the fever returned.

It went on that way for the next day and night. Sarah was often quite lucid, but just as often not. Many were the times when she cried out her fear. Thaddeus knew her horror of violent death. He imagined that witnessing what she had was haunting her dreams.

Doc Winslow came periodically. Thaddeus bombarded him with questions whenever he showed his face. It was the same every time. "How much longer will she be like this?"

"The quinine should help."

"What if it doesn't?"

"Don't see no reason why it won't."

"When is it going to start working?"

"It's working now. She'd be worse without it."

But Thaddeus could hardly believe that. He'd never seen anyone so lost in the throes of fever. She was half out of her mind with it. The only ones he'd seen this bad were the men injured during the war and they, down to the very last, had died.

But Sarah wasn't going to die. Not if he had anything to say about it.

For the first time in his life, Thaddeus wished he believed in God. He wished there was a being watching over them. Someone he could turn to and ask for help in this moment of desperation, for he wasn't ever likely to need help more than now.

Sarah had asked him once, "What have you got to lose by believing?" and Thaddeus knew she was right. Did it matter if he believed? If there really was a God, as she professed, wouldn't he hear a plea no matter who spoke it? He wasn't asking anything for himself. She was the one who believed. She was the one who should be allowed to live.

Thaddeus cleared his voice, feeling very much the fool, but he spoke anyway. "If you're there," he said softly, almost to himself, "if you really exist, please help her." His eyes filled with tears. The medicine wasn't working. As far as he could see, despite the doctor's assurances, she was only getting worse.

He waited a long time, watching her as she grew steadily restless and more ill. He was half afraid to touch her, knowing her skin would feel like fire beneath his hand. "Please," he begged the Almighty. "Please don't let her die."

He watched her for hours. Again and again, he changed the cool, wet cloth that covered her entire body. She cried out and fought him at every changing, but he insisted and she finally quieted. His body grew stiff sitting in the chair beside the bed. His eyes burned and still he watched her. Was it his imagination? Was she resting more easily? Was her skin a bit less flushed and slightly cooler? He couldn't tell anymore. He'd watched her for so long that he couldn't trust his own judgment.

It was the morning of the third day. Thaddeus had spent an exhausting night, the worst yet. During the night, she'd complained of the cold and refused to lie still. He'd come as close as he was ever likely to get to crushing despair. How much longer could this go on? At last she seemed to be resting a bit more comfortably. His head was slumped against his chest as he sat beside the bed, when he heard a soft voice. "Are you the one who's been drowning me in ice water? When I get out of here, you're going to suffer for that."

Instantly wide awake, Thaddeus grinned down into blue eyes that although still fevered were a lot less glassy. His hand reached for her forehead and he breathed a sigh of relief to find her skin only slightly warm. "How do you feel?"

"Like I've been trampled by a herd of horses."

Thaddeus's smile grew into a chuckle at her nasty tone. "Are you mad at me?"

"Let's say, I could be happier." Her glare was as

unfriendly as it was ever likely to be. "I'm thirsty."

Maybe Sarah could have been happier, but Thaddeus couldn't. He thought his heart just might break with the happiness that filled him to overflowing. She was going to be all right. She might not be completely well for some time, but eventually she would be. Thaddeus couldn't stop smiling.

Something happened then. A peacefulness and a deep sense of security and trust suddenly filled his being, and he knew. It wasn't quinine that had saved her, it was God. No matter his previous denials, he knew The Almighty existed. He couldn't believe otherwise. The proof of it lay in this bed.

The sight of his grin didn't raise Sarah's spirits any. She couldn't remember why she was aggravated, but she was. A scowl twisted her lips. "What are you grinning about?" And then she remembered. But did she? Was it a dream? Had Thaddeus really been kissing Annie? Sarah knew she had to think. She could be angry for nothing. She wasn't sure.

"Me? Was I grinning?" He held the glass of water to her lips. "Just a little now. Easy."

Sarah took a mouthful, swallowed, and cried out in pain. Her throat felt as if it were filled with shards of glass. "My throat," Sarah whispered, her hand coming to press against the pain.

"Is it sore?"

She shot him a look of annoyance. Of course, it was sore. What kind of a question was that? Did he think she always cried out when she drank water? "Were you feeding me glass while I was sick?"

Thaddeus laughed. "If I thought it would make

you better, I would have fed you cactus spines."

Sarah murmured a low sound, unable to find the strength to answer him right now. God, but she was tired. She'd never known such utter exhaustion.

That afternoon Thaddeus sent word to the ranch saying they wouldn't be back before a week. He figured it would take at least that long before she could travel.

And when Doc Winslow made his next visit, Thaddeus felt his first sense of relief in three days.

"Who's sick here, me or you. Get up!" Sarah grumbled as she shoved him. Lord, but the man slept like the dead.

"What?" Thaddeus asked as he lifted his head from the pillow.

"I need water."

Thaddeus turned to face her and reached a hand to her forehead. He smiled at the cool touch of her skin. "Your fever is gone."

"I'm thirsty."

Thaddeus grinned. "I love you."

"Is that why you were kissing Annie?" she blurted out.

"What?"

Sarah stared at his confusion for a long moment before she realized she was talking about a dream. The amazing thing was she'd had the same dream over and over again. Even now, knowing it hadn't really happened, she couldn't completely shake her anger. "I was dreaming you were kissing Annie."

Thaddeus laughed. "Were you? Is that why you were so ticked off?"

"I don't know. I think I was just feeling so bad."

"I know, darlin'," Thaddeus said as he hugged her gently against him. "How are you feelin' now?"

"Weak and sore. But most of all, thirsty."

"I'm leaving in the morning," Jake said as he stared into a glass of whiskey. The golden color reminded him of her hair. She was the most beautiful thing he'd seen in a long, long time. He licked his lips, anxious to begin their friendship. His imagination came up with a dozen ways the beauty could bestow her thanks for his saving her life, each more deliciously erotic than the last. He couldn't wait to find out exactly how she'd go about it.

Annie smiled as she slipped out of her red dress. The first step of her plan was accomplished. Jake would be working at the ranch. All he had to do was keep his eyes open and they'd soon find the silver.

She poured herself a drink and took most of it in one swallow. Her petticoats followed her dress to the floor. Standing before him in only a corset and stockings, since she almost never wore drawers or a chemise, she grinned, unconcerned that she flaunted her nakedness. "She probably knows."

Jake forced his mind from his daydreams and frowned at being interrupted. "Who probably knows what?"

"Sarah. She must know where he keeps it. If you sweet-talk her some, you might find the silver a lot sooner than watching Payne."

"My thoughts exactly."

"You ain't goin' sweet on her, are ya?"

Jake wanted Sarah like he'd never wanted another woman in his life. Still, he realized the need to keep Annie happy. There was no telling what she might do if riled. She might ruin everything in a spurt of jealousy. Jake shot Annie a stern look. His eyes widened with surprise as he noticed for the first time her state of undress. "Be serious. Do you think someone like that could fit into my life-style?"

"Just remember that, honey. Especially when you're pumpin' into her."

Jake grinned. He tried not to let himself dwell on that all-too-enticing picture but was helpless to prevent his body from reacting. Luckily, Annie would imagine his response was due to her half-naked state. "You think that will happen, do you?"

"I haven't the slightest doubt. All you have to do is turn on the charm." Annie walked to the bed and sat on its edge. Her legs spread in invitation and she leaned back on one arm. "Of course, it couldn't hurt to get in a little practice."

Jake's smile was sinfully wicked as he placed his drink on a table and slowly began to remove his clothes. Annie was a whore. She didn't care who she spread her legs for. All she wanted out of life was personal gratification. But even more than that, she wanted money.

What made her so bad was she didn't care what she had to do to get it.

Jake looked down at the exposed, already-moist

pink flesh between her thighs and felt a surprising twinge of ill-timed revulsion. Odd. He wondered why Annie suddenly made him feel this measure of disgust. He'd known her and her kind for years and had never before questioned their morals. Why, now, did the sight of white, spreading thighs appear less than enticing? Why, instead, did the memory of blue eyes and a sweet smile inflame his senses?

Something was happening to him. Something he didn't understand. If he didn't know better, he might imagine himself in love. Jake almost laughed aloud at the thought. Imagine, Jake Blackman in love. Jesus, Annie would get a good laugh out of that.

Still, if he was honest—and despite everything he'd become over the years, Jake was that—he had to admit the woman had some hold over him. He didn't know as yet what it was, but he sure as hell was going to find out.

With a softly uttered groan, Jake reached for the woman before him. But it was Sarah he saw . . . Sarah, he touched.

"You want any more?"

"Thaddeus, I'd appreciate it if you wouldn't hover over me. You're beginning to get on my nerves."

"Am I?" he grinned as he sat at the side of the bed, took her tray, and placed it on a nearby chair. "I reckon there are things we could do to calm them some."

Sarah might have been over the worst of her illness, but she was far from feeling her normal self.

The fever had left her entire body sore, but that was nothing compared to the ache in her shoulder. Top off her discomfort with another of those damn dreams, and Sarah was far from her usual good humor. She thought her husband's teasing entirely inappropriate and sneered her resentment. "Is that all you can think about? God, I can't imagine a man more obsessed with — with —" Sarah helplessly allowed the sentence to falter.

"Loving you?" Thaddeus asked. He shrugged away her obvious objection. "You might say I'm obsessed with it. Especially since you came so damn close to dyin'."

Sarah bit at her lip, her eyes lowered to the sheet as she fidgeted with the material. "I'm not feeling myself," she said in lieu of an apology. "I didn't mean to bite your head off."

"I know, darlin'," Thaddeus breathed in a long sigh. "In a few days, we'll be on our way back home. You'll be feelin' better by then."

Sarah's eyes grew teary and sadder than ever. "I miss Emily."

Thaddeus nodded in understanding.

He was straightening up their room when he mentioned, "That fella that saved your life asked me for a job."

Sarah felt a moment's apprehension. "You didn't agree, did you?"

"Now, honey, I know how you feel about killin', but the man is down on his luck. He saved your life. What else could I do?"

"He didn't save my life. It was because of his interference that I was shot." Sarah's face twisted into a mask of disgust as she remembered. "The poor cowhand didn't have a chance. He shot him quicker than you'd swat a fly."

"The cowhand was roughin' you up. Everyone agrees."

"He was drunk. The problem could have been settled without guns."

Thaddeus imagined he understood her reasoning. She was the most peace-loving woman he'd ever known. It was natural that she'd feel a sense of unease at having Jake come to the ranch. But she'd get over it, he was sure. "Maybe, but that's not how Jake saw it."

Sarah felt an almost horrifying sense of foreboding. Something terrible was going to happen if that man came to work for them. She just knew it.

"Thaddeus . . ." Sarah refused to meet his gaze, feeling a bit foolish as she forced herself to speak her worst fears. "I've had the same dream three times. That man Jake has a gun pointed at you, while you're kissing Annie."

Thaddeus laughed. "Someone would have to hold a gun on me to get me to kiss that woman."

"It's not funny!" she snapped. It took a moment before she could force herself to go on, so real was the fear. "After kissing you, Annie laughs and walks away, and then Jake shoots the gun. I try to warn you but I can't get the words out." She gave a soft groan as she remembered clearly the horror. "It's just like I'm trying to warn you now and you won't listen."

Thaddeus's gaze narrowed with suspicion and he felt just a bit unnerved as he read the fear she couldn't begin to hide. "Are you tellin' me you have some kind a special powers?"

"Of course not." She looked at him then, her gaze filled with pleading. "But the dream must mean something. Why else would I have it over and over again?"

Thaddeus shrugged for an answer and then sighed. "Be reasonable, Sarah. I can't tell the man he's fired 'cause my wife had a dream."

"Tell him you don't need any more hands."

"I've already told him he's welcome."

Sarah's lips tightened and she shot him a nasty look, obviously ready to argue further but never getting the chance when Thaddeus reiterated, "I've already told him, Sarah." He shook his head. "I can't go back on my word."

Annoyed that he wouldn't take her seriously, she turned her back to him. Still terribly weak from the fever she'd suffered, she soon drifted off to sleep, only to have that horrifying dream once again.

Chapter Sixteen

The trip had sapped nearly all her strength. Thaddeus had driven the wagon as slowly and carefully as possible, but the road was littered with holes and rocks. Sarah hadn't realized just how rough the ride was likely to be, until she suffered the bone-jarring thuds the springless wagon imposed.

She was home at last. A planned short three days had turned into a long two weeks. She felt tired but wonderful, even if she had a ways to go before her strength returned.

More than once she'd suggested that they send for the baby. Lord, but she'd missed her so. But it was impossible. She'd been too weak to care for Emily and Thaddeus had his hands full caring for her. Sarah felt a large measure of guilt knowing her daughter must be suffering, unable to understand why her mother was gone.

Held in Thaddeus's arms, the toddler glared her resentment upon spying her mother at last. She wasn't about to make this reunion easy. Clearly, she was angry at being left behind.

"Want to give Mommy a kiss?" Thaddeus inquired, watching the child's pouting mouth and downcast eyes.

Emily purposely turned her head away and buried her face in his neck. Amazingly, her anger didn't extend to Thaddeus. When he'd brought her from Lottie's cabin, she'd soon forgotten his desertion and settled herself comfortably in his arms.

Thaddeus watched with a helpless expression as Sarah's delighted smile grew sad. He didn't know what to do. "Lottie said she cried for you every night."

"I imagine she's a bit upset. I don't blame her. I guess I'd be angry if I thought my mother had forgotten about me."

Emily turned to look at her mother, her arms tight around Thaddeus's neck. Obviously, she didn't know what to make of Sarah's attitude. She watched her mother carefully, waiting for her next move.

"Why don't you put her down on the bed," Sarah offered. "She'll be fine in a minute."

Thaddeus did as she asked. He was soon puttering around the kitchen, putting up a pot of coffee and slicing into a cake Kate Spencer had delivered to them upon their arrival, as Sarah wondered how to go about breaking through Emily's anger.

Sarah smiled as her daughter put her thumb into her mouth, clutched at the ragged blanket she slept with every night, turned her head, and purposely ignored her mother. Even at nine months, the child had already developed a strong stubborn streak. But

331

Sarah imagined she knew how to coax her daughter back into her usual good humor.

"Emily," she called out in a gentle singsong voice. "Did anyone see my Emily? Did you, Thaddeus?" she asked, never taking her gaze from the tiny child who sat, her back ramrod straight, on the bed.

"Can't say as I have," he answered, while gentle laughter danced in his dark eyes.

"I wonder where she's gone off to. I'd surely hate to lose her. I love her very much."

"I know you do. But I reckon she's a might upset."

"With me?"

Thaddeus nodded.

"Because I was away so long?"

He nodded again.

They were talking around the child, but Emily was listening to every word. Sarah wondered just how much she understood.

"Doesn't she know I didn't want to be away?"

Thaddeus shrugged.

"Well, if she's unhappy here, I certainly can't make her stay. Do you think we might find another little girl? I surely love little girls."

Emily's pouting lips began to quiver.

"Of course, I love my Emily most of all. Too bad I can't find her."

By now tears were streaming over the child's chubby cheeks and Sarah thought her heart just might break. She sat up and with one hand reached for her daughter. A soft smile curved her lips. "Emily, come to Mommy."

With a short hiccupping sound, Emily crawled up her mother's legs and body, never stopping until she laid her little head upon Sarah's breast. Sarah gazed down at her daughter and smiled as her fingers threaded through silky brown curls. "I love you, darling. I'm sorry I was gone so long." Silently, she promised she wouldn't be leaving this baby anytime soon.

"Every time I see him, I remember the man he killed." Sarah's voice was low, filled with dread. "I can't feel relaxed around him."

"I wouldn't want to tell you what he makes me feel," Kate Spencer remarked as she eyed the man in question. Jake slid his foot into a stirrup and mounted his horse in one graceful movement.

"Kate!" Sarah whispered in shock.

"I never said I'd do anything about it, did I?" the young woman returned defensively, as laughter filled her eyes. "But I got eyes, don't I?" She petted the baby that lay sleeping on his stomach over her lap.

"What about Will?"

"Oh, I love Will, but that don't mean I went blind the day I married him."

Sarah laughed and then said softly in agreement, "He is a fine-looking man."

Kate's grin was downright wicked. "Honey, he's

better than fine. I can't rightly say I've ever seen a more handsome man."

Jake moved his horse past the two women and gave them both his most enticing smile. His eyes held to Sarah's a long moment before he tipped his hat and murmured, "Ladies." A moment later, he moved on.

Sarah couldn't control the shiver of revulsion. She didn't understand why, but this tall, exceedingly handsome man terrified her.

She sighed with dismay, for she hadn't a doubt, by the look they'd exchanged, that the man had heard most, if not all, of their conversation. She was mortified. Her cheeks blazed painfully.

"No need to get yourself in a fuss," Kate remarked. "I'm sure the man knows he's a looker."

"Oh, God," Sarah groaned.

"He's a gentleman, Sarah. I think, judging by the way he looks at you, that he finds you attractive, but he's not about to do anything about it. You should feel flattered."

Sarah shook her head. "I don't, and you don't know that for sure."

"He knows you love your husband."

"Suppose he doesn't care?" For some reason, Sarah knew that to be the case. Why she would think that, she had no idea. He hadn't once done anything . . . at least not anything she could put a name to.

"He's been here a couple of weeks. Has he ever once treated you with anything but respect?"

334

Sarah sighed and shook her head again. He had treated her respectfully, but the looks he often shot her way were anything but. Was it her imagination? Could it be all in her head? Sarah knew it wouldn't be fair to tell Thaddeus of her suspicions. Suppose she was wrong and the man lost his job because of it?

Sarah kept her distance, practically hanging on to her husband or whoever else was close by, whenever the man showed himself. Somehow she knew it dangerous if he should find her alone. She silently prayed that he'd soon tire of the backbreaking work and meager pay and be on his way.

Sarah followed Thaddeus up the mountain's gentle slope and deep into a thick copse of trees. The underbrush would have been impossible to get through had they not been on horseback. The small glen they entered was entirely surrounded by huge trees. Thick branches came together above their heads, forming a ceiling of sorts, blocking out most of the sun's rays. It was quiet, damp, and cool. It was the most private place Sarah had ever seen, perfect for what they had in mind.

Thaddeus tied his horse to a low hanging branch and turned to help Sarah from the saddle. By the time he had spread a blanket upon a large, flat rock and unsaddled both horses, Sarah had emptied their picnic basket. From his saddlebags, Thaddeus took a bottle of wine and two glasses.

Sarah's eyes widened. "Where did you get them?" she asked, her gaze on the delicately stemmed glass.

"I picked them up the last time I was in town." He shrugged as if they were hardly important, when in fact they were. He'd been waiting for weeks to get her out here and had imagined a thousand times how they would sip from these very glasses. "Thought they'd come in handy sooner or later."

Sarah knew, even though Thaddeus appeared not to want to admit it, that he was trying to set a romantic scene for them. Her love and appreciation for this man shone like fire in her eyes. For a long moment, neither spoke but simply enjoyed looking at one another.

Finally, she smiled and placed the dish of cold fried chicken between them. To the chicken she added biscuits and a chunk of sweet cheese, while Thaddeus poured the wine.

"I baked a blueberry pie for dessert."

"That was very nice of you, but I have something a lot sweeter in mind for dessert."

Sarah didn't miss the wicked look in his eyes. She laughed merrily.

"Take off your clothes."

"Now?" she asked with some surprise, never bothering to deny the real purpose behind this picnic. "We didn't finish eating yet."

Thaddeus shrugged as he pulled off his boots. "No sense waiting till later. Besides, it's a known fact that food tastes better if you eat it naked."

Sarah successfully squashed the need to laugh, although not without some effort. "Can't say as if I've ever heard that before."

"Haven't you?" Thaddeus grinned, his eyes widening with supposed amazement. "I'm surprised. I thought everyone knew that."

"Are you sure?" she asked doubtfully.

Thaddeus's expression turned serious. "As sure as I've ever been in my life."

Under his watchful eye, Sarah did as he asked. A few minutes later found them naked, sitting facing one another, as they ate their picnic meal.

It wasn't easy to eat. Now and then the chicken got stuck in her throat as she followed the direction of his gaze. Lord, his eyes fairly blazed with the passion he held at bay. Sarah shivered with longing. He was dragging out their meal, knowing the longer they took the more eager they'd be to touch.

His eyes darkened with fire as she started to brush at a crumb that had dropped to her breast. "Don't," he whispered, through an obviously tight throat. "I'll take care of it." And to their mutual pleasure, he did. His tongue slid across her breast and disposed of the crumb. With a gentle flick of his tongue and a nip of his teeth over the darkening tip of her breast, he left her flushed and aching for more. Without a word spoken, he proceeded to attack the piece of chicken still in his hand.

"We probably should have waited till later to eat."

Thaddeus shook his head. "The waiting makes it better."

"I can't," she said, her face flaming at her

337

daring. "I want you to do that again."

Again he shook his head. "If l do, I won't be able to stop this time."

Sarah raised her gaze to his dark eyes and whispered, "I don't want you to stop."

Thaddeus cursed, knowing he had no willpower against this woman. Despite his best intentions, he couldn't wait a moment longer. He came to his knees and reached for her. Within seconds she was impaled upon his arousal, her legs wrapped tightly around his hips. His mouth, hard and hungry for hers, refused to release her lips even to breathe. She didn't care. She didn't want to breathe. She didn't need anything but to be in his arms.

Thaddeus held her against him, her soft flesh in the palms of his hands as he drove wildly into her. He'd waited too long. He'd wanted her too long.

He felt her grip his shoulders, her head falling back, her mouth open as she gasped for air, her eyes closed with the ecstasy that wracked her body. He felt her tighten around his engorged flesh and groaned as he allowed himself the pleasure of release at last.

They were gasping for their every breath. Thaddeus groaned into the dampness of her neck, "Witch! I wanted the first time to be slow. I wanted to pleasure you for hours, but you drive me wild."

"I'm glad," she said, breathing heavily against his thick hair.

"Can we eat now?" he asked some moments later, his face still buried against her throat.

"What would you like to eat?" Sarah teased in a throaty whisper, uncaring that her cheeks heated with color. She was usually too embarrassed to join him in these wicked conversations, even though she knew he loved to listen to her talk like this. She bit at the inside of her mouth as she listened to his groan.

Thaddeus raised his head and shot her a stern look. "Control yourself, Sarah."

Sarah burst into laughter at his pained expression. "Poor baby," she soothed as she petted his hair and cheeks, then dropped a light kiss on his nose.

Sarah sighed as she finished the last bite. "I don't know what it is, but this meal was really good."

"I told you," Thaddeus arrogantly returned.

She shook her head. "I think it was the fact that we ate outside."

"Nope, it was eating naked."

"Well, I have to admit that cleaning up your crumbs gave the chicken a special flavor."

Thaddeus nodded. "And you did a good job of it."

"Amazing," she shook her head, "but I don't remember you dropping so many before."

Thaddeus said nothing but simply grinned.

"Does your theory extend to drinking as well? This wine is delicious."

Thaddeus smiled, put the remnants of their meal into the basket, and moved closer to

339

her half-reclining form. "You're delicious."

His mouth touched gently against hers, his beard and mustache teasing her flesh and bringing a groan of renewed anticipation from deep in her throat. "You like that, do you?"

"Mmmm," she sighed with delight as he brushed his facial hair over her skin. "I like it very much."

"Let's try this, then," he said as he slid down the length of her.

"I . . . I don't . . . think you should," she said between short gasps.

"Why?" he asked, his dark gaze taking in the glazed look in her eyes.

"Because, before wasn't enough. It's been forever since we . . . I don't want to wait any longer." Her heart was pounding in her throat, cutting off her ability to breathe. "I don't think I can."

Thaddeus chuckled. "Yes, you can. We both can."

Sarah moaned as his mouth held to hers. His tongue delved deep into her mysterious warmth, taking from her all he could. She was dazed by the time he released her lips and shivered as his beard feathered over her skin. He was driving her insane. It had been weeks since the accident . . . weeks since she'd enjoyed his loving.

Sitting before him naked had stirred her more than she could have imagined. His dark gaze upon her body had left her shivering with the need for his touch. She'd never be able to survive this torment. She wanted him and she wanted him now.

He was sliding down the length of her when she

gasped, "Later," then pushed him to his back. "Do that later. I can't wait any longer."

Sarah straddled his hips and leaned down to take what she would of his mouth. Her tongue found no obstacle to prevent its penetration into his heat, while she slid his hardened sex deep into the burning depths of her body.

Their mutual groans of delight mingled as their mouths fused together. Sarah used him for her pleasure and Thaddeus was never happier that she did. She moaned and clenched her teeth. Arching her neck, she dragged air through her parted lips, the hissing sound only seeming to add to their immeasurable pleasure. Again her mouth joined to his and she ate hungrily of his taste, delighted in his texture, breathed deeply of his scent. She couldn't get enough. She'd never get enough.

"I love you," she murmured, the words almost lost in his mouth, even as she slowly raised and lowered herself upon his shaft. It was too good. Nothing could be this good. "I love this," she moaned, her eyes closing against almost intolerable pleasure.

"What?" he managed, although he couldn't imagine how. She was driving him mad and he could hardly utter a coherent sound with the need she'd aroused.

"This," she said as she pressed her hips hard against his. Her mouth created a trail of fire over his chest as her tongue licked his distended nipples. "The things you do to me. The things you make me feel."

"Show me," he gasped. Her hot breath brushed against him. He thought he might go mad with the need she instilled. "Show me the things you like."

Sarah pulled back and smiled. "You're not allowed to move," she said as she swung herself away from him. "Promise?"

"Do I have to?"

Sarah laughed at his almost childish whine. "If you want me to show you, you must."

"I promise," he said dutifully. Moments later, he cursed his thoughtless pledge, for he had cause to wonder if it were possible to live through this torment.

Her mouth was everywhere. She was killing him with the fire of her tongue, the nipping of small teeth, the softness of full lips. He couldn't stop the groans of pleasure nor the rising of his hips, as the searing heat neared his sex. He couldn't breathe. He needed her mouth on him like he'd never needed anything in his life.

"Sarah, my God," he moaned, his body stiffening as if in shock as she sucked him deep into liquid fire.

He had to force down the sudden lump he felt in his throat. His eyes grew suspiciously damp. No woman had ever loved him like she did. No woman had ever been so unselfish. There were no words. Words would have been insignificant. They couldn't begin to tell the depth of his feelings. His love. His happiness. His thankfulness that she had come into his life.

342

"Enough," he whispered as he brought her face to his. He kissed her deeply, reveling in the warm, sweet taste of her. "Come to me, Sarah. Come to me now."

Sarah did as he asked. Again she straddled his hips. Their eyes locked as did their bodies, but they didn't touch anywhere else. It was a silent communication, and each knew it joined more than their bodies. It joined their souls forever.

They knew without saying that when the blinding, insane ecstasy came upon them, the world would fade into nothing. They knew there was nothing but these two lovers, forever.

Sarah sighed a heavy breath and collapsed upon him. Blissfully, she accepted the aftershocks of their loving. "It's getting better," she said against his hair-matted chest. "I didn't think it could get better, but it has."

Thaddeus chuckled. "That's because it's been so long."

"Why did you wait?"

"I wanted to make sure you were completely healed. I wanted you strong."

Sarah grinned and raised her head to glance at his satisfied expression. "Why? Why strong?"

"Because I didn't want you to just accept me. I wanted you to take what you wanted."

"Well, I did that."

Thaddeus laughed. "I reckon you could say you did."

Sarah rolled off his body and smiled as he reached

343

for his shirt. A moment later he had rolled the small piece of paper around the tobacco, licked its edge, and put a light to one end.

She was nestled against his side as she watched him take a drag on the cigarette. A thin stream of blue smoke was exhaled. "Why do you smoke?"

Thaddeus shrugged. "Habit, I guess."

"Do you like it?"

"Not as much as I like you."

Sarah smiled. "Let me try it."

Thaddeus shot her a look of surprise and then, saying nothing, handed her the cigarette.

After her fit of coughing eased, when she could finally breathe again, Sarah made a face that described well her disgust. "Yuck. That stuff is awful. How could you like it?"

Thaddeus grinned at her gasping. "I didn't at first."

"But you kept smoking anyway? Why?"

He shrugged. "I was a kid, trying to act like a man."

"It can't be good for you."

Thaddeus looked at the cigarette and remarked, "Probably not."

"So stop."

He put the cigarette out. "I've stopped."

Sarah grinned. "Just like that?"

"Well, I will have to find something else to do with my hands and mouth." He leered at her. "I think I'll probably miss sucking the most."

Sarah answered his wicked grin with one of her

own. "Oh, I could probably help you out there."

"I was hoping you could," he said as his mouth lowered to hers.

"It's beautiful here. I'm so glad you found this place," Sarah said, her hands cushioning her head against the flat rock as she took in the sight of the surrounding thick forest. The air smelled of pine and damp earth, of Thaddeus and Sarah and their moments together.

Thaddeus grinned as his wife lay naked and relaxed at his side. The thin blanket beneath them didn't go far toward supplying comfort, but they had been so anxious, so greedy for one another, that they'd hardly noticed at first. "The next time I'll gather up some pine needles before we lie down."

Sarah grinned. "I didn't mind."

"That's because you were on top."

Sarah giggled and glanced his way, her cheeks growing pink as she remembered her daring. The way she'd almost attacked the man was downright disgraceful, and she knew he wasn't going to let her actions go by without a comment. "Do you think it's all right for us to lie here like this? You don't imagine anyone will—"

"No one will see a thing. We'd hear anyone long before they come near." He turned on his side, and grinned as he ran his hand over her gently rounded belly. "It's a little late to be worryin' about our lack of privacy now, don't ya think?"

Sarah pursed her lips in a prim fashion and refused to look his way. "I've worried about it from the first."

"You didn't act like it."

"No?" A chuckle slipped out before she could stop it. "Well, here and there I might have had something else on my mind."

"You're a wanton, lady."

Her eyes widened with surprise. "Really, Thaddeus, *wanton* and *lady* are hardly synonymous. A woman can't be both."

"You can."

Sarah's laugh was low and decidedly wicked. "Do you think so?"

Thaddeus nodded, his eyes narrowing as he studied her reaction. "I wouldn't have thought the word *wanton* could make you so happy."

Sarah laughed at his amazed expression. "It's not the word, it's the fact that you liked it."

"How do you know I liked it?"

Sarah rolled to face him. She propped her head up on one arm. "Because you can't stop grinning."

Thaddeus moved the hand that had been rubbing over her belly and hips to her breast. Gently he cupped her, his finger playing with the dark tip. He breathed a long, deep sigh and closed his eyes with the pleasure of having her beside him. Not a year had passed since he'd come upon her in the snow. He might not have been happy, at the time, that this woman had been forced upon him. He'd thought then that he was satisfied, content with his solitary

346

life, but Thaddeus knew now he'd only been existing without her. He hadn't known what it was to really live until he'd found her. He moved closer, so his mouth was within inches of her soft flesh, knowing he couldn't remember ever being this happy.

Sarah leaned just a fraction closer and sighed with delight as he took her softness into blazing heat. "Thaddeus, I want to talk to you."

"Talk," he said, the word muffled as he continued with the pleasure.

"I can't, if you keep doing that. I can't think."

Thaddeus grinned and leaned away. Still, his hand never left the softness of her. Gently, he swung her breasts back and forth as she spoke.

"I want to bring Emily to visit with my parents. They're dying to see her."

"You got another letter?"

Sarah nodded. "Will brought it back from town yesterday." Sarah wasn't unaware of Thaddeus's unhappy expression. "Can't you leave the ranch for a bit? We won't be gone that long."

"The weather might not hold. August is almost over. We could get hit with a storm within the next month or so."

"We would be back by then."

Thaddeus shrugged and then shot her a questioning look. "You're sure you want me to go with you?"

Sarah laughed. "First of all, I couldn't get there alone. And why would I want to? I want everyone to meet my husband."

"You sure?" he asked doubtfully.

347

"Of course I'm sure. What's the matter with you?"

Thaddeus shrugged again. "I ain't never had a family. I wouldn't know how to act. I'll probably embarrass you."

"You're being ridiculous," she said, not believing for a moment that a man like Thaddeus might feel insecure when it came to meeting his in-laws. "Are you trying to find an excuse to get out of taking me? Is that it?"

Thaddeus grinned. "No. I'll take you, all right. Just don't say I didn't warn you."

"Why?" She eyed him suspiciously. "What are you planning on doing?"

"Nothin'." Thaddeus grinned as her eyes narrowed. "You surely are a suspicious lady."

"It seems to me you're giving me reason to be suspicious. What are you thinking?"

"I was thinking that I might forget there were people around and kiss you or touch you where I shouldn't."

Sarah laughed at the thought. "Where?"

"Here, maybe." Thaddeus ran his thumb over the hardening tip of her breast. "Or here," he said as his hands left the soft, enticing flesh and moved to the juncture of her thighs.

"Well," she gasped as two fingers slid into her slippery warmth. "That could probably prove to be embarrassing." She took another sharp breath as he dragged his fingers over her warmth and settled unerringly on the tiny hard, sensitive flesh. "But I imagine in eighty or ninety years, my family will get over it."

"Suppose they never get over it?" he asked as he raised himself higher above her.

Sarah groaned, laid on her back, and parted her legs to allow him easier access. He caressed the tiny nub of her passion with expert touchings as she sighed her pleasure, "Then that's too bad, isn't it?"

He shouldn't have come. It was insane. He'd known when he saw them leaving the ranch what they were about. Once he'd seen them together, he should have left. What madness kept him here? Why did he torment himself by watching?

In a wild moment of raw agony, he wondered why he didn't kill them both. But he knew he wouldn't. He'd never loved anyone before. He'd never known himself capable of suffering this kind of pain. And even though she'd caused it, he couldn't hurt her. He could never hurt her.

Jake could hardly breathe. He leaned heavily against a tree and never realized the tears that blurred his vision. Fool! Did you think she'd spurn him? he wondered. Everyone knew how she felt. She never hid the fact that she was in love with her husband.

Jake groaned. He hadn't known. He hadn't imagined her feelings ran so deep or that she'd show them quite so deliberately.

She was a lady. He hadn't ever imagined a lady could act so brazenly . . . could do the things she was doing. He'd thought only whores acted like that, but he'd only known whores. What else did he have to go by? He'd barely said more than a few words to her since he'd come, but Jesus God, he wanted her so desperately. He wondered how he could survive this kind of wanting.

A hard glitter of determination entered his eyes. He'd make her forget this man. He was going to have her. If it was the last thing he ever did in this life, he was going to have her.

Chapter Seventeen

"What the hell are you doing in town?" Annie snapped, then grinned hopefully. "Did you find it?"

Jake glared at the woman suddenly standing at his side. He turned his attention back to his drink and took a long swallow. "Not yet."

"You've been out there over a month. Don't tell me you haven't noticed anything."

"I've been breakin' my ass for over a month. What the hell do you think a cowhand does all day? You think I have nothing better to do than watch the boss?"

"I've been waiting too long for this, Jake. You better not be shitting me."

The corners of Jake's mouth turned down with disgust. His blue eyes grew hateful and glittered like shards of ice. His hand gripped the short glass until his knuckles grew white, so tightly, in fact, that it was a wonder it hadn't shattered into a million pieces. But his voice grew oddly calm. Perhaps too calm. "Or what? I don't much take to threats, Annie." The words were hissed through clenched teeth and were a threat in themselves.

Annie stamped down her flash of annoyance and willed aside the anxiousness that plagued her every waking minute. She was a smart woman, especially wise in the way of handling men. It was easy enough to see that this man needed sugar, not her sharp tongue. "I wasn't threatening you, darlin'," she said, her expression all sweetness and smiles. Her voice grew softer, more calming as she ran the palm of her hand up his back and down again to cup and squeeze his hard buttocks. "You look tired. Why don't you come upstairs? I'll give you a special treat."

Jake's first thought was to refuse her offer. Twice a month, he made the twenty-mile trip to town. Once there, he spent most of his time taking his frustrations out on Annie in bed. Not that she wasn't good. Annie knew her stuff, but damn it, it wasn't Annie he wanted.

Jesus, he was going crazy with this wanting. He couldn't think beyond a beautiful smile and gentle blue eyes. Seeing her cavorting with that bastard had nearly driven him insane. His lips curved into a self-deprecating smile. Perhaps it had. The sight of her naked had haunted him awake and asleep ever since. He couldn't look at her without remembering the smooth silkiness of white skin . . . of full, heavy breasts with dark nipples, of long, delicious legs, even while he cursed the fact that he hadn't been the one she rode.

Jake knew he was damn near out of control. As far as he could tell, there was no silver, probably never had been. He didn't care. All he knew for sure was that nothing and no one had ever possessed his every thought before. He hadn't imagined it possible that a woman could ever hold such power over him. He'd never known this degree of wanting. He'd give anything, do anything, to have her come willing into his arms. He'd pledged to himself that that day wasn't far off. He wouldn't be able to survive if he had to wait much longer.

She'd smiled at him today, and he'd almost reached for her and taken her off right then. Silently, he cursed the fact that he hadn't given in to the impulse. After she realized what he had to offer, she'd come to him again and again. He grew dizzy imagining the pleasure of that moment. They'd go away together. For her, he'd work, he'd slave. There was nothing he wouldn't give her. Jesus, loving her was tearing him apart. Damn his luck. Why couldn't he have met her first?

In the meantime, Annie was here, waiting for him to finish his drink. He might as well take what was offered. Until he had Sarah, nothing else mattered a damn, anyway.

Annie smiled as she watched him sleep. As a lover, he was getting better every time they came together. There was a desperate quality to his movements and kisses that hadn't been there before.

He wanted Sarah. Annie had been around long enough to know when she was being used in place of another. She didn't mind. It was to her benefit that another was appealing. Besides, if he was that crazy about her, Annie wouldn't have long to wait. Soon, now, things would come to a head.

Three guns were due to arrive by the end of the month. With those men backing Jake, the silver would soon be hers. Too bad Jake wasn't going to live long enough to spend his share. Annie needed it all; half wasn't near enough. Her mind wandered to dreams of owning the best and fanciest whorehouse in San Francisco. Yes, it was too bad about Jake, but a partnership was out of the question.

Sarah was terribly disappointed. She had so wanted to see her parents again . . . to show off her baby and her husband to her friends. Lord, but the women she knew back home would all flock to the mountains if they even suspected men like Thaddeus lived there. The planned trip had been only two days away when Emily had come down with a raging fever. It was out of the question that Sarah would take a baby so desperately ill on a journey as long and exhausting. No. Her visit would have to be put off. And because of the weather, she most likely wouldn't see her family until next spring.

Emily was better now, but she lacked her usual energy and spirit. Sarah watched her carefully. It would be a while, she imagined, before Emily was herself again. In the meantime, snow already coated the mountain's higher elevations. There was no telling when fall would turn suddenly into winter.

Thaddeus didn't dare leave now. Already, he and the men were busy with the herd, gathering them closer to the base of the mountain and making sure enough feed was brought out to their pastures, so they might survive the first snowfall. No, a trip right now was out of the question.

He should have worn his heaviest coat. Jesus, but it was cold. His hands inside heavy cowhide gloves were freezing and he had another six or more horses, if his count was right, to bring down.

He wouldn't be able to work much longer. The light was fading. Soon it would be too dark to see. He couldn't wait to sit himself before his warm stove and have Sarah fuss over him.

Thaddeus felt a prickling sensation run up his spine. Was someone out there? His gaze moved slowly over the tree-lined landscape as he tried to separate shadows. His instincts, till now, had always been good. Thaddeus smiled. Nothing. He was thinking crazy. His mind was playing tricks on him. Odd, but he wasn't as nearly at ease as he usually was when alone. No doubt it was the responsibility he felt toward Sarah and Emily. He knew they needed him. Nothing could happen to him lest they might suffer. A moment later he shrugged away the peculiar sensation.

He shouldn't have.

He heard the sound, far off in the distance, some seconds before he felt the jolt. He'd been shot before. Twice during the war he'd taken a bullet. He knew the sensations, the burning, the pain. He knew why his left hand had gone suddenly numb.

With his good hand on his gun, Thaddeus toppled from his horse. He lay there for endless moments, waiting for his attacker to come to finish him off. He waited until it was dark. Either the bushwhacker had figured his one shot had done the trick, or he was too scared to come closer. Either way, Thaddeus knew he was long gone.

His arm hung uselessly at his side, his hand numb as he struggled to mount his horse. Despite the cold night, he was sweating with the effort it took. He had to get back. Lying still had eased the flow of blood, but it was running down his arm now, puddling inside his glove.

He should have waited, but he couldn't. Not any more. He didn't give a damn about the silver or the gunslingers that were due to arrive in a few weeks. As far as he was concerned, Annie and the rest could go to hell. He couldn't wait another minute to feel her against him, to breathe her scent, to sample her taste. Now. He had to have her now.

Sarah was alone with Emily when she heard the

sound of a racing horse stop abruptly outside her cabin. A second later footsteps were heard racing toward her porch, then someone was pounding at her door.

"What?" Sarah asked as she wrenched the door open. Jake was standing there, hat in hand, his eyes wild with anxiety. She'd never seen him anything but calm. Something terrible must have happened. "What's the matter?"

"He's hurt. He's asking for you."

"Oh, God," she moaned, as her hand came to calm a pounding heart. Jake didn't need to tell her who. No one but Thaddeus would be asking for her. "Oh, God," she whispered again as she felt her legs give out.

In an instant Jake was there, holding her tightly against him. He'd sampled this little glimpse of heaven the night he'd shot the cowboy, but he couldn't know that holding her, really holding her, could feel this good. He'd never imagined anything could be like this. He closed his eyes against a sensation that rivaled pain, unable to believe he had her in his arms at last. He forced aside his groan, lest she realize just how much he loved holding her in his arms. She couldn't know. Not yet.

Jake forced his mind away from her delicious softness. "Calm down," he said, knowing it was too late. His heart ached that she should feel this pain, but he couldn't undo what had been done. "Get a coat and one of the women to watch the baby. I'll saddle you a horse and get Will to bring a wagon."

"How bad is he hurt?" Lottie asked as she came quickly from her house to watch over the sleeping child.

"I don't know." Sarah was obviously wild with fear for her husband. So wild, in fact, that she'd never thought to ask. "Will's getting a wagon." She shook her head. "I can't wait. I'll be back as soon as I can."

"Is anyone with him?" she asked as she rode her horse alongside Jake's.

"No. I had to leave him to get help," he said, and Sarah knew the first inkling of suspicion. Why hadn't she seen Will? Where was the wagon he was supposed to be bringing?

"Is it bad?" she asked for at least the tenth time, only to receive no answer again. Sarah brought her horse to a stop. Something was wrong. If Thaddeus had been hurt, why couldn't she get Jake to tell her how badly or where he was?

"What's going on? You said you'd tell Will to bring the wagon." Sarah couldn't remember anyone running toward the barn. No horses were brought from the corral. "But you didn't, did you?"

Jake realized his mistake. This woman was too smart to fool for long. The only reason she'd come with him was because she thought her husband was hurt. Damn, he should have told Will to fetch the wagon. He could have told him Thaddeus had been hurt. It didn't matter if they found his body tonight.

Jake didn't bother to answer her questions. In an instant, he scooped her from the saddle and gathered her into his arms. He held her there, his arm a band of steel just below her breasts, effectively stilling any movement. "I won't hurt you," he said softly, almost against her ear.

"What?" she asked, unable to comprehend this sudden action. He started moving his horse again, leaving hers behind. "What are you doing? Jake, answer me! What are you doing? Where is he?"

"Don't matter no more where he is. He won't be coming back."

"No! Oh, my God, no! What have you done?" she asked, her eyes wide as she braced herself to hear the worst.

"I had to do it," he said, his eyes soft with sympathy. "Don't you understand that?" He touched a fingertip to her cheek. "I love you. I don't care about the silver. I couldn't wait any longer."

"Wait for what?"

"For you. I couldn't wait for you to leave him. I had to do it."

Sarah could have asked again what he'd done, but she couldn't bring herself to say the words. She didn't want to know. If she didn't hear him say it, there was a chance none of this would be real. But it was. She knew without being told that Thaddeus wasn't hurt. He was dead! Jake wouldn't dare touch her unless he was dead. "Noooo!" Sarah screamed, the sound echoing throughout the forest, her wailing cry proof of her heartbreak. The pain crashed into her chest, leaving her breathless and aching. "No," she shuddered against the pain.

It was this madman's fault. He'd killed Thaddeus. She couldn't allow him to get away with it. He had to pay for what he'd done. He had to suffer for the horror he'd wrought. "Let me go," she cried as she struggled wildly for freedom.

Jake tightened his hold. He crushed her against him, stealing what was left of her breath as he calmly insisted, "You're coming with me."

"I can't!" Her whole body stiffened with dread, but she couldn't allow the horror of this moment to flood her mind. Not now. She had to think. She had to get away. And she'd never escape if she couldn't think. "Emily! I can't leave her. I have to go back."

"No!" he snapped. "You won't be going back. You belong to me now."

"Oh, God," she moaned aloud. "Please. Don't take me away from my baby. Please!"

"We can send for her. You can't go back."

"Jake, please." She turned to him, her eyes huge as she pleaded. "If you love me, take me back. I promise I'll go anywhere you want. I'll do anything you want. Just don't take me away from Emily."

Jake shook his head. His eyes were sad. He didn't want to see her cry. His hand wiped away the tears that had fallen over her cheeks. "I promise we'll send for her, darlin'. I promise."

Sarah shivered at his gentle touch. He was insane. There was no other answer for it. How could he believe that she'd willingly go away with her husband's

360

murderer? How could he think she'd leave her baby?

She didn't know what to do, but fighting him or pleading was getting her nowhere. She tried to force a calmness she was far from feeling. God in Heaven, help me! she silently prayed.

They rode for a long time. Sarah wasn't sure just how long, but the sun had been down for what seemed like hours before he finally brought his horse to a stop.

"You'll feel better once I have a fire going." And at her shiver, he said, "You should have worn a heavier coat." His smile encompassed many things— his sympathy for her plight, gentleness, caring, but most of all and most terrifyingly, love. Sarah felt nothing but horror when he whispered softly, "Don't worry. I'll keep you warm."

She forced back the scream that threatened, knowing she had to play his game. She had to keep her wits about her or never escape, and above all else she had to escape. She couldn't leave Emily. She needed her baby now more than ever.

"Here," he said, handing her a blanket. "Wrap this around you and rest while I make us a fire."

Sarah took the offered blanket with a smile. She hadn't shivered because of the cold. She was terrified. She'd never known anyone could suffer such fear and live. Now that they'd stopped, what would happen? The man was mad. She didn't know what to say, how to act. Suppose she did something that upset him? Suppose he killed her and left her body here, for the wild animals to feed on? Sarah shivered at the thought. What would happen to Emily? She shook her head. No, he wouldn't kill her. Not if he loved her as he'd said. Had he really killed Thaddeus? Her heart ached at the thought. The pain squeezed at her chest and took away her breath. Please, God, don't let him be dead. She didn't know how she could go on if he was.

If he was alive, he'd come for her. She knew he would. But she couldn't count on Thaddeus now. She had to take care of herself. She had to find a way to escape, but until then, she'd do as she was told.

He wasn't going to make it. His arm was bleeding still. He was losing too much blood. How much farther? How much longer could he last?

His strength was ebbing fast. The night was growing colder, and the deep shadows of trees and underbrush began to sway before his eyes. He let the reins go, knowing his horse would find his way back. Sitting slumped over the animal, he held onto the saddle with his good hand.

He could hear her. Damned if couldn't. And she sounded so close. His mind was playing tricks. He wanted her with him so badly that he was imagining the sound of her voice. Thaddeus smiled, knowing how Sarah would fuss at his injury, knowing as well that he would love every minute of it. Lord, but he couldn't wait to get back.

He spotted the campfire and frowned. Who was

out here tonight and why? He tried to think. No one was supposed to be out here, were they? Was he heading in the right direction? Damn, he had to clear the wooziness from his brain.

Thaddeus reached for his gun. Silently, it slid from its holster. He wondered if, in his condition, he'd be able to hit anything.

"Feeling better?" Jake asked as he came to sit close to her side. Much too close.

Sarah inched slightly away. "I'm warmer," she said. In truth, her hands had stopped shaking. Her mind had become focused on one fact: If she couldn't escape, she would kill him. No matter how gruesome the thought, she would do it.

It was imperative that Jake let down his guard completely. He had to relax in her company. The problem was, she wasn't that good of an actress. How did a woman get her kidnapper to relax when she was terrified of him?

Sarah smiled and prayed he wouldn't notice the quivering of her lips. "Have you been planning this long?" Her voice shook, but she was positive he hadn't noticed.

"I've been in love with you from the first moment I saw you."

Sarah's eyes widened.

"I know you're surprised. I was, too. This hasn't ever happened to me before."

"When?"

363

"In town. I saw you drive in that afternoon. That's why I was so close when that cowboy came up to you. I killed him so you'd realize how much I loved you."

Sarah gave a silent moan. Oh, God. This was madness. He'd killed a man to prove his love. He was insane. How was she going to get out of this?

"Why didn't you tell me?"

"You never gave me the chance. Every time I got near you, you'd hurry off somewhere."

"A married lady can't . . ."

"I know," he interrupted. "I think that's what I love about you most of all. You were so true to your man. I know you'll be the same with me."

God in Heaven, help me!

"You will give me time, won't you, Jake?"

"Time for what?" His eyes narrowed suspiciously.

She shrugged. "My husband just died." Sarah nearly strangled on the words. She couldn't stop the shudder that spread through her body as she prayed her words a lie. "I can't very well . . ."

"You don't want me?" he asked. His body stiffened; his voice grew hard, his eyes suddenly cruel. He was on the edge of violence and Sarah couldn't think how to bring him back. "But you smiled at me," he said, as if that were reason enough for this horror.

"No, it's not that. It's just . . ." She breathed a long sigh and prayed the words she sought were the right ones. "I can't go from one man to another in a matter of minutes. You have to give me time."

"Do you want me?" he asked. Both knew every-thing, perhaps even her very life, depended on her answer.

He was watching her closely. His eyes glittered with insane light, easily seen with the flickering fire. "Of course, I want you." She almost choked on the words. "It's just . . ."

"Then nothing else matters." He nodded and breathed a great sigh of satisfaction. His voice grew soft again as a smile curved his handsome lips. "I love you. Don't think of anything but my loving you forever."

His mouth closed over hers as he pulled her stiff form into his arms. Sarah prayed the terrified groan that had slipped from her lips would be mistaken for one of yearning. It was.

Jake forced her lips apart, his tongue delving deep into her softness, raping her sweetness, taking, never thinking to give in his madness. "I saw you," his voice trembled as he covered her cheeks and throat with a dozen kisses. "I saw you with him and I wanted to die." His voice was tormented by the memory. "Tell me you were thinking of me when you were with him. Tell me," he groaned, his desperation obvious as he covered her mouth again with rough, breath-stealing kisses.

Sarah stiffened and inwardly recoiled at the thought. He'd been watching them. Oh, God, how awful! She wanted to rail at him. She wanted to swing her fists into his handsome face. How dare he do something so vile! But Sarah knew better than to

365

let this man know her thoughts. She tried as best she could to relax and allow his kisses. She had to make him believe it wasn't revulsion she felt.

Her arms moved to his shoulders. He groaned at her touch, his heart pounding furiously against the wall of his chest. She loved him. She might not have said as much, but her actions proved it beyond a doubt.

He held her tighter. He couldn't believe the joy. He'd never known a woman's lips could be so soft or a mouth so luscious. His whole body shuddered as she slid her hands down his sides. God, what heaven to be touched by her.

Sarah's hand slid over the butt of his gun, to the center of his back, and then to his gun again. It took her a second. The handle faced the wrong direction, but she finally slid it from its holster and pressed it against his side.

"Let me go, Jake," she said against his lips.

But Jake was too far along in his dreams of loving her. He never felt the hard barrel of the gun in his side. He never heard the words.

"Jake," she said, more forcefully this time as she pressed the gun harder against him. "Let me go."

The sexual fog took a long moment to lift, but when it did, Sarah faced a man crazed with rage.

"Put your hands behind your head." And when he hesitated, she pressed the gun more painfully against him. "Do it!"

Slowly, Jake loosened his hold on her and watched with burning eyes as she slid off his lap. On her knees, Sarah moved to his side and then behind him. "Don't move," she said. "I'll use this if I have to."

Jake did as he was told. He remained perfectly still until Sarah returned with the rope that had looped around his saddle horn.

"Put your arms down and behind your back."

Again Jake did as he was told.

Sarah knew the minute she laid the gun on the ground that it was a mistake. Jake didn't hesitate a second but swung on her with all the fierceness of a wild animal. He swatted the gun out of her reach even as a giant fist slammed heavily into her mouth. The blow snapped something in her neck. She felt the snap and then the huge amount of blood as it gushed from her mouth. In a second it covered her jaw and dribbled to her dress, but Jake never noticed. All he knew was betrayal. She had tricked him and she was going to suffer for it.

"Bitch! Dirty whorin' bitch! You're like all the others. I thought you were better. I thought you were everything."

Sarah moaned, only half conscious after taking yet another blow. She saw stars as this one landed just beneath her eye. She never felt his hands reach for the collar of her dress. She didn't realize he'd ripped the garment clear to her waist. It wasn't till later that she felt the cold. Chill caused her to shudder uncontrollably as she lay naked on the grass, beneath him. Only then did she notice her clothes in a torn pile at her side.

The sound of her moans finally penetrated his

mad mind and he realized what he'd done.

"Oh, God," he sobbed at the destruction. "Sarah, I'm sorry. I'm so sorry." She was crying now and the sound was tearing at his heart. "You're not like the rest, darlin'," he cooed tenderly. He held her gently as her body was wracked with sobs. "You're beautiful. You're sweet and so innocent. God, I love you."

He heard her again. Was it a cry or a laugh? He couldn't tell, for the sound was almost instantly muffled. He was imagining things, of course. Sarah couldn't be out here. Sarah was at home with Emily, awaiting his return.

His horse broke suddenly through the underbrush. He was staring at a couple moving beneath a blanket. Thaddeus thought to turn his head. What he was seeing was private and not for others to look upon. But in the soft glow of the fire, he caught the wild look in her eyes.

She was desperate, wild in her need for help, but Thaddeus imagined her half-crazed look to be one of surprise.

For an endless moment, he simply stared. It wasn't Sarah. It couldn't be Sarah. She wouldn't be out here. She wouldn't be lying with another man. But she was. The proof was before his eyes. He wanted to deny it, but he couldn't. At that moment, his soul shriveled up and died. He only wished his body could do as much.

He couldn't breathe. Something was gripping at

his chest. Was it horror? Pain? He couldn't tell. An instant later, it exploded. Too late, Jake Blackman had heard his approach. He stood naked, his eyes searching wildly for his gun. He needn't have bothered.

The old Thaddeus had returned full force. Without thinking, he raised his own weapon and pulled the trigger. He didn't stop until the gun was as empty as his soul.

His eyes were blank, devoid of any emotion as he watched her come to her feet. The blanket covered her from shoulder to foot, but he knew she was naked beneath.

Thaddeus looked from the man lying dead at her feet to her wild-eyed expression. Tears streamed down her face. Idly, he wondered if she cried because he'd killed Jake or because she had finally been discovered. It didn't much matter. He wondered, too, how long this had been going on and then realized that didn't matter either. Nothing mattered but that he never lay eyes on this cheating whore again.

She was crying or laughing, maybe both. He couldn't tell for sure. "Oh, God, Thaddeus. He told me you were dead. Thank God," she groaned. The words came from the depths of her soul. "Thank God."

She was good. He had to hand her that. If he hadn't seen her betrayal with his own eyes, he might have believed every word she said. God, why did he have to see it? The sight would haunt him awake and asleep forever. It would have been better, so much better, if he'd never known. "I want you off my land before first light. If you're still here by then, I'll kill you."

"No!" she cried as she realized at last his words. "No! You don't understand." Thaddeus thought she had been with Jake because she wanted to be. She laughed at the absurdity. She couldn't let him think that. She had to make him understand.

She ran to him. Her foot caught on the blanket, pulling it from her hold. She never noticed. Naked, she clung to his leg and pleaded. "Thaddeus, please. Let me explain."

Calmly, frighteningly, he only whispered in a menacing tone that promised death, "Don't let me find you here tomorrow."

Sarah shivered. She never felt the night's cold air against her naked skin. It was the look in his eyes that brought on the shivering dread.

Her hand tightened over his thigh as she pleaded. "No, Thaddeus, it's not what you think." She cried out as she tripped over a root and fell, the horse shying away from her frantic movements. "Thaddeus, please, I swear you're wrong."

His mouth split into an eerie, almost insane grin. Filled with disgust, his eyes moved over her naked form, sprawled upon the ground. He didn't say another word, but simply turned his horse around and left her alone with the horror this night had brought.

* * *

370

Sarah felt no fear at being left in the wilderness alone. She knew she should have been afraid, but she couldn't manage the emotion. She wasn't cold, she wasn't even angry at being so falsely accused. All she knew was the greatest sadness imaginable. It increased with every breath, with every heartbeat, until she wondered if she could survive the crushing weight, the pain.

She wouldn't think now. Not now. She had to get dressed. She had to get back. If she could talk to him for just a minute, she could make him understand. She knew she could make him understand.

Sarah's hands trembled as she pulled on her clothes. She was freezing, but it wasn't from the night air. A cold terror had lodged in her chest. It didn't matter how many layers of clothing she wore. She somehow knew she'd never feel really warm again.

She kicked dirt over the fire and ran to the horse. A soft groan was torn from her throat. She had to saddle it. She didn't know how to ride bareback. Soft pleading prayers slid from her lips as she hurried about the task. Time was of the essence. She had to find Thaddeus and explain this terrible misunderstanding.

It was almost three hours before Sarah managed to find her way back. Twice she'd thought that she recognized the area, but she'd been wrong. She didn't know this country well enough to travel easily at night.

The sound of the horse's hooves brought someone to her door. Thank God, it was Lottie. Sarah sighed with relief as she slid down from the saddle. "Lottie, oh Lottie, thank God. Something terrible has happened."

"I know," Lottie said, then moved out to the porch and closed the door behind her, barring Sarah's way. "He's inside."

"Good," Sarah said, determined to put to rights this crazy misunderstanding.

"No. You can't go in." And when Sarah appeared to ignore Lottie's words, the older woman took her by the arm and gave her a sharp shake. "He's sitting there with a gun. If he sees you, he'll—he'll—" Lottie couldn't voice her terror of what might happen. "You can't go in there."

Sarah shook her head. "He won't hurt me," she said with more confidence than she felt.

"Oh, God," Lottie groaned as Sarah moved past her and on into the house.

He was sitting at the table, his rifle lying upon the scrubbed surface. His arm was bandaged, his face tight and pale, his eyes as hard and lifeless as the devil's own. Sarah gasped at the sight. He'd been shot. Thank God, it was only his arm. She shivered, remembering how Jake had led her to believe him to be dead.

"Darling, oh darling," she said sympathetically as she moved to him. Her body trembled at finding him injured, but she was filled with untold relief upon seeing the injury was only slight. But Thaddeus never raised his gaze from the table. With his good hand, he shoved her away. Sarah trembled with apprehension, knowing it was going to take some talking to convince this man that what he'd seen wasn't what he'd seen at all. But she had every confidence she could.

"Thaddeus?" The name was spoken as a question.

Thaddeus took his watch from his pocket. "You got five minutes to pack. You'd better hurry, 'cause I'm going to burn whatever you leave."

"Wait. Thaddeus, please, let me explain. I know it looked bad, but—"

"Four minutes and forty-five seconds," he said, never taking his gaze from the watch.

"Stop that and listen to me. He told me you were hurt. I went with him only because I thought you were hurt."

Thaddeus's eyes raised with disbelief. Not bad. She'd come up with a damn good story. Only, she was mistaken if she thought it mattered now. Nothing mattered. She was talking to a dead man. He'd seen them together. Nothing she could say could make a difference now.

"I'd never willingly leave Emily. You know that."

"Never thought you would," he said with a shrug, as if the thought mattered not at all.

"If you know that, why would you believe I'd go with him?"

He never saw her bruises, never realized her ripped dress. All he could see was a liar, a woman he had trusted, a woman to whom he had given his heart, his very soul. A woman, who like all the others, had done him false.

He felt an almost insane wave of rage. Thank God. He needed the anger desperately, for the pain lingered just beyond every breath. He couldn't allow pain of this magnitude. Somehow he knew he wouldn't survive its strength.

Thaddeus watched her with blank eyes for a long moment before he smiled, but the smile caused shivers to run down her back. He glanced at his watch again. "Four minutes."

Sarah took a deep breath and tried again. "I know it looked bad, especially since you came upon us like that. But you've got to believe me."

"Three minutes and—"

"Thaddeus, listen to me. He shot you and then kidnapped me. He was insane. He said he loved me. I was terrified. I tried to fight him. I thought he'd surely kill me. He kept hitting me over and over again. Look at me! Look at my dress. You can see I wasn't willing."

Thaddeus refused to raise his gaze above his watch. He wasn't about to listen to any more lies. "Two minutes."

"I tried to stay calm for as long as I could. It wouldn't have helped things if I panicked." She took a sharp breath as she remembered the horror. She knew she was babbling. She was repeating some of what had happened out of sequence, but she was so nervous and time was so short that she didn't know where to begin. Thaddeus was a man of ice. She

374

didn't know how to convince him. "He was just about to—to—when you came."

"One minute. You'd better start packing."

"I'm not leaving. You're going to stop this nonsense and listen to me."

Thaddeus, enraged at her order, came to his feet. He was momentarily a bit unsteady due to the loss of blood, but even so, Sarah was no match for his superior strength. His good hand clamped on her arm and swung her hard against the door. The force of contact brought a groan from her lips. Neither noticed.

Tiger growled, low and threatening, at her mistreatment, and was rewarded with a curse and a hard look from his master.

A moment later she was outside. She almost fell off the porch at his shove but managed at the last second to hold on to the railing. "Wait!" she said as a bundle of clothes were thrown at her.

"Emily is at Lottie's place. You can stay there till morning. Then I want you off my place." His voice lowered with disgust. That he despised her was clear in every word he spoke. "Don't ever come back."

Sarah cried out and threw herself at him, but the door slammed in her face, causing her head to thud hard against the solid wood. An instant later and she would have been inside, but the door had permanently interrupted her flight. She groaned again and shook her head, fighting off the wave of dizziness caused by this second blow. Wild with horror, she pounded on the heavy door . . . pounded until she heard the wooden bar fall into place. "Please listen to me," she cried, hardly able to speak so choked was she with tears. "Thaddeus," she whispered, her voice almost as shaken as her body, "please."

She couldn't believe it. This couldn't be happening. But it was. It took a few moments before the reality of this night actually sunk in. But once it did, Sarah straightened her back and glared at the man she knew would be standing on the other side of the door. The hurt hadn't started yet. At the moment, all she could feel was anger at his ill-treatment, and for that she was thankful. "All right, Thaddeus, you win. It looks like you've found your excuse to get rid of me. I guess . . ." her voice choked up with unshed tears. She swallowed and tried again. "I guess . . ." Her voice broke. She wouldn't let him hear her cry. He wouldn't know how she hurt. He wouldn't.

Sarah took a deep, steadying breath and fought back the tears that threatened. She wanted to say more, but didn't know what or even where to start. She kicked the bundle of clothes at her feet off the porch. "Go ahead and burn the clothes; I don't want them. I don't want anything from you." She turned then and moved down the three steps that led to the ground. Her back had never been so straight nor her head held so high.

Sarah smiled politely and refused Lottie's plea to stay the night. She refused as well Zack's company on her trip to town. She'd be perfectly all right, she promised. No need to take the man from his home.

376

A smile was plastered to her face as she gathered Emily and her things. With Lottie's and Zack's help, she managed to mount Jake's horse. It took some doing, what with the baby sleeping in her arms, but Sarah carried what she could. The rest was tied to the saddle and pushed into the saddlebags.

She never looked back. She never saw the big man standing in the light of his cabin door. She couldn't have seen the empty, soulless eyes. She never realized his utter despair. She never knew it matched her own.

Thaddeus felt a rush of fear for her safety, that she'd chosen to travel at night, and then laughed in ridicule at the emotion. She was no concern of his. He didn't give a damn what happened to her. Her kind could take care of themselves.

He closed the door as she disappeared from sight and leaned his back heavily against it. It was over. Fool that he was, he'd believed her to be everything good. Now he knew the truth. If he lived through this torment — and judging by the pain that ripped through his guts, he doubted the possibility — he swore he'd never look at another woman again.

Chapter Eighteen

Sarah smiled, or at least gave a weak semblance of a smile through stiff throbbing lips, at Becky Smithston's concern. She hadn't known where else to go. She had no money. Taking a room at the boarding house was out of the question. There was no way she could pay for it.

Becky, the owner of the town's only restaurant, was one of her few friends. Tonight she'd silently proclaimed herself Sarah's staunch supporter. Thank God. Sarah knew she'd never need a friend more than she did on this night.

To her credit, Becky never asked what had happened. Sarah had come knocking at her door at four in the morning, her clothes in tatters and her face swollen. All Becky did was make a soft exclamation of surprise, then usher Sarah and Emily inside and upstairs to her private living quarters. There, in a spare bedroom, Becky settled them for the night.

"I can't pay you," Sarah said through stiff, swollen lips.

Becky shot her a look of annoyance. "Don't you

worry none about that. We're friends, aren't we? I don't expect payment for doin' the neighborly thing."

"I can work."

Becky shook her head. "Maybe later. When you're feeling better, you can help me downstairs. That will more than take care of your board." Becky smiled encouragingly. "I can't afford to pay much, but tips are pretty good on Saturdays, when the cowhands come into town. A woman as pretty as yourself will soon have a little nest egg set aside."

Tears of gratitude slipped over bruised cheeks. One eye was growing more purple by the minute and swelling at an alarming rate, hampering her vision. Upon entering the room, she'd glanced into the small mirror above the dry sink. No one would call her pretty tonight. Sarah didn't know how to thank this dear woman. She'd hardly known her long enough to call her a friend and yet she was going out of her way to help. Her blue gaze told Becky she'd never forget this kindness.

Becky studied Sarah's face for a long moment and then sighed, trying, albeit not very hard, to hide her disgust. "I'll get you some water. You'll feel better after you clean up." A moment later, she left the room.

Sarah knew Becky imagined Thaddeus to be the culprit behind her injuries. The boot he'd thrown had hit her above her eye and given her a small cut, but that had been an accident. No, her bruises weren't the results of Thaddeus's handiwork. Still, Sarah didn't bother to correct that impression. Some men beat their wives regularly. It didn't matter that Thaddeus would never, had never, raised a hand to her. What he had done was so much worse. Sarah didn't want anyone to know he had thrown her out. No, the truth was too mortifying. It was better if everyone believed she'd left him because of his abuse.

Sarah tried to shake away the memory, an impossible feat. Her heart was heavy, its weight crushing her chest and prohibiting regular breathing. She found herself continually gasping for her next breath.

Sarah stiffened her spine. She was strong. She wouldn't wallow in self-pity. She had to think. There were plans to make and Emily to see to. She couldn't waste her time with useless tears. Later. Later would be time enough to think about his mistreatment.

The only problem was that once she was in bed, with Emily cuddled warmly against her side, Sarah couldn't stop thinking. It was over. Really and truly over. The fact that he'd forced her to leave in the middle of the night, never listening to a word of explanation, proclaimed that truth loud and clear. Did he know she'd left the ranch? Did he think she was at Lottie's? No doubt, he simply didn't care. Knowing the truth of his feelings hurt more than any accusation, any mistrust, any violence he could have bestowed.

The heavy ache in her chest stole her breath, and Sarah wondered if she could survive this amount of pain. She groaned at the knifelike agony that penetrated to her soul, wondering if it were possible to die of heartache. Sarah imagined it possible, but knew she would someday overcome this torment. She had Emily to think of. The baby needed her, and for her sake, she would survive.

Despite her fatigue, Sarah couldn't lose herself in sleep. Again and again, the scenario replayed itself in her mind. He hadn't looked at her. Had he, even for a moment really looked at her, he would have known the truth.

She'd been battered. And if the bruises were only just beginning to become apparent, he would have noticed if just for a moment he'd put aside his rage.

But he wouldn't believe her, wouldn't listen to her explanations. Sarah gave a long sigh of sorrow and disappointment. He'd wanted to believe the worst, wanted to believe her unfaithful. Sarah couldn't imagine why. But it was so.

She groaned at the many aches and pains that wracked her body. She'd been roughly treated and needed someone to comfort her. Why was it whenever she needed comfort the most, there was no one? Sarah took a long, steadying breath. She wouldn't cry. Self-pity was useless. Tears would gain her nothing. And yet, despite her pledge, they slid silently to her pillow. It wasn't until the first signs of light crept over the horizon that her exhausted body overcame her torment and she finally gave in to the need to sleep.

Will Spencer heard the sound of a door slam. He opened his eyes and blinked his surprise at the flickering light that filled his cabin. Damn it to hell, something was on fire! He scrambled from the bed, dressed only in boots and drawers, and raced outside, coming to a sudden stop. Amazed, he simply stood there and watched.

Thaddeus was holding Emily's crib in his uninjured arm. With a roar that bespoke his agony, he suddenly swung it from his side and into the fire. He stared at the blaze for a long moment. It wasn't until the crib had become engulfed in flames that he suddenly turned away. He glared at Will, noticing him at last. Leaving the fire unattended, he walked into his house and again slammed his door.

"What is it? What's happening?" Kate asked her husband as she hurried to his side, barefoot and fumbling with the belt to her robe.

"I don't know. Thaddeus is burning something."

"Now?"

"He just threw Emily's crib into the fire."

"Oh, my God, why? What happened?"

Will shook his head and glanced at the cabin's closed door. "From the look he just shot my way, I'd say he wasn't in the mood to say." His arm came around his wife and pulled her close to his side as they walked back to their home. "I reckon we can wait till tomorrow to find out."

As it turned out, he'd have to wait three days. It took that long before Thaddeus ran out of whiskey.

Sarah tried not to smile. Every time she did, her lip cracked again. Darn, she thought, as she licked away the tiny drop of blood. When was this going to heal? She hadn't realized how easily she bruised. Granted, she had never had reason to realize it before. Jake had been far from gentle, but Lord, he'd only hit her twice. At least she thought it was twice. Thinking back, she realized she'd been so frightened she'd probably never know for sure. Three days had gone by, and instead of healing, her bruises had grown until her face now sported the most amazing combination of colors. Right now dark blue, with tinges of sickly green and yellow, circled her swollen eye, while her cheek and lip were a paler version of the same colors.

It was barely dawn. She left Emily to sleep, knowing Amy Stanley, her usual sitter when in town, would soon be there to watch over the baby. Sarah crept down the back stairs to the kitchen and put up a huge pot of coffee. She had placed an enormous bowl on the table, next to a basket of eggs, when behind her Becky gave a loud yawn and asked, "What are you doing up? Doc Winslow told you to stay in bed."

383

Sarah smiled. Darn, if her lip didn't start bleeding again. "Becky, I'm perfectly all right. I can't stay in bed all day and expect you to wait on me. You have enough to do."

"You don't look all right."

"It's just my face. And that will heal soon enough."

"What are you going to do?"

"Well, I thought I'd help out with the cooking. I'd rather not wait tables until I look a little—"

"I meant what are you going to do about your husband?"

Sarah stopped cracking eggs into the bowl. Her hands trembled uncontrollably, while the rest of her grew very still. Her eyes filled with tears. She took a few shaky breaths and swallowed several times before she was sure of her voice. "Nothing. There's nothing I can do."

She gave a weak smile and wiped at her eyes with the back of her hand. "I figured, if you let me work here for a while, I could save enough money to get back to my family."

"Are you sure?"

Sarah tipped her head, a quizzical expression in her eyes as she waited for her friend to go on. "Sure?" she prompted.

"Sure you don't want Thaddeus to know about the baby."

Sarah's eyes grew wide with terror. Her whole body stiffened. "He can't know. He can't ever know.

Dr. Winslow swore he wouldn't say anything. Becky, please, you've got to promise me you won't—"

"Take it easy. I'm not going to say a thing. Far as I'm concerned, the man don't deserve you. And your baby is probably better off without him." Becky's shrug was meant to show her nonchalance, but the sound of the frying pan slamming upon the stove disallowed the casual movement. She cursed. "Never could take to a man who abused his wife. I think—"

"He didn't," Sarah defended before she even thought to stop the words.

Becky turned to her, her mouth hanging open in shock. "What?"

"Nothing."

"What didn't he do?"

Sarah shook her head. "Nothing." It was obvious she didn't want to talk about it, but Becky wasn't a woman to be put off. She wasn't about to take no for an answer.

"He wasn't the one who hit you?"

Sarah swallowed, breathed a long sigh, and shook her head again.

"Then who the hell did? Jesus Christ! You mean to say someone beat you and he didn't do a thing about it?"

Sarah didn't say anything. She couldn't. The whole mess was so sordid, so horrible, she couldn't imagine telling anyone.

"Are you protecting someone? Have you taken a lover? Is *he* the one who beat you?"

385

Sarah moaned. If word got out about Thaddeus's treatment, then everyone would believe just that. She couldn't bear the shame of it. "It's a long story."

"I got the time. Let's hear it." It never occurred to Becky that this was none of her business. She'd taken Sarah's problems on as her own when she'd offered her her friendship. She figured she had every right to know what the hell was going on.

Becky sat Sarah at the small kitchen table and, over coffee, listened to the story.

"Damn," she muttered once Sarah had finished. "And he never let you explain?"

Sarah shook her head.

"He just threw you out in the middle of the night?"

Sarah shrugged. "He suggested I stay with Lottie for the night but insisted I was to leave at first light.

"Heartless bastard."

Sarah smiled and said nothing.

"So you're fixin' on going back to your folks?"

Sarah nodded again. "After I make enough for my fare."

"I could loan it to you."

"Oh, no." Sarah shook her head. "I couldn't borrow the money. There's no telling when I'd be able to repay you. Besides, I couldn't travel now. I don't want my family to see me like this."

"They'll think Thaddeus did it, and you don't want that, right?"

Sarah only stared into the cup of cold coffee.

"Why are you protecting him?"

"I'm not," she said defensively.

"Yes, you are. He might not have hit you, but the man's a heartless bastard. He doesn't deserve protection."

"I'm not going to protect him. I'm going to tell my family everything. I just don't want them to see me like this." Sarah sighed, then came to her feet. "It's getting late. Your customers will be looking for breakfast and nothing is ready."

Will came the next day. He couldn't look her in the eye as he handed her a roll of bills. "I've been looking for you since this morning."

"What's this?"

"Thaddeus said to find you and give it to you." Will didn't bother to mention that Thaddeus had been half out of his mind with liquor at the time. He probably wouldn't remember giving him the money by the time he came out of his drunken stupor.

Sarah's smile was the saddest he'd ever seen. She should take it. Being his wife gave her every right to take it, but she knew she wouldn't. She wasn't about to let him ease his conscience by paying her off. She shook her head. "Tell Thaddeus thank you, but I don't want or need his money."

"What will you do?"

"What I've always done. I'll work."

"Are you going to stay here?"

Sarah knew what she was going to do, but she wasn't about to tell this man. She didn't want Thaddeus to know. He had given up the right to know anything about her four nights ago.

Thaddeus groaned and rolled over. The pain in his head was unbearable. He'd been drunk for days. He couldn't remember how many, exactly. All he knew was every time he started thinking, he reached for another bottle. Thankfully Zack had brought back six when he was last in town. Thaddeus had found it to be the only way to blot out the pain.

He opened his eyes and moaned again as blinding pain shot through his head. He had to stop. Actually, he had no choice but to stop. Last night had seen the last of his whiskey.

He sat up, and with elbows resting on his legs, he held his head in his hands. His arm ached like bloody hell. Probably should have gone into town and seen the doctor, rather than let Zack take care of it. But he hadn't exactly been thinking clearly that night. Actually, he hadn't been able to think clearly since.

Through bloodshot eyes, he looked beneath the bandage and groaned. The wound was festering. He'd have to go to town before he lost the damn thing or died. Thaddeus didn't much care if he died, but as far as he could remember, he'd never once seen a one-armed rancher.

* * *

Thaddeus had never felt so sick in his whole life. He couldn't tell if he was hung over or still drunk. Maybe a little of both, he reasoned. Silently, he swore he was never going to touch another drop of whiskey for as long as he lived. The ground swayed as he rode his horse over the dirt road. Town had never seemed so damn far away before.

Thaddeus felt a great shiver vibrate throughout his body. Sarah and Emily had made this trip alone at night. God, what could she have been thinking to leave in the middle of the night? Why hadn't she waited till morning? Why hadn't he insisted? Or at the very least told one of his men to accompany her? Thaddeus gave a short self-deprecating bark of a laugh, then groaned at the pain the sound brought about. No sense fooling himself. At the time, the danger had only been a flickering thought. He'd been unable to think much past his own suffering.

Thaddeus pushed aside his fears and tried to center his thoughts on what she'd done. She deserved none of his concern. The woman was no better than a whore. He wondered again how long she'd been cheating. The thought was apt to drive him mad. He couldn't think of anything else but his wife in another man's arms.

Thaddeus smiled as he remembered her plea not to hire Jake on. Too bad he hadn't listened to her then. He might have saved himself a pack of trouble.

Odd that she had chosen that particular man to take as a lover. He'd thought she didn't like him all that much.

Damn, but the woman belonged on the stage. She was good. The best. She'd had him convinced that Jake, despite his good looks, was the least appealing man she knew.

Thaddeus frowned as he remembered how she always reached for him when the man was close by. He hadn't thought much of it at the time, but now he wondered why. Was it all a ploy to throw him off guard? He shook his head at the thought. No. It hadn't been an act. He knew Sarah's aversion to violence. She couldn't forget how Jake had killed the cowboy. Why then had she taken up with him? Him of all people?

Doubt suddenly filled his mind, but Thaddeus determinedly pushed the emotion aside. It couldn't be. He'd seen what he'd seen. There was no denying that.

She'd been naked and under the blanket with him. The sight of it had torn his heart out, almost killing him on the spot. Thaddeus knew he'd never feel anything but pain again. He could see it now as if it were happening at this very moment. The tormenting picture was clearly imprinted on his mind; he'd never forget anything about it.

The fire burned low, giving off minimal light, but more than enough for him to see them struggling. *Struggling!* Despite the pain, Thaddeus's eyes widened. His face grew pale beneath his tan. He looked as if he'd received yet another shock and his stomach lurched, ready to empty itself again. Was it true? Had they been struggling? Or were they simply wild for one another?

Thaddeus searched for an answer. It came amid a low groan of horror. Her clothes had been thrown carelessly around the small campsite. He could see them even now, as they lay ripped and discarded.

Ripped! he shuddered. *Jesus Christ! Her clothes had been ripped!* Vaguely, he remembered the condition of her clothes as she'd entered the house. He'd hardly looked. Purposely, he'd kept his attention on either the table or his watch. But when he had looked her way that one time, what had he seen? *Think! God damn it, think! What did you see?* Her blouse! Most of the buttons had been missing. The sleeve at her shoulder had been torn. Her lips or something had been bleeding. The bottom half of her face had been streaked with dried blood.

Thaddeus cried out a long, mournful sound of agony, as he realized what he'd done. She'd been innocent and in desperate need of his care. And he, like a madman, had ignored her pleas and thrown her out into the middle of the night.

Thaddeus had never known such remorse. Why hadn't he believed her? Why hadn't he listened? Why had it taken the memory of that night to confirm what he should have known from the start?

Despite the pain in both his arm and head, Thaddeus hurried his horse's gait. He had to get to town. He had to find her. He didn't know how, but he had to convince her to forgive him. She had to. He couldn't make it without her.

Thaddeus breathed a sigh of relief as he remembered. She loved him. After he explained everything, she'd forgive him. "Please, God, I swear I'll never make her unhappy again if she'll forgive me."

At the edge of town, Thaddeus brought his horse to a sudden stop. It took him a minute to remember. Will had said she was staying at the restaurant. Would she still be there? Please, God, let her be there.

Becky Smithston stood across from where he sat, glaring down into his ashen face. He was so damn sick that he couldn't stop the room from spinning around him. But he didn't mistake the disgust he heard in her voice. "I don't want you here."

Thaddeus shot her as hard a look as he could muster in his present condition. "It's a public restaurant, isn't it? Where is she?"

"Who?"

Thaddeus glared. "Sarah."

"Sarah who?"

"Becky, I'm warning you . . ."

"She don't want to see you."

Thaddeus breathed a long, silent sigh of relief. She was still here. He wasn't going to have to search for her. "Where is she?"

"It don't matter none. She won't see you."

Thaddeus got up from the table. On shaking legs, he pushed past the woman, ignoring her protests, and walked into the kitchen.

Sarah was at the sink, washing a pile of dishes when he entered the room. He must have made a sound, because she turned and looked in his direction. For just an instant, a smile lit her eyes. But it was gone faster than a blink, and Thaddeus knew she was remembering what he'd done.

He gasped at the sight of her face. "What happened? My God, did I do that?" Had he gone over the edge of reason and never remembered? Had he actually struck his wife?

Silently, Sarah turned her back to him and continued with her chore. "No," Sarah said, never offering further information.

If Thaddeus held any lingering doubts, the sight of her face put to rest the last of them. Five days had passed since the infamous night and she still showed signs of abuse. She had fought Jake off, as much as she was able. Fool that he was, had he only stopped to think, stopped to look, he would have known the truth from the beginning.

Thaddeus couldn't remember ever being so glad someone was dead. He was glad Jake had died at his hands. He deserved that and more for daring to touch his wife. Thaddeus had only one regret. Jake's death had been too quick. The man should have suffered for what he'd done.

Thaddeus moved into the room. Sarah could hear

his footsteps. She looked his way again, her gaze emotionless, and said, "Don't touch me. I don't want you to touch me."

Thaddeus felt searing pain slice into his soul at the flatness of her tone. He swayed but forced his mind to rise above the pain that wracked his body. He had to think. "Sarah, I've got to talk to you."

"And why should I listen, Thaddeus? I can't remember that you allowed me the same consideration."

"You'll listen because you're a hell of a lot better person than I am."

Sarah smiled, then licked at her swollen lip. "I can't disagree with you there."

Thaddeus probably loved her the most when she smart-mouthed him. God, but he wanted to hold her. He could hardly think of anything other than holding her. But he had to. He had to, or chance losing her forever. "I was out of my mind with jealousy. I know now that I was wrong. I've come to take you home."

Sarah dried her hands on a towel and faced him. Her eyes widened with some surprise. He looked awful. His face was haggard, his eyes bloodshot, his skin almost chalky beneath his tan. Determinedly, she pushed aside her concern and shook her head. "I'm going home, but it won't be to your house."

"You don't mean that. I know you love me."

Sarah nodded. "You're right. I do love you, but loving you isn't everything."

His voice rose in frustration. "What are you talking about? Of course, it's everything. What's more important than the way we feel about each other?"

She breathed a long, calming sigh. "Trust. Respect. I need them both, and you don't have any to give."

Sarah took yet another deep breath and looked at the floor as she went on. "You can't expect me to go back, knowing that you might throw me out tomorrow over another imagined infraction. I can't live like that."

His voice was hard and tight, as if he couldn't bear the memory. "I didn't imagine seeing you naked with another man. I was mistaken about the circumstances, is all." Thaddeus groaned softly. He was feeling worse by the minute. He'd probably never been more ill in his entire life and he couldn't take the time right now to do a damn thing about it. "Look, I was in shock. You have to understand. I didn't know what I was doing." He tried to touch her, only to have his hand brushed firmly away. "Sarah, nothing like that will ever happen again. Can't we start over?" he pleaded, his voice so ragged, so raw in his suffering, that Sarah almost turned to him.

Her heart was heavy in her chest. Tears filled her eyes, but still she remained firm in her resolve. "I'm sorry." She shook her head. "I can't go back."

"You mean you won't."

Her shrug told him clearly he could believe whatever he wished. "I have work to do," she said, hoping he'd soon give up and leave her alone. She didn't know how much more she could take before she ran to him and threw herself in his arms.

The idea of taking her by force came to mind, but Thaddeus knew that wasn't the answer. She had to come to him of her own accord. He'd never be satisfied with anything less.

Still, he knew there was no way he was going to let her go. No way. Only right now, his arm was aching so damn bad he couldn't think clearly. He knew he should stay and plead his cause, but he had to get over to the doctor. The room was spinning around his head. He was so damn sick. If he didn't get there soon, he was liable to fall on his face. He didn't have much strength left.

"I've got to go, but I'll be back," he said as he staggered out of the kitchen. Just beyond the doorway, all choice was taken from him. As he'd feared, he fell flat on his face. A table and two chairs went crashing to the floor in splinters beneath his weight. Someone screamed and Sarah raced into the dining room.

Chapter Nineteen

"I'm not sure I can save his arm."

Sarah had been waiting for what felt like hours before Dr. Winslow came out of the room. His words should have brought on a sense of panic, but Sarah couldn't muster the emotion. Not over an arm. An arm meant nothing compared to his life.

Her eyes filled with tears and she shook her head at the doctor's words. "It doesn't matter," she said, knowing of course that it mattered very much indeed. Thaddeus could hardly do what was necessary to run his ranch with only one arm. Still, there was no choice. He couldn't be allowed to die. If it meant losing an arm in order to live, so be it. "Please, God," she silently prayed, "all I ask is that you save his life."

"I'll know in a day or so. I've got a poultice drawing on the wound right now." Doc Winslow gave a helpless shrug. "We'll see."

"Can I see him?"

The kindly doctor shook his head. "I gave him

something for the pain. He won't know you're there."

Sarah nodded in understanding. "That doesn't matter. I just want to sit with him for a bit."

Sarah sat beside his sleeping form for the rest of that day. He was worse the next day and the next. For three days the fever raged, and Thaddeus wavered between life and death. All anyone could do was sit and pray that this man was strong enough to survive. On the fourth morning, Sarah arrived at the doctor's office early as usual, only to pass a man she'd never seen before, on his way out.

A few words with the doctor brought tears of happiness to sparkle in her eyes. He was over the worst of it. He was going to make it.

Sarah smiled upon finding him, if in some discomfort, quite lucid. He watched in silence as she moved toward him, a soft smile curving her lips. Uninvited, she sat in a chair beside his bed. "I can see by your coloring you're feeling better today."

Thaddeus nodded. "Doc said I came close to losing my arm."

Sarah nodded, knowing how the doctor had each day delayed his decision, hoping the next few hours would see some improvement in the red, puffy skin around his wound. "For a time it was very close."

"He said the thought of losin' my arm didn't bother you none. Why?"

"An arm isn't worth dying over."

"And you wanted me to live?"

Sarah frowned. "Are you being ridiculous again? Why would I want anything else?"

"I didn't treat you right. You have every reason to hate me."

Sarah allowed a long, shaky sigh as she nodded in agreement.

"But you don't?"

"I've never hated you." She smiled. "Well, perhaps I have, now and again, but I've never wanted you dead."

"I really messed up this time, didn't I?"

Sarah shook her head and avoided looking into his eyes. She didn't want to talk about their troubles. Not now. Perhaps not ever. "You shouldn't think about that now. You should concentrate on getting well."

Thaddeus grinned at her simple answer, then scowled as he complained. "They put the most god-awful-smelling stuff on my arm. Jesus, it stinks."

Sarah laughed and wrinkled her nose. "Now you know how I felt."

Thaddeus looked at her, saying nothing for a long moment. He hadn't been able to think too clearly these last few days. And now that he could, he didn't know what to say. He wanted to tell her that he loved her. He wanted to beg her for forgiveness, but he'd tried that before and it hadn't worked.

There was one fact he couldn't deny. He couldn't

go on without this woman. Life wasn't worth the effort without her. "You're so beautiful," he said, the words coming before he thought to stop them.

"Thank you," Sarah said with a smile, knowing she was anything but. The swelling on her face had gone down, but discoloration was still evident, if only slight, around her eye. She felt suddenly uncomfortable at his long, almost hungry stare. "I'd better be getting back. Becky will be needing my help."

Thaddeus grabbed her wrist with his good hand. "Wait. We have to talk. Don't go yet."

Sarah shook her head. "We've already talked, Thaddeus. We've said all—"

"I haven't said near all I've got to say."

Sarah leaned back in the chair, the movement breaking his hold. Silently, she waited for him to go on.

"First of all, I want to tell you that the ranch belongs to you."

Sarah started with surprise, almost coming out of the chair. She perched on its edge again, her eyes wide with amazement. "What are you talking about?"

"I've just now signed it over to you. So if you want to go home . . ." He shrugged his good shoulder, never finishing the sentence.

"I don't want it. You can't do this."

"I already did it. I reckon it don't much matter if you want it or not. It's yours."

400

"I'll sign it back. I don't want it. I have to go."
Sarah came abruptly to her feet and was gone before Thaddeus could say another word. It was three days before she returned.

She walked into the room, knowing he was much better if still weak. The only reason he had remained at the doctor's office was because there was no one to look after him. "You look much better today."

"So do you."

"Thank you."

"All the swelling is gone."

She nodded at his comment. They were talking to one another like strangers. Sarah had never, even when she'd first come to his home, felt more ill at ease.

"I shouldn't have come," she said, and wondered why she had.

"Why did you?"

She shrugged, having no answer.

"It's because you love me," he said, only his statement sounded oddly like a question.

"I'd better go."

"Wait. Don't go." He took a deep breath and then rushed on, as if he were afraid any hesitation would find her running from the room. "Won't you please let me explain why I did it?"

Sarah watched him for a long moment. She didn't want to hear his excuses. She didn't want to know the reason behind his actions. She could never feel sure of him again. They couldn't start over. It was impossible. "I'm afraid it won't make any difference," she said softly, and Thaddeus knew a terror unlike anything he'd ever known.

Still he had to try. He couldn't make it without her. She had to know that he'd follow her anywhere and ask her every day for the rest of his life to forgive him. "Let me try?"

Sarah nodded and leaned back in the chair.

"I have to start at the beginning."

She nodded again. Saying nothing, Sarah waited for him to go on.

Thaddeus hesitated then, not at all sure how to begin. "It took me a long time to get over Annie. When she left me, she came to town and worked here, in the saloon."

Sarah's eyes widened with shock. She hadn't ever imagined. She could only guess what that would do to a man. "My God," she breathed.

"Those days, most everybody looked at me with pity. I couldn't stand it. Hardly ever came into town after that. At least not for a very long time." He took a deep breath. "One day, some fella made a crack about enjoyin' my wife. I'll never forget his snicker." His eyes grew hard with the memory. "He never did it again." Thaddeus sighed, the sound of his own disgust evident. "I reckon you could say I was pretty down on women for a long time after that." Thaddeus watched her for a moment before his voice lowered and he said, "And then you came.

"I was mean as hell to you at first. One look at you and I knew it could happen again. I was afraid. I was afraid I'd love you and you'd leave me, just like she did."

He looked down at the sheet, his fingers twisting the smooth fabric as he spoke, and Sarah could have sworn he was embarrassed. "Only, it didn't happen again." He raised his gaze to hers. "I never loved Annie the way I love you. I suffered when she left, but that was mostly pride." His voice grew choppy and strained. "When you left, I thought I would die. I wished I could."

"Thaddeus . . ."

"Come back to me."

Sarah shook her head. She was overwhelmed. She hadn't even imagined anything so horrible. His mother and his wife? Good Lord, no wonder the man was so terrified of loving.

Mistaking her shock for a negative response, Thaddeus anxiously pressed on, "What more do you want? What more can I do? I can't let you go. If I have to, I'll follow you and beg you every day to come back."

Thaddeus breathed a long sigh. "Sarah, I loved you even as I swore love didn't exist. I couldn't let myself believe or chance being hurt again. I came to believe in God because of you. There's nothing I wouldn't give you, nothing I wouldn't do for you."

403

Sarah shook her head. "You can't believe in God to please me. You have to believe in him for yourself."

"I do. Don't you understand? I know he has to exist, because only God could have made someone like you."

Sarah closed her eyes, swallowed past the lump in her throat, and moaned, "Lord." That did it. There was no way she could refuse this man. He might not be perfect. She almost laughed at the gross understatement. He was far from perfect. He was the most stubborn, opinionated, thickheaded man she'd ever loved. He had the foulest, quickest temper, almost unbelievable pride, but she couldn't imagine her life without him.

"You can't leave me, Sarah. You're the only woman, the only human being in my whole life, that's ever loved me. I can't let you go."

Tears blurred her vision as she whispered, "The next time you try to throw me out, I'm going to take a frying pan to your head." She sniffed and then swallowed. "I might have to stand on a chair to do it, but I'll beat some sense into you."

Happiness filled him to overflowing. He could hardly breathe with the force of it. "I can't throw you out. Remember? The ranch belongs to you."

Sarah leaned back in the chair again. "So what happens the next time?"

Thaddeus grinned. "There won't be a next time. I have every reason to believe we'll live happily ever after and never fight again."

Sarah's laughter was dry, filled with disbelief. She reached for his forehead. "No doubt you're delirious. Has your fever returned?"

Thaddeus took her hand and brought it to his lips. "Delirious maybe, but not from fever. I think it's from happiness." He laughed at her suspicious expression. "All right, so maybe we'll fight once in a while." He shrugged as if the matter were of no importance. "I love you more every time you smart-mouth me, anyway."

Sarah grinned, her surprise obvious. "Do you?" Her eyes danced with devilish light. "I could give you a lot of reasons to love me, then," she teased.

"Don't," he pleaded, his gaze growing serious again, his dark eyes filled with fire. "Just tell me you love me. Tell me you'll stay."

"I love you." She glared at his smug expression. Lord, but she hated it when he looked so almighty pleased with himself. "You knew that all along, anyway. And I'll stay." Sarah tried to free her hand from his crushing hold. She couldn't. "Besides," she continued, her voice light, almost carefree, as if she weren't telling him the most important thing he'd ever heard in his life, "I figure if I have to go through with birthing this baby, I shouldn't be the only one to suffer." Sarah grinned down at his suddenly shocked expression. "You did have a hand in it, after all."

Thaddeus imagined it was impossible to know

greater happiness. His eyes grew suspiciously moist, his hand almost crushing hers as he brought it to his mouth. It took him a long moment before he could gain control of his feelings. When he did, he suddenly felt capable of conquering the entire world. He laughed, but the sound was more of a whoop that spoke clearly of unbearable joy. And then his gaze grew warm, wicked, and more inviting than any sick man's should, "Actually, if I remember correctly, it wasn't my hand I had in it, at all."

Two days later Annie paced the small floor of the sheriff's office. "What do you mean it was self-defense? How can you know that?"

"Mr. and Mrs. Payne were there. They each made a statement."

"So? And you imagine them both so pure they wouldn't ever lie?"

Sheriff Brown's eyes narrowed as he watched the whore nervously twist her closed parasol. "Why would they lie?"

"Maybe she was running off with him and her husband found out. Maybe he shot him in cold blood."

"When I found him, the man was as naked as the day he was born. I doubt he was going anywhere at the moment, 'cept maybe to hell."

Annie opened her mouth, ready to further argue

406

her point, when the sheriff cut her off. "Might as well save your breath. All the evidence points to their telling the truth. Jake Blackman tried to abuse another man's wife. If it was my wife, I would have blown his head off." He didn't bother to add what he would have done to him first. Even a whore didn't have to hear that kind of talk.

Annie turned on her heel and slammed out of the office. Damn the man! Just because Sarah batted her eyelashes, he believed every damn thing she said. He hadn't been there. How did he know the truth?

Jake wouldn't have risked everything for a single toss in the sack. Something must have happened and that stupid sheriff believed anything he was told.

Annie shook her head with disgust. What else could he do? He didn't know their plans. He didn't know that a man like Jake could have had any woman he wanted. He didn't have to abuse anybody.

"I don't like you walking around this town alone."

"Don't be ridiculous. Nothing's going to happen."

"Sarah, I'm not being ridiculous. It's not safe for a woman to be alone on Saturday night."

"I'll hurry along. I won't look anyone in the eye. I'll keep my eyes on the ground like a good little—"

Thaddeus's lips tightened, just a bit annoyed. "Go ahead. Make fun. Laugh. Tomorrow we're going home."

"You're not ready." She shook her head. "Not yet."

Thaddeus reluctantly gave in to her insistence, knowing he didn't have much of a choice. She was right. He wasn't ready for the long ride home. He'd yet to regain even half his strength. "I'll move to the boarding house tomorrow. After a few more days, I'll be all right."

Thaddeus was right. She should have made arrangements for someone to walk her to her room, or at least should have left earlier. It was almost dusk, and the street was alive with men of every size, description, and stage of inebriation. They blocked the wide sidewalk, where they gathered outside both saloons. Sarah wondered why these men, who spent most of their lives in the great out-of-doors, stood outside. Did they prefer the clean air of the night to the smoke-filled, over-crowded rooms? Or were they simply waiting their turn to visit with the women upstairs, as Thaddeus had once suggested?

It didn't matter. What mattered was she couldn't very well move among them in their present state. No doubt there were some, perhaps more than a few, who would see to her well-being. But it was the others, the boisterous, rowdy ones, who caused her a moment's pause. She knew Thaddeus was right. It wasn't safe for a woman to travel these streets alone on a Saturday night. The smart thing to do was to avoid these groups in their entirety.

Sarah slipped between two buildings, using the dark alley to bring her behind the buildings to a road, unused except for deliveries. It was much darker here but she breathed a sigh of relief, knowing she could move about with some degree of safety. In seconds she'd be at the back door of the boarding house, where she and Emily had taken a room three days ago.

Sarah hurried along, imagining herself quite safe using the back street. She was just beyond the saloon's open window, when she heard someone issuing a stream of vile curses. It was done in a whisper and Sarah couldn't be sure, but she thought it was a woman. And then, "I want him dead and the sooner the better."

Sarah stopped in her tracks, her eyes widened with amazement. Someone was calmly planning a murder and she'd just heard the order given. Good God! What was she going to do?

Sarah's heart was pounding so loud that she wondered if it could be heard above the murmured conversation just inside. She pressed herself against the wall, so frightened that her entire body trembled, knowing she had to hear more. She couldn't

409

just walk on by and ignore this, not if she could somehow prevent disaster.

Some poor, unsuspecting soul was targeted for murder. Sarah could do nothing about it. She'd go to the sheriff, of course. There was nothing else she could do. But first she had to hear more. She had to find out who was the intended victim.

"You know what to do," the voice drawled on. Sarah's brow wrinkled into a frown. Had she heard that voice before? If so, where? "The Cheyenne," the whispering continued, "are giving the settlers up north a ways a bit of trouble. No one will question an Indian raid. Especially if there are no survivors." There was a moment of silence and then, "This is very important. There can't be any survivors."

"What about the women?" a man asked. "Every ranch has a few women."

"What about them?"

"You want them dead as well?"

"What do you think an Indian would do?"

"First rape and then—"

"Exactly."

Another male voice cut in, "There're babies. Two that we know of. I don't have no hand in killing babies."

"Don't worry about it," the whisperer said, the voice low and filled with cold, terrifying menace. "You just do what I paid you to do. I'll take care of them."

"When can you be ready?"

"It'll take a few days. I want to look the place over. I'll be in touch."

Sarah heard a door close and then the low voice again. "You two boys interested in a little fun upstairs? It's free."

"Maybe later," a man answered. Sarah heard a chair scrape over the floor. "Figured I'd give the tables a try."

Sarah hadn't realized she'd been holding her breath. It was only when the door closed again that she released a long, silent breath. "You look in' fir someone special like, darlin'," came a sudden if slurred voice behind her. Sarah gasped and spun around. She found herself facing a whiskered old man, hunched over, bowlegged, and more than half drunk. "If you're lookin' for a man, I could—" Sarah grunted as she pushed the old man aside and almost ran the width of the next two buildings. She was breathing heavily as she rounded a corner and hurried down another alley. Moments later, she was in the sheriff's office.

"And you can't remember where you heard that voice before?"

Sarah shook her head. She was calmer now that she was safe inside his small office, sitting across from his desk as she spoke. Sheriff Brown listened carefully, asking an occasional question, but mostly

411

he let her tell her story. The telling of it did little to relieve her anxiety, however. She felt so helpless. Who were the would-be victims? And why? Why would anyone want them dead? "I'm not even sure I've ever heard it. I only know it sounded familiar."

"How?"

Sarah shrugged and gave him a helpless look.

"You think it was a woman?"

"I'm almost positive."

"Did she have an accent?"

Sarah hesitated, then her frown brightened into a smile. "An accent! That's it. It's not so much that she sounded familiar. She sounded different."

"Was it a southern drawl?"

"No. Neither was it eastern. It was just a little different."

Sheriff Brown nodded and made some notes on a piece of paper.

"What about the men? Did they have accents?

"Not as far as I could tell."

"How many do you figure there were?"

"Three, I think. There could have been more, I suppose, but I heard three different male voices."

The sheriff nodded his head. "Gunslingers." He grinnèd. "And not particularly smart ones, either. I saw them ride in together this afternoon."

"Does that matter?"

He shrugged. "It wouldn't usually make a difference, but with something like this . . ." He took a deep breath and then sighed, obviously thinking out loud. "Sounds to me like they didn't know till they got here what they hired on for. Folks are bound to remember three strangers, especially after . . ." He shrugged, for neither of them knew who or exactly how many were about to die.

"Not if people think Indians did it."

Sheriff Brown grinned and then nodded toward Sarah. "I forgot about that. You're right, of course. So, let's see what we've got. A woman is planning a murder. She's hired on at least three men. Disguised as Cheyenne, they will attack a ranch or farm near here."

"A ranch. I heard someone say a ranch."

"All right. They're going to attack a ranch near here. There'll be no survivors."

Sarah groaned with despair. She'd given him so little to go on. How could the sheriff help when he wouldn't know until it was too late who needed his help? "I should have moved closer. I should have looked."

"You might be dead right now if you had."

Sarah came to her feet, her body filled with nervous energy.

"You did real good," he grunted as he came around the desk. "Now leave the rest to me. I'll find out what's going on."

Sarah nodded and gratefully accepted his company on the short trip back to her room.

Chapter Twenty

Johnny Lewis, the deputy sheriff, groaned as he rolled off the woman. Exhausted and content, he smiled at her flushed, happy expression. No matter her obvious experience and no matter how odd the notion, Johnny somehow found Sally adorably innocent. She was pretty and young and always eager for him. Maybe he was crazy, but there was something about her eagerness that convinced him he meant more to her than just another customer.

Johnny knew she liked their time together as much as he did. But did she consider it special? He was going to have to ask her about that real soon, because lately he'd been thinking that maybe he'd ask her to go away with him. Maybe if they went someplace where nobody knew what she'd been, maybe she wouldn't mind a little respectability and a few kids. God knew he was tired of being alone. He figured it would be nice to have this woman waiting for him at the end of a day's work. He imagined the lusty nights they'd share. The thought of being the only man in her life was becoming more important every day.

Johnny played with a soft, round breast as she cuddled against his side. She'd be hot for more in a few minutes. If he wanted to get any information, he'd have to start now before both of them began thinking on other things.

"You seen those three gunslingers ride into town?"

Sally shrugged. "I seen them hangin' around downstairs."

"Anybody special they take up with?"

"Not so as you could tell," she said, then added conversationally, "I had one of them a couple of hours ago."

Johnny stiffened slightly, trying to understand why the idea of her being with another should bring on such anger. Damn, you'd think he was new to it or something. He knew what she was, and until he could convince her to leave with him, he would have to accept it. "Did he talk much?"

Sally grinned. "Nothin' special. Told me I did a real fine job and that he was comin' into a lot of money soon. Promised to take me away with him when he did." She shrugged. "You know, the usual things."

"Reckon I don't know," Johnny said, feeling more than a bit annoyed. It wasn't unusual for her to mention her clients. But lately, it was sure to get him riled.

415

"Most every man I see tells me that. They all want me forever," she giggled, "or until they get soft again. Whichever comes first."

His mouth thinned into a straight, tight line. Yeah, he definitely had to do something about this. It was bothering him more each day. His voice was harsher than either expected when he asked, "How much money? Did he say?"

"Nope. Said somethin' about silver, though."

"What about the other two?"

"I saw one of them with Annie. She was sitting on his lap while he played cards." Sally hesitated a minute and then continued with, "Now that I think about it, I saw her goin' upstairs with two of them."

"When?"

"I don't know." She shrugged. "Earlier."

Johnny figured the sheriff would be interested in hearing this, but he knew the information would have to wait a bit. Sally had reached between his legs while they talked and was playing right nice like with what she found there. There was no way he was going to leave this bed. Not anytime soon.

"Do you know Annie?" Sheriff Brown looked slightly embarrassed. "The first Mrs. . ."

Sarah cut him off, remembering all too clearly her first and hopefully only meeting with the woman. Her face still burned at the memory. "We've met."

"Could it have been her voice you heard?"

Thaddeus had been brought to the boarding house just that morning. Sarah had settled him moments before the sheriff had come to their door. "What are you talking about?" Thaddeus asked from the bed. His gaze moved from the sheriff to his wife and back again.

"Could it?"

Sarah frowned. "I only heard her talk once, and it wasn't in a whisper."

"Think. Could she be the one?"

"Would one of you tell me what's happening?"

Sheriff Brown glanced at Thaddeus and sighed. "Mrs. Payne heard someone planning a murder."

Thaddeus stiffened and, despite his weakened state sat straight up in bed. "Jesus! Where? How?" His gaze moved accusingly to his wife, his eyes hard with anger. "Why didn't you tell me?"

Sarah shot her husband a look of annoyance. "I didn't tell you because you give me more than enough trouble when I have to go out."

"Sonofabitch! You're not leaving this room again. Not without me." He glared as she rolled her eyes toward the ceiling. "I told you it wasn't safe for you to be out alone. A woman needs protection."

"And what could you do? You're as weak as a kitten."

"Goddamnit, Sarah! I—"

417

"Listen, folks, would you mind workin' this out later?" Sheriff Brown cut in. "This is important.

"Think, Mrs. Payne. Could it have been Annie you heard?"

"It could have, but I'm not sure."

"Why do you think Annie's involved?" Thaddeus asked.

"She was seen goin' upstairs with two of the men." Sheriff Brown had the grace to color. He wasn't used to talking about so sensitive a subject within a lady's hearing.

"Sheriff, I want to know what's goin' on."

Sheriff Brown sighed. He pulled a chair from the corner of the room, turned it to a position where it could be straddled, and leaned his arms across its back as he faced Thaddeus. "Mrs. Payne came to my office last night. She heard a woman and three men planning a murder. Appears like they're gettin' set to take out a whole ranch."

"You mean kill everybody?" Thaddeus asked, his eyes wide with shock, his concern obvious.

He nodded. "Looks like they're fixin' to disguise themselves as Cheyenne. The woman's the ringleader and she wants no survivors."

"Why?"

Sheriff Brown shrugged. "Don't know all the whys and wherefores yet. My deputy heard that one of the men was boastin' about comin' into some money. Silver was mentioned."

"Silver!" There followed a long moment of silence before Thaddeus murmured, "Jesus! Does she hate me that much?"

"Who? Who hates you, Mr. Payne?"

"Annie. She wants the silver. Always did. She thinks I've been mining it. Won't believe there's not enough on the whole damn mountain to keep her for a year. Even if there was, I don't want no part of workin' in a black hole the rest of my life."

Sheriff Brown never looked more serious. "Do you have two babies on your ranch?"

Thaddeus nodded, and Sarah gave a soft little cry of fright.

"Then, I reckon we know where they're gonna hit."

"Jesus," Thaddeus murmured again as he tried to get up.

Sarah pushed him to his back again. "Don't move," she ordered. "You're not going anywhere."

"I'll have my deputy go out to your place. He'll get the women back to town while the men get things ready."

"I have to be there."

"No, you don't," Sarah insisted.

"It might not happen for a spell. One of the men mentioned they wouldn't be ready for a few days. Besides, the others look like they're aimin' to have themselves a bit of fun, for the time being."

"That won't last long. Annie never was a patient sort."

"Jake!" Sarah gasped. "Do you think—?" She

didn't finish her sentence, her eyes so huge they almost appeared to swallow her face.

"What? What about Jake?" Sheriff Brown shot her a puzzled look.

"He said . . ." Her brow creased as she tried to remember exactly what Jake had said. "He mentioned silver. He said he didn't care about the silver." Sarah looked at the sheriff. "Do you think he was in on it?"

Sheriff Brown shrugged. "I reckon it don't matter none." He came to his feet. "What matters is that I get word to your people." He nodded to Thaddeus, touched his fingers to the brim of his hat, and murmured, "Ma'am," as he left the room.

Thaddeus awakened from his nap to find Sarah standing at the mirror over the dry sink. She was placing her bonnet on her head and pushing a few strands of golden hair beneath the brim. "Sarah, I'm warning you. If you dare leave this room, I'll—"

"What?" she snapped as she turned and glared in his direction. "You should know by now that I don't take kindly to threats."

"I wouldn't have to threaten you if you were obedient. Damn you. How can I rest? How can I sleep while wondering if you're going to sneak out the minute I close my eyes?"

"I won't be sneaking out, Thaddeus. When I

leave, I'll tell you clear enough."

Thaddeus groaned his frustration.

"All right," Sarah sighed, understanding his fear for her even though she believed it misplaced. "If it will make you happy, I'll make sure I'm not alone."

"I'll be able to ride in a few days. Promise me you won't go anywhere until then. Promise me."

"I have to go to the apothecary, Thaddeus. You're almost out of your medicine."

"To hell with my medicine. Stay here."

Sarah sighed again. The man was so thickheaded, it was a miracle she could keep her temper. "I'll ask Mrs. Stanley to send someone."

"Fine."

True to his word, Thaddeus was ready to ride in three days. What he wasn't ready for was the argument he was getting from his wife. Actually, *argument* was the wrong word. She simply ignored his every demand.

"I don't know what you think you're doing. You're not coming with me."

"Yes, dear," Sarah remarked sweetly as she continued to ready herself.

"Sarah, it's dangerous. I can't take the time to worry about you."

"Then don't."

"If you're there, I'll be half out of my mind with fear for you."

"Seems to me you're half out of your mind in any case."

Thaddeus glared in her direction. Not that it did any good. "You're not leaving here."

Sarah hummed a little tune as she pulled on her boots.

"Did you hear me?"

"I heard you."

"Where the hell did you get that?"

"What?" Sarah asked, never looking in his direction as she slid a shirt into the waistband of her spilt skirt.

"Sarah." His voice was low and filled with warning.

"What?" She pulled her hair back and pinned it beneath a wide-brimmed hat.

"What do you think you're doing?"

Sarah smiled. "I'm getting ready to ride home, of course."

"You're not going."

"Yes, dear," she said as she buckled a gun belt around her hips.

"Jesus Christ! Are you going to tell me you're ready to shoot someone? You?! The only woman I know who just about goes loco at the thought of violence?"

"I'm going to do whatever it takes to make sure you're safe."

Thaddeus sighed and sat on the bed. He wasn't nearly as strong as he'd like to be, but he couldn't wait another day. Every gun was needed to save his ranch. "What about Emily?"

"Emily is staying in town with Mrs. Stanley. She'll be fine."

"She's going to miss you."

"And I'll miss her."

"Sarah, I can't let you do this. You're going to have my baby."

"And you're going to be there with me. I'm going to make sure of it."

He couldn't fight her. He simply didn't have the time or the energy it would take. He couldn't stop her, but he sure as hell could make sure she didn't get hurt. "All right. You can go, if you promise to listen to everything I say." And when his words brought about no response, he asked, "Will you promise?"

Sarah grinned. "I promise."

"Out of the question. I won't do it." Sarah's angry gaze moved from her husband to the secret door, which she'd believed only a wall that butted up against a solid mountain, and back again. She shivered with revulsion as she saw the ladder and the deep black hole it disappeared into.

"Sarah, you promised you'd do anythin' I say."

"I wouldn't have if I'd known you expected me to live in a pit for the next few days. I'm not staying down there." Sarah eyed the black walls with disgust. "I'm not even going down there."

"It's the only place I can be sure of your safety."

"What about the others?"

"I'm not concerned about anyone but you."

"Kate and Lottie are staying with their men. They're not hiding in a hole."

"Kate and Lottie are different."

"Really?" Sarah's hands came to her hips as she glared her resentment. How dare he imply that she wasn't as good as these women. "And just what makes them different?"

"I don't love them," he shouted as he lowered his head and glared at her almost eye to eye. "That's what."

Sarah's gaze softened, understanding the fear he felt for her. How could she find fault when she knew the same? They had finally found each other again. She couldn't bear the thought of losing him. She sighed and moved within inches of his chest. "Darling, I'll take every precaution. If things get bad, I promise I'll go into the cave."

Thaddeus took her in his arms and crushed her tightly against him. His hold told of his desperation. "If anything happens to you . . ."

"Nothing is going to happen to either of us. Nothing," she promised as she raised her mouth to his kiss.

By nightfall, a dozen men were in position. Six from the ranch and six more, including the sheriff,

424

from town. Sarah stayed within the protective walls of her house with Kate and Lottie. The women baked for hours on end, trying to ease some of their pent-up tension. Along with the baking, they made pot after pot of black coffee and dozens of sandwiches, which would be given to the men throughout the long night. Things went on that way for the next two days. It was in the wee hours of the third night that they finally came.

During the lulls in conversation, one or another of the women would wander toward the window and peer out, trying to see what they could between the cracks in the shutters. The tension was unbearable. The night appeared more silent than most. Even the crickets had quieted. The lack of sound brought chills up Sarah's spine. Why should there be such total silence? Was someone out there?

Sarah had her answer when Tiger growled. All three women were instantly alert. The dog could hear something, sense something. It was about to happen. Quietly, calmly, Sarah took her gun and placed it before her as she sat at the table. The first man who broke through that door would die. She didn't care what happened to her, for she knew if he got that far, Thaddeus would already be dead.

Sarah heard the wild, horrific screams. The eerie sound sent chills up her spine. A moment later she saw the flicker of flame through the cracks in the wooden shutters. The barn was on fire. Thank God, Thaddeus had thought to bring the animals out to pasture. Sarah shivered, knowing that they would certainly have burned to death if still inside. Not a man came from his hiding place as they tensed, laying in wait for the criminals to show themselves.

She was terrified. Her entire body trembled with the fear of this coming moment, yet she almost breathed a sigh of relief knowing this endless waiting was over at last.

Her gaze moved to Lottie and then Kate. Both women offered weak, nervous smiles, and Lottie murmured almost beneath her breath, "Here we go, ladies." And Sarah, as promised, extinguished the lights. All three women were armed. They waited in silence for their men to do what had to be done and then come to them.

The place appeared deserted. Where the hell was everybody? Fires raged in three separate outbuildings. In a few minutes, they'd have burned the entire place to the ground, and still not a soul showed himself. If anyone was here, which he was beginning to doubt, they were obviously unwilling to defend their homes.

The plan had been to burn them out and, when they emerged from the flaming buildings, to shoot every last one of them dead. It was simple and would be over in minutes.

426

Tom Macon, the leader of the three men, grinned. This was damn easy pickings. Annie had warned them that her ex was good with a gun. But as far as he could see, not one man on that ranch had any guns. They had been prepared for a fight, but it looked to him as if everyone had scattered at the first sign of trouble.

"I don't like this," Annie said as she stood half hidden behind a large boulder and watched the ranch burn below. "It's not normal for everyone to be gone. Someone must be there."

"They're probably shiverin' behind their doors. Guess it's time we got them to come outside and play." Tom grinned as he mounted his horse. Dressed as an Indian, war paint and all, he looked chilling against the light of the flaming buildings.

"Be careful," Annie called softly after him. Not that she cared if he lived or died. She just wanted to see this job done before something happened to him.

She watched as the two other men also mounted their horses. A few moments later, all three raced into the yard below. Even from here, she could hear the sounds of their screams. It ran chills down her spine.

Thaddeus watched as the riders came toward him. He knew the ranch appeared to be deserted. That, of course, was the plan. His nerves were stretched to the limit as he strained for control. It was imperative that he wait. Wait until they returned to finish their dirty job. All three, or never get a chance to hold these men to account. He was crouched behind a wagon. "The rest of the men stood or lay in the dark shadows of the few buildings that had so far escaped the torch.

Three riders came to a stop in the center of the yard. "Damn, if this don't give me the willies. It ain't natural for a place like this to stand empty."

Tom Macon ignored the man's comment and nodded toward the main house. "Let's see what we got inside."

Thaddeus's mouth grew instantly dry and his heart thundered in his chest as he watched the three men drop to the ground and into a crouched position. Bent almost in half, they ran toward the stone cabin. They were out in the open and moved quickly for the cover the shadowy porch provided. They never made it. It was impossible that Thaddeus would allow them any closer to Sarah. A barrage of firing guns exploded in the night. Contrasted against the sound, the raging fires appeared little more than a whisper on the wind. The men rolled for cover, one of them beneath the very wagon where Thaddeus lay.

A cruel smile curved Thaddeus's lips as he placed a gun to the man's temple. His voice was hardly more than a whisper. "Easy. Just take it easy." His free hand moved quickly to divest the gunman of his weapons. "You're out of it now."

One man lay mortally wounded, moaning as a

few men gathered around his prone form. None were about to come to his aid. In truth, there was no aid possible. At least three bullets had crashed into the man's midsection. A hole the size of a fist had ripped his belly open. Blood was pumping through his fingers and puddled on the ground at his side as he whimpered his fear.

The third man was already dead. It took a few moments before those defending the ranch could believe it was over. For three days they had waited for battle and it was over within seconds.

Thaddeus knew he'd never rest until he found the culprit behind this dastardly deed. Annie. If he had her here now, he wouldn't have thought twice about killing her. She didn't deserve to live. The hell of it was, she'd most probably get away with it. How would the law prove her to be behind this would-be massacre?

The fires were soon put out. The barn was a total loss, but Thaddeus figured the loss had been well worth it. Everyone was safe at least for the time being. He couldn't ask for more.

Sarah and the two women had coffee and breakfast ready for all. Heartfelt thanks were offered and accepted.

The men were tired and obviously anxious to get back to town. Sheriff Brown had his prisoner shackled, his hands behind his back, his feet tied with a rope that ran from foot to foot under the horse. Thaddeus eyed the man with real menace.

This man would have killed them all if he'd gotten the chance. Even Sarah would not have escaped his murderous intent. "Leave him to me. I'll get him to talk," Sheriff Brown said as he mounted his horse. Thaddeus realized, for the first time, just how civilized he had become. It wasn't that long ago when he wouldn't have thought twice about putting a bullet between the man's eyes.

It was almost light. Warm rays of sunshine were fast chasing away the last of the darkness, when the men finished their coffee and the large, tired group started for their own homes.

"We'll pick Emily up later," Thaddeus said as he and Sarah watched the men leave. One arm slid around his wife's shoulders and pulled her close to his side. "We can both use a few hours of sleep first."

Sarah smiled as she nuzzled her head into the warmth of his chest. "I'm so glad it's over."

Thaddeus knew it wasn't, but even he couldn't have imagined the horror that would befall them next.

Chapter Twenty-one

Annie cursed nonstop the entire twenty miles back to town. They were all incompetents. Every damn one of them. She couldn't count on anyone to do the job and do it right. First it was Jake. The damn fool had let what lay between his legs control his thoughts and actions. She supposed she should consider herself lucky he hadn't ruined all her plans. And then these three. Annie wasn't sure how they were found out. How they'd walked into a trap. It was enough that they had. Damn them all to hell.

Annie couldn't depend on anyone but herself. It had been that way since she was a kid. She should have known better.

An evil smile turned ordinary lips into an ugly grimace. She knew a way. She'd get what she wanted, all right. She'd had enough of this pussy-footing around, damn it! She'd waited long enough!

* * *

Annie laughed. Jesus, it was so easy. Why the hell hadn't she thought of this before? She held the baby before her. It had been ridiculously simple to take the child from her bed. No one had seen her enter and leave the boarding house by the rear door. Annie gave a low sound of merriment. By the time anyone thought to wake the baby from her nap, she'd be long gone.

Emily whimpered her fear, knowing instinctively that this woman offered no safe harbor, and received a sharp slap to the side of her head as a result. "Shut up, brat! I'll tell you when you can cry."

Oddly enough, Emily, who wasn't yet a year old, seemed to understand her danger. Her pretty little lips and jaw quivered, and tears slid from huge blue eyes. Still, nary a sound came to break the quiet, muffled pounding of the horse's hooves.

As brazen as could be, Annie rode out of town. Once she dropped the kid off somewhere deep in the thousands of miles of woodland that covered these mountains, she'd return to the ranch and give them her ultimatum. Annie had every confidence that before this day was over, she would be the sole owner of that silver mine, and Thaddeus, Sarah, and probably this brat as well would be dead.

Things looked like they were going to work out just fine from where Annie sat. Just fine indeed.

All she had to do was offer them the baby for the signed deed to the place. Annie knew they wouldn't refuse.

* * *

"You're not wanted here," Sarah said as Annie slid to the ground and tied her horse to the hitching post.

Annie grinned. "Oh, I think you'll want me here, all right. As a matter of fact . . ."

"What the hell do you want?" Thaddeus asked, suddenly appearing at his wife's side, his voice grim, his dark gaze filled with disgust. His arm moved in a protective fashion around Sarah's waist and he pulled her back just a bit, as if just being in Annie's company might somehow contaminate his wife.

"A deal."

Thaddeus's mouth twisted with hatred. His first thought had been to kill her. Now that he'd pulled his emotions into some sort of control, he only wanted this woman off his land. Still, he instinctively knew she wouldn't dare show her face lest she had—or thought she had—the upper hand. He was better off knowing this enemy. "What kind of a deal?"

"I want the silver."

There was no sense telling her there was no silver, or what little there was of it was hardly worth the effort it would take to mine it. The woman had her mind set. Nothing he could say was going to change it. "And why should I give it to you?"

"If you know what's good for you, you'll sign the deed over now."

"Or what?"

433

"Or I'll never tell you where the kid is."

Sarah felt the beginnings of an almost overwhelming terror squeeze at her heart. A buzzing sounded in her ears. She couldn't think. She was afraid to think, afraid to know. It couldn't be. It couldn't! She took a deep lungful of air and staggered as she realized what this woman was about. She didn't have Emily. Mrs. Stanley wouldn't have handed the baby over to a woman like this.

Annie grinned at Sarah's obvious suffering. "It was easy enough. No one stopped me. They probably still think she's sleeping."

Sarah's lips pulled back into a grimace of hate. A low rumble of sound came from deep within her chest. Even to Thaddeus, a man who loved her to desperation, the hatred that had suddenly overtaken his wife was a chilling sight to see. She reached for his gun. It happened faster than a blink.

"You have five seconds," Sarah said as she leveled the weapon on the woman. "Where is she?"

Annie grinned. She wasn't afraid of this whining bitch. No one was going to shoot her. Not if they wanted the kid back. "After you deed your land over to me."

A shot rang out and Annie gasped at the sight of her boot. A good-sized chunk of it had been blown away. She could see her exposed toe and the empty place where her big toe was supposed to be. Pain the likes of which she'd never known was slowly invading her brain. "You stupid sonofabitch!" Annie cried. Her eyes hardened with unbelievable hatred. "Do you think I'd tell you now?"

Another shot smashed the woman's ankle. "Jesus Christ! Stop her," she screamed as she fell to the ground. But Thaddeus was almost as stunned as the injured woman. He found himself incapable of doing anything but watching this gentle, peace-loving wife of his turn into a tigress. She who had never before shown this capability for violence. She who had hated the thought of using a gun, of taking a life, was now inflicting untold pain upon this villainous woman. He couldn't believe it.

"Where is she?" The sound of Sarah's voice hissed like a snake. It sent chills up Thaddeus's spine.

Annie's eyes narrowed with hatred. Spittle formed at the corners of her mouth as she screamed. "You dirty bitch! You whorin' . . ."

The gun exploded again and Annie's eyes widened with shock. The bullet had almost hit her knee. Another few inches and she'd be crippled for life. What was she doing? Sonofabitch! She'd been so shocked she hadn't remembered the damn gun. Even now the pain was so great she could hardly bring her shaking hand to her pocket.

"Where is she?" Sarah asked again, knowing no sympathy for this animal. There wasn't a doubt in anyone's mind that Sarah was going to kill Annie. Not one of the half-dozen people suddenly gathered around were of a mind to stop her.

"Wait! Stop! Damn it! I didn't hurt her," Annie moaned as she stalled for time. "You got no cause." She had to get her hands on that gun. She was going to see this woman dead, if it took the last of her strength. If it was the last thing she ever did.

"Where is she?" Sarah asked for the third time, while not a flicker of pity for this woman's suffering entered her eyes.

Another shot rang out, this one bringing a scream of torment as the derringer was sent flying from Annie's hand. Blood squirted everywhere. Tiny specks of it covered Annie's face, then heavy amounts coated her dress.

"If you kill me, you'll never find her." Annie amazed herself that she managed to stay coherent, so great was her suffering. God, but she'd never known pain like this before.

"I won't kill you. But before I'm finished, you might wish I had." A horrific grin twisted Sarah's lips, and Annie knew she'd met another as heartless as herself. She'd find no pity here. "I haven't started on your other leg yet. Now, where would you like the first one?" Sarah's voice promised a painful death. Thaddeus was positive he'd never heard the promise so clear. "How many do you think you can take before you tell me?" The words were said so calmly, so quietly, that not one among the small gathering doubted her intent.

Annie knew she'd lost this battle. She couldn't bear the pain of another bullet. She couldn't bear the pain of those she'd already taken. "On the way to town," she gasped for every breath, trying to ward off the pain. "She's in the woods where the road turns twice."

Sarah glanced at her husband's shocked expression and said, "Put her on her horse." She was like a different person. And it wasn't only her actions. Her features had contorted into such hatred that she was barely recognizable.

Thaddeus did as he was ordered. A quick glance at his men and a nod of his head brought all six to their saddles within seconds. Every one of them knew the chances of finding the little girl were slim. Anything could have happened to her. And if she'd already wandered off . . . Not one person dared to think beyond that thought.

Lottie sat across from Annie, a gun in her hand, while every man from the ranch scoured the woods for a sign of the child. "If you know what's good for ya, you'd better be tellin' the truth."

"I told you where she was." Annie was nauseous from unbearable pain and hardly in any mood to chitchat with this stupid cow of a woman. She was gasping as she tried to keep the pain under control. When the hell were they going to get her some help? The rags they'd wrapped around her wounds had stopped the bleeding, but the pain . . . "Is it my fault that she's crawled off?"

Lottie laughed. "Whose fault do you think it is?"

Annie didn't answer. She wasn't in the mood for talking right now. She couldn't think beyond the pain that clouded her mind.

* * *

Emily knew that if she waited, her mommy would come for her. She was tired and hungry, but hardly afraid at all. She was glad the bad lady had put her down. She didn't like her. Her mommy wouldn't like her, either.

Emily looked around her. Everything was so big, but that wasn't really any different. Everything was always big. She sat where she'd been left, her blanket gathered at her side, her thumb in her mouth, knowing mommy would be there soon.

She watched an ant crawl from beneath a dry leaf. She watched it walk across her blanket and then on to another leaf. She pulled the blanket more closely around her and rocked back and forth as she sucked her thumb. She sucked her thumb until her eyes began to close. And then she rolled onto her side and slept.

"You're lying. Emily isn't here," Sarah said as she moved to stand before the woman. Thaddeus's gun was no longer in her hands. For that, Annie was thankful.

"I left her here. I swear it." Annie knew better than to cross this woman again. The stupid bitch had probably maimed her for life. She'd get even, of course, but she'd have to wait a bit for that. She'd have to wait until she could think again until this pain eased a bit.

438

"Where?" Sarah asked, trying to keep the panic from her voice. She wanted to tear this woman apart limb by limb. She couldn't remember a time when she'd so wanted another to die . . . and die a horrible, painful death.

"She can't be far," Thaddeus said as he guided his wife from Annie's presence. There was no telling what Sarah might do next. He'd never thought she could shoot someone. Not his woman. How often had she shown her abhorrence for violence? And yet when it came to her own, she'd shot Annie again and again, never giving a thought to the damage she'd inflicted.

Sarah looked up at Will as he dashed into the clearing. "She was here. This is a piece of her blanket, isn't it?"

Sarah didn't know whether to be filled with joy or wild with fear. She had been here, but where was she now? How far could a ten-month-old baby crawl before she got tired and fell asleep? Sarah refused to think about the animals that filled this forest. Nothing was going to happen to her baby. Nothing!

The men from the ranch spread out. In a line, they walked slowly through the thick underbrush, while Sarah called out every few feet. "Emily! Emily, can you hear me? Answer Mommy."

They retraced their steps and started again, careful to search every thick area of brush.

"She couldn't have gone this far, Thaddeus." Sarah knew she was on the verge of panic. She

439

didn't know how much longer she could hold back. She had to find her. She had to!

Sarah looked at her husband with huge terror-filled eyes, which silently begged for this nightmare to pass. "She's so little. She couldn't have gone this far!"

"A little further, darlin'. Just a little further and we'll turn back."

It was then that they saw her and the man who held her in his arms walking down the rise. Johnny grinned as he tickled the child beneath her chin with a dirty finger. "I was just wonderin' what I was going to do with this. Lucky you folks happened by. She's got a real good pair of lungs."

Thaddeus wasn't surprised that they'd never heard Emily's cry. The huge trees and the thickness of the underbrush could easily muffle many a sound.

"Emily," Sarah groaned as tears began to roll unheeded down her cheeks. "Thank God, Emily," she shuddered as she took the trembling baby into her arms. Within seconds, both mother and daughter were hugging like they'd never let each other go.

Sarah couldn't stand. Her legs simply wouldn't hold her weight. Without a sound, she slumped to the ground and held her daughter in her lap. It took no effort to close out the rest of the world.

Thaddeus and Johnny stood facing each other. "You still lookin' for a woman to see to your needs?"

Johnny's eyes widened as they moved to Sarah

He couldn't believe his luck. Damn, all he'd done was track a deer. He'd expected his old sergeant to put up a stink that the deer had crossed over to his land. Instead, the man was telling him to take his woman. He couldn't believe it. A huge grin spread across his lips and exposed brown tobacco-stained teeth, one recently lost. "You mean you're finally willin' to let her go?"

"Sorry." Thaddeus shook his head, while a hard gleam entered his eyes. "I'll never let her go. But there's another back a ways," he nodded over his shoulder.

Johnny licked his lips and then shrugged. Too bad. If he had his druthers, he would have chosen this one, but he had to admit any woman was better than no woman at all. "What she look like?"

Thaddeus shrugged. "Pretty enough. Fact is, she's got a few holes in her right now, but I reckon she'll be ready to service both you and Joe in a week or so."

"And she'd be willin' to live up there?" Johnny nodded over his shoulder in the direction of his far-off mountain. He hadn't found a woman yet who wanted to live up there . . . no matter how many lies he told them.

Thaddeus's only answer was to laugh with incredulity.

"So how do I keep her, then?"

"That's your problem. If you lay off the whiskey, she won't be able to sneak away without you hearin'."

441

"And she's mine to keep? How come?"

Thaddeus knew a jury would think twice about sending a woman to prison. Not many ended up there, no matter how vicious their crimes. Especially if they swore real pretty like that they had had no hand in any wrongdoing.

No one had seen Annie take Emily. He was sure of that, or someone would have tried to stop her. True, she'd admitted to taking the child, but she'd only admitted it to Thaddeus and Sarah. The baby had been found a mile or so from where she was supposed to be. Thaddeus had no doubt that Annie could lie her way out of this somehow. Especially after the brutal treatment she'd suffered at Sarah's hand.

The only way to rid himself of Annie's evil presence and make sure she never got the chance to harm his family again was to give her to Johnny and his partner. Thaddeus forced aside his smile. Justice. He remembered the squalor in which these men lived. Jesus, he couldn't find a better form of punishment if he'd searched the world over. There wasn't a prison in the whole damn country as dirty as Johnny's shack.

"One condition."

Damn. Johnny knew it. It couldn't be this easy. Nothing ever was.

"If she gets free, I'll come and get you," Thaddeus said, his eyes promising death. Thaddeus knew she never would. Even if she managed to get away from these two, Annie would never find her way down Johnny's mountain. The whole area was filled with boxed canyons, the terrain so rough that, most of it had to be made on foot. No, once she was atop that mountain, Thaddeus wouldn't worry about her evil presence again. But he felt better putting a little fear into this man.

"Christ! What the hell has she done?" Johnny felt a shiver of fear run over his entire body. He didn't cotton to having his throat slit in his sleep, just so he'd have a woman to diddle with now and then.

"She's dangerous. I won't lie to you. She kidnapped my daughter. I want her dead, but the law ain't likely to oblige. If she gets loose, my wife might kill her. I don't want no more trouble."

Johnny grinned. "You ain't got no cause to worry. I'll keep her chained." Johnny grinned. "I've got a collar that'll fit real nice like around a woman's neck. She won't be leavin' the shack, not with five dogs to get by." He shook his head, his eyes filled with satisfaction as he thought out his plan aloud. "No, she won't be goin' nowhere."

Annie's features were contorted with agony. She'd never known pain to equal this horror. Still, her eyes were huge and filled with uncertainty as Johnny carried her off. Wisely, she offered no objection, knowing this might be her only chance to escape the gallows. Those left behind watched in silence as every step he took brought him closer to his home and sealed Annie's fate forever.

443

"Why did you let him take her?" Sarah asked as she moved to her daughter's bed and checked her again, as if she hadn't done the same at least a hundred times the last few hours. "Why didn't you take her to town? She should go to prison for the rest of her life."

Thaddeus lay on his back and grinned up at his beamed ceiling. "She is in prison. As long as Johnny and Joe are alive, she'll never get free."

"Suppose she kills them. Then what?"

Thaddeus shrugged. "I don't have a doubt that she'll try. But if she does, she'll probably starve to death. Johnny's got some mighty fierce dogs guarding his place. They ain't about to let anybody in or out."

"Were you afraid I'd get in trouble for shooting her? Is that why you did it?"

"Nope. I figured she might sweet-talk her way out of the whole thing. I don't want her in our lives anymore. Reckon her being up on that mountain takes care of that for good."

"But—"

"Darlin', I don't want to talk about her anymore."

"Don't you?" Sarah smiled as she settled herself at his side for the night. "What would you like to talk about, then?"

Thaddeus slid Sarah's gown over her head and

threw it to the bottom of their bed. "You. I thought you hated guns."

"I never said I hated guns. Actually, I'm very good with a gun. My sister and brother and I used to shoot at targets. I always won. What I hate is violence. The thought of killing someone with a gun makes me ill."

"You could have fooled me. I've seen gunslingers that didn't have half your stomach. You didn't even flinch when Annie was covered with blood."

"I never noticed."

Thaddeus grinned. "You sure are a mean lady."

Sarah chuckled. "So you think I'm mean, do you?"

"Like a tigress protecting her cub. Damn, but I never saw anybody so calm. How many times were you plannin' on shootin' her?"

"As many times as it took." Sarah shivered as she remembered her terror, wondering at Emily's safety. "I was going to find out where Emily was."

Thaddeus laughed as he snuggled her tightly against him. "She probably won't ever walk on that ankle again."

"She should have thought of that before she took my baby."

Thaddeus crushed her against him. "Lady, you sure relieve my mind some." His hand ran up and down her back as he nuzzled his face in her hair and breathed her delicious scent. "I feel right safe like just bein' your husband."

Sarah's eyes glittered at his teasing. A smile

touched the corners of her mouth. "Do you? Why?"

" 'Cause the sorry fool who tries to hurt anyone you love can count himself lucky to end up in one piece."

"You could have done worse, and you know it."

Thaddeus chuckled, knowing the truth behind those words. He put his hand on her flat stomach and thought for a moment about the child who grew inside. His heart filled with peace and contentment as he thanked God for bringing this woman into his life. "I figure it's probably time to start that extra room. This house is bound to get a mite crowded in the next few years."

Sarah smiled and cuddled against her husband. "Are you still planing on six children?"

"Darlin', I only told you six 'cause I didn't want to make you nervous."

Sarah's laughter was low and wicked. "How kind of you to worry over my nerves. How many do you really want?"

"Well, I reckon twelve to be a right nice number."

Sarah's eyes widened with shock. Her voice was tiny when she finally managed, "Twelve?"

Thaddeus nodded. "Maybe more."

"More?"

"Who can say? I got a powerful lot of lovin' saved up for you. And I expect it's goin' to last a while. His mouth slid from nuzzling her hair and cheek to her neck, and then down in a long, deliciously slow path to the tip of her breast.

Sarah squirmed as he grazed his teeth over the sensitive flesh. "Ah, Thaddeus," she said, trying to keep her mind on their conversation.

"Mmmm," he murmured as he took her breast deep into the heat of his mouth, while his hand slid lower over her stomach.

"Six. No more than six." And when he didn't respond, but seemed more interested in what his mouth and hands were touching than her words, she said, "Thaddeus, answer me."

Thaddeus loomed over her, a smile teasing his lips as he eased her thighs apart. "Not good enough. I want twelve."

"Six, Thaddeus." She shot him a deliciously wicked look. Her hand slid low over his belly and then cupped his sex. Her eyes sparkled in the soft light of a candle, an unmistakable promise of pleasure in her gaze.

Thaddeus groaned as he imagined the years ahead and the delights she held in store. There was nothing on earth he wouldn't give this woman if it were within his power to give. "Sarah, I reckon I'll never love another soul on this whole earth the way I love you." His body trembled as he rocked his hips into her hand. A soft moan of pleasure rumbled from somewhere within his chest at the delicious sensation of her tightening her hold. "As long as you belong to me, it doesn't matter how many we have." He took a shuddering breath as he forced aside the need to

447

enter her now with hard, swift strokes.

Thaddeus kissed her for a long, breathless moment. His tongue swirled into her depths, delighting in her taste, her texture, her scent.

Sarah smiled and asked, "You're sure?"

Thaddeus moaned as he eased himself slowly into her moist heat. His eyes closed against the pleasure. "Jesus God," the low groan was torn from his throat. "Don't you know?" His body trembled as strong muscles tightened and squeezed around him. "As long as I have you, I have everything."